THE FAREDENE TRILOGY

LIE A LITTLE

To Love a Lot

DEBRA DELANEY

POOLBEG

Published 2020
by Poolbeg Press Ltd
123 Grange Hill, Baldoyle,
Dublin 13, Ireland
Email: poolbeg@poolbeg.com

A catalogue record for this book is available from the British Library.

ISBN 978178199-401-6

www.poolbeg.com

Acknowledgements

To Claire Dean, my editor, critique buddy and friend, without whom this book would never have been written – it was you who asked me to write it.

Your excellent editing and research skills have been vital to this project, and I know you have worked tirelessly, often until the early hours (mainly without complaint ☺), to ensure this book came to fruition – and on time.

What can I say about your insightful critiquing? There were times when I wanted to strangle you as you pushed me to improve my plot, telling me I could do better, pulling me up on every little thing! Your comments were priceless – and your suggestions invaluable. But I knew you were right.

I will never be able to thank you enough. That said, you've had enough praise now – I don't want it going to your head.

DEDICATION

In fond memory of a dear friend

Part of the Faredene Saga

Prologue

Liverpool, October 1877

No one thought it unusual to see the pale young woman sitting on the park bench overlooking the boating lake. She was there most days, even when, like today, it was bitingly cold. Apart from the occasional word with a passing nanny or their small charges, she was sitting very still, almost as though in a daze. But the calmness on the outside didn't reflect the confusion behind Victoria Kavanagh's eyes, her inner turmoil.

It was a year today since her father had died and she'd finally had enough of feigning being in mourning. She was glad he was dead. She was tired of wasting her life and wanted to do something with it. Make a difference to the world – even a small one. If she carried on the way she'd been going, she knew she was in danger of losing her mind.

But how was she going to lay the past to rest once and for all?

Her mind wandered over the years as she reflected back. The events were so clear it was almost as though they were taking place right before her eyes.

Her beautiful mother stood by her dressing table, holding her torn white slip so that her small breasts weren't exposed. Scooping five-year-old Victoria into her arms as they cried together. Though Victoria wasn't sure why they were crying, other than her mother was sad again. Countless tears on her mother's lashes quickly wiped away.

"It's nothing, darling. Silly Mother smashed the vase, that's all."

Even at that young age, Victoria felt her mother wasn't telling the truth. But she had no one she could ask. Unlike most girls of her social class, she didn't have a governess, because her mother had taught her herself. Bridie O'Shea, the housekeeper, just said, "Little pigs have big ears." Or "Curiosity killed the cat – don't ask questions, lass." And she couldn't ask her father, because that would make him angry and somehow, when he got angry, her mother always cried or had a silly accident.

When her father was at work, there were moments of sunshine with her mother, who would sometimes play the piano and smile. But as he entered the front door, the music and laughter would stop – it was as though a menace had settled on the house.

She wasn't sure when exactly she'd realised her father beat her mother. But the image of her nine-year-old self, screaming at her father to let go of her mother's hair and let her get out of bed, still caused a knot in her chest.

Victoria would never forget the terrible scream that just a year later had caused her to scramble out of bed. The image that plagued her from then was one of her father trying to help her mother because she'd fallen down the stairs. Her head was at a funny angle and a thick red substance dribbled from the corner of her mouth. She was staring past Victoria, her eyes blind.

After that, life changed, her father's anger always lurking just below the surface, often erupting. Bridie said he was consumed by grief and guilt at her mother's passing, but Victoria didn't understand. She was sad, too, but *she* didn't bellow at him!

At ten, there was no need to go to school. Instead, it was decided that she'd help Bridie around the house and occasionally work with her father in the shop. She liked the draper's shop. Although she preferred it when he went out and left her in charge, so she didn't have to worry about making his eyes turn black with anger.

When he was out in the evening, Victoria would go into the kitchen to see Bridie, who'd slip her a piece of lardy cake or a scone. Then the old woman would give her a cuddle in the battered armchair as they warmed their stockinged feet by the stove, but always with the strict warning: "Don't tell your father – he wouldn't like you sittin' here like this, lass." Victoria knew Bridie was right – he wasn't a nice man.

At thirteen, she'd been looking through a trunk containing her mother's clothes when a terrible realisation had struck her as she'd fingered a tear in her mother's slip that had been darned. And from then, she believed her father was responsible for her mother's death. From that day, she hated him.

Life in the main was rigid and frightening when he was around – the house deathly quiet. Except when her father's friends came round. Then, the house was no longer quiet. She'd stay up in her room, avoiding the loud men, who'd place their hands on her bottom at any opportunity and laugh when she screamed.

"Leave the girl alone," her father would say, but again, always with a laugh.

Sometimes she'd stand on the landing outside his

bedroom door and listen to the noises he made with the vulgar women he brought home. They weren't the harsh voices and cries she'd heard coming from the room when her mother was alive – and these strange sounds were frequently followed by laughter.

Bridie often said, "I'd be out of this house of sin if it weren't for you, little one."

She never would explain what she meant, but she seemed to know when Victoria was afraid and envelop her in her arms.

"There now, my love, you're safe with Bridie."

At twenty-three, Victoria felt nothing but relief when her father died suddenly of a heart attack. Her cousin, Patrick Davenport, had handled all of her father's affairs and assured her that she was financially secure if she lived sensibly. But she didn't want to be sensible – that was just another word for boring. In some ways life had been better since he'd gone, but the future stretched before her. Endless years of a lonely, childless spinster's life.

She knew she'd never marry. Never allow a man to own her – slap her. She'd found letters and papers after her father's death and knew that her mother had been a relatively wealthy woman before they'd married. But on her marriage, she and everything she owned became the property of her husband.

Victoria knew that since the law had changed a few years back, if she were to marry, she could still own property. But once married, she'd no longer own her own body. She wouldn't be able to stop her husband from beating her if he felt like it, or to protect her children from his anger if he was that way inclined. So *no*, she'd never marry. She was no one's property.

❖ ❖ ❖

Victoria shifted slightly in her seat as she remembered how her visits to the park had begun. They'd started innocently enough.

Short in stature with a formidable character, the housekeeper had dried her hands on her frilled apron and looked at Victoria sternly, but her eyes were kind.

"Where are you off to, lass?"

"I'm going for a walk around the park."

"Good. You've hardly been out the door these last weeks. Make sure you wrap up warm – there's a real nip in the air."

When Victoria had reached the park, the spring sun had provided little warmth as it hung above the boating lake. She'd shivered and fastened the top button of her coat before taking the path around the perimeter. The park was busy, nannies taking their afternoon constitutional with their small charges in tow.

Drawn by the sight of a small boy with a mass of blond curls tottering towards the lake with his toy sailing boat, she'd felt a prick of alarm as she realised that his nanny was deeply engrossed with her counterpart, who was pointing to an infant in the pram.

Quickening her pace to catch up with him, Victoria kept just enough distance so as not to alarm him.

"Hello. That's a lovely boat."

"It's mine," he dimpled, his hazel eyes shining.

"Well, you are a lucky boy."

"I got it for my birthday. I'm four now," he said proudly.

Victoria smiled for the first time in weeks. "My, you

are a big boy. And what's your name?" She glanced over at the nannies, who were still oblivious.

"My name's Tommy."

"Well, Tommy, I really think you should wait for Nanny before you put your nice new boat in the water." Stooping to his level, she felt a sudden urge to pick him up and hold him close.

"Master Thomas, come here this minute, you naughty boy! What do you think you're playing at, young man?"

The nanny's voice was harsh and the boy's face crumpled.

"He was going towards the lake and *you* weren't watching him!" Victoria rounded on the woman, her brown eyes flaring.

Without a word, the nanny grasped the boy's hand and marched off, pulling him along as she engaged once more in conversation with her friend. As Victoria watched them march away, she wanted to call after him, tell him it wasn't his fault, he'd done nothing wrong. She resolved to be *very* careful who she chose as a nanny for her own child.

Then a sinking feeling had washed over her as she acknowledged that she'd never be a mother. Much to Victoria's embarrassment, Bridie had taken her to see the doctor when she was seventeen and hadn't yet begun to have a woman's monthly cycle. After examining her, he'd told her she was unlikely to bear a child. Bridie said it could be a blessing, as children could bring great heartache. Victoria didn't believe it was a blessing – she thought God had decided she wasn't fit to be a mother, punishing her for some sin she wasn't aware of.

Since then, the desire for a child had become a gaping hole in her chest that nothing could fill and she'd been drawn to the park day after day. No one had any idea how much time Victoria spent watching the children – it was her secret.

Then just a few weeks ago, she'd come close to the edge of destruction when she'd offered to call at the apothecary for some liniment for Bridie's arthritic knees while on her daily walk. As she'd turned the corner into Hancock Street, she'd almost collided with a fat, dishevelled woman with wild, matted hair pushing a battered pram with three small children around her ankles.

"Get on with yeh, you little bleeders. And don't come back until you've got that bag full of cinders or I'll scalp yer backsides!"

"But, Mam, I'm starvin'," said a waif of a girl, her eyes enormous in a dirty face.

"I told youse – I ain't got no bleedin' money for food. I'll keep Bertha wi' me. Now, get gone before I lose me temper."

Victoria stood transfixed as the stick-thin children scurried off.

"What yeh bleedin' looking at, yeh snooty cow!" the woman, her teeth blackened, dirty hands on hips, challenged Victoria.

Unable to think of a response, Victoria had crossed the road and rushed on.

After a moment, she'd stopped and looked back to see the woman leave the pram, along with the baby, outside the pub and enter The Nag's Head.

Victoria had been incensed. How could she leave the infant unattended! She rushed into the apothecary, made her purchase, then marched back to the public house and the pram. The baby sucked on the filthy rag she was holding. Peering through the dirty window, the loud woman could be seen sitting at the bar, laughing raucously, downing what looked like a large glass of gin – mother's ruin. The desire to take the baby away from the ghastly woman was overwhelming.

Lifting the infant out of the pram, Victoria's nose crinkled at the stench – she was nothing like the pampered babies in the park. But as she gurgled, Victoria thought she could just go, taking the child with her – give her a better life.

She jumped as the door of the pub swung open with a bang and a man staggered out, falling back against the door.

"Hey, Pol, some tart's messing wi' yer nipper," he slurred.

Victoria plonked the baby back in the pram and ran, her heart pounding in her chest.

Was she really going to steal a child?

Yes! she was. If the drunkard hadn't come out when he had, she'd have stolen a child.

That night, horrified at what she'd almost done, dismal thoughts had flashed through her mind. The bottle of laudanum, left over from when Bridie had fallen and hurt her foot, and a long, endless sleep . . .

Victoria's mind returned to the present. She knew suicide was a sin. She believed that, just as she believed in God. He wasn't always there to make every little thing right. Even to save her mother. Bad things happened. But she wanted to believe in Him, in something good. And she wanted to live. To laugh and make a noise without fear.

The park had become like a drug Victoria knew she couldn't do without. It brought exquisite joy and pain at the same time. But she also knew she had to find a way to stop.

"God, if you *are* real, please help me to find happiness and I promise I will always help others," she bargained.

Part 1

Chapter 1

Bridie crossed to the window, pulled back the heavy velvet curtain and peered out at the ink-black sky that was mottled with balls of white cotton.

"Sure, I wouldn't put a dog out on a night like this," she said as she dropped the curtain. "Why not give Mass a miss?" she suggested, her grey eyes full of concern.

Continuing to put on her thick wool coat, Victoria didn't answer.

"You spend too much time brooding, lass. Aww, sure, it would be grand if you'd just stay home and have the craic, maybe even a glass of sherry."

"Sorry, Bridie, but I have to go. You get off to bed," she urged, knowing full well Bridie would wait up.

"There's not a pick on you and that wind will have you off your feet."

Sighing, her voice heavy, Victoria said, "I know you can't go, not with the roads so slippery, but I need to and I'm not going to let a bit of snow stop me." She fixed her hat firmly on her head.

Victoria could see the older woman's face in the reflection of the mirror, wrinkled with worry, and Victoria loved her for caring so much about her. She'd tried on many occasions to make Bridie understand that even though her father was no longer dominating them, she wouldn't be walking out with or courting anyone. Bridie, bless her, was ever hopeful that she'd come out of herself. But Victoria didn't know how to snap out of it. She was trying – these last few weeks, she'd really tried. She'd even stopped going to the park to watch the children, but this had done nothing to improve her mood. She missed seeing the children, telling herself that it was for the best, hopeful that one day, the longing would die inside her.

She turned and kissed the old woman on the cheek.

"I'll be back before you know it. I think it'll do me good to go," she said, pulling on her kid gloves.

Victoria was unprepared for the icy blast that met her as she stepped outside into the empty square. Her boots sank into the thick layer of snow and soon, her feet were wet and frozen. She struggled to lift her dress clear of the snow while keeping her balance and sodden skirts flapped against her legs, adding to her misery. Despite what she'd said to Bridie, she knew the service wouldn't make her feel better, but she felt compelled to go – it's what her mother would have wanted her to do.

If her father had died before her mother, life would have been so different. She should have protected her mother, stopped him from hurting her. Once again, the guilt of standing by while he destroyed her softly spoken mother weighed on her. But why didn't her mother take Victoria away? She knew the answer – she'd asked herself the question many times before. Fear. Her mother was too afraid, too gentle to save them.

By the time Victoria reached the church, she was drenched and grumpy. As she took her seat, she felt a tapping on her shoulder.

"Bridie not with you tonight then, Miss Kavanagh?"

Bett Turpin, the nosy cook from next door, was the last person Victoria felt like talking to, but she smiled tightly.

"No, Mrs Turpin. Her legs are too bad to cope with the slippery roads."

"Aye, well, at least you're here to say a prayer for your poor sainted father and mother."

Victoria nodded. *Sainted*? That was a joke. Her father could never be called a saint and she wouldn't be praying for him. Outside the home, they'd appeared to be the perfect family. What a farce. It was true what they say – no one knows what goes on behind closed doors. No one heard him shouting at the slightest provocation, or saw him dragging his wife across a room, her arm twisted up her back, almost breaking. Victoria turned back round in her seat, pretending to listen to the service, lost in her own thoughts.

As Bridie always said, "God can't be sortin' out every little problem – He just gives you the strength to cope until you sort them yourself." Even if God could give you what you asked for, Victoria knew she'd never allow herself to have what she craved: a loving husband and children. But if He was listening, surely He wanted her to do something with her life, not waste it sitting at home until she went mad with loneliness and boredom.

As the choir sang the closing carol, Victoria's attention was drawn back to the present. She waited until the aisles cleared – she had no intention of walking back with Mrs Turpin.

The clatter of feet broke the silence as two altar boys, their surplices flapping, scrambled down the aisle and out of the door to join their families. She shivered, suddenly cold. The main doors had been left open and an icy wind swirled around the church, dispensing the previously cloying warmth.

She walked briskly to the rear of the church and paused by the carved wooden screen that surrounded the baptismal font. As she adjusted her coat and pulled on her gloves, she heard a sound like a small animal in pain. She looked around then bent to peer under the pews, expecting to find a kitten or a puppy, but she couldn't see anything. Then she heard the sound again, only this time it was more a whimper.

Curious, she peered into a dark corner behind the font. She could see a bundle and as she approached, she detected a slight movement. She bent gingerly and, with finger and thumb, lifted the corner of a worn, faded quilt, gasping in amazement to see a baby. Its lips were blue and its skin tinged grey. It began to cough as it choked on mucus that rattled in its throat.

Victoria picked it up and carried it into the light, the baby floppy, limp and lifeless in her arms. Instinctively, she turned it over and tapped its back in an attempt to dislodge the obstruction. It coughed weakly. It felt cold – deathly cold. Frantically, she looked around and called out.

"Help. Is there anybody there? Can someone help me? *Anybody*?"

Her voice echoed around the empty church. She undid the buttons on her coat, wrapped the quilt tightly around the baby, thrust the bundle inside and, with a pounding heart, ran from the church. Her mind focused on not falling and injuring the child, melting snow seeping into her skirts, she negotiated the icy pavements of the maze of streets that stood between her and her home.

❖ ❖ ❖

Victoria burst through the front door and ran down the passage to the kitchen, shouting, "Bridie. Bridie, quickly!" Her voice was raspy from the cold, fear and exertion.

She placed the bundle on the rug in front of the fire, removed her wet coat and flung it on the floor. Bridie, who'd been sleeping in the armchair, looked from Victoria to the bundle to the discarded coat, trying to make sense of what was happening. Victoria began pouring boiling water from the brass kettle into a large enamel bowl.

"Add some cold water to the bowl, quickly," she ordered. "And I'll need towels and some old sheeting. Do as I say!"

Bridie, looking bemused, scuttled off. Victoria began to unwrap the bundle. A boy, she thought, a baby boy who will die if I can't save him.

When Bridie returned, Victoria was gently lowering him into the warm water before massaging his tiny frozen limbs.

"Holy Mother of God!" gasped Bridie, crossing herself. "Where did you get that child?"

Victoria ignored her and issued another order.

"Tear the sheeting into broad strips and place the olive oil by the fire to warm."

When she felt the water had warmed him sufficiently, Victoria dried him swiftly then rubbed him vigorously with the oil. Gradually, the infant's skin took on a more natural appearance, so she swaddled him in the sheeting and a large towel before thrusting him into Bridie's reluctant arms. Victoria heated some milk, adding a spoonful of honey, which she poured into a cup. Then she took the baby back in her arms, still fending off Bridie's questions.

With great care, she dribbled the warm fluid from a spoon into his mouth. Instinctively, he tried to suckle, but the milk spewed out. After several attempts, she managed to get him to swallow a little of the liquid, only to see him vomit it back as he was seized by yet another violent coughing fit. Feeling desperate, she persevered every few minutes until some of the milk stayed down and his breathing eased.

He fell into a fitful sleep and Victoria placed him in a basket by the fire, watching over him while explaining to Bridie how the infant came to be in their care. Eventually, she agreed to let Bridie help her to remove her wet boots and saturated stockings before leaving the kitchen to change out of her damp clothes. She returned wrapped in a thick dressing-gown, looking even whiter than usual. Glancing at the baby to check he was still breathing, she slumped at the table, overcome with fatigue.

Bridie pushed a steaming cup of cocoa and two slices of hot buttered toast in front of her.

"Come on. Drink up and eat that toast, lass," she urged. "I've a feeling we're not going to be sleeping much tonight."

Not wanting to offend the exhausted-looking older woman, Victoria obeyed, muttering her thanks.

Over the next few hours, Victoria barely took her eyes off the child for fear he'd deteriorate and need a doctor. Bridie sat with her, despite Victoria urging her to get some sleep. When at Bridie's insistence she explained for the third time how she'd found the infant, Bridie shook her head in disbelief.

"It's almost morning. Once we've had breakfast, I'll run and fetch Father O'Reilly before he does the morning service. He'll need to find the buggers who left this little one to perish."

"No. We'll keep him warm and nurse him for a few days until he's stronger."

"What are you blatherin' about? We can't keep him here!"

"Just a few days, then we'll see what the priest has to say," she promised.

"I'm not sure we should wait. Father O'Reilly will know what's best." Anxiety etched Bridie's face.

"Please. It's Christmas Day and he'll be busy. Give me a couple of days to make sure he survives," she cajoled, grasping Bridie's wrinkled hand.

"How's it going to look if he dies and we didn't tell anyone you'd found him?" Not waiting for a reply, she added, "We could be done for murder."

"I won't let him die. If he doesn't show signs of improving, I'll fetch the doctor, I promise."

Bridie began to tidy the kitchen, still shaking her head and muttering.

"Dear God, if you've got a plan in mind for this child, I wish you'd share it with me."

Victoria wasn't ready to tell Bridie what was *actually* going on in her mind – she wanted to keep him. But at the back of her mind, the question lurked: had she, in a moment of madness, stolen him? No! she told herself firmly. She'd called out for help, but there was no one left in the church. No one wanted him but her.

Later in the day, Victoria and Bridie exchanged small Christmas gifts – a picture of Our Lady for Bridie, a mother-of-pearl hair comb for Victoria. Although Victoria thanked and hugged her gratefully, she knew her best present was sleeping soundly.

For the next few days, Victoria and Bridie tended to the baby between them. He was now taking milk and his movements were stronger, but his breathing was far from normal. Not wanting Bridie going out of the house in case she was tempted to go to the church and speak to the priest, Victoria had rushed out to the apothecary to buy a baby's bottle.

Instead of going to the nearest one, where people might know her, she'd raced to one on the other side of Liverpool. Guilt coursed through her. She was selfish! He'd thrive best with a wet nurse, but she couldn't risk bringing one to the house. A wet nurse would mean he'd be taken away and in her heart, she felt his best chance of a happy life was with her.

On the sixth day, after extracting Bridie's promise that she'd tell no one, Victoria conceded to Bridie's request to go out to fetch fresh milk and flour – she couldn't exactly hold her prisoner. While she was out, Victoria decided that it would be safe to wash him.

He was about three months old, with fine features and long limbs. Thick brown hair curled onto his forehead and his large eyes were fringed with dense dark lashes. He was kicking his legs and his thin arms were flailing. She smiled tenderly. He even has brown eyes like me, she thought.

"How could they leave you to die, little man?" Tears smarted.

As she leaned over him, his tiny fingers grabbed the gold chain dangling from her neck. She laughed as she disentangled her jewellery from his grip.

"You little scamp!" Impulsively, she kissed his tiny hand.

She'd never divulged to anyone just how much she'd longed for a child, how the ache to nurse a child was a physical pain. And how could she explain that the emotion growing within her since she'd held him was now so strong it threatened to overwhelm her? Her chest felt tight with fear that she might not be able to protect him. Intuitively, she gathered him in her arms and held him close, her cheek against his.

"I'm going to find a way to keep you forever," she whispered. Shocked at hearing her admission aloud, a rare smile played on her lips and she held him high over her head. "Did you hear that, young man?" she shouted. "I'm going to find a way to keep you!"

Victoria knew that she'd have to devise a plan – a web of deceit and lies. She could tell people that he was a cousin's child who had been orphaned and she'd taken him in. People might suspect that he was her illegitimate child, but she'd deal with that when the time came – it was too important not to. And she'd have to get Bridie's cooperation – that wouldn't be easy.

One thing Victoria knew for certain was that Bridie loved her. Since her own mother's death, Bridie had been the only woman in her life. She'd been Victoria's nursemaid as a child, as well as doing the cooking and cleaning. She'd worked hard all of her life and was particularly proud of how she'd helped to raise Victoria.

When Bridie returned, Victoria had a pot of tea waiting. She began to put the provisions away, saying casually, "Would you do me a favour and feed the baby? He always takes more milk for you."

"Even at that young age, they know when they're in experienced hands."

Bridie took the child from the basket and began to feed him, a faraway look on her face.

"Isn't he a handsome boy?" Victoria asked.

Bridie, intent on the task in hand, merely nodded.

"You and I saved his life, Bridie."

Still, the old woman didn't respond.

"I think we should keep him. Give him a loving home."

Bridie spluttered and got to her feet with surprising agility. She thrust the boy into Victoria's arms as though he were burning her fingers.

"Jaysus! We can't do that. It's against the law! It would be a mortal sin."

"It was a mortal sin to leave him to die."

"That may be so, but two wrongs don't make a right. Anyway, how would you explain him if a gentleman wanted to marry you?"

Victoria gave a harsh laugh. "Good God! Do you honestly think I'd ever marry after what I witnessed in this house?"

Bridie flinched – they'd never spoken about her father's treatment of her mother.

"Now, there's no need to take the Lord's name in vain. Besides, not all men are like your father."

"Well, I'm not prepared to take that chance. In any case, I'm twenty-four years old. I don't exactly have male admirers queuing up. Come to think of it, I don't even have *any* male acquaintances other than Patrick. Apart from my hair and maybe my eyes, I'm nothing to look at, so I'm not going to worry about putting off prospective husbands."

"You're not an unattractive woman."

Victoria ignored her remark.

"They'll take him to Myrtle Street Orphanage and

you've always said you'd never send a dog there. We can't condemn him to that."

"I think we should send for Father O'Reilly." Bridie stuck her chin out.

Tears of frustration slowly leaked from Victoria's eyes and rolled down her cheeks. She wiped them away angrily.

"Please, Bridie. Please help me. Even if I could find a man I trusted, you know I'm not like most women. How could I ever expect a man to marry me when there's virtually no chance I could give him a child? I want a child of my own, Bridie. Surely you can understand that." Victoria thought she saw something in Bridie's face, some sense of understanding, a softening. She continued, "We have to keep him safe. I'll ask Patrick to help me."

Bridie's brow creased. "He's a bigwig lawyer. You can't ask him to break the law. Once it's done there will be no turning back. Think about what you're taking on before you go jumping in with both feet. Will you do that for me?"

"I'll think about it, that much I can promise you." Victoria hugged her.

"Go on with you!" Bridie said as she settled her weary bones in the armchair.

A week later, Victoria was sitting in the kitchen almost nodding off as she gazed at the child nestled in the crook of her arm. She loved the feeling of his warm little body in her arms, his eyes staring intently at her face. She'd looked after the baby single-handed. She felt Bridie was testing her resolve and was determined not to give in. Even though the baby was sleeping better and recovering well, she'd checked on him constantly throughout the night. The 24-hour vigil was beginning to take its toll and disorientated by a lack of sleep, she was on the verge of collapse.

She jolted awake at the sound of rapping on the back door and froze.

"Bridie, 'ave you got time for a cuppa, love?" a loud voice called.

Victoria recognised the voice – it was the cook from next door. Since her father's death, Mrs Turpin had occasionally taken to calling in for a cup of tea with Bridie. Victoria eyes darted to Bridie, who was stood at the table making bread.

Before either of them responded, the door opened and a rotund woman with white hair and several chins waddled in.

"I just thought we could put our feet up and have a natter for a few minutes." She looked at Victoria, surprised to see her there, then her chins wobbled slightly as her mouth hung in astonishment at the sight of Victoria cradling a child.

Bridie stood immobile, her hands sunk into the dough on the large, well-scrubbed wooden table.

"Mrs Turpin, how are you?" Victoria said, rising, trying to steady her breathing.

"Err, I'm all right. Sorry to have disturbed you. I can see yer busy," she said, nodding at the child.

"This is my cousin Alice's baby. I'm just looking after him for a while. Her husband is unwell and she's too busy nursing him to care for the child." Victoria was amazed at how swiftly she'd invented both a cousin and a story.

"Aye, he's just here until his dad's on the mend," Bridie added hurriedly.

Victoria looked at her gratefully.

"Oh, I see. Live local, do they?" Bett asked.

"No, they live in Manchester," Victoria answered, cutting her short, knowing how much the woman loved gossip. "If you don't mind excusing us, Mrs Turpin. Bridie's very busy at the moment, now we have the child to care for." She rose and stood holding the door open with one hand, the baby in the other.

"Aye, course. P'rhaps I'll see you tomorrow, Bridie."

"Aye, perhaps, Bett. But it's best if I give you a shout when I've got time. As yeh can see, I've got me hands full at the moment," Bridie said, wiping her sticky hands on her apron before taking the child from Victoria. She watched the woman waddling down the yard. "It'll be killing her not knowing all the details." She turned to Victoria, who was trembling slightly. "Aww, lass, you're as determined as yer da at times. Don't look at me like that – yeh know it's true. And you know I couldn't love you more if you were me own child. I want you to be happy, yeh know that an' all."

"Do you think she believed us?" Victoria asked, her breath coming fast.

Bridie took the place in the armchair Victoria had vacated.

"Go to bed, lass. Get some rest – I think you're gonna need it," she said gently. "I'll take care of the little fella. And don't worry – Bett Turpin will get nowt more outta me. I've been keeping the secrets of this house for over twenty years and I won't be telling that nosy old goat any more than she's had from you already. But this is just the beginning, lass. There'll be a lot more questions and judging you before you've finished with this business. Mark my words."

Victoria embraced the old woman and then dutifully went upstairs. As she undressed, she discarded her clothes in a heap. They had to get far away from anyone who knew them, and fast. But for now, she was too tired, her mind too befuddled to think clearly. She fell into bed, where she slept soundly for fourteen hours.

When she woke, she tore downstairs in a panic. The baby was safe in the basket and a huge fire crackled in the grate. Smells of freshly baked bread and Irish stew filled the kitchen. Bridie, in a spotless starched apron, was setting the table.

Without looking up, Bridie said, "Supper won't be too long. You've just enough time to take a bath."

It was at that moment that Victoria felt she might have got Bridie on her side.

The following day, Bridie listened as Victoria outlined her plan, pulling a map from the drawer.

"I'm going to sell the house and look for some shop premises in one of these towns . . ." She pointed to the two towns she'd visited on buying trips with her father, outwardly excited and confident. She was determined not to voice any of her concerns. It was important Bridie and Patrick believe that she knew what she was doing, that she was thinking clearly. "Nobody will know us and I can pass myself off as a widow. I can open a shop and do dressmaking. We can have a new life. Make a home and be a family." She held her breath, looking at Bridie expectantly.

Bridie cupped her chin. "I'm not sure about all this, lass. I don't relish the idea of living a lie, or moving, but yer right – you can't stay here. I know you well enough to know you're as stubborn as a mule. So if yer mind's set, I won't be able to change it."

Victoria was stunned – Bridie wasn't going to go with her . . . She went to speak, but Bridie held up her hand to stop her.

"But I've not seen a spark like this in you since yer poor mam passed, God bless her soul." Bridie crossed herself. "There's been times I thought you might just fade away and join her. So if this little lamb . . ." She gestured towards the basket. "Well, if he's what you need to be happy, then I guess I'll go along with it."

Victoria felt the tension leave her shoulders. She went to hug Bridie, who held up her hand again.

"But only if Mr Patrick agrees."

"Bridie, you're an absolute darling and I love you." She squeezed Bridie, planting a kiss on her sagging cheek.

Bridie turned her head away, blushing.

"Well, let's see what Mr Patrick says and then we'll go from there. He might see some flaws in this plan o' yours."

"Very well." No matter what Patrick said, she wouldn't give up the boy, but it would be much easier *with* his help.

Victoria understood why Bridie thought she was stubborn, as one morning she'd gone into the kitchen and stated quietly, "I hate my father." She wouldn't explain to Bridie why – Bridie wasn't the only one who could be tight-lipped. But from that day, Victoria barely spoke more than two words to her father, answering his questions with ill-concealed contempt. No amount of raging from him or coaxing from Bridie could get her to give in.

"Jaysus, he's like a raging bull. Can yeh not just speak to him?" Bridie would plead.

But no, she couldn't. Victoria wasn't her mother. Bridie was right – she had her mother's heart, but a band of steel ran through her core like it had her father.

Chapter 2

Although Patrick was nine years older than Victoria, he'd always been kind to her. Occasional afternoons spent at his home were some of Victoria's happiest memories. Her visits had ceased abruptly shortly after Patrick left for boarding school, when his mother and his younger sister, Martha, had died of tuberculosis. Victoria had asked her mother if they could still call on Patrick and her uncle during school holidays, but her mother had said, "I'm afraid your father will never allow it now. Please don't ask him, as it will make him cross." And that was the end of it.

Then as she got older, she'd begun to write to Patrick – grateful for a connection outside her dismal home. Following her father's death, Patrick had been a tower of strength and they'd begun to grow close again. She felt sure Patrick would help her, but there was only one way to find out.

On Saturday, Victoria began to make final preparations for his visit, knowing that the way to Patrick's heart was through his stomach. Despite his wealth, he rented a shabby suite of rooms close to his practice. He constantly complained about his housekeeper's slipshod ways and poor culinary skills but did nothing to replace her. Victoria suspected her gentle cousin was a little afraid of his imperious housekeeper.

"Jaysus, lass, we've cleaned this house from top to bottom. Mr Patrick could eat his dinner off the floor, never mind the table."

"I just want to make sure everything is perfect."

"I don't think a clean house is gonna lessen the shock of what you're about to tell him, lass. I just hope he's got a strong ticker or you'll be getting the doctor out to him."

"I'll lead up to it gently."

"Gently! There's no way to put this gentle."

Victoria could hear Bridie laughing mirthlessly as she went back to the kitchen.

Nervously, Victoria checked her appearance in the mirror over the mantelpiece. She was wearing a day dress that she'd made herself in a soft-peach embroidered cambric. She'd swept her hair up in a tight bun, hoping it added a couple of years to her appearance. Patrick knew full well how old she was, but she wanted to portray herself as a responsible woman and potential business owner, as well as a capable mother.

She turned as Bridie came back into the room and stationed herself by the window, from where she could get a good view of Stanley Square.

"Well, at least the little fella's sleeping. We don't want him crying and putting the cat among the pigeons before you've had a chance to soften Mr Patrick up a bit." She dodged behind the curtain. "Jaysus, Mary and Joseph! Mr Patrick's carriage has just turned the corner." She crossed herself, looking to Victoria for instructions.

"Will you just calm down! Let him ring the bell, then answer the door and take his driver to the kitchen after he's stabled the horse."

Victoria began to breathe deeply in an effort to control

her own nervousness. She must appear composed at all costs.

The sound of the doorbell echoed through the house. Victoria could hear her cousin chatting to Bridie as he no doubt removed his hat and coat. Smiling, he appeared, his bulk filling the doorway to the drawing room.

"Hello, Vicky! Lovely to see you. This invitation was a welcome surprise. I was worried you were unwell, but I see you're glowing." He crossed the room and planted a kiss on both cheeks.

"Good to see you, Patrick," she beamed with genuine affection.

She handed him a large glass of brandy, which he proceeded to sip noisily with his back to the fire. He was over six feet tall but appeared shorter because he had a permanent stoop.

"The house looks splendid, my dear." Patrick lifted his head and sniffed the air like a hound scenting a fox. "What are we having?"

"All your favourites," Victoria smiled.

Job done – she'd succeeded in the first part of her mission.

Somehow, throughout a lavish luncheon of soup, sirloin of beef, apple pie and cheeses, Victoria managed a little small talk, asking Patrick if he'd enjoyed his Christmas and New Year break at his friend's lodge in Scotland, enquiring about his latest cases. Feeling increasingly edgy, she ate little. Her whole future might rest on this meeting.

At last, they returned to the drawing room. Patrick held his second large brandy in his doughy hand.

"What is it, my dear? You seem jumpy and you hardly ate a thing. And you're awfully pale all of a sudden, if you don't mind my saying."

"Patrick," she ventured, "I need some advice."

"Of course, my dear. What can I help you with?"

She took a deep breath and spoke. "I want to sell the house and buy shop premises."

Patrick began to chuckle. "What nonsense is this?"

"It's not nonsense. It's something I want to do and I need your advice." Her eyes flashed. "I want to open a drapers and a haberdashery, and offer a dressmaking service."

Patrick leaned back in his chair as though to get a better look at her.

"Vicky, you have no need to work. Your father provided well for you and it's all been invested wisely. You have an income for life if you live quietly. Why risk your capital in a business? You've no experience. It would be disastrous."

Victoria knew she had a little of her father's temper. If she didn't control it now, she wouldn't obtain Patrick's help.

"Patrick, I don't want to live quietly. I've done that most of my life. I could easily run a draper's shop. I've done bookkeeping and stocktaking. I worked on the counters alone for a month during the flu epidemic and I've even been on buying trips with my father. I've always made my own dresses. I made this one . . ." She held her arms wide, her eyes narrowed defiantly – Patrick had touched a raw nerve.

"Vicky, my dear, I really don't understand. What on earth has got into you? Why do you want to work?" His voice was gentle now.

"I'm bored and lonely, if you must know. My life is wasting away. My entire life has revolved around this house. It's like a prison. I don't want to rot here forever."

"My dear girl, there are many charitable organisations that would be delighted to acquire the services of a bright young woman like you."

"That's not what I want to do. I want the challenge of a business, something that's mine."

"But what about marriage? I may be your cousin, but even I can see you're attractive."

"Patrick, were you aware my father was a tyrant?" She didn't allow him to respond. "He was a bully and a violent brute. He made my mother's life hell. I will *never* marry." She shook her head.

"Even so, Vicky, I . . ." He shifted uncomfortably in his chair. "You're right . . . er, I do know something about the situation. My parents did try to persuade your mother to leave, but . . . er . . . well, she never felt able. But we . . . We're not all tarred with the same brush."

"Do you know how I envied the freedom of your home, where Martha and I could run, play, laugh and even shout if we wanted?" Victoria remembered how Patrick's father had chased them round the garden pretending to be an ogre.

"Of course I remember. But you could have that in your own home. You're still young. You might change your mind. Don't you want a family? I'm sure you'd make a wonderful mother."

Victoria didn't answer. He stared at her, waiting for a response.

Silently, Victoria rang the bell to summon Bridie. As arranged, Bridie entered the room with the baby wrapped in an embroidered quilt. She handed him over to Victoria, casting a sideways glance at Patrick as she sidled from the room. Patrick's eyes were wide, his brandy sloshing onto his lap. He moved his mouth to speak, but no sound came. When he found his voice, he exploded.

"Where on *earth* did that child come from?"

Victoria began to tell him how she'd found the boy in the church on Christmas Eve.

"Christmas Eve! Are you out of your tiny mind? I take it you have informed the police?" His face was scarlet.

Victoria shook her head defiantly. "No. There's been no reports of a lost baby, or of parents abandoning one and changing their minds. I want to keep him. I'm going to give him a home."

Victoria knew it was now or never. It was time to open her heart and be as honest as she could. If she was to secure his help, this was the only way.

"You've just said I'd make a wonderful mother. I can't expect you to understand fully the need a woman feels to have a child. But the one thing I do know is that I'm unlikely to bear one of my own. The doctor told me when I was younger. It's like a gaping hole in my chest, and it's getting bigger and more painful. Every time I see a child or hear its laughter, it's like a knife to my heart." She stopped short of telling him about her visits to the park or the child she almost stole.

Patrick's eyes were steely. "My dear, not reporting that you found him was a criminal act. Even if I wanted to help you, it's impossible. I cannot become involved in any way. But I'm sure you would be allowed to be his guardian if you went through the correct channels."

Victoria felt her eyes stinging and fought in vain to hold back the tears.

"Patrick, I can't risk losing him. I don't want to be his guardian. I want to be his mother. I feel so very empty and I want . . . *need* to be a mother. I'm doing this with or without your blessing." As the tears flowed, she kissed the baby's head.

Patrick came to her side, hovering helplessly, attempting to get her to accept his handkerchief.

"Please stop blubbering, my dear."

"I just want help to sell the house and find shop premises. You've no need to get involved with the baby." She was unable to stem the flow.

"I'd be aiding and abetting. I could be disbarred!"

"Not for simply helping me to sell the house."

"I'm staggered by what you have done. I'm sorry, Victoria, but it's out of the question!" Patrick shook his head as he rang the bell.

Bridie appeared almost immediately, which made Victoria suspect that she'd been lurking behind the door eavesdropping.

"I'm leaving," said Patrick. "Please fetch my coat and tell my driver I'm ready."

Bridie, her face anxious, scurried off.

Victoria made one last appeal.

"Please give it some thought. I'm determined never to marry. This is my only chance to have a child and I don't know what I'll do if I lose him. It's only been a couple of weeks, but I love him with all of my heart. No one else wanted him. I saved his life! I *am* his mother already. I have no one else to turn to. Please help me."

Patrick looked at her tear-stained face. She knew he cared for her – she was his only family. Despite his obvious annoyance and concern over her actions, he bent to kiss her cheek.

"I'll have to consider all the implications. I'll be in touch."

With that, he left the house without waiting for Bridie to show him out.

Victoria held the baby close as she watched him stumble absentmindedly to his carriage. He was no doubt wondering how to get her to give up the child. She swallowed down her frustration.

The following few days passed slowly. Every knock at the door filled Victoria with dread in case Patrick had decided to inform the authorities. Bridie didn't improve the situation, muttering about how Patrick would never agree to the plan, but at least she hadn't let Mrs Turpin back in the house.

It was a Saturday morning when Patrick arrived unannounced. Victoria was in the parlour sewing a frock for the baby when Bridie showed him in and hovered nervously until Victoria asked her to leave, taking the sleeping child with her.

"Vicky, I'll come straight to the point. I still think this is madness. But I know you didn't have a pleasant childhood and I can't stand the thought of you being unhappy for the rest of your life. You're so damned stubborn, I expect you'll do it without my help anyway. I can't quite believe I'm saying this, but I'm going to help you."

"Oh, Patrick, thank you." Victoria jumped up and flung her arms around his neck, kissing his cheek and almost overbalancing him.

"Steady on, old girl. I've not finished yet. How about I buy this place from you? It will speed up the process, get you out of Liverpool quickly. Besides, it's time I had a place of my own."

"Oh, Patrick, would you? I-I don't know how to thank you."

"I just hope we don't live to regret it."

"We won't, I promise. I'll make this work."

"Hmm, well, I've made enquiries. It seems a ship left for America on Christmas Eve. And given that the church where you found him is close to the docks, I suspect his parents were on board. Damned silly time to sail, if you ask me – the seas will be rough at this time of year – but I expect that's why there was a large number of poor Irish emigrants, as passage would have been cheaper."

Almost an hour later, Patrick left, once more seeing himself out. Victoria was glowing with excitement and could barely contain herself as she flew into the kitchen, where Bridie was feeding the baby.

"Well?" said Bridie. "What's happening?"

"Bridie! Oh, Bridie. We can keep him. Isn't it wonderful!" She took the baby from Bridie and smothered his face with kisses as she intermittently told Bridie what Patrick had said. "Patrick's taken the quilt the baby was wrapped in when I found him to make some discreet enquiries and see if it confirms his theory."

"Enquiries! Surely not with the police? Tell me he isn't doing that, lass."

"No. He felt he couldn't use any of his police contacts, but he knows a private detective, so he's going to get him to investigate."

"A private detective?"

"Yes, who'd have thought Patrick would know a private detective!" A broad grin lit up her face.

"Well I never. If Mr Patrick is helping, maybe we can make a go of it. I still have me concerns though, lass. I doubt it'll be as easy as you think it will." Bridie sighed as she filled the copper kettle.

Victoria hesitated. In for a penny . . .

"Bridie, now we know we're keeping him, he has to have a name."

"Aye, lass, I suppose he does. What have you come up with, then? No doubt you've already thought of summat."

"Sean."

Bridie didn't answer, moving her pursed lips from side to side, mulling it over. Eventually, she gave her verdict.

"It's a bit modern, but I like it."

"Would you like to choose a second name?" she asked, praying Bridie didn't pick something old-fashioned.

"Hmm . . . What about Christian?"

"I like that. Sean Christian. It suits him. Why Christian?"

"Well, at least he'll be a Christian in name, 'cos we won't be able to have the little lamb baptised in church, after all."

The thought had occurred to Victoria, but she hadn't allowed herself to dwell on it. Now, she wondered what other difficulties would present themselves as they began this new life.

Chapter 3

A month later, Victoria was glad she'd chosen to wear her best coat with fur collar, matching hat and muff as she paced up and down excitedly on the cold platform at Lime Street Station in Liverpool. Patrick had established that the quilt was of a traditional Irish design peculiar to a small area of County Mayo, so he was reasonably sure that no one would lay claim to the child later. Now, all she had to do was get away before anyone discovered her secret. Bett Turpin was still poking around, but so far Bridie had risen to the challenge of keeping their meddlesome neighbour at bay.

As the train hissed to a stop, she waited for passengers to alight. Victoria wondered if Faredene – being over thirty miles from Liverpool – was far enough away to keep their old life a secret. She certainly hoped so. Having been there with her father the year before he died, she felt the thriving market town would be a good place to raise her son. She was incredibly nervous at the prospect of meeting Patrick's solicitor friend, though. Her experience of the opposite sex had been extremely limited – and in the case of her father's friends, unpleasant.

"May I help you with your bag?"

An extremely handsome, elegantly dressed gentleman

held open the door to a first-class compartment so Victoria could climb in. Taking her bag, he lifted it easily into the overhead rack. Thanking him for his help, she placed her coat, gloves and other accessories on the seat next to her as the man took the seat opposite. Conscious of his grey eyes staring at her, she'd have preferred him to sit further down the compartment. She looked out of the window as the train pulled away, avoiding his penetrating gaze.

"I'm James Brakenridge. I hope you don't mind my introducing myself, but as we are to be travelling companions, it seems impolite not to do so." He inclined his head in greeting.

"Not at all. Victoria Kavanagh."

"Travelling far?"

"Er, yes. I'm going to Faredene."

"What a coincidence! So am I," he smiled. When Victoria didn't respond, he continued, "I live there – Faredene Hall. And you? Are you visiting someone?"

Victoria felt unnerved by his unflinching stare and his questions. Was it appropriate for her to chat with him? Her mother had died before she'd had the opportunity to teach Victoria how a lady should behave, particularly around gentlemen. She couldn't just ignore him, so she decided to practise her story on him.

"I'm recently widowed." She indicated the black dress she'd chosen for the occasion, making sure he could see her mother's wedding band, which she was wearing to give authenticity to her words. "I'm looking for business premises and a home for myself and my son."

As James began to ask questions about her business, she could feel her excitement growing as she outlined her plans. It was far easier to talk to this stranger than she'd expected. Other than Patrick and her father, this was the longest conversation she'd ever had with a man and she was surprised how pleasant she found it. He was so encouraging and seemed interested in her plans.

"If there's anything I can do to assist you in your venture, I would be happy to oblige, ma'am. I have a number of business contacts in the area." He smiled broadly.

As the train approached Faredene, Victoria looked out of the windows on both sides, amazed at how quickly the journey had gone. On one side of the tracks were open fields with a hillside beyond. On the other side she could see the canal running parallel with the track, town buildings flanking the towpath. There was an abundance of greenery and the horizon seemed bigger somehow, so different from the crowded skyline of Liverpool. It would be a wonderful place to live, away from the grime of the city. She could take her son out into the surrounding countryside for picnics and walks along the towpath.

Screeching and straining, the train came to a halt and she rose from her seat, hastily pulling on her coat and reaching for her gloves, eager to be off and begin her search for their new home, their new life.

James helped her down with her bag. He bowed slightly, his blond hair falling forwards, and kissed her hand, sending a tingle of excitement rushing through her. She'd never experienced this type of feeling and blushed again, hoping he wasn't able to determine the effect the simple action had had on her.

"Good day, Mrs Kavanagh. I hope your search is successful and that we will meet again soon. If you move to Faredene, I'm sure we'll run into each other – it's a small town. You must allow me to take you to luncheon, to welcome you to the area," he said before striding off to his awaiting carriage.

Having refused Mr Brakenridge's offer of a lift in his carriage, Victoria donned her gloves before she walked off the platform into Station Road and over the canal bridge, passing a few small shops before The Crown Hotel came into view. It was rather shabby, in need of a new coat of paint at the least. But she hadn't risked booking The Royal Oak in case she was recognised from her previous visit with her father. Nervously, she checked in as Mrs Kavanagh.

Victoria tipped the porter, who'd put her valise just inside the bedroom door. Her room was small, as run-down as the rest of the hotel, but at least it was clean. She didn't care what the room looked like. This was her first time in a hotel alone, she'd spoken to a charming man on the train and with any luck, she was about to buy a shop. Best of all, she had a son. Her life was changing.

"Victoria Kavanagh, you are taking part in the world!" She flopped back on the bed, laughing.

Having washed quickly and tided her hair, she returned to the lobby and took a seat from where she could see the entrance. At noon exactly, the doors swung open and a man with dark hair walked in. Victoria couldn't help watching, fascinated by his gait. He had a slight limp and held his right arm close to his body. Conscious that she was staring, Victoria looked at her hands in her lap.

At the very moment Victoria settled into her hotel room, thinking what a nice man James Brakenridge was, he was arriving home at Faredene Hall. Ignoring his butler's greeting, he stalked through the entrance.

"Where's your mistress?" he barked.

"I believe Mrs Brakenridge is in her room, sir."

The butler took the hat and coat that were thrust at him, his disdainful look going unnoticed as James strode across the large entrance hall before taking the wide, curved staircase two at a time. Without knocking, he threw open the door to his wife's room and crossed directly to where Lydia was sitting at her bureau. Swiftly, she pushed the letter she'd been reading in the drawer.

"Not still writing to that stupid friend of yours, I hope."

Ignoring his remark, she stood up, her voice wavering as she asked, "Have you had a successful trip, James?"

Seizing her, he ripped at the buttons on the bodice of her rose-coloured silk gown. Lydia struggled as she attempted to push his hands away.

"Not now, James. Please, I need to go to the nursery to see Charles."

"That's what servants are for. I've been away for three days and you *will* do your duty."

As he threw up his hands in annoyance, she tried to manoeuvre around her husband.

Blocking her way, he sneered, "I've just spent some time with a lovely young woman. Long dark hair, big brown eyes – positively glowed. Why can't you ever look excited?"

"I don't need to hear about another of your conquests, James."

Managing to sidestep him, she once again moved towards the door. But James grasped her blonde hair as she slid past, dragging her backwards towards the bed.

"Please, James. I beg you, please."

James grabbed her shoulders, smirking at the look on his wife's face.

"I love it when you look scared. Maybe that's why you do it. Perhaps it's all part of a game."

"Don't be ridiculous, James."

James gripped her face, squeezing her cheeks hard.

"Don't you dare call me ridiculous," he growled. "And she's not *yet* a conquest, but she will be. I had to amuse myself, imagining biting one of her girlish breasts as she prattled on about the business she's opening." Snatching Lydia's hand, he pressed it hard against his trousers. "Can you feel how aroused she's got me? It's more than you can manage. Either I have *you* now, or I get someone up here from the servants' quarters again. Your choice."

"James, no. Not a maid. Why do you feel the need to humiliate me with the servants? You have plenty of other women you can use."

James laughed. "I didn't *think* you'd want me to take my ease downstairs."

He shoved her face down on the bed. Hauling up her skirts, he tore at her undergarments, pushing her face into the covers to muffle his wife's sobs.

Edward Caldwell had seen the woman watching him walk across the room. Most people stared – until they got used to seeing him. He, on the other hand, had never got used to being an object of pity, to causing women to look away as she had. Born with his left leg shorter than the other and a deformed right hand, he'd been fortunate that his parents hadn't allowed him to wallow in self-pity. Despite the pain it caused him, he'd learned to write with it, avoiding the wrath of the teachers any left-handed boys had faced.

"You have a brilliant mind. You mustn't let your deformities hold you back, son," had been his father's mantra.

Edward tried to remember it every day of his life. But it hadn't made school life any easier – James Brakenridge and his followers had seen to that. Even going on to study law at Oxford, receiving a first-class honours degree and passing the bar, hadn't made him feel whole.

He scanned the lobby. There was only the beautiful dark-haired woman with high cheekbones and full lips who'd been staring. He took a deep breath before he made his way to where she was sitting. He removed his hat and bowed slightly, smiling warmly.

"Mrs Kavanagh?" he enquired.

Victoria almost laughed when he called her Mrs. He was the third person today and it still sounded odd. She'd better get used to it – she wouldn't want people to think she was gurning at them.

Regaining her composure, she extended her hand. He took it and kissed it in a business-like manner.

"Edward. Edward Caldwell. May I sit here?" he asked, indicating a chair opposite hers.

"Yes, please do."

He went on to explain how he and her cousin had become close friends at university, expressing his fondness for Patrick and his respect for his rise in the legal profession. He then produced a sheaf of papers and handed them to her one by one.

"Patrick was a little vague as to your exact requirements, so I have viewed a number of properties for you to consider. I hope you will like the ones I have selected to show you."

Victoria scrutinised the papers. Trying to take in all the details was difficult as she was hit by the sudden realisation that she, too, was a little vague about what she wanted. In her mind, she could picture the shop, their home, but the list of rooms and sizes on the papers did little to inspire her.

"With your permission, I will escort you to see the available properties and show you the town at the same time." Edward placed the papers back in his leather briefcase ready for their departure.

As Victoria stepped into the carriage that was waiting outside, she was extremely grateful she wouldn't have to view the properties alone. Edward wrapped a thick plaid rug across her knees and she tried not to look at his hand as he adjusted the rug, but it was clear he had difficulty moving his twisted fingers. She wondered if it was painful but resisted the urge to say she could manage, nervous of embarrassing him or hurting his feelings. As he climbed into the carriage, she noticed one shoe was built-up. The shoe, she assumed, was helping him to walk straighter. Life was cruel at times.

Victoria groaned as she climbed back into the carriage several hours later. They'd looked at far too many properties, in her opinion, which were completely unsuitable, and all of her earlier enthusiasm had evaporated.

"I can see you're disappointed," Edward said as he took his seat. "Patrick gave me no indication of your budget. Some of the properties I've shown you can be bought very reasonably. Completely refurbished, the last one would provide a decent amount of space."

"I'm sorry. I don't want to appear ungrateful. It's just that I'm not simply looking for a shop. I want to find a home, somewhere I can raise my son."

"So, the Rows, with only one outhouse and standpipe to service the entire street, are not for you, then?"

Victoria couldn't tell if he was teasing her but answered in the same manner.

"I'm sure the mill workers who live in that area are all very decent, hardworking folk, as you pointed out. But peeling paint, broken windows and faded, torn curtains definitely aren't to my taste."

"What about the third property, then? It was in a good part of town."

Their definition of good was clearly at odds. Victoria could smell the fishmongers next door to the vacant property before she saw the lines of fish laid out in morbid display. And the store itself had been littered with the debris of a sudden departure – she'd had to breathe through her mouth as the smell of mould, damp and decay had warred in her nostrils.

"I'm afraid it would take too long to refurbish. I want to move quickly." Victoria stopped abruptly, her face taut. She didn't want him asking why she needed to move in haste.

Edward was staring at her. "Don't look so worried. I understand. Some of them *were* awful, weren't they?"

"They were *all* pretty dreadful." A smile tickled her lips.

"Which do you think was the worst?"

"That's hard to say. It's a close race."

"Was it the butchers? That grey apron and the rotting meat with flies crawling all over it was ghastly, wasn't it? And what about that poor sheep in the back waiting to be slaughtered?"

"That was a particularly bad one."

"Or the empty grocers with the cockroaches and the brown furry thing?"

"Hmm. Perhaps the grocers."

"I thought so. I don't think I've ever heard anyone scream so loudly. I thought you were going to jump into my arms."

Victoria blushed. "Well, it was a very large mouse."

"Large? The blasted thing was enormous. Joking aside, I didn't want to tell you at the time, but it was actually a rat."

"Thank you for enlightening me. Is that supposed to make me feel better?"

"Never mind about you. Look what it's done to my hand!" he said, a grin playing as he held up his malformed hand.

Victoria stared at him, shocked that he could make light of his own abnormality. She felt the corners of her mouth rising.

"It *was* enormous. You're lucky it didn't take your *entire* hand," she joked at last, hoping it wasn't inappropriate.

Edward's shoulders shook. "Come on. I did have one or two more properties, but I think we'll skip them and just go to the last one on my list. I've a feeling it will be more to your taste. First, though, I will show you the better part of town. I don't want you to have been put off Faredene altogether."

The carriage took them along the broad, bustling high street. Edward pointed out the town square, the theatre, the guildhall, and several affluent-looking shops, hotels and taverns. She looked avidly for a drapers – there was an apothecary, a baker, a florist, a tea room . . . in fact, it appeared all manner of shops, but she couldn't see a drapers. Could she dare hope there wasn't one?

The carriage turned off the high street and continued up a steep hill.

"This is Hampton Heights. I want to show you a very important place," he explained as the carriage toured a series of wide streets of fine-looking three-storeyed houses. He pointed to one of them. "There! What do you think?"

"It's a nice house, but why are you showing it to *me*?"

"Because that's where I live with my sister. I wanted you to see where your first friend in Faredene lives."

He has such a nice smile, she thought, and she was especially taken with his cleft chin . . . She really needed to stay focused.

"You're my second friend, actually. I met a James Brakenridge on the train. Do you know him?"

Edward surveyed her for a few moments. Victoria could feel herself colouring under his gaze and she wished desperately that she could stop blushing every time a man looked at her. She was meant to have been a married woman, for goodness' sake. She was relieved when at last he spoke.

"Yes, I know him. And what did you make of him?"

"I found him quite charming. He showed a particular interest in my business plans. He wasn't dismissive like some men might be of a woman."

"Umm, from what I hear, he's a very successful businessman. Fingers in lots of pies, predominantly in Liverpool and Manchester."

There was something in Edward's tone that she couldn't put her finger on – was it dislike? she wondered.

Edward said seriously, "The real reason I brought you here was to show you the park."

They stopped outside a pair of large iron gates, through which an extensive park could be seen. On the far side was a boating lake and a bandstand surrounded by formal landscaped gardens, edged by bare trees with frosted limbs stretching into the grey skies.

"The park can also be accessed by a smaller entrance just off the high street. I use it when I want to walk home from my office."

Momentarily, her mind slipped back to the park in Liverpool, where she'd sat watching other people's children – now, she had one of her own.

"Penny for them," Edward said.

"S-sorry. I-I was just taking in the view," she lied.

"Let's go and see this next property, then. I think you'll like this one."

The carriage travelled back down the hill and headed onto Centenary Lane, pulling up outside a large corner store, ideally situated just off the busy high street.

"This area is expanding rapidly and as you can see, there are lots of large, well-kept houses for about half a mile before they give way to open fields. Even the rats wear top hats."

Victoria pursed her lips. Was he making fun of her because she wanted well-heeled customers? She stared at him.

"The area is known as Centenary Gardens, as most of the houses have gardens," he continued.

"Really? I'd never have guessed," Victoria added in the same vein, noting that he seemed to be waiting for a reaction.

She looked out of the carriage windows. Immediately around the store were a number of prosperous-looking shops and offices. She felt a prickle of excitement.

Chapter 4

The premises for sale was a run-down drapers. Large, dusty windows displayed a selection of grubby, outdated garments, bolts of sun-faded fabrics, bobbins of cotton and skeins of wool.

"You will be pleased to know it is currently the only drapers in town, although I understand there are some stalls on the market selling inexpensive fabrics." Edward's eyes crinkled at the corners. "This used to be a thriving business at one time, but since the owner's death, his daughters have rather neglected things. Such a waste. Don't let the Sisters Grimm put you off – they don't come with the premises."

"Grimm, is that *really* their name?"

"No, you'll see what I mean. Shall we go in?"

As they opened the door, a bell jangled. A dirty doormat greeted the visitors, sending a small cloud of dust onto Victoria's skirts. A girl shivered as she appeared from the back of the shop, a worn brown shawl around her shoulders, her arms wrapped across her body. Edward stated his name – he was obviously expected. He excused himself and followed the girl, leaving Victoria to sit on one of the rickety chairs.

Her nose scrunched – what was that weird smell? A

mixture of stale cooking, lavender and something else . . . Camphor. She couldn't resist having a nosy. The black-and-white marble floor was in good condition. She ran her hand along the glass tops of the display cabinets – they'd look good if they were clean. The mahogany fitments that lined the walls had seen better days, and everything looked dull and worn from years of neglect. But if the premises could be brought up to standard, this could be the very place! Her stomach somersaulted at the thought that her plan might come to fruition.

Edward reappeared and escorted her down a dark corridor with several doors leading off, at the end of which was a small, cluttered parlour. Heavy velvet curtains blocked the light. Only the flames from the fire relieved the gloom. The room was crowded with large items of furniture, every surface overflowing with china ornaments. Despite the freezing temperatures outside, it was unbearably hot and claustrophobic. Two elderly, identically clad women in black perched on a horsehair sofa. They barely glanced in Victoria's direction. She wondered how they could sit in such warmth while the shop assistant was left shivering.

"They have asked their assistant to show us round." Edward gestured towards a girl, who was waiting by the door.

"Ma'am, sir," she curtseyed.

The birdlike girl looked embarrassed as the sisters went back to reading their Bibles. How they could see in this light was beyond Victoria.

Everywhere was shabby, dated and in need of decorating, but even so, it felt right. In addition to the small parlour was a large drawing room and a dining room. The kitchen was dark but big, with a walk-in pantry and scullery, complete with large wooden sink and a tap.

"Did you say there are six bedrooms, Edward?"

"Yes, four on the first floor, plus two more and a storeroom in the attic. Every room has gas lamps fitted and there's a small indoor water closet."

"Pardon me, sir, but there's a privy and washhouse in the yard, as well. So staff don't have to use yer facilities, like," the girl piped up nervously.

"Is there a separate entrance to the living accommodation? I'd prefer not to have to enter and leave via the shop or yard every time I come home."

"Yes, ma'am. The misses never use it, but there's another door just here. So you have a proper front door to yer house, like," the girl said, pulling back a thick, dusty curtain.

Victoria thanked her for showing them around. She'd have liked a second look in each room, but the smell was making her feel nauseous. Once outside, she took a deep breath. Despite the mess and the awful odour, Victoria couldn't describe the feeling even to herself. She just knew this was it! This would be their new home.

"I must apologise for the sisters' behaviour."

"You definitely gave them the right name. What a pair of old misery guts. And the smell . . . was that them?"

Edward laughed. "You're very refreshing. Not like most ladies. You say what's on your mind."

Victoria felt strange, but it was a good strange. She wasn't used to laughing, let alone making others laugh.

"What do you think of the shop?" he asked, nodding in the direction of the premises.

They paused to look back at the shop frontage before climbing into Edward's carriage.

"I love it."

As they made their way back towards the town centre, Victoria couldn't stop grinning as they discussed the merits of the property.

"If you can buy it at a reasonable price, it would be relatively inexpensive to restore it to its former glory," Edward stated.

She quizzed Edward and he suggested what he thought she should offer, which was well within the budget Patrick had suggested.

"I have a good feeling about this place. We could make a life here. I think once we're settled, even Bridie will like it."

"Bridie?" Edward tilted his head to one side.

"Oh, Bridie's my maid. She looked after me as a child and now helps with my son. She's very dear to me."

Edward nodded his understanding. Victoria thought he'd probably be teasing her about her criminal activities if he knew the truth – that they were getting out of Liverpool before anyone discovered she'd kept a child who wasn't hers. Worse still, maybe he'd be horrified.

She believed Bridie would stick to her story, keeping that Turpin woman and any other gossips at bay. But if Father O'Reilly were to ask her about the child, Bridie would find it impossible to lie to him. The prospect of losing the baby and endless lonely days loomed large, giving her the courage to decide. With a look of determination, she turned to Edward.

"As long as the Sisters Grimm definitely don't come with the shop, make the offer you suggested, please."

Edward agreed to visit the spinsters first thing the following morning.

"Would you care to join my sister and me for dinner this evening? I know Anne would be delighted to meet you."

Victoria hesitated. Dinner with a man other than Patrick was a rarity for her – it might be the perfect end to the day. But what if she made a fool of herself? Ran out of things to say? His sister had probably been groomed on how to behave.

Edward sensed her hesitation. "There will be no rodents, sheep waiting to be slaughtered, or miserable old women."

"I couldn't put you to so much trouble."

"I can assure you, it would be our pleasure. I promise that the food will be better than the boiled potatoes and beef they serve at The Crown." His gaze held hers while he awaited her response.

Despite her nerves, Victoria found herself accepting the invitation. Being bold was all part of her new life.

At seven o'clock that evening, Victoria surveyed herself in the mirror. She hoped her black afternoon dress would be suitable for the occasion, having been careful only to pack gowns that suggested she was still in mourning. Then she added long gloves and her mother's pearl necklace, managing to secure her abundant hair with clips and the mother-of-pearl comb Bridie had bought her for Christmas.

She walked down the steps into the hotel foyer, where Edward was waiting. His blue eyes ranged over her as he approached, smiling. She felt disconcerted by his gaze but returned his smile as he escorted her to the awaiting carriage.

On arrival at his home, Edward ushered her into an elegant hallway. As a maid took her cloak, she noticed that the pretty young woman who sauntered down the stairs was clearly imbued with more confidence than herself.

"How do you do?" the woman asked, gazing at Victoria with apparent interest.

"I'm very well, thank you," Victoria answered, annoyed at her own lack of poise compared to the younger woman.

"I'm Anne. Sorry, I should have been downstairs before you arrived to greet you properly. How very remiss. Edward will be most displeased."

"My sister is always late," Edward grinned.

The girl tapped his head playfully with her fan.

"Don't believe a word," she said to Victoria as she slipped an arm through hers and led her into the drawing room, leaving Edward standing in the hall.

Anne chatted as if she'd known Victoria all of her life and the light-hearted banter between brother and sister made for a relaxed atmosphere. By the time dinner was announced, Victoria's nervousness had dissipated and she began to enjoy herself. The delicate light from the candelabra masked her blushes as Edward teased her about the rodent from earlier. She'd never been teased before today, but she could tell from the twinkle in his blue eyes that it was just his way and she found herself smiling with them.

She broached the subject of her son with care and thanked God when they were sensitive enough not to ask searching questions as she briefly told them her husband had died of a tumour before her son was born. Feeling comfortable in their company, she shared her ideas for the shop if her offer was accepted.

"Your eyes do sparkle when you talk about your plans. Edward, you were right – she is endearing." Anne giggled, looking from one to the other as if gauging their reaction.

"Anne!" Edward said sharply, almost knocking over his wine glass.

"I'm sorry, Victoria. I never know when to keep quiet, do I, Edward?"

Victoria could feel her cheeks burning. When she could eventually bring herself to look up from her plate, she was relieved to see Edward's cheeks had also taken on a pink tinge. He pushed his hand through his hair – he was as embarrassed as she was. Then he grinned. He's incredibly attractive, she thought.

Thankfully, Anne breezed over their discomfort, leaving Victoria trying not to think about the fact that a man thought she was endearing. It had been quite a day, not just because of the momentous decision she'd just made for their future, but also because she'd spent it in male company – someone who wasn't her father or Patrick. In fact, two men, if she counted James Brakenridge.

Victoria tossed and turned all night worrying about Bridie and Sean, interspersed with thoughts of James and Edward, and her plans for the house and store. By dawn she was up and dressed, prowling restlessly around her hotel bedroom.

She wondered how much higher she'd be prepared to go with her offer for the property should it be declined. The prospect of not finding suitable premises and her plans coming to nothing filled her with dread. If she had to pay a bit more and tighten her belt, so be it.

Edward arrived at The Crown just as Victoria was taking morning coffee. His face was grave.

"I am afraid they will not accept a penny below the asking price. To my mind, they are making a mistake. They will never get that for it. Their greed will stop them from securing a sale."

Victoria felt her heart sink. She might have considered raising her offer just that morning, but the full asking price was far more than she could afford. She knew she should consult Patrick. She had big plans for the shop's improvement and the decorating of her new home. If she paid the sisters the asking price, by the time she completed the refurbishments she'd have a lot less to live on until business picked up.

She mulled it over for a few moments. She had to have the shop, no matter the price.

"I've thought about nothing else all night," she said eventually. "I'm certain I can make a go of it. I'd like you to go back to them, please, and offer them the full amount."

"Victoria, I must advise against this. I have no knowledge of your financial position, but the price is exorbitant. I could always go back with a counter-offer, but from what they said this morning, I doubt they would accept."

"Please submit the offer as I asked, Edward. I know it's the perfect property and this is the right town for what I have in mind. It'll be worth the sacrifice."

"If you're sure. But wouldn't you like to speak to Patrick first? At that price, I'm certain it won't sell in the meantime."

"No, Edward. I'm quite sure."

She knew she sounded irritated, but there was no point in asking Patrick's opinion. He'd try to talk her out of the purchase – and that wasn't an option.

While Edward went back to see the sisters, Victoria

remained in the restaurant. She was tense about the amount she was paying but was determined to push ahead with the move regardless.

He returned an hour later. The offer had been accepted and he could start the purchase if she wished. His furrowed brow didn't go unnoticed by Victoria.

"You think I've been a fool?" Her voice was more definite than she felt.

"No. I think the price was too high, but the plans you outlined are sound. Anne's already talking of bringing her friends to order dresses. But it has to be your decision."

Victoria took a deep breath. 'I'm confident I've made the right choice. Go ahead with the acquisition please, Edward."

Excitement and trepidation fought a battle in her head as she travelled back to Liverpool. She'd missed Sean and Bridie far more than she thought possible and could scarcely wait to share her news. She thought about Edward's look of disappointment when she'd declined his invitation to lunch after giving him his instructions. He'd been so kind that she'd felt compelled to explain it was the first time she'd been apart from her son and that she wished to get home as soon as possible.

As she let herself into the house, the distant sound of Bridie humming in the kitchen brought a small smile to her face. Bridie, busy removing a pie from the oven, hadn't noticed her arrival. Victoria threw her gloves on the dresser and picked up her son from his crib. To her delight, he smiled and gurgled as she kissed him. Bridie turned round, startled, almost dropping the earthenware dish.

"Holy Mother of God! Sure, you frightened the life out of me!"

Victoria placed Sean back in his crib and embraced the old woman.

"I've found a shop! We could be moving before Easter!"

"What! So soon? You're barely giving us time to breathe, lass."

Victoria pulled away, her face stern.

"We can't wait, Bridie. We don't want people around here asking any more questions."

"Well, while you were away, I sincerely hope you gave a lot of thought as to how we're going to keep the child's origins a secret, lass. I don't fancy getting banged up for this, or worse." She shook her head.

Victoria could see the old woman's mind churning, possibilities running away with her.

"I can't promise difficulties won't arise at some point. But as far as everyone will know, my husband died of a tumour before the baby was born. I'll say he ran a drapers and that I helped there on occasion."

"Sure, you seem to have it all mapped out, I'll say that much for you. I just hope you're not making a mistake."

"Oh, Bridie, wait until you see how nice it is!" She clapped her hands together. "The kitchen and scullery will be newly decorated for you. The light in the drawing room is simply wonderful because of the two windows. I can't wait for you to see it."

Bridie nodded her approval.

"And you, young man, will have a nursery in one of the back bedrooms that gets the afternoon sun. Would you like that?" she asked, bending over the crib and tickling the baby. "Look, Bridie, he's excited, he's smiling!"

She went on to describe the details of her trip, the kindness of James, her meal with Edward and his sister, though she said nothing about Edward's deformities – she wasn't a gossip. Finally, she explained how she believed the business would run, expanding on the plans she'd made for their future.

"You see. You're proving my point. Yer already getting to know people. We'll need to keep to ourselves if we're to keep our secret safe."

"Bridie, I refuse to let your worries spoil my mood. Everything will be simply wonderful, I just know it."

Patrick called round later that day. Victoria didn't feel she could lie to him, so with trepidation, she told him how much she'd paid.

"Have you gone mad, Vicky? I just hope you're going to be careful with what you spend from now on. I gave you a fair price for this place." He waved his hand, indicating the house. "I've liquidated as many of your stocks and shares as I could for you, but we're still in the midst of a depression. The financial panic a couple of years ago hit everyone hard. Having to sell in a hurry has meant you've made some considerable losses. I should never have helped you. You've behaved recklessly, in my opinion. And now you've made me behave irresponsibly, too. I just hope you know what you're doing, young lady."

"Just be pleased for me, Patrick. I've not been this happy since . . . well, since ever," she laughed. "I'm going to *make* this work. You'll see."

Edward had just finished having dinner with his sister and they'd retired to the drawing room. After pouring himself a brandy, he sat back in his chair by the fire. Anne positioned herself on the floor beside him. Putting her arms across his knees, she rested her chin on her hands and stared up at him, as she always did when she wanted something from her doting brother.

"Come on, Edward. Tell me what you really think of the lovely young widow."

"Anne, you're incorrigible."

"Come on, spill the beans. You're certainly putting a lot of effort into looking after her."

"I told you even before I met her that I was going to take good care of her. I owe it to Patrick. If he hadn't come up and spoken to me, befriended me on my first day at Oxford, I might not have settled in. In any case, my first year at university would have been dreadful. We might have had limited contact over the years, but I've not forgotten what he did for me."

"Yes, yes, I know all that, but I also saw the way you were looking at her. So what do you *really* think of her?"

Edward smiled but stayed silent. His eyes had a faraway look to them.

"Tell me, or I'll just invent my own version. Do you still think she's 'endearing'?"

Edward laughed. He found it difficult to resist his young sister anything.

"Yes, actually, I do, if you must know. I don't know how she manages to look so vulnerable yet independent at the same time."

"Ooh, Edward, I do believe you're falling in love!"

"Possibly." He tilted his head to one side.

"Why, Edward, I can see you're picturing her face right now. Aren't you? Don't deny it. You really have got it bad!"

"You, missy, need to keep out of your brother's business." He touched the tip of her nose with his index finger.

Anne smiled affectionately. "I like her, but if she's going to steal my brother away from me, she'd damned well better be good enough for you."

"I don't think you have any need to worry about that, little one. She won't be interested in me." He patted her affectionately on the head.

"Why ever not?"

"My deformities hardly make me a catch."

"Don't put yourself down. Anyway, it's hardly noticeable with your shoe. You walk really well now and as for your hand, it's just not important. You have a handsome face and are the cleverest man I know. Father and Mother always said you were incredibly smart.

"Besides, I know you're besotted with her, but she's not *that* attractive." She lifted a finger to halt Edward's response. "The way you spoke about her after showing her round, I was expecting a real beauty. She'd be lucky to have you. Any woman would be. I'll be keeping an eye on her to make sure she doesn't mess you around," she added before they both fell silent.

Chapter 5

Victoria looked at the bare rooms. China and glassware were carefully wrapped and packed into tea chests brought down from the attic, while trunks of spare clothing and shoes, plus boxes of books and other items, were lined up in a spare bedroom. The house was a large, seven-bedroom property on Stanley Square in one of the most desirable areas of Liverpool. This was the only home she'd ever known and there *were* some happy memories – of times spent alone with her mother. But these were tainted by thoughts of her father's rages, her mother's tears, her mother's murder at the hands of her father . . . No. There was nothing for her here.

Thanks to Patrick buying her house, they'd be settled in Faredene long before Easter. He seemed delighted at the prospect of his new home. He'd even agreed to purchase several of the larger items of her furniture, though she suspected he'd done that just to help her financially. And great wonders – Patrick had also given his formidable housekeeper notice and had already started interviewing prospective candidates.

"One damned woman was worse than the one I've got now, telling me what time I'd eat supper and that there would be no food in the bedroom. She had a full blasted list of things she wasn't prepared to do. I'd have thought one would have been grateful for the work, considering times are hard."

Victoria had laughed. "You definitely don't want another tyrant. Perhaps someone younger," she'd suggested. "That's it. Someone who has moved with the times, who is less frosty, would be perfect for you."

"Yes, I think perhaps you're right. Anyway, I have some more candidates tomorrow, so fingers crossed, old girl."

"Well, your expanding girth won't suffer if you don't find anyone, that's for sure."

"Victoria, I don't know what's got into you. But I like it. Reminds me of when you were a child. I used to think you'd be a feisty madam," he'd winked.

Victoria hoped he'd be happy in this house. Give the place a new lease of life and create better, more joyful memories – maybe even get married. Now there was a thought . . .

He'd offered to supervise the day of the move and organise everything with the removal company, allowing Victoria to travel to Faredene a week or two early so she could begin putting the place in order before Bridie arrived with Sean. Victoria suspected Bridie would be tempted to sneak in a few of the older items they'd discarded and she hoped Patrick would be firm with her, not bribed to look the other way with slices of Bridie's apple pie.

Victoria considered the enormity of what she was about to embark on as a heavy April shower clattered against the windows of the train compartment, now bound for her new home. Bridie had given her word that she'd keep Victoria's secret and she knew the old woman would guard both it and Sean with her life. All she had to do now was make a success of the shop and their new life – they were both depending on her. And Patrick, he'd put his reputation and career on the line.

Maybe, despite her longing for a baby, she wasn't cut out to be a mother. Would nurturing come naturally? After all, motherhood wasn't just about the first few months – she potentially had years of challenges ahead of her!

Whatever problems she faced, she'd just have to deal with them. She wasn't happy before she found him. All Sean had done was bring joy and purpose to her life, and now she had the chance to do something worthwhile, to make friends and enjoy life.

Her thoughts turned to her conversation with Bridie the previous night. Everything but the essentials that Bridie and the baby would need for up to two weeks had already been packed for the move and she'd joined Bridie in the kitchen as she had done on so many occasions since finding the baby. Perhaps it was the end of an era that caused Bridie to open up to her for the first time.

"Was my father always violent and cruel towards my mother?" Victoria had asked, unsure if she really wanted to know.

"No, lass. When they were first married, when I first came here, he was kind to her and they were much in love. He'd always had a temper, caused ructions, but those days he'd just bang his fist on the table. Then after a while, it were like he were two people – one minute he were kind and loving, the next he were lashing out. He was always sorry afterwards, mind, but yer mam grew to hate him – and he knew it."

She glanced at Victoria, no doubt checking she was coping with the truth before continuing.

"Well, knowing how your mam felt towards him only made him madder, lass. Fit to be tied, so he was. Used to lose his head. He still loved her in his own way, but he couldn't stand to see the way she looked at him, the disgust in her eyes. How do you come back from that? She knew she'd made a mistake marrying beneath her. She were an educated lady, while he'd dragged himself up by his bootstraps.

"As I understand it, both she and Patrick's mother were orphaned as young women, but they both had decent trust funds. Your aunt never wanted yer mam to marry yer da. Somehow, she sensed the bad in him, something desperate. But yer mam did it anyway.

"When she lost two babbies, one after the other, the second living for just two hours, she became maudlin. Sure, wouldn't get out of bed most days. That got yer da in a right old state. He needed a wife, wanted a son, and she couldn't give him either."

"I must have been a real disappointment."

"No. He loved you, lass. Thrilled when you were born, he was. And yer mam was better than she'd ever been, now she had you. But she never got over losing the babbies. As you got older, she enjoyed being with you. Brought her to life a bit, you did. But he could see the way it was going – you were yer mam's girl and would look at him with the same dislike she did. Then after she passed away, with every year you looked more like her. It pained him to look at you."

"Why did you stay, Bridie? I know you weren't happy here."

Bridie took a deep breath then and as her shoulders slumped, she began to explain.

"Sure, we lived in Doolin in County Clare. It's a grand place. On a clear day you could see the Twelve Pins mountain range in the distance. But the Potato Famine hit Ireland hard. Crops kept failing each year. We were starving. Then when we lost our daughter, Moira, me husband, Aiden, sort of gave up living. When he passed, there were nowt for me to stay for. I still had some family there, but the place had lost its wonder for me.

"I thought about just lying down on their graves and waiting to join 'em. But some bit of me deep inside told me to get outta Ireland. So I made me way to Dublin. Used Shanks's pony most of the way – got a lift on a cart when I had the chance."

Victoria's eyes were wide, her lips parted. She had no idea Bridie had ever been married, let alone had a child. She leaned forwards in her chair, not wanting to miss a word.

"I found bits o' work where I could along the way, often begging. Sometimes I even had to steal food just to stay alive. In Dublin, I found work in a laundry. I intended to save up and make for America. Get as far away from me memories as I could. But the bloke running the laundry were a right dirty bugger. Couldn't keep his hands to himself. So as soon as I'd managed scrape together enough for me passage for the short journey over to Liverpool, I took the next boat.

"I were overcome with guilt. Maybe Moira and Aiden would have survived if we'd left Ireland sooner – done summat different."

Bridie took a deep, juddering breath, then waited in silence for several minutes.

"When I got to Liverpool, nobody wanted to hire me. Resented the Irish coming over and taking their jobs. After a week of walking the streets, sleeping rough, I were in a terrible state. This city weren't a safe place for a woman alone at night – sure, it still isn't. Some would fleece yeh soon as rob yeh."

Victoria could see the old woman was struggling to hold back the tears and she took her hand gently.

"I thought about going into the workhouse, but there were no fight left in me. So I just sat on a bench. It were opposite some shops. One of them was yer da's place. I sat there all day, occasionally asking people to spare a few coppers. I saw him looking at me through the window a few times, thought he might get the police to move me on. But I didn't care. I didn't have the strength to move."

"Oh, Bridie, I had no idea. It must have been terrible for you." Victoria stroked the old woman's hand.

"Anyway, when he were leaving to go 'ome, he walked up to me. I'll never forget, he said, 'Are you hungry?' Just like that. I must have looked half-starved. I thought he were gonna suggest I did summat bad for the money – some men don't care what you look like. But yer da, he handed me a butty wrapped in greaseproof. I think it were his own lunch. I took it and started to eat, just nibbling at it, even though I were starving. It were like I'd forgotten how to eat.

"Then he said he recognised me accent. Told me his folks were from County Clare. Sure, he asked me if I could cook and clean. He said yer mam needed help around the house and so he fetched me back here."

"So what did my mother say when he just turned up with you? Was she angry?"

"Another woman might have refused to let me over her doorstep, the state of me. Must have looked a holy show. I were filthy and I must have stunk to high heaven. But yer mam were kindness itself. Made me strip off and bathe in the scullery. Gave me a clean frock to wear – it were an old one of hers. I were a lot slimmer then." She jiggled her ample belly before continuing. "It were just a plain green one, but it were the nicest dress I'd ever had. And that were that. I had a home here in England with yer parents and I never went back to Ireland.

"Sure, yer da were beside himself when yer mam died. His carrying on with women and gambling got worse. Even though I were still right grateful to him, I'd have gone if it weren't for you. But I knew he were a good man underneath and I felt that even when the demons were on him, he wanted me to stay here and look after you."

Victoria had wanted to ask Bridie about the night her mother died. Why her mother had never left. But she could see how tired the old woman looked. It had taken a lot out of her, talking about the past, so she'd simply kissed Bridie's cheek and they'd gone to bed, each lost in their thoughts.

Victoria wondered if she'd blocked out any nice memories of her father. Bridie had said he was a good man underneath. How was that possible? In some ways, the knowledge that her father had been kind at times made it more difficult to believe you could trust any man . . .

She was jolted from her reverie as the train pulled into Faredene Station. On the short walk from the station, she managed to wind herself up like a tightly coiled spring. Almost as soon as she'd checked into The Crown Hotel once again, Edward arrived with the final papers for her to sign and the concerns she fully intended to keep to herself burst out.

"I'm sure lots of people dream of running a successful business, but that doesn't mean that they're capable. Do you think I've been impetuous? You do, don't you?"

"You are bound to be anxious, but I don't think you have much to worry about. As I explained before, the shop used to be a gold mine – and that was without dressmaking."

"I hope you're right. I'm afraid it might all be a big mistake." She didn't tell him what a large proportion of her capital she'd spent on the purchase, or how angry Patrick had been.

"I admire your decision. I understand from Patrick that your husband left you sufficient for your means. Not many newly widowed women with a small child would take such a big step, especially not moving to a new town. That shows your courage and I believe in you," he ended, smiling.

She'd never known anyone to smile so often. He didn't let his handicaps affect him.

"Thank you, Edward, that means a great deal."

She felt reassured. She had to stop doubting herself, because tomorrow the store would be hers. But of course, she'd only told him part of her concerns. She'd said nothing about her fears of not being a good mother, or how she'd have to keep lying about her past to almost everyone, including him. What a framework on which to base their friendship. It went against every bone in her body.

Chapter 6

Victoria was glad she'd accepted Edward's offer to escort her to the store. Legs like jelly, her stomach churning, they set off in his carriage. Despite the earliness, weak rays of April sunshine were peeking through the clouds. The town centre was already bustling, making her feel a little more optimistic about the future.

"Just look at everyone! And at this hour. The shops must be doing well based on the number of packages people are carrying." She knew she was babbling like an excited child. Feeling her colour rising, she focused her attention back on the road.

There were three large carts parked outside the shop as they drew up and men were loading furniture. The two sisters scarcely acknowledged their arrival as they fussed over every item leaving the premises. It was the young girl they'd seen on their initial visit who greeted them.

"Good morning, sir, ma'am," she said, brushing the front of her faded skirt nervously.

Victoria smiled at her warmly and Edward returned the greeting before turning to Victoria.

"I am afraid I have a meeting, but if you will permit me, I will call on you again soon."

"Thank you so much, Edward. You've been most

helpful." She was genuinely touched by his kindness.

As he got back in the carriage, she turned to look at the girl, who was fidgeting anxiously.

"Is anything the matter?" Victoria asked.

"I'm so sorry, ma'am. I wasn't sure what to do this morning. The misses said they're not payin' me for today but I were to come in as normal and you'd decide if you were keeping me on. I thought about trying to sort the stock, but the misses said I were to leave it, as it were all included in the price and it were up to you to sort in your own time. So I've just been helping them pack up the last of their things." She shrugged apologetically.

Victoria tried not to show her displeasure at the sisters' attitude but couldn't help raising her eyebrows.

"That's fine. I'll pay you for today, don't worry. What's your name?"

"Millicent Gibbs, but everybody calls me Milly."

"Well, I'll call you Milly, as well. You definitely don't look like a Millicent." Victoria appraised the honest, smiling face of the waif who was as thin as a pike staff with dark blonde hair and slightly protruding front teeth. "Would you like to stay on, Milly?"

Milly nodded enthusiastically.

"Well, let's see how we get on today and we can talk about it later. Does that work for you?"

"That would be smashing. I mean yes, ma'am."

Victoria surveyed the disarrayed stock scattered around the shop shelving, her nerves forgotten for the moment as her naturally organised mind took over.

"Start by taking all the supplies from the shop into the stockroom and then sort it all into type of fabric and colour. Put anything that's faded or damaged in any way to one side."

"Yes, ma'am, right away." Picking up a pencil, pad and a bolt of fabric, she headed through the door, practically skipping.

Victoria followed her into the stockroom at the back of the shop and her heart sank as she took in the huge quantity of fabric strewn everywhere.

"It were neater than this, ma'am, honest. Well, you'll know that from yer visit. But first thing this mornin', the misses were looking for some pieces that they wanted to take with them. Proper fancy stuff. I hope you don't mind me explaining, but I were worried you'd think *I'd* left it in this state or pinched summat."

"That's quite all right, Milly. You don't have to be afraid of speaking to me about anything."

Victoria wondered for a moment if she should confront the Sisters Grimm about taking stock that now belonged to her. No doubt they'd taken what they considered the best pieces, as Milly implied, but she didn't want to start her new life on a disagreement. She just wanted them gone so the place would feel like hers and they could begin their new life – safe and with a past of her own design.

"Well, Milly, this looks like a job for two. Shall we get started?"

"Right you are, ma'am."

As they began working, Victoria asked Milly about the barbers next door. She wasn't used to being around men and had some reservations about the opposite sex frequenting the neighbouring store, even though Edward had already assured her it was where he went and that it was a very respectable establishment.

"Oh, you've no need to worry yerself about that, ma'am.

All of his customers are from this side of town, so there's no riff-raff."

"Well, that is a relief. What's he like, the barber?"

"Mr O'Brien? He's all right – a decent bloke. His wife's okay – a bit uppity at times. But they'd help you out if you were stuck. They're both from Ireland originally and say they're going back when he retires."

They chatted amiably as they worked, about the stock, the customers, life in general, and Victoria took a real liking to the girl. It took several hours before they'd sorted everything and she was pleased to find that having been kept out of direct sunlight, the fabric in the back room wasn't faded, albeit much of it was dusty or dated.

"What do you think of this, Milly?" Victoria gestured to a bolt of rose damask. "I think it would make lovely curtains for the drawing room."

"Aye, ma'am. And there's that pale blue. P'rhaps for a bedroom."

"That's not a bad idea. Let's see what else we can use."

They managed to find something suitable for each room. Any dress fabrics Victoria considered too old-fashioned or spoiled, therefore unsuitable for her shop, were set aside. Next, they cut away any damaged, grubby or discoloured pieces and placed them with any remnants.

"If you don't mind my saying, ma'am, but you can still get good money for these pieces. This one . . ." She held up a piece of yellow-and-white gingham. "If you place a paper pattern around the faded bits, you could just about make a blouse."

Milly looked at her. Victoria didn't want to offend the young girl or discourage her from having ideas, but she had no intention of starting her new business with substandard stock. She chose her words carefully.

"Milly, do you know of anyone who could make use of them? If so, you may take them."

"What, all of them?" Her eyes stuck out on stalks.

"Yes, you're welcome to them all."

"Cor, thank you, ma'am. I can hardly believe it. Are yeh absolutely sure?"

"Yes, I'm certain. I'm pleased you'll be able to make use of it."

"Blimey! Wait till me sisters see this lot. They'll think I've finally cracked, done those two old bats in and nicked this lot."

Victoria spluttered, stifling a laugh.

"Blimey, me and my big gob! I'm so sorry, ma'am. I wouldn't speak like that about you."

"It's all right, Milly. I've already got the measure of the Sisters Grimm."

Milly smothered a grin. "That's the perfect name for them."

Once all the fabric was sorted, the piles were lined up along one side of the room. Then they categorised the threads and lace pieces in a similar fashion. She realised that she'd have to get rid of the unsuitable stock at rock-bottom prices, so began thinking of inventive ways to sell them. She was tired and dusty, and her back was breaking – she'd begun to wonder if she was cut out for a full day of hard work. Milly looked like a gust of wind would blow her over, but she was showing no signs of fatigue.

Victoria was itching to discuss her concerns about her ability to make a success of the shop with someone. However, as there was no one around but Milly, she decided it wouldn't do to let the girl see any doubts that were troubling her. She'd just have to keep them to herself for now.

Milly looked across, studying Victoria.

"Are you all right, ma'am? You look right done in. If you don't mind me saying, that is."

Stretching, Victoria hastily painted on a smile.

"My back *is* killing. But I was just worrying about Bridie, my housekeeper. She's looking after my son on her own. I'm concerned it might be too much for her." Surely this wasn't giving too much away . . .

"You've got a baby! What's his name?"

"Sean."

"How old is he?"

"Seven months, so quite the handful."

"Aye, they can be at that age. I'm the eldest of nine, so I've had to do me fair share of minding the young 'uns. I can cope with the skriking. It's when the little buggers start running around that the real problems start," she ended with a laugh, covering her mouth with her hand. "Begging yer pardon, ma'am. I'm ever so sorry about me language."

Victoria laughed despite her surprise. "That's quite all right, Milly. But not in front of the customers."

"Oh no, ma'am. I know how to mind me p's and q's. I just forgot meself again, 'cos yer so easy to talk to."

Victoria thought Milly would be a tonic to have around. Once they'd finished in the shop, they toured the property room by room, avoiding the ones the men were still emptying. It was hardly surprising they were still here given how cluttered everywhere had been. Nevertheless, when she saw the sisters looking at her critically, she felt like shoving them all out of the door.

Having noted all the repairs that needed to be done,

Victoria went back into the shop. Feeling overwhelmed by the amount of work required before they even opened, she leaned against the wall for a moment, reprimanding herself silently. Come on, woman. This is what you asked for – a child, a purpose, no more boredom. She almost laughed out loud. She didn't think she'd ever be bored again.

She called Milly into the shop and asked her what hours she worked.

"I work seven days, eight till six thirty. Monday to Saturday I'm in the shop. Sundays I do the cleaning. Every fourth Sunday I get to finish at two."

Victoria was unsure how to respond. Was she being naïve? She knew that most working people slogged for long hours for a pittance. Even Bridie worked long hours. But at least she had every Sunday off, even when her father was alive, and she could stop and put her feet up for a rest whenever she felt the need.

At last, she said, "Did neither of them ever work in the shop?"

"No, ma'am, but I had to run any decisions by them."

No wonder the business had been declining. Milly deserved better – she'd proved her worth today. Victoria resolved to begin repaying her bargain with God by treating her employees fairly.

The Sisters Grimm emerged and announced their departure.

"Everything to your satisfaction?" they asked in unison.

They both looked at Milly as though she were a dirty dishrag. Victoria guessed they were wondering if Milly had told her about the stock they'd pilfered. She matched their disdainful manner.

"I believe all is in order."

She didn't know these women well, but what she'd seen, she didn't like. She'd be glad to see the back of them. As far as she could see, they were snobbish, tight and lazy, which was confirmed moments later when they paid Milly for her week's work. The slightly taller of the two looked pointedly at Victoria.

"You realise you're paying her for today. It's not our responsibility to pay her for helping you settle in."

"I'm perfectly happy to pay Milly for the *whole* day. Even though I suspect you've had her slaving for a pittance for years and had her packing your belongings this morning."

"Well! I've never been so insulted."

"If you don't want to hear any more of what I've got to say, I'll thank you to take your leave before I change my mind and insist you leave behind the stock you've taken that by rights belongs to me."

When they left without a word of thanks to Milly, Victoria was disgusted, shutting the door with a bang as they left. She turned to find Milly doubled over with laughter.

"I'm so sorry for laughing. It's just you've made me day."

Victoria smiled tightly. "I probably shouldn't have said anything, but they *are* awful old bats. I don't know how you stuck them."

"Well, I'm glad you did. It was worth a day's pay."

"I had half a mind to trip them up on the way out." Suddenly serious, Victoria asked, "How old are you, Milly?"

"I were nineteen last month, ma'am. I've been working here since I were ten."

"Nine years! And have you ever enjoyed working here?"

"Blimey, no, ma'am. But it's close to our house and Mam needs me nearby so I can help with the little 'uns when I get home. It's not so bad now some of them have grown up a bit. But Mam doesn't need so much help now, so I might not have stayed here much longer. I've been offered a job on one of the fabric stalls down the market. It would be all right in the summer, but in the winter, standing outside all day is no fun. The cold cuts right through yeh."

"Was there anything you liked about working here?"

"I love working with all the nice fabrics, and some of the customers are lovely. But as you've noticed, the misses weren't very nice. They're a pair of Scrooges and a right pain in the pinny. An' I had lots of ideas for improving things, like, but they said it weren't me place to have ideas."

"What sort of things did you suggest?" Victoria was intrigued to know what the spinsters had chosen to ignore.

"Well, I suggested doing a new window display each month, perhaps with different colours and fabrics to match the season. Like yellow and green in spring, and rich colours in December." Milly's fingers fidgeted.

"Milly, I'd like you to continue working here. You won't be expected to do any housework and will get every Sunday off, unless we have a rush order to finish, in which case you'll be paid extra for that day. And I'd very much like you to continue coming up with ideas. Never feel afraid to approach me."

"That's real kind of you, ma'am, and I'm ever so grateful, honest. But I'd prefer to work seven days if possible, so me money won't go down."

"Milly, I can assure you, you will *not* be paid less."

She went on to explain Milly's duties in more detail, outlining how she'd be trained in both dressmaking and bookkeeping. Milly's eyes were alight with a mixture of relief and excitement.

"Thank you so much, ma'am. Me mam'll be made up."

As she spoke, the shop bell jangled and a tiny woman walked in carrying a basket.

"Mam, this is Mrs Kavanagh an' she's agreed to keep me on. Ma'am, this is me mam, Edith."

As she introduced them, Edith handed Milly a gingham cloth, from which Milly took two thin slices of bread and dripping.

"Thanks, Mam, I'm starving. Me stomach thinks me throat's been cut," Milly said, taking a hungry bite.

"It's very good of you to keep her on, ma'am." The small woman spoke directly to Victoria.

She noticed the woman was birdlike, just like Milly, and that she had her daughter's hazel eyes and smile. But she looked careworn.

"I'm sorry, ma'am. I should have brought extra food." The woman glanced at her empty basket, her discomfort obvious.

"That's quite all right." She suspected that this woman had to watch every penny. "I'm intending to pop to the bakers down the lane later, but at the moment I'm not hungry – I had a large breakfast," she lied.

She'd actually been far too excited to eat breakfast and could feel her stomach rumbling. She hoped it didn't betray her.

"Well, I'd best be off. Kitty's watching the baby and our Teddy, and you know she can't be trusted for long. Ta-ra."

Chapter 7

While Victoria pored over the long list of jobs that had to be done, Milly was dispatched with messages to various tradesmen. She'd also been given cash to purchase cleaning materials from nearby shops. She returned in record time – clearly, the girl didn't dawdle.

"The tradesmen all said they'll be along to give you estimates. I told them to be sharp or they'd miss out on the job, 'cos I know you want it done quick. And I didn't need the cash, 'cos the hardware shop has set up an account for you. I told him he couldn't be expecting a business owner to be paying cash for every bar of soap or cloth," she said proudly.

Milly could certainly think for herself.

"Well, I'm glad that's all organised. And the cleaning?"

"Oh aye, and me mam said she's happy to come in and give the place a good scrub. She said to thank yeh for the work, ma'am."

While Milly had been out, Victoria had nipped to the bakers, where she'd purchased two large iced fingers, one each for Milly and her. Milly reacted as if she'd been given the Crown Jewels.

"Aww, ma'am, that's ever so kind of you. I'd save half for our Teddy, but the rest of them will be in when I get home and it'd cause an uproar," she added, licking her sticky fingers.

Those tight old biddies. Victoria doubted they'd ever shown Milly even the smallest acts of kindness.

As they sipped their tea, Victoria asked, "Did the sisters keep a list of suppliers?"

"There's a book in the stockroom I used to use to list the items that came in, but it's a bit out of date. You see, they didn't buy much in the last couple of years. They lost interest but still expected the place to make money."

Milly rushed off, returning with a large, dusty volume. As Victoria scanned the entries, Milly gave the ins and outs on all the suppliers they'd used in the past.

"Faircloughs were always late with their deliveries and the fabric would sometimes have faults halfway through the bolt. I think they thought they could get away with selling any old rubbish to the misses. And they were right – they did," she giggled.

Faircloughs was the supplier Victoria had visited with her father and she was happy to avoid using them in case they recognised her. She'd make some initial purchases from one or two other local suppliers Milly recommended, giving her some breathing space. After that, she could arrange for more suppliers to visit the shop so she could select the bulk of her stock and discuss pricing.

The skies were just beginning to darken as Victoria locked up. She was looking forward to getting back to the hotel and resting. Milly stood beside her, a large parcel tied with string hanging in each hand.

"Have you got far to go carrying those parcels, Milly? You've worked hard today and they look heavy."

"Only to Halton Row, ma'am."

Victoria remembered Halton Row – it was in the deprived area on the other side of town. Poor Milly. What a place to live. Victoria doubted she could be as cheerful as Milly if she lived there.

"I can give you the fare for the omnibus, if you like." She knew the Sisters Grimm had paid Milly for the past week, but she suspected most of her meagre wages would have to go into the family pot, leaving nothing for fares.

"That's kind of you, ma'am, but I'll be fine walking. I do it every day."

"But today you have heavy parcels." Victoria reached into her purse and took out a coin.

"Really, ma'am, there's no need. This is the first day in nine years I've ever enjoyed me job. I'm not tired. In fact, I feel like I could dance 'ome. We'll make good use of this fabric. Me mam and sisters will be made up when they see it. But I'm gonna hide it under the bed us girls share, 'cos if me dad sees it, he'll sell the lot down the pub for beer money. I'm glad you came to live here. I think yer lovely, ma'am." Milly blushed.

Although tired, after listening to Milly, Victoria felt inspired to walk back to the hotel, so they strolled part of the way together until Milly left her with a cheery wave and more thanks. Victoria grimaced. Her feet were killing, but at least she was going to have a hot bath, a decent meal and a bed to herself. She'd always known that poor people had to share rooms and even beds – of course she did – but they'd always been nameless faces, people she didn't know, somehow unreal. She'd always had her own room and it hit home that her life had been far more sheltered and privileged than she realised. Life in Faredene was going to be a revelation.

❖ ❖ ❖

By the middle of the following day, Victoria had accepted estimates for the work on both the shop and the living accommodation, insisting work begin immediately and continue over the weekend. What mattered most was getting the job done swiftly and to a high standard. In some cases, she felt she was paying over the odds, but despite Patrick's warnings about her not overspending, saving money wasn't her priority at the moment.

Victoria had decided that she wanted to offload the unsuitable stock quickly, so she sought out Milly, who was at the new workbench making curtains for the house.

"Milly, would you like to take a trip to the market for me?"

"Certainly, ma'am. What would you like me to fetch?" she asked, already laying down her sewing.

"I don't need anything fetching. I'd like you to speak to the fabric stallholders and see if any of them would be interested in buying the stock we put to one side. What do you think?"

"Aye, ma'am. I can think of a couple of 'em who'd definitely be keen. They've got a real eye for a bargain."

"Here, take this and get yourself a pie from the bakers for your lunch as you're passing."

Victoria handed Milly some coppers. The girl was painfully thin and Victoria couldn't be sure she even got breakfast.

"Thanks, ma'am, what a treat."

Milly was all smiles at the prospect of both a pie and a paid trip to the market.

"Tell the stallholders if they're interested, to come to the shop at six thirty this evening. Let them know that all stock must be paid for in cash," she added as Milly was leaving.

When Milly returned, she gave Victoria most of the money back.

"I got me pie – meat and potato. I grabbed it from the market instead 'cos it's cheaper. You pay through the nose at the bakers."

She'd found someone she could really trust in Milly, she thought happily.

That evening, two stallholders arrived pushing barrows. They were both eager to buy the goods, which led to some arguing about who got which bolt and haggling on price. Victoria looked on bemused as the two men pulled a bolt of chenille back and to between them – she thought they might actually come to blows. Just as she was about to intervene, Milly stepped forwards.

"Now come on, youse two. If yeh don't stop arguing about it, I'll go back to the market and ask Fat Finnegan to come and have a gander. You both know he'll want the lot."

"Now, Milly, there's no need for that. You can have that 'un if I can have the green tweed," the man said to his companion, who was clutching the bolt tightly.

"Aye, all right, then," the older man said, putting the bolt on his pile.

In the end, they bought all the unsuitable stock and the stockroom smelled fresher, the last traces of the sisters gone.

The next morning, she'd made a buying trip to Blakes, a warehouse that Milly believed sold a good range of fabrics, situated behind Erlington Mill. When Victoria told the owner, Mr Blake – an angular, bearded man with vapid eyes and onion breath – that she was stocking her new store, he'd suggested that he show her round the warehouse personally. He must have thought her naïve enough to buy all stock from him at any price when he'd handed her the bill, but then she'd shown him she wasn't as green as she looked.

He'd smiled patronisingly until she said, "I will take all of this on account on net thirty-day terms, with a 35 per cent discount on the prices you've just given me."

Dumbfounded, he'd stammered, "That's . . . er, not possible, I'm afraid. These are the very finest fabrics."

"Mr Blake, if you want my business, those are the terms I expect. And when I increase the volume I buy from you, I expect the discount to increase accordingly. Do we have a deal, or shall I take my business to Faircloughs?"

"But, ma'am, Faircloughs don't have fabrics of our quality."

"Mr Blake, do you want my business? It's very simple. Either you do or you don't." Although her legs were trembling, she'd managed to hold out a steady hand.

For what seemed like an age, Mr Blake had ummed and ahhed, lifted his hand up, put it back down by his side. Victoria didn't flinch and kept her hand held out. She'd seen her father negotiate in this direct, firm manner on many occasions. Although she didn't speak to him, she'd listened and learned when he'd explained that the key was to tell them what you wanted and then stay silent. "It unnerves them," he'd said once. She'd remembered this incident particularly well because she also knew her silence had done the same to her father – at least when he wasn't in one of his rages.

Eventually, Mr Blake had stammered, "Deal." Shifting

uneasily on his feet, he'd taken her outstretched hand, shaking it weakly.

"Good day to you, sir. It's been a pleasure doing business."

Victoria was thrilled – it had worked. She might have paid too much for the shop and over the odds for the refurbishments, but she didn't intend to spend her life being pushed around – not any more.

She'd written to several companies while getting the place ready for Bridie's arrival and spent much of her time dealing with their salesmen, checking samples and ordering from catalogues. Now, all she needed was customers. She hoped her mother would have been proud of her. Edward would be. She imagined his smile. Honestly, woman, get a grip.

In just over a week, the exterior of the shop had been painted dark green and gold, and an elegant sign reading "Centenary Store" had been erected. The shop windows had been covered with old newspaper on the insides in the hope that passers-by, unable to see in, would be intrigued as to what changes were taking place inside. Victoria wanted people to know the shop was changing hands and that this would no longer be the dusty, old-fashioned establishment it had been before. Her shop would be elegant, a special place to shop.

When Edward called in, he ran his good hand along the newly polished counter.

"So, when are you having the counter French polished?" His expression was unreadable.

"What do you mean? They've been done! Can't you tell? I think they look wonderful."

"Whoa! Calm down. I thought you were going to lynch me – they've come up like new."

"You're such a tease. I've not met many solicitors, but I'm sure they're all more serious than you."

"Sometimes you just have to learn to laugh at yourself, not take life too seriously." He held up his misshapen hand.

Victoria didn't know how to respond. After a few moments, she realised she'd left it too long to say anything about his hand. Not that she knew what to say. Instead, she went back to safe ground.

"I want my customers to feel special. Especially if they're getting a gown made. I know many of them will currently be getting their gowns designed in London or even Paris. I have lot to live up to."

"If the ladies of the town have heard about the way you tackled the Sisters Grimm, I think they'll be too scared to shop anywhere else," he laughed. Then noticing her grimace, he quickly added, "I'm joking, Victoria. You have nothing to worry about. The sisters have moved away, no one will have heard. Besides, if the quality of your gowns is as good as the shop, they will be running to your door."

She hoped he wasn't just being nice but accepted his praise without contradiction.

Before the week was out, she'd also had a visit from a potential customer, which appeared to confirm Edward's opinion. She was adding the final touches to the windows, when the door rattled.

"We're closed," Milly shouted.

The rattling grew louder. Victoria rolled her eyes. Couldn't people see they were shut?

She unlocked the door, about to tell the rotund, well-dressed woman that they'd be opening next week, when the woman barged in and stood in the middle of the room, casting a critical eye over the changes.

"We're not open yet, madam," Victoria said, suddenly conscious of her untidy hair and apron.

"I'm aware of that. Anne Caldwell told me the drapers was in new hands. You're a widow, I understand. Mrs Kavanagh, is it?"

"Yes, and you are?"

"Mrs Hornby-Smythe."

"How do you do, Mrs Hornby-Smythe. May I help you?"

"Not at present. You've refurbished, I see."

"Yes, do you like it?"

"It's certainly an improvement. More in keeping with the town." She took the gown Milly was holding that they'd been about to add to the window display. "Is this a dress you've made? I heard you were going to be offering dressmaking."

"Yes, that's one of my designs. We're also going to be selling accessories." Victoria pointed to the matching gloves and bag in the window.

"Hmm. Very good. Well, I'll leave you to it. You'll need to find a husband before too long, though. It doesn't do to have a single woman in trade. Makes married women uneasy." On that, she turned on her heel and left.

As the door closed, Milly snorted loudly.

"My goodness, Milly. Please tell me all of our customers aren't like that."

"No, ma'am. Quite a few are toffee-nosed, but she's definitely the worst."

"Well, she seemed to like the dress. And I'm sure she'd have said if she thought the shop wasn't up to her standards."

As Milly finished the window display, Victoria rearranged the curtain for her new changing cubicle for the fifth time. After adjusting the gilt chairs an inch to the left, she stood back and surveyed them. No, that still wasn't right, she thought as she put them back where they started. If she could just entice people through the door, she was sure they'd be impressed by the range of stock on offer.

Victoria couldn't rest with Bridie and the baby in Liverpool – she was missing Sean dreadfully. She knew Bridie would do everything she could to take care of him, but she worried in case he became ill. Would she notice? And if he needed a doctor, would Bridie be able to call one without divulging his parentage and compromising Patrick's position?

Feeling she couldn't wait to see him, she dispatched a note to Patrick arranging for Bridie and the baby to travel to Faredene on the Monday. They would have to stay with her at the hotel until they could move into the shop, but at least that way she could see them every evening.

From the note Patrick sent in reply, she had the distinct impression he'd be more than happy to have Bridie out of the way while he supervised the loading of Victoria's belongings:

> Vicky dearest,
> While my stomach tells me to keep Bridie here for longer, I will dispatch her on the first train Monday morning. There are only so many times I can listen to *Danny Boy* being hummed while I eat my breakfast and keep my sanity.

Chapter 8

Monday morning, as the train puffed into the station, Victoria looked eagerly for the first glimpse of Bridie and Sean. Seeing Bridie's anxious face peering from the compartment window, Victoria felt deflated – she wanted Bridie to share her excitement. She pulled open the compartment door and helped Bridie to alight. She hugged her and then took the sleeping baby from her arms, smothering his face with kisses.

Bridie spoke wearily. "Don't wake him, lass. He's been cranky all morning. He's teething. I've only just got him to sleep."

"Poor lamb. Well, his mummy's missed him," she said shyly, having never referred to herself as mummy before. But it felt good, natural. "Is Mummy's brave boy teething?" She couldn't resist kissing him again.

"You'll spoil him, lass," Bridie tutted.

Shaking her head but with a smile on her face, Bridie went to supervise the porter as he removed the bassinet and bags from the goods wagon. Victoria watched Bridie limp along the platform. Realising her arthritis must be playing up, she resolved to get her to rest once they reached the hotel.

"Bridie, the new house isn't quite ready, so we'll be spending a few days at The Crown Hotel before moving in."

Bridie stared, her mouth open.

"How are we supposed to manage in a hotel with a baby?"

"The manager has made the staff aware and they've assured me everything we need will be on hand. Everything will be fine, you'll see."

"We should have stayed at the house until everything was ready, instead of all this messing around. You can't be expecting the staff to be running around after us. It'll spell disaster, all this. And sure, I won't sleep a wink, not being in me own bed. I don't know. What will you be thinking up next?"

"Bridie, don't be mad. I was missing you both and wanted you here. You're going to love your new home. I've thought of everything! Besides, as much as Patrick appreciates your cooking, I'm sure he'll want his new home to himself. We can't deny him that when we have somewhere else we can go."

"Aye, well, I'll say one thing. This place, it's green – reminds me of Ireland. I've missed seeing swallows and swifts arriving in spring. All yeh got in the city were pigeons."

As Bridie wasn't raising any more objections, in the hope of distracting her, Victoria began pointing out things of interest on their short carriage journey to the hotel.

Bridie had her own room, as she needed her rest so she could cope with Sean during the day, which meant Victoria had been pacing the floor the previous two nights, trying to get the teething infant to sleep. But in the early hours of Thursday morning, the night manager tapped softly on the door of Victoria's room.

"I'm extremely sorry, Mrs Kavanagh. We've had a complaint from one of the other guests that a crying baby is keeping him awake."

Victoria pushed a tendril of hair from her face, staring steely-eyed at the thin, harassed-looking man.

"What exactly do you want me to do about it? Can't you move the other guest?"

"I'm afraid I've tried that, but they've refused." He looked at the floor and shifted uncomfortably before holding out a small glass containing a dark liquid. "If you don't mind, madam, may I suggest a small dram of whiskey? It's known to be effective for settling them."

Victoria took the glass, even though she had no intention of giving her son alcohol.

"We'll be leaving later today."

Victoria closed the door abruptly. It wasn't the man's fault and she shouldn't shoot the messenger, but that's exactly what she felt like doing.

Although the furniture was due to arrive later that day in just a few short hours, they still weren't meant to be moving in for another few days. She'd wanted everything to be perfect for their first day in their new home, with everything already in its rightful place, but it seemed there was no alternative – she wasn't prepared to back down now. She desperately needed sleep. Looking at the glass in her hand, she considered drinking it herself, even though she'd never tasted whiskey. Sean's wailing only seemed to get louder and in desperation, she wondered if it would do any harm – for Sean, that is, not her.

Nervously, she dipped her little finger in the liquid and then allowed Sean to suckle. She repeated the process several more times and eventually, he dozed off. She was desperately grateful that she could now get some sleep, but she was also filled with a sense of self-loathing. She felt a failure as a mother – and this was definitely something she'd have to admit at confession when she next went.

Victoria had no idea how old Bridie was, but what was clear was that she wasn't the only one who was worn out looking after Sean. She'd said she had a husband and a baby, and she'd worked in the Kavanagh household for thirty years, so she had to be knocking on a bit. But when she'd asked in the past, Bridie's answer was always the same. "I'm as old as me tongue and a little bit older than me teeth." Was she being too hard on her? Expecting too much? Whatever her age, she was too old to look after a baby night and day. Something had to be done if she was going to make a success of the business. But for now, she'd committed them to moving later that day and the clock was ticking, as it was beginning to get light. Maybe she should have tried holding her tongue.

After little more than three hours' sleep, Victoria dragged herself out of bed – she had to be at the shop early before the furniture arrived. Looking in the mirror on the dressing table, she frowned at the dark circles under her eyes before creeping over to the washbasin and splashing her face with cold water. Sean was finally sleeping peacefully and after the night she'd had, she needed him to stay that way for a while longer.

After receiving assurances from Bridie that she could cope, Victoria peered outside to look for the carriage she'd ordered. April showers brings May flowers, that's what Bridie always said. Well, this was one heck of a shower, so hopefully it would bring plenty of flowers.

Bracing herself, she lifted her skirts and rushed down

the steps of the hotel, climbing hurriedly into the carriage. Despite having been outside for just a few moments, the heavy rain had soaked through her coat to her white blouse, which clung to her uncomfortably on her journey.

A while later, her tiredness and damp clothes forgotten for a moment, she admired the newly painted pale cream walls of the drawing room. Even though it was dank and dark outside, the little available light from the two large windows gave the room an airy feel. Although desperately tired, she also felt a surge of optimism. Her new home! She'd chosen it herself and she was now in charge of her own destiny. She *would* make this work or die trying, she told herself resolutely as she heard footsteps running up the hallway.

"Blimey, it's raining cats 'n' dogs out there," Milly said, coming through the door as she removed her sodden, faded shawl from her shoulders.

"You're wet through. Let's light the fire and get dried off before we start," Victoria suggested, already shovelling coal into the grate.

"Blinking showers. It's been raining like this since four when I got up."

"You got up at four!"

"Aye, with Mam and Dad, there's eleven of us to get breakfast for. And some of us have to be at work for six. Me dad's a drayman at Paynes Brewery, and our Cora and Agnes are in service but still live at home. Agnes hates her place, though – the cook's a right dragon.

"David and Sam work at Erlington Mill, and Bert delivers parcels and runs errands for shopkeepers before and after school." Milly touched the fingers of one hand with the index finger of the other as though ticking them off before she continued. "Our Kitty helps Mam – she takes in washing. But Kitty can be a little terror at times. Our Teddy, well, he's just different. An' he's right lovable. And Harry, he's the baby of the family."

"That sounds like a houseful."

"Aye, it is. But it's not as crowded as when most of us kids weren't earning. Then, Mam and Dad had to rent out upstairs, so we only had the two rooms."

Despite the obvious poverty in which they lived, Victoria felt a little envious of the large Gibbs family and doubted they'd ever have known loneliness. Perhaps now she had a little family of her own, the feelings of isolation that had always been part of her life would diminish. But for now, her priority was to get her business up and running as fast as possible.

The furniture was due to arrive about noon, so to fill the time, Victoria and Milly began hanging the new curtains they'd worked hard at making all week. The drapes in the drawing room looked elegant and Victoria smiled. Her new home and her dreams for the future were finally coming together.

A huge van drawn by two carthorses clattered to a halt outside the shop and the unloading of her furniture began in earnest. Milly, list in hand, directed the sopping men to the various rooms, while Victoria dashed about the house ensuring that each item was placed in its chosen location. Floors were continuously mopped as the rainwater from the men's soaked boots seemed to travel to every room.

Despite the continuous downpour, the job was completed by mid-afternoon and the men were sitting on upturned crates by the fire, drinking tea as steam rose from both their clothes and their cups.

"Right nice place you've gotten here, ma'am, if you don't mind me sayin'." The gaffer nodded appreciatively, taking in the room.

"We'll soon have it looking like a home," Victoria agreed, already in love with it.

The door opened and Edward entered carrying Sean, supporting the child's back with his bad hand. As Bridie slowly made her way up the corridor, the gaffer rose and held out his large, beefy hand for Edward to shake. She noticed a slight movement in Edward's face and realised how difficult it must be for him to shake hands without flinching.

"I was just saying to your good lady, you've a fine house, sir." The gaffer looked around the room admiringly once more.

Before Edward had the chance to answer, Victoria spoke in a rush, blushing fiercely.

"This is Mr Caldwell. He's a friend of mine," she continued. "I'm a widow," she added, which only made her blush deepen.

She didn't know why she found it necessary to explain to these men, but the way Edward had looked so natural carrying Sean and the assumption that she was his wife made her feel strange and uncomfortable. She could see Edward struggling desperately not to smile as she ushered the removal men out, slipping each one a few coins with her thanks for working through the rain. Regaining her composure, she returned to the drawing room.

"Thank you, Edward. It was so kind of you to collect them for me, especially at such short notice. I felt very presumptuous pushing a note through your office door this morning."

"Not at all. It's my pleasure. I promised Patrick I would look after you. And besides, I wanted to meet this young man." He smiled and touched Sean's cheek.

Suddenly, there was a squelching sound and an acrid odour spread across the room.

"Oh, dear Lord, I think someone needs changing," Edward said, retching as he held Sean dangling as far away from him as possible.

Milly laughed. "That's men for you. They only want the smiling end of a baby, not the end that smells like a midden. Would you like me to change him for you, ma'am?"

Leaving Sean in Milly's care, Victoria took them on a tour of the building. She was proud that she'd managed to create a comfortable home in such a short time, even if it had cost her a small fortune – though she'd never admit that to anyone. She knew Bridie wouldn't give her true reaction to the place until they were alone. They were close, but in company, Bridie always adhered strictly to the conventions of mistress and servant.

As Edward made his departure, Victoria returned to the kitchen and found Milly watching over Sean napping in his bassinet.

"Milly, would you mind sorting the box of ribbons that arrived this morning?" Victoria jerked her head slightly in Bridie's direction.

Milly gave her an understanding nod and left without a word.

As the door closed, Bridie broke her silence.

"Well, lass, you've outdone yerself. It's just grand." Pointing to the comfortable armchairs by the fire, she continued, "I can just see me and you here having the craic of a night."

Victoria smiled, pleased Bridie seemed more her former self.

"But, lass, yer should have mentioned about his leg and hand. I kept finding meself looking at his hand. And he's a right nice chap. I didn't want to offend him, like."

"I'm sorry, Bridie. I completely forgot. I was so tired and pleased to see you both, it slipped my mind."

"What happened to him? Do you know?"

"No, but I expect he was born that way."

"God works in mysterious ways, lass. No doubt He's given him the strength to cope with it."

Sean was sleeping, so Bridie was dispatched to unpack her personal possessions in her own room while Victoria joined Milly and got on with emptying the rest of the packing crates. By the time they'd finished and returned to the kitchen, Bridie had made herself at home and was making a simple supper using the groceries Victoria had had delivered earlier.

"Milly, would you like to stay for supper?" Victoria asked, feeling it was the least she could do as the girl had worked so hard.

"That would be smashing. Thank you, ma'am," Milly accepted shyly.

Bridie looked put out, but Victoria couldn't work out why. She wasn't generally mean-spirited.

After supper, Victoria paid Milly for her week's work.

She looked at the money in her hand before declaring, "You've given me too much, ma'am."

Victoria smiled. "I've given you what you're worth. Now off you go. I'll see you tomorrow."

Milly gulped. "I can't believe it. I only got one raise from the misses in nine years. I'll never let yeh down."

"I'm sure you won't, Milly. Now, get yourself home."

When she went into Sean's room to kiss him goodnight,

Bridie followed her in and handed her a small plaque in a frame.

"It's for above his bed, lass."

Victoria read the words with a lump in her throat. Then she hugged Bridie and kissed her on the cheek before placing it on the dresser by his crib. She knew now that she had Bridie's full support.

May Love Connect Us,
Faith Guide Us
And God Protect Us.

Chapter 9

A week later saw another day of driving rain. Despite Sean sleeping though the night, Victoria had slept fitfully, disturbed by dreams of an empty shop and her explaining to Edward – her husband! – that she'd mislaid their baby. Waking with an uneasy feeling, she'd felt compelled to check Sean was sleeping peacefully in his nursery. He was fine, but the uneasy feeling persisted. She wasn't sure if it was the thought of the empty shop or Edward being her husband and potentially Sean's step-father that disturbed her most.

Her stomach felt like it was full of hopping frogs, never mind butterflies! Whatever it was, excitement or nerves, she wouldn't be able to eat breakfast.

Sitting at the table playing with her food, she was desperate to get down to the shop and reveal to the world the shop's transformation.

"Are you worried about the shop, lass?" Bridie asked.

"No. I'm sure it'll be a success," Victoria lied.

Bridie raised an eyebrow, eyeing her sceptically.

Wanting to change the subject, Victoria asked, "Why didn't you want Milly to stay for supper last night?"

"I'm just worried. We're living a lie and the closer people get, the harder it'll be to keep it a secret. Sure, I'm just bothered if it all comes out, we'll end up in clink. I don't think I could take it." She made as if to shake the image away.

Leaning forwards, Victoria clasped Bridie's hand. "Trust me, Bridie, no one will find out. I promise you – we won't end up in jail." She spoke with more certainty than she felt.

At eight o'clock, Milly and Victoria grasped the newspaper and pulled it from the windows with a flourish. She wasn't sure what she'd expected to see. Crowds of people gasping in delight at her window display. Throngs of people shoving to get through the door first. Perhaps that was a bit much, but the deserted lane and lone pedestrian, almost hidden by his large umbrella, made her heart sink as he scuttled past without a glance.

It was late morning before their first customer ventured through the door. Milly dashed forwards to offer the woman a chair while Victoria asked what she required.

Looking somewhat bewildered by the attention, she said in a small voice, "Brown darning wool."

Victoria looked despondently at the coppers on the counter after the woman had departed clutching her purchase. So much for my first sale. A bit of wool. If her father could see her now, he'd be laughing. She could practically hear him saying, "You thought you were clever refusing to speak to me, girl, but I could have taught you plenty about trade."

As the weather improved, a trickle of customers came into the shop, but not enough to alleviate her niggling anxiety.

As though reading her thoughts, Milly piped up,

"Don't worry, ma'am, it's always quiet when it rains. It'll pick up. You'll see."

"I hope so, Milly." More than you'll ever know, she thought to herself.

Victoria knew that she had enough money to fund the shop for some time, but the thought of her small savings dwindling made her uneasy. Everyone was relying on her – Sean, Bridie and now Milly.

She walked around the shop and storeroom, thinking of the small fortune she'd spent on the vast amount of fabric and haberdashery. It all looked wonderful, but it wasn't going to bring in any money if she couldn't sell it.

She was determined to prove to her father's memory that she was better than him. Her business *would* be a success, and she *would* do it while helping and caring for those around her. But if the business was going to flourish, she couldn't rely on word of mouth. Come on, think, you stupid woman. How can you attract custom?

Slowly, a plan formed in her mind. Leaving Milly to deal with the sprinkling of customers, she spent the afternoon drawing out an advertisement for her dressmaking services for the local paper. She also penned some flyers that Milly's brothers and sisters could push through letterboxes for a few coppers after they'd finished work each night.

On her return from Mass on Sunday, Victoria took charge of Sean. No matter how she tried, she couldn't shake the feelings of disappointment. In the weeks before the move she'd built up images for her fantastic new life. A thriving shop, the joys of motherhood. She'd pictured herself always immaculately groomed. Calm and in control as she drifted from her flourishing business to her adoring, well-behaved baby.

The reality had been very different. Most of the time she'd looked bog-eyed, her hair scraped back, baby drool and stains on her shoulder. She'd definitely not drifted anywhere – instead, she'd torn between the shop and Sean, constantly worrying that she was neglecting both of her babies. The number of customers in the shop was still pitiful – yes, on the whole they'd been impressed by what she'd done. But if trade didn't pick up soon, she, Bridie and Sean would be pleading with Patrick to take them in – or worse still, heading for the workhouse.

Sean's teething had settled with the help of a bone teething toy mounted in silver, but he was still grizzly. Other than when pacing the floor of the hotel trying to get him to sleep, Victoria had been too busy to pay him much attention in recent weeks and she longed to spend time alone with him. She needed to re-establish herself as his mother in his mind. Was she grateful to Bridie for her support and how well she cared for Sean? She loved Bridie. But that didn't change the fact that if Sean kept holding his arms out to Bridie instead of her, she might just be tempted to creep into Bridie's room while she was snoring her head off and smother her.

Forcing her attention back on her son, she looked at his chubby face. It was the first time all week she'd really looked at him. She was amazed at how much he'd changed over the months since she'd found him. He was now a plump, alert baby who was charming everyone he came into contact with.

"I won't let you down, little one. You can trust your mummy. And I won't kill Bridie, don't you worry."

Everything would be all right.

As if to add his agreement, Sean burbled at her.

All right, so she'd jumped into this new life. She'd barely given herself time to think it through properly. And maybe they should have stayed in Liverpool. But it was too late and now was *not* the time to think about it – she'd be back in the shop tomorrow. For now, she wanted to drink in her son. Even the smell of him – at least, when his nappy wasn't full – filled her with love, lingering on her clothing. No matter what challenges lay ahead, she was grateful for the chance she'd been given. Sean was all she needed to give her the strength to make this work.

Victoria had been living in Faredene for two months and was desperate to get out of the mourning clothes she'd been wearing for the husband she'd invented. When Anne had asked when Victoria's husband had passed away, she'd said it was the previous April, meaning that as more than a year had passed, she'd been able to discard her black gowns without contradicting her story. Smiling broadly, she now donned her pale blue coat and matching gloves then turned to Bridie.

"I'm off into town. I'll be a while as I want to look round the shops."

"Aye, righto, lass, but don't yeh want a spot of lunch first? I've got a nice steak and kidney pie in the oven."

"Let's save that for supper. I'm not hungry and I might call in at a tea shop, so I'll get something there if I'm peckish."

"Fair enough, lass. I'll see yeh later."

Victoria cringed as she walked through to the shop. You liar, Victoria Kavanagh. You're lucky God doesn't strike you dead. She didn't want to lie to Bridie, but it was for her own good – she didn't want her worrying. She knew Bridie was concerned about her growing friendships with Edward and Milly. If she knew she was meeting James Brakenridge for lunch, it would be another worry added to her list.

Her arrangement to meet James had come about innocently. Yesterday, he'd been coming out of the barbers as she got back from the bank. Having noticed she'd discarded her mourning attire, he'd invited her to luncheon. At first she'd refused, which resulted in her feeling vain and foolish when he'd pointed out it was simply the welcome meal he'd proposed at their first meeting on the train. Eventually, she'd agreed but insisted she make her own way there.

When she arrived at The Vaults, James was waiting for her in his carriage. He jumped out and escorted her inside. He was courteous as ever and asked how she was enjoying Faredene, listening to her eager responses, nodding his approval in the appropriate places and not interrupting. At the mention of how helpful Edward had been, he enquired how she knew him. She explained that he'd managed the shop purchase for her and that he was an acquaintance of her cousin.

"He's a decent solicitor. It's good he found a profession where he isn't hindered by his obvious deformities. At school, some of the boys gave him a hard time. Dreadful, really. Unfortunately, Edward blamed us all for it. I'm sad to say he took a particular dislike to me."

"That doesn't sound like him. Why on earth was that?"

"It's embarrassing, really, but I was athletic, captain of various teams. I don't blame him for it. I understand why it made him feel inadequate. He didn't have a built-up shoe then and his limp was very pronounced. His leg is a lot shorter, you know. Some of the boys . . . well, they called him Cripple Caldwell. Made terrible fun of him. Children can be so cruel."

Victoria put her hand to her heart. "That's dreadful. Poor Edward."

"Yes, it is. It's made him a very bitter man."

"That's so out of character. He's normally so cheerful and self-depreciating."

"All a thin veil, I'm afraid. He has a nasty temper. I've suffered his wrath many a time."

"That sounds unfair."

"I made the mistake of trying to stand up for him, as it just made him hate me more. Can't stand the sight of me now. It's perhaps best not to mention my name to him."

"I won't. I do understand how hard it must have been for him, but he shouldn't have blamed you."

James shrugged hopelessly.

"What about you, James? You said on the train that you have a business in the town."

"I have several businesses, many of which are in nearby cities. But really, Victoria, I am frightfully boring. Tell me about how you intend to grow your business and entice the ladies of Faredene into your store – now that would be more interesting."

Victoria told James of her plans and how she hoped to expand in the future.

At the end of the meal, James signed the bill. When he offered her a lift, she explained that she wanted to look in the shops on her way home and would prefer to walk. He kissed her hand swiftly, wished her every success and said he hoped they'd meet again one day. She felt foolish for imagining it was anything other than a welcome-to-Faredene luncheon.

Edward looked up from the papers he was reading and tried to hear what the voice he recognised – the voice he hated – in his outer office was saying. The door to his office opened and James Brakenridge strode in, Edward's clerk hovering uncertainly behind him.

"It's all right, Perkins. I'll see him without an appointment on *this* occasion. Please close the door on your way out."

The clerk must have noted the scowl on his employer's normally genial face, but he backed out and closed the door.

"Just thought I would let you know. I have just had lunch with the lovely Vicky Kavanagh."

Edward gripped the edge of his mahogany desk.

"Ah, I *was* right. You *are* after her." He sneered at Edward.

"My relationship with Victoria is nothing to do with you, Brakenridge."

"We met once on the train, you know. She's filled out a bit since then." He made a lascivious gesture as if holding large breasts. "Still, at least she has that virgin schoolgirl way about her that I like. Hard to believe she's been married."

Edward balled his left fist, a vein popping out in his neck. "You stay away from her!"

"I will do what I like, but you can have her after I have finished. If I stick a bun in her oven, maybe you can beg her to marry you, like you did with poor Charlotte. There again, perhaps Victoria would prefer to throw herself under a train, as well. You're not exactly marriage material."

"You bastard!" Edward stood, his face purple.

"Don't worry. I'll take my time. Maybe you'll even get

to poke her first. A cripple like you mustn't get many chances to get his leg over, whereas I can bed a real virgin every day of the week if I want to."

"Perkins!" Edward bellowed.

The nervous-looking clerk opened the door.

"Kindly show this *gentleman* out. He is *not* to be admitted again. Under *any* circumstances! Is that clear?"

Edward heard James' laughter as he passed his office window.

Chapter 10

Victoria felt sure her business was now on a steady track as each week, revenue had increased. Despite the slow start, several ladies had ordered gowns. Mrs Hornby-Smythe had been so pleased with her gown that she'd recommended Victoria to several of her friends, meaning that her order book had grown considerably, with some ladies booking appointments for their entire wardrobe for next year's London season.

"Do yeh want anything special for yer supper tonight, or are you all right having what I make? I'm asking 'cos I got some stuff that will go off in this heat if I don't use it up. It's so blinking hot, nothing's lasting," Bridie said.

"I'll take whatever I get, Bridie," Victoria answered distractedly as she watched her son.

She estimated Sean was about ten months old and he was already asserting his independence. If he was put on the floor, he'd scuttle off on his hands and knees, looking for things to investigate.

"Bridie, look! He's trying to stand!" Victoria said, gazing proudly at her son as he tried to pull himself up using the edge of the sofa before plonking back down.

"They all do it, you know. To hear his mam speak, you'd think he were the first child to try to walk," Bridie ended on a laugh, looking at Victoria's adoring face. "Lass, I can't believe the transformation in yeh. You've blossomed. There's a twinkle in your eyes. And as for yer figure. Well, that's filled out smashing."

"Bridie, really!"

A few months ago, Victoria would have blushed like crazy. Now, she laughed, enjoying the compliments. She knew she'd changed. And she knew Bridie was proud of her.

"Will you be all right to watch him now, Bridie, while I go down to the shop?"

"Aye, lass, you go on. I'm gonna open a few windows. Me teeth are sweating an' it's still early."

Victoria bent to kiss Sean on the top of his head and left the room smiling. Bridie had laughed and joked more in the last few months than Victoria ever remembered her doing in Liverpool.

A few hours later, bending over her workbench, where she was pinning together the last pieces of a duck-egg blue tea gown, Victoria rubbed the back of her neck. Then she leaned back and stretched her arms above her head to relieve the tension that was developing. She could hear Milly advising a customer on her choice of ribbon for a hat.

How life had moved on in just a few months, she thought contentedly. She was a mother! The ache in her body to bear a child hadn't gone – she still yearned to feel a child growing inside her, to feel her child suckle – but she was able to control the feelings by holding Sean in her arms.

As for Edward, he was so kind and she found herself looking forward to his visits. She'd been in the habit of dining with Anne and him once a month, and felt she and Edward had a great deal in common. She enjoyed Anne's company in small doses but found her a little snobbish on occasion. Just last week she'd tried to discourage Victoria from speaking to Mrs Parkinson simply because her husband ran a shop.

"You don't want to associate with *them* – they're in trade. I know you have your little shop, but that's different. You can afford to be selective about who patronises your establishment now."

Victoria had been firm. "Any lady who can afford to purchase a gown from me will be treated with respect. As for friendships, I judge people on their behaviour, not on their source of income."

Anne's pretty face had been haughty, but she hadn't retorted. Edward had quickly changed the subject.

Her reverie was broken by the sound of Sean's loud, urgent wails and Bridie's shrieks. Jumping up from her seat, she tore round her workbench, catching the material she'd been pinning, which fell to the floor along with the pot of pins, scattering everywhere. Holding her skirts, she dashed towards the workroom door, almost tripping in her haste. She shoved the kitchen door open with such force that it slammed against the wall as she took in the scene.

Bridie was stood transfixed. Sean lay rigid on the floor beside the kitchen table, the teapot smashed on the floor beside him. His bare legs were flailing, his hands balled into fists as he roared. His skin was bright red where the scalding liquid had soaked him.

She picked him up. Holding him away from her, not wanting to hurt him further, she darted into the scullery and plunged him into the large wooden sink. Urgently, she began to pump cold water over him. She had no idea if it would work, but instinctively felt the need to cool his scalded limbs.

"I only turned me back for a second! I'd just been mashing the tea ready for lunch. Just a second, that's all I turned me back for. He must have pulled the tablecloth." Bridie paced back and forth, wringing her hands. "Oh, dear God, what have I done? I'll never forgive myself if I've scarred that child!"

"Bridie, Bridie! Hush. Go and ask Milly to run for the doctor. Tell her to shut the shop. Quickly, now."

Victoria continued to run water over him, praying the bright red blotches would fade. She could feel her heart thumping wildly in her chest, her breathing shallow. It was as though time stood still while she waited for the doctor. Unable to think of anything else to do, she kept the poor mite submerged in the water and began to sing, repeating a lullaby over and over. His whimpering continued as his little arms wrapped themselves around her neck, his damp cheek to her face.

"Right, let me see what's happened here."

Doctor Owain Farrell, a sandy-haired young man of medium build with a warm smile, bustled into the room. He headed straight for the scullery, glancing at Sean then Victoria, whose dress front was drenched, her sleeves sopping to well past her elbows.

"Getting him into the water was quick-thinking. Well done."

"I had no idea if it would help. I just wanted to soothe him. It seemed like the right thing to do at the time."

"Well, it will certainly have helped. Now, let's get him on the table and see what needs to be done. Come on now, woman. Get this table cleared," he barked at Bridie. "You're no use bawling." He turned to Victoria. "Lay him down here." Taking small scissors from his bag, he cut

Sean's clothing away, talking to him softly. "There, there, young man. This isn't so bad now, is it?"

Victoria couldn't drag her eyes away from the red weals covering most of his chubby little legs.

Having examined him closely, Doctor Farrell announced that it could have been a lot worse. Taking a pot from his bag, he smeared a paste over Sean's legs and began to wrap them in cotton wadding as he continued to wail and struggle to get away.

"Now now, little man, no need to carry on so."

Once Sean's injuries had been dressed, Doctor Farrell gave Victoria a note, instructing her to send someone to the apothecary with it.

"Give him one drop every four hours. Until the pain subsides, the best thing would be for him to sleep. I'll call again tomorrow. And take that worried look off your face. I doubt there will be any permanent scarring. But you will need to watch him from now on. I've seen far too many children with burns and scalds. Children's faces marred, lives ruined – and that's the ones who survive."

Victoria felt like she'd been scolded. Doctor Farrell was a kind man and a good doctor. She knew he meant well, but his words affected her deeply. Had she been wrong to trust Bridie with her son? She was meant to be taking care of him. Part of Victoria wanted to take Bridie by the shoulders and shake her. She shouldn't have turned her back on him. She said she'd watch him.

Victoria's anger frightened her. She didn't want to become like her father. Deep down, she knew it wasn't Bridie's fault. She only had herself to blame. She'd promised herself months ago she'd get help for Bridie and she'd let all this time go by without doing anything.

Should she sell the business and find a small cottage where she could look after her son properly? That's what a good mother would have done. She'd longed for this child, prayed for him. In fact, she believed he was a gift from God. Yet, here she was, spending most of her time running the business. Leaving him to be raised by another woman, when she knew how Bridie struggled.

She felt deeply ashamed. Especially when she was forced to admit that she didn't want to give up her new life. But by working, she was building a future for Sean, as well. Surely that was part of being a good mother, a responsible mother, she reasoned.

That afternoon, Edward called in as he generally did two or three times a week. Touching her hand gently, he said, "Vicky, you are an amazing mother. A remarkable woman, in fact. I can see the love in your eyes every time you look at him. As for running your business, as long as you don't expect him to help with fittings for the likes of Mrs Hornby-Smythe, I'm sure he'll be very proud of you."

His words brought a lump to her throat and unable to speak, she busied herself, straightening Sean's covers. It was a relief to know he didn't think badly of her, but she wouldn't allow it to ease her conscience.

Later that day, while Sean slept, Bridie sat in her chair by the fire brooding, wiping her eyes when she thought Victoria wasn't looking. Victoria left the room briefly and went down to the shop to speak to Milly. She had a plan, but it would take careful handling if she was to avoid making Bridie feel worse than she already did.

Milly was busy putting bolts of fabric back on the shelves having just served a customer with several pieces.

"Is the little fella all right now, ma'am? I went for

Doctor Farrell 'cos he's always so nice. Not like the other miserable old bugger – jumped-up quack, he is."

"He's sleeping. But I can't afford to let anything like this happen again. Is your sister Agnes still unhappy where she's working?"

"Yes, ma'am. She's hoping to find summat else." Milly turned round to give Victoria her full attention.

"Do you think she'd like to work here, helping Bridie with the cooking, bit of light housework and looking after Sean?"

"Really, ma'am? She'd snatch yer hand off. She's right fed up where she is an' our mam doesn't want her going to the mill 'cos the dust gets in the lungs. And our Agnes can get a cough at the drop of a hat."

"Could you ask her to come for an interview? Bridie isn't going to take kindly to someone coming into her territory, so I need her to approve the engagement. And we'll have to tread softly."

"Don't worry, ma'am. Agnes is a good girl. She'll know how to be diplomatic. If it were our Kitty, it might be a different matter. But you can trust Agnes."

"And I need someone to do the cleaning and laundry twice a week. Do you think your mother would be interested?"

"I don't know what to say now. I'm ever so grateful to you for giving her a chance. She'll be made up. She needs every penny, 'cos she can never rely on me dad's money. He drinks half of it away most weeks. Anyway, you don't need to know about all our troubles."

Victoria didn't know whether she was amazed or appalled at the ready acceptance of her father's behaviour. But then she never truly understood why her own mother had stayed with her father when she could have taken Victoria and run away before it was too late.

Sean had woken several times in the night but was now sleeping soundly as Victoria spoke to Bridie while they ate breakfast.

"Bridie, I'm so sorry. I feel terrible that I've put so much on you over the last few months. Will you ever forgive me?"

"Dear God, don't ask *my* forgiveness, lass. It were my fault. I should have been watching him." Bridie stifled a yawn. "I'm so sorry, lass. I've tossed and turned all night. I feel right guilty. I were distracted, like. I couldn't remember where I'd put the cake I'd made yesterday. I'm sure someone must have moved it on purpose."

"Bridie, who on earth could have moved it? No one comes in here accept Milly and it wouldn't be her. And Sean's hardly capable."

"I know yer right, lass. I keep misplacing things and then finding them in right strange places. There's no one to blame. I'm getting to be as much use as a square wheel these days, lass."

"No, Bridie, it's my mistake. I let you down. But it won't happen again. I've arranged for Agnes, Milly's sister, to come here this morning so you can interview her. If you're happy with her, she'll be your assistant."

"You don't need two people. It's throwing money down the drain. Sure, I don't want you wasting money. Do you want me to leave? I'll understand. I want the truth now." Bridie's eyes glistened.

"Bridie, listen to me. You heard the doctor. He sees lots of injuries like these. We just need some help, that's all.

I'm as much to blame, leaving you to shoulder everything while I run the business. Now, I'll hear no more of it. It's time I thought of you for a change – you've done enough for me over the years."

Agnes, who was a smaller version of Milly, arrived promptly, looking like she'd been scrubbed to within an inch of her life. Her blue dress was faded in places and had been made from fabric Victoria had given Milly from the old stock. Bridie was at a loss as to what to ask, so Victoria took over, explaining her duties and emphasising how fortunate she'd be if taken on to be trained by someone as experienced as Bridie.

"Oh, yes, ma'am, I know." She looked at Bridie. "I'd consider it an honour if you'd teach me proper, like. An' I'll work ever so hard. I'm a quick learner, ma'am."

Victoria looked at Bridie, waiting for her response.

"Well, you know your manners, girl, I'll say that for you. Sure, I think we can give this a try."

Victoria breathed a sigh of relief.

Once Agnes had left, Victoria went on to explain that Edith would now be in every Monday to do the washing and Saturday to do the rough cleaning, leaving Bridie and Agnes to see to the running of the house and to care for Sean.

"If yer sure that's what you want, lass. I know I'm not pulling me weight an' I feel bad about it. But it's a full-time job looking after the little 'un."

"Bridie, I need you – and so does Sean. You *are* our family. So no more talking about you not doing enough."

When Edith arrived to discuss the weekly cleaning, Victoria was humbled by the tiny woman's gratitude.

"I'm ever so grateful, ma'am. Not just for me, but for employing two of me girls. It's such a weight off me mind." As she spoke, she continuously rubbed the pads of her thumbs against her fingers in a nervous habit.

Victoria's eyes were drawn to the fading yellow-black bruise around her left eye – no doubt one of many she'd suffered during her life. Her dress was clean but the collar and cuffs were badly frayed and she'd tried to repair the holes in her boots by stuffing them with old newspaper, which was sticking out. It occurred to Victoria that they'd both probably dressed in their best to see her.

She wondered if she should supply her staff with uniforms. Yes, she was sure this was the right thing to do for her staff. Besides, if any of her staff were seen by her clientele, she wanted them to look smart. As all the dresses would be made in-house from cheaper fabric bought from her supplier at cost, all she had to do now was source a supplier for boots.

The doctor returned three more times to check on Sean's scalds. Within a few weeks, the marks had all but faded on his legs and arms. The scars on Bridie's and Victoria's consciences were deeper and would take longer to heal, though.

Chapter 11

The September morning brought with it the first chill of autumn and Agnes had the kitchen fire glowing as Victoria indulged in her habit of playing with Sean for a short while before going down to the shop. She warmed her hands in front of the fire and as he hurled one of his wooden blocks across the rug, she realised he must be almost a year old.

"Bridie, you do realise this young man here must be nearly one! How did I miss that? It's gone so fast. I'll never know when he was *actually* born, but I want to mark it in some way. I know what we'll do. Sunday would have been my mother's birthday, so he'll share her day. I don't know why I didn't think of it before."

At that moment, Agnes returned to the kitchen. Victoria put her finger to her lips to silence Bridie – they needed to be careful Agnes didn't hear them talking about not knowing Sean's birthday.

"It's nippy out, so I've laid all the fires in case you want to light them later, ma'am," Agnes said as she began to clear the breakfast things, seemingly oblivious to the conversation she could so easily have overheard.

"Thanks, Agnes," she said, turning her attention back to Bridie. "Let's have a birthday tea for Sean on Sunday."

"He'll not know the difference – he's far too young. But if that's what you want, lass, I'll bake a little cake," Bridie stated as she finished her cup of tea.

"I could make it. If you'll let me, Bridie?" Agnes glanced hopefully in Bridie's direction. "It would be good practice for me, with you watching me, of course."

"We'll see. Sure, I don't want it messing up, now."

Victoria tried not to smile. In the short time Agnes had been with them, Victoria had already noticed Agnes had a flare for cooking. Perhaps it was the lack of food she'd suffered from that gave her such an appreciation for it, but Victoria suspected that before long, her culinary skills would surpass Bridie's excellent but traditional dishes.

"A cake would be lovely and I'll invite Edward. And perhaps Milly and you, Agnes, would like to come with some of the little ones."

"Not too many of them, mind. It's just a tea party." Bridie bristled with horror, knowing how many of them there were. "We don't want the house overrun."

"Most of them are too old. Perhaps we could just bring the three youngest – Teddy, Kitty and Harry," Agnes suggested, looking at Victoria.

"It'll be nice for him to have other children to play with," Victoria agreed.

"Aye, as long as they're not lousey!" Bridie whispered, but not quietly enough.

"Bridie, I'm sure they won't be!" After kissing Sean, Victoria left the room, shrugging and mouthing "Sorry" to Agnes.

Edward arrived first and presented Sean with a wooden rocking horse for his birthday.

"Edward, it's beautiful. But you shouldn't have! It's too much."

"I wanted to get something big and in the way so you would have to think of me as you struggled to get past it."

"Honestly, Edward. Are you *ever* serious?"

"Far too often in my job, so I am afraid you are stuck with my silly jokes."

"They're not silly. Actually, you're quite funny . . . for a boring man." Her face was deadpan.

Edward threw his head back, laughing. "Victoria, I do believe you have just made a joke!"

"Actually, I think it's my second. I don't know what's come over me, or where that came from, so don't get too used to it."

A clattering in the hall signalled the arrival of Milly and Agnes, along with Teddy, Kitty and Harry, whom they had yet to meet. Milly had told her previously that Teddy, at eleven, was still like a small child. Harry, the baby of the family, had been two in July. Kitty, who was six and often had the job of taking care of Teddy, was in Milly's words, "a little madam with a heart of gold".

Following a knock on the kitchen door, Milly entered with Harry in her arms, smiling. She was followed by Agnes, who went straight over to Bridie, offering to help with the remaining preparations for tea. Victoria wasn't prepared for the appearance of the other two visitors as Kitty came through the door, her back to the room.

"Come on, Teddy, they won't bite yeh."

Long red hair cascaded down her back over her worn dress and as she turned round, Victoria was taken aback. All the other Gibbs offspring had either their mother's buck teeth or, as Milly had explained it, their father's big conk. One or two unfortunate ones, Cora and Sam, had both. Kitty, on the other hand, had enormous green eyes, her mother's button nose, a rosebud mouth and a smattering of freckles. This child's beauty was at odds with the environment in which she was growing up.

Teddy was just as Milly had described – small for his age and stocky. His face was round and he was smiling broadly. It was the happiest face Victoria had ever seen.

Edward immediately came forwards, holding out his hand. "Hello, Master Teddy. I'm Edward. We have the same name."

"No, I'm Teddy. T-e-d-d-y," the boy said slowly.

"Yes, of course you are. Silly me! I guess that makes you young Teddy and me old Teddy," he laughed, not realising that the name would stick in Teddy's mind forever. "Would you like to play with Sean, Harry and me?" Edward crouched on the floor with the three boys.

"Cor, would yeh look at that cake! Will I get a slice if I'm good, 'cos I've promised me mam an' our Milly I won't let 'em down?" Kitty piped up, staring wide-eyed at the sponge cake Agnes had made.

"Yes, of course, but after we've eaten the sandwiches," Victoria laughed.

"Blimey! Butties, too? Are they jam or dripping?"

"There's ham, cheese and egg." Victoria stifled a smile.

"'Ay, it's dead posh 'ere. Am I gonna get a whole slice of that cake to meself?" She eyed Victoria suspiciously.

Victoria couldn't help being amused. "I don't see why not."

Even Bridie was beaming as she piled sandwiches onto a large serving dish.

"I've never seen this much food, 'cept in shop winders,"

Kitty said, pointing at the plate of sandwiches. "This is gonna be the best day of me life! I'll remember what yeh said though, Milly. I won't stuff 'em all in me gob at once," she said seriously.

None of them could help smiling and Kitty looked at their faces, bemused.

As the afternoon wore on, Harry, a sullen child, tried to monopolise Sean's toys, much to Milly's embarrassment when Sean cried as toys were snatched from his hands. Despite Victoria's assurances that it was fine, Milly scolded him, explaining crossly that he shouldn't take things that weren't his.

"He's a right little bugger, ain't he?" Kitty said to Edward, gesturing at Harry with her thumb.

Edward looked like he was struggling to breathe as he tried desperately not to laugh. Milly put her head in her hands and groaned.

"He's still a baby," Edward managed to get out at last.

"Aye, I suppose yer right. He ain't learnt how to behave in posh company like me."

All of the adults fought to contain their laughter while Kitty continued chattering, ignorant of the effect she was having.

"This 'ere teddy is nice," Kitty said, picking up the bear Victoria had bought Sean. "Bit tatty-looking, though. His fur's a bit like your baby's hair – all over the place," she added, stroking the fur down. "You should call him Tatty Teddy," she finished, bouncing the bear up and down on her knee.

Milly rolled her eyes, cringing, while everyone else chuckled. Despite her total lack of etiquette and decorum, it was impossible not to like Kitty.

"So, old Teddy, what 'appened to yer hand? Was yeh born a bit funny like our Teddy?"

The room went silent as the adults looked from Edward to Kitty, whose face was full of innocent concern.

"Do you mean this?" he said seriously after a beat, his eyes wide, holding up his contorted hand.

Kitty nodded, momentarily silenced by his tone.

"No, it wasn't always this way. It was mangled by a great big brown bear. Just like this . . ." He raised both of his arms in the air, making his fingers claw-like as he chased Kitty around the room, growling like a bear.

Skirting past him, Kitty hid under the table giggling. "Quick! Under here youse lot before the bear takes a big chunk outta yer backsides."

Teddy scrambled beneath while Edward, still growling, proceeded to tickle Harry and Sean.

It took some time to calm the children. Victoria was relieved that despite Kitty's insensitive question, there had been no sign of Edward's temper James had warned about.

Bridie was reluctant to engage with Teddy at first but was impressed how kind and gentle he was with Sean and Harry. By the time they'd eaten tea, both Teddy and Kitty had won everyone's hearts. Even Bridie was saying they should come again.

When they were alone, Bridie voiced her thoughts.

"Kitty's a right character, but I hope they leave Harry at home next time."

"Bridie!"

"That Harry is heading for trouble, you mark my words."

"Bridie, how can you say that? He's just a baby. He won't understand why Sean has so much when I suspect he has no toys. He's probably not learned to share."

"Aye, well, unfortunately, he'll have to get used to it, 'cos that's how life is. But it does more harm than good for some to see how the other half live."

Victoria wondered if Sean's family had been as poor as Milly's. Poorer even. Life could be harsh. Much of where you ended up was dictated the moment you were born.

"With her looks, if they'd been born into a wealthy family, no doubt Kitty would have been looking forward to a future of parties, suitors and a good marriage. And I'm sure Teddy's speech would have been far more advanced than it is."

Bridie had a different opinion.

"Rich folk don't like the stigma of someone like him in the family. Sure, he might have been kept locked away upstairs with just one maid caring for him. Or worse still, sent to an asylum and forgotten about – nothing but a coffin to look forward to."

Victoria shivered at the thought.

Chapter 12

"The wind would blow the bloomers off a nun!" Milly announced as a gust of wind blew her into the shop. She was clutching her thin shawl, her hair in disarray.

"You pop in the back and get yourself tidied up. We have a busy day ahead," Victoria said as she checked the order book.

Victoria was now so busy that she had to devote most of her time to dressmaking as many of her customers were recommending her services to family, friends and acquaintances. Edward's sister, Anne, who was becoming increasingly nosy, had also been so delighted, if somewhat patronising, with her first evening gown and day dresses that she'd brought along several of her wealthy friends.

"Victoria, you really are a treasure. They're as good as the gowns from London. I will definitely send my friends and help you to build your little clientele," she said, twirling in front of the gilt mirror.

She is so condescending, Victoria thought irritably, then immediately rebuked herself for thinking badly of Edward's sister when they'd both gone out of their way to welcome her to Faredene. Smiling brightly, she thanked Anne for the compliment.

"So, how are you and Edward getting along?" Anne asked as Victoria helped her back into her own clothes.

"I'm not sure what you mean. Has Edward said there's a problem? I thought we got along very well."

"Come on, Victoria," she giggled. "I like you, you know I do. But I love Edward and I have to look out for him – he really has no one else. It's clear to me that Edward is besotted with you. I would like to know if you feel the same."

"How I feel about Edward is my business. And our relationship is between the two of us, no one else. I'm sorry, Anne, but I'll thank you to mind your own business."

What gave Anne the right to question her about Edward? As for him being besotted, surely not!

"There's no need to be so touchy, Victoria. Sometimes I think you've never had a friend before. You certainly don't know how to treat one."

Victoria was flummoxed. Was she touchy? Anne was right about her not having friends, but then Milly was a friend, and she didn't stick her nose in Victoria's business.

Thankfully, she'd been saved from having to answer as Anne, looking disgruntled, returned her attention to her new gown and the exquisite embroidery that Olga had added. Olga, a middle-aged Austrian woman who spoke fractured English but was a superb needlewoman, had been a lucky find. Her skills had enabled Victoria to customise each gown and add to her exclusivity.

Milly had been put in charge of the shop and a junior assistant had been taken on to cope with the growing trade. Bridie spent most of her time with Sean, as though afraid to take her eyes off him in case he had another accident. Agnes was still under Bridie's strict supervision as she went about her duties, with Bridie picking up on every little thing not done to her satisfaction. Agnes was an exceptionally quiet girl, who arrived promptly at six thirty every morning. Despite Bridie's occasionally sharp reprimands and critical gaze, Agnes did everything with a smile and appeared to have a genuine respect and fondness for Bridie.

Edith came in twice a week as arranged, occasionally sporting new bruises. She worked swiftly and never stopped for a cup of tea, despite Bridie's offers.

"I'd love to, but I've to get back. Kitty's looking after Teddy and Harry," was always her response.

Occasionally, she'd give a little more detail, explaining her reluctance.

"Kitty's good with them, but I never know what I might find when I get home. Last week, she nearly set the place on fire! She'd decided to bake a loaf. Flour every-bloody-where. Dough stuck in Harry's hair. Teddy with me lard all over his face. If she hadn't wasted what precious bit of stuff I had in, I might have laughed. Her dad gave her a right hiding when there was no bread with his supper."

Victoria hated the thought of Kitty being hit. In fact, it made her blood boil. The girl shouldn't be missing out on school to look after Teddy and the baby, either, but Victoria didn't think she had the right to interfere. Victoria was dismayed when she discovered that much of the Gibbs family income found its way into the alehouses in the Rows.

"Dad comes home legless most nights, but it's not so bad these days. Mostly he just falls asleep, and Mam doesn't get as many shiners," Milly had explained.

Regardless of how the money was spent, Victoria had no regrets about employing any of the Gibbs family. Even

Milly's younger brother, Bert, now delivered parcels to Victoria's customers, pushing a smart cart that was bigger than he was. Together with Olga and the other staff, they were helping her to make her dream a reality and her profits were increasing. As she placed the previous week's takings in her bag and donned her hat ready to go to the bank, she felt a rush of pride at the thought of her growing bank balance.

Victoria struggled to hold her hat in place as she headed towards the bank, leaves swirling around her ankles. She wondered if Edward would drop by later. There was no denying she missed him if he didn't visit for a few days. Despite Bridie's concern about Edward getting too close to Victoria, he appeared to be charming even her, as she'd giggled like a young girl when he'd teased her recently.

"Bridie I don't know what makes me want to marry you most – those gorgeous Irish eyes of yours or your scones," he'd said.

He was wonderful with Sean, as well, and bought him small gifts: a wooden engine, a jack-in-the-box, a spinning top. Often, she'd look up to find him gazing at her and even she'd worried that his feelings were more than friendship. Despite mulling it over many a night when she should have been asleep, she was still confused about how this made her feel. She'd even imagined being enveloped in his arms while he told her he loved her, but these images would swiftly turn to ones of her father grasping her mother's arm tightly, or her mother crouching in a corner sobbing.

Having deposited the week's takings, she pulled her gloves on in the doorway and glanced up and down the street before stepping out into the wind. She felt slightly disappointed James wasn't here today. Following their first luncheon, she'd run into him a few weeks later just as she was leaving the bank and he was entering.

"Victoria! You must have lunch with me. I've had a frightfully boring morning and I'm in need of cheering up," he'd said.

Once again, they'd dined at The Vaults. Victoria didn't feel at ease as she did in Edward's company and when James' eyes had ranged over her, she'd found it unsettling. But he never said anything improper.

Since that day, they'd happened on each other on a few other occasions, which had also led to them dining together. She'd tried to convince herself that the meetings were just by chance, although she knew she'd started to go to the bank with the takings at the same time each week in case he should be there.

Surreptitiously, she looked around today, but he was nowhere to be seen. She frowned slightly, disappointed she hadn't seen him for three weeks. There was nothing in it – she didn't imagine them having a relationship – but he was always so agreeable and amusing. Who was she kidding . . .

Just as she got close to the tobacconists, James stepped out of the doorway.

"Victoria! What a pleasant surprise."

"James, how lovely to see you," she blushed, embarrassed that she was actually delighted to see him.

"Come, we must have lunch. It's been an age since I saw you last and my luncheon date has cancelled. Not that I mind – he's a frightful bore. Dining with you will be far more enjoyable. We had a table booked at The Royal Oak, if that's acceptable to you?"

He's just a friend like Edward, she told herself as she allowed him to lead her to the hotel in the centre of town. She'd never allow it to go any further, so surely there was no harm in it . . .

As they entered, the manager nodded to James and led them to a private dining room adjacent to the restaurant. Victoria faltered – she couldn't dine alone with him.

"Victoria, have you not realised yet that you have nothing to fear from me?" James asked, sensing her hesitation.

"But my—"

"Surely you're not worried about your reputation. I merely wish to dine with you and I already had this room booked for my business acquaintance. But if you don't trust me . . ." He looked wounded.

"No, of course. It's fine. Shall we go in?" she said, feigning confidence.

They chatted happily as they waited for their soup. Once the waiter had served, she was sure she saw James cast his eyes towards the door and the waiter left the room. She suddenly felt nervous. Surely they shouldn't be left entirely alone. Tension knotted in her chest.

James listened patiently as she talked about her business.

"Enough about my life. I must be boring you, James. We always talk about my business and my life, yet I know nothing about you." Victoria looked at the door, willing the waiter to return.

"Do I give you the impression I am bored?" he asked pointedly.

"No. Not at all. You're always very attentive. I just can't understand why you're so interested in ladies' fashion. I feel I monopolise the conversation."

Putting his spoon down, he put his hands to his face and groaned.

"It's not ladies' fashion I'm interested in, you must know that."

"James, I . . . James, what is it?"

Victoria rose from her seat and went to his side. He didn't answer.

"James?" Tentatively, she put her hand on his shoulder. "What on earth is wrong?"

Turning and putting his hands on her waist, he buried his head against her chest. She tried to pull away.

"It's you! Don't you see what you are doing to me? You are in my bones. You are coming between me and my senses."

Still holding her close, he stood up. She gulped as she felt his hot breath on her neck. He looked down on her startled face.

"James, I'm sorry, I . . . No. Please, l-let go of me." She tried to pull away.

"Victoria, don't deny what we both want. I've felt your reaction when I brushed your hands with my fingers. You knew what I was suggesting. Never once have you recoiled. Today, I saw you looking around for me. I know you always go to the bank at the same time every week. It's because you want to see me. I know it is."

"James, I—"

"Don't deny it. I deliberately stayed away for three weeks. Trying to overcome your bewitchment. You are torturing me, you know you are."

"James, I'm sorry if you feel I've misled you, but you must unhand me!" Panicking but afraid of offending him, ashamed that on some level he was right, she tried to push him off.

"Don't pretend with me, Victoria. You have toyed with me. Pulled me in. Played with my affections. Now, I need you to release me from my misery. I ache for you."

Grasping her hand, he pulled it down so she could feel his stiffness. He pressed his lips against her, kissing her hard, his tongue forcing its way into her mouth. Victoria had never been kissed. If this was how it felt, she hadn't been missing out.

"James. No, I . . . Get off me this instant!" She shoved him off, backing to the door.

"Victoria, don't do this. We can give each other pleasure. You want me, I know you do," he shouted after her as she threw open the door.

Horrified at her own stupidity, Victoria looked back at him as she stepped out into the foyer, almost colliding with Mrs Hornby-Smythe just as she and three of Victoria's other clients were about to enter the main restaurant. Victoria smoothed her skirts, trying to regain her composure. James appeared behind her looking angry and disarrayed.

There was no mistaking the shock on the ladies' faces. Had they heard what he'd said? Her face scarlet, Victoria scurried out onto the high street. Still trembling and flustered, she took her handkerchief from her bag and mopped her brow.

She was such an idiot! Stupid, stupid, stupid! she admonished herself all the way to the park.

Sitting on a bench by the lake as she had done many times in Liverpool, she clasped her hands to still their trembling. Desperately wishing she could turn back the clock, she gulped deep breaths as she tried to calm her thoughts and make sense of what had happened. She knew she wasn't blameless. She'd wanted his attention. But now she regretted it deeply.

It was late afternoon before she felt composed enough to return to the store.

"Ma'am, could you assist with this fitting?" Milly asked as she walked through the door.

Grateful for the distraction, Victoria plonked her gloves and hat behind the counter and entered the fitting room.

Chapter 13

The following day, Victoria was feeling guilty. James had looked so upset. She hadn't intended to lead him on. She was very inexperienced at dealing with men, but she assumed that both Edward and he understood they were just friends. Or was she merely being dishonest with both them and herself?

Victoria had to accept it was all her own fault as she got ready to meet Anne. Anne was still being a little huffy with her since Victoria had refused to discuss her relationship with Edward with her. She hoped today they'd be able to put the matter behind them, as they were due to meet for a Women's Guild charity luncheon in aid of poor families in the area. She'd taken to attending monthly events to help the charity, fulfilling the promise she'd made to God to help others. It also provided an opportunity to meet local ladies who could potentially become customers.

Victoria sat half listening to the ladies in her group chatting about their own children. She realised with disapproval how when their little darlings behaved, it was down to their own perfect mothering skills. Whereas if the child committed some misdemeanour, it was the result of inadequate guidance from the nanny, nursemaid or unsupportive husband. Anne looked irritated. As a single woman and childless, she couldn't join in the conversation. She stared at Victoria as though mulling something over.

Victoria turned away, her gaze coming to rest on Mrs Hornby-Smythe, who was engaged in conversation with a group of women, who seemed to be sending surreptitious glances in her direction. Was it her imagination, or were they talking about her? She shifted uncomfortably in her seat.

Abruptly, Anne interrupted the group, bringing everyone's attention back to her, leaving Victoria no more time to wonder about Mrs Hornby-Smythe.

"Maybe you should be like Victoria, whose husband died before her child was born – she doesn't have those problems. Has to be the man and the woman in her household. Heart-breaking. How did it happen, Victoria? Was he ill for a long time? Did you know he was ill and still marry him, like in tragic romance novels?"

Victoria was livid. She'd previously answered some of these questions for her when they were in private. Admittedly, she hadn't actually been widowed, but Anne didn't know that. It was a thoughtless thing to do, using Victoria's life to get attention for herself.

Ignoring Anne's question, she brought the topic back to the poor and needy children of Faredene. Anne's lips pursed. So much for putting their differences behind them. No doubt she'd be sulking even more now, spoilt little madam!

"Perhaps, ladies, we should return to the reason for our luncheon – the destitute. While our luncheons are wonderful and raise money for them, I feel we should do more. There must be so many unfortunate widows and families who need our help. And do we really *need* to have a luncheon in order to donate money to them? Can't we give at other times, as well? Surely the money would be better spent on giving a bigger donation than filling our faces when they're lucky to get one pitiful meal a day."

"Our luncheons are a civilised way to contribute to the fund for the disadvantaged," said Mrs O'Brien, the barber's wife. "But sure, you might have a point regarding the widows – perhaps we should look into that. There again, giving families in general too much money would merely get them thinking they could have more babies. Back in Ireland, they breed like rabbits. Almost every family has ten or more they can't feed."

"I'm sure we can all understand where your sympathies lie, Mrs Kavanagh, but widows have a duty to take another husband." Mrs Hornby-Smythe looked at her pointedly.

She hadn't realised Mrs Hornby-Smythe had joined the group and tried to avoid making eye contact with her. She knew it was a dig at her remaining a widow. Before she could tell her that not all women wanted another husband, Mrs Erlington took up the mantle.

"I for one agree with you, Mrs O'Brien. They're just the same here. We give them enough already. And I don't feel we should encourage them to have more children. They simply need to learn household management. How to live within their means. If my housekeeper overspends, she has to answer to me. That's the problem with these people – they squander their money down the alehouses. It's enough that my husband gives them jobs in our mill. I really don't see why we should just give them money to waste."

Many of the underprivileged of the area worked for the woman's husband, with children labouring for twelve hours a day from the age of ten to help support her lifestyle. The hours were so long that men were employed to oversee that workers didn't fall asleep on the job and small children were expected to squeeze between the machinery to clean it. It was no wonder children often lost fingers or were crushed, even killed.

Victoria banged her teacup forcibly on the table. "I hardly think giving them food and clothing is squandering. Are you so blind you can't see what's under your noses? People live hand to mouth."

"I agree, Victoria, dear. What do you suggest?" asked Mrs Payne, whose husband owned the local brewery.

"Shoes. Shoes and food," Victoria said. "Children can't concentrate in school if they're hungry. And we're coming into winter, so they can't be expected to walk to school if they have no shoes. Surely we can donate shoes our own children have outgrown, plus set up a fund to buy food to be distributed at the school.

"By giving direct to the children, at least we'll know they've had one decent meal. That way, the money isn't frittered on non-essentials. Education is vital if their lives are to improve. We were educated – surely they deserve the same opportunity, too."

"Education is wasted on them. What do they need to learn to read for? Besides, they have limited intelligence," Mrs Hornby-Smythe said.

"Because some of them are bright, incredibly bright, and they deserve a chance in life, that's why. If you took a child from a mill family at birth, looked after it and educated it, who knows what it could achieve."

Some of women tittered. Victoria's blood was boiling – they didn't know about Sean, but it felt like they were insulting her son.

"All of my staff are paid a decent wage and provided with uniforms. If you don't care about the welfare of your own workers, at least you must recognise that if they're cold and hungry, they aren't as productive. Surely you can all see the sense in that?"

"Really, Victoria. You seem to think you are quite the champion of the lower classes. Are you sure your husband ran a drapers and not a soup kitchen?" Anne asked, giggling behind her hand.

"You make some excellent points, Victoria. I am sure the ladies on the committee could look into organising something along those lines," Mrs Payne said.

By the time Victoria had finished, despite looking disgruntled, even Mrs Erlington said she could see some logic behind the idea. Victoria strongly suspected she was afraid to go against the other ladies, who were now agreeing to her idea. Only Anne and Mrs Hornby-Smythe looked like they'd been sucking lemons.

Despite the demands of home and work, Victoria had joined the Women's Guild because she wanted to help people. At last she felt they'd be doing something really worthwhile to help the less fortunate. She didn't care who organised it as long as the children got help, but she intended to see it happen. She hadn't stuck her neck out and risked losing valuable custom for nothing.

As they were leaving, Victoria decided that now was as good a time as any to tackle Anne. Although she risked losing both her custom and that of her friends, she'd have to insist Anne respect her privacy. She may as well get everything off her chest today.

"Anne, I must insist that you do *not* raise the matter of my personal life for the entertainment of your friends."

"Oh! But I don't understand. How can you accuse me of that? I'm surprised at you, Victoria. I was simply trying to get the ladies interested in you. If they feel sorry for you, it's more likely they'll frequent your little *shop*." She scowled petulantly. "I'm offended that you'd think otherwise of me, frankly. Mind you, after your little outburst over lunch, I'm not sure why I bothered – they're hardly going to be queuing up now."

"Most of them are already clients. And I don't want my private affairs aired for all and sundry in future."

"Well, don't expect me to try to help you again. And don't think I haven't heard about your little *liaison* with James Brakenridge. You act all sweetness and light, but now I know different. I'd always suspected that you were playing fast and loose with Edward's affections. And now I have proof. Or are you going to claim Mrs Hornby-Smythe is a liar?

"I won't let you hurt Edward. He and I have been everything to each other since our parents died. I can't believe I encouraged him when you first came here. Well, that's certainly going to change. I intend to warn him about you. You are no lady!" And with that, she flounced off into her carriage.

Well, at least she wouldn't have to worry about avoiding Anne for a while. But knowing people had been talking about her was horrendous. She cringed at the thought of Edward finding out about James. But what on earth was Anne talking about – playing with Edward's feelings? She was just friends with him, that's all. He'd never even flirted with her – or she him, for that matter, that at least she was certain about. Wasn't she?

That's the second disastrous luncheon in a week,

Victoria thought. Maybe I just need to stay at home and focus on my business and family.

When Edward called later that evening, Victoria tried to explain what had happened between Anne and her but soon realised there was little she could say . . . Especially when she didn't want to mention James. Nor did she want to speak of Anne's accusation that she was playing fast and loose with his affections. And she definitely couldn't confide in him about Sean's birth.

After umming and aahing, eventually she gave up. It was obvious Anne hadn't had the same problems getting her point across when Edward said, "Anne is just a caring, sensitive young woman. She believed she was helping you and now she feels hurt. But I completely understand why you don't want to discuss your husband's passing at a ladies' luncheon. Let's just put it behind us. Anne is a dear girl. I'm sure she won't harbour any ill feeling towards you."

Victoria bit back her retort. It wasn't his fault. She couldn't blame him for thinking his sister was a caring person. She certainly didn't want to come between them. That he knew about James made her cringe – she was just glad he'd not mentioned it. But Mrs Hornby-Smythe was a vicious gossip! She'd like to stick a pin in her behind at her next fitting . . .

Victoria sat at her desk. Opening the morning's post, she stared at the small spidery writing. It was Mrs Hornby-Smythe, cancelling her appointment. So no opportunity for a pin to slip, then. She picked up the next envelope – another cancellation. Putting it to one side, she hurriedly opened the rest of her post. There was a bill from the butcher and two more cancellations. This had to be because of her private luncheon with James Brakenridge. Wonderful. Now everyone thought she was a loose woman and didn't want to do business with her. Or perhaps it had been her outburst yesterday. Or was Anne behind this? She slammed the letter opener on the desk.

Milly knocked tentatively on the door. "Mrs Brakenridge is here to see you, ma'am."

Mrs Brakenridge? That's all she needed, just when she was trying to put the encounter behind her. But why on earth would James' mother wish to see her? Perhaps she was here to yell at Victoria for leading her son on . . .

As she walked into the shop, her step slowed. She looked around in confusion. The only person she could see in the shop was an elegantly dressed young woman. Perhaps Milly meant Miss Brakenridge and she was James' sister. He'd never mentioned a sister, but then he'd never mentioned his mother, either. In fact, he'd still told her nothing about himself.

Surely he wasn't married. Someone would have told her. But then why would they? Nobody knew she'd been having luncheons with him until this week. No, it couldn't be that. But it would certainly explain the cancellations. She clasped her hands behind her back to stop them from trembling.

"Miss Brakenridge?" Victoria ventured nervously, her fingers crossed in her mind.

The woman was taller than Victoria, her tone not unfriendly.

"It's Mrs – Mrs Lydia Brakenridge. Is there somewhere we can talk privately?"

Victoria escorted her visitor through to the drawing

room. She felt a sudden chill crawl down her spine, which was nothing to do with the coldness of the room.

"I must apologise for the lack of a fire. We don't use this room during the day."

"That's quite all right. I called unannounced. I will keep my coat on."

"May I offer you some tea?" Victoria asked, her hand outstretched, indicating that the other woman take a seat.

"No, thank you. If you don't mind, I will come straight to the point."

"Please do." Victoria sat on the edge of her seat. Please, please be his sister-in-law or *any* relative, she prayed silently.

"Mrs Kavanagh, I believe my husband has been endeavouring to make you his latest . . . How shall I put it? Perhaps blunt is the best way. His mistress."

No, no, no! Please let her have misheard.

But she knew she hadn't.

"I can see you are shocked, Mrs Kavanagh."

"I am most definitely not anyone's mistress. I mean, I don't understand. You said your name was Mrs Brakenridge. I can see you're not his mother. Is James your h-husband?" she asked, suddenly feeling nauseous.

Lydia smiled slowly.

Victoria was reeling. Why was this woman smiling? At least it wasn't a sneer. She didn't even look angry, come to think of it.

"Yes, James is my husband. Lucky me. James told me about your dalliance himself."

"What? Why? What? Why would he do that?"

"I can see you are distressed. You have gone quite pale. Should I call your maid to fetch you a glass of water?"

"No, thank you. I'm fine. Or at least I think I am." The last thing she wanted was Bridie or Agnes coming into the drawing room.

"He can be very charming. You wouldn't be the first."

Victoria didn't allow her to finish. "I can assure you, I am not involved with your husband. Not like you think. You must believe me. I'm so very sorry, but we have had lunch together on occasion. However, I swear to you that I had no idea he was married. I am guilty, though. Guilty of being taken for a fool.

"I confess, I was taken in by his charms – until our last meeting, that is. And I had no idea of his intentions, you must believe me, Mrs Brakenridge. As far as I was concerned, he was just a friend who was welcoming me to the area. There has been no dalliance. Mrs Brakenridge, I'm not looking for *any* relationship. Far from it."

Victoria was mortified. She *had* liked him. Maybe she'd encouraged him. Regardless, she had no intention of becoming anyone's mistress. She realised his wife was speaking again.

"Are you sure you're all right?"

That this woman could be kind to her made her feel even worse.

"I'm fine, really. I-I just need to know you believe me."

"Why, I believe I do." She smiled wanly. "I am used to suffering the indignity of him having a mistress. Usually acquaintances of mine, indiscretions with my maids.

"I heard about your private luncheon. From him, as it happens. And later from a certain righteous lady. Gossips can be so cruel, pretending to care when truthfully, they are just malicious."

Victoria knew who she was talking about: Mrs Hornby-

Smythe. That horrible woman had wasted no time in spreading rumours. Or was it Anne? Nothing would surprise her.

"Mrs Brakenridge—"

"Lydia, please. Let's dispense with the formalities."

"Mrs Brakenridge . . . Lydia. I honestly had no idea your husband was married," she repeated. "In any case, I can assure you that I'm not involved with him. I met him accidentally on the train on my first visit to Faredene and we merely chatted. We got on and I thought we were friends. However, the last time . . ." She hesitated, embarrassed, unsure how to continue. "Well, the last time we met, quite by chance, he did make advances." She could feel her cheeks burning, her neck blotching. "But I'd already decided I wouldn't be seeing him again. I feel terrible. He made me feel I'd led him on."

A small mirthless laugh emitted from Lydia.

"Victoria . . . I hope I can call you Victoria, because we are about to discuss matters only friends should. But first, I want you to know, I put the gossips straight. I told them I knew about the luncheon, that I had been intending to join you but had been unavoidably detained as my son, Charles, was feeling unwell. I assured them that you and I are friends and that they were quite mistaken about you."

"Thank you, thank you *so* much. But why on earth would you do that?"

"Because I know you are not to blame. You are not having an affair with my husband, as Mrs Hornby-Smythe gleefully suggested, because if you were involved with him, he would not have come home following your little rendezvous and raped me."

Victoria gasped.

"I do hope I haven't shocked you too much."

Victoria shook her head, but she was stunned – so stunned, in fact, that words wouldn't form.

"While he was asserting his manhood, as he calls it, he said this time it was your fault he was forcing himself on me. That he'd wasted weeks and paid for several luncheons manipulating you. Not bumping into you at the bank for weeks was apparently his best move. He said . . . Again, pardon me for being vulgar, but he said having not seen him for so long, he thought you would be ready for it."

Victoria opened her mouth like a fish gasping for air.

"He said that he wanted you because you behaved more like a virgin than a widow – different from the usual conquests.

"I should be congratulating you. I think you're the first not to have fallen for his rather obvious charms. You have put quite a dent in his ego." Suddenly, she started to smirk, then she laughed softly.

Victoria watched, bemused, not prepared to admit she *had* been taken in by his charms.

Over the course of the next hour, Lydia confided in Victoria how unhappy her marriage was. How her husband had taken several mistresses since their marriage. She told of his violence, the drinking and the gambling.

Victoria was appalled. She couldn't help wondering if this was similar to what her own mother had gone through. Men really were pigs – except perhaps Edward and Patrick. And her son, of course – her son would be different.

She knew there was nothing unusual about men taking mistresses with their wives' blessing, but she was horrified how easily James had manipulated her. And how she'd allowed it. She was equally ashamed of her attraction towards him. She was even more thankful she didn't have anything worse to tell this woman sitting in front of her. Her stomach churned at the thought. Albeit it there *had* been something exciting about James, there was no denying it, she was embarrassed to admit now.

As she was leaving, Lydia said, "You and I must be seen together soon to quash the rumours, for both our sakes. Perhaps we could meet in the park with the boys. I always think the park is at its best in the autumn – not so crowded and full of colour."

Victoria readily agreed. Regardless of saving her reputation and limiting any damage to her business, she found she wanted to help Lydia, that she wanted to see her again.

"Mrs Hornby-Smythe is a dreadful woman. I don't know how I'll be able to face her next time she comes into Centenary Store."

"But you must, my dear. Perhaps this will help. She's a dreadful snob and the reason she insists everyone use her full name is because she was called Ethel Butts until she married. Her father was a blacksmith, not a gentleman farmer as she would have you believe. Just call her Ethel and she'll know that I've told you. That should keep her quiet for a while."

A few days later, Victoria took Sean to the park to feed the ducks and meet Lydia with her son, Charles. Charles was a replica of his father with the exception of his eyes, which were blue like Lydia's. Victoria couldn't hide her pleasure when Lydia said the same thing many others had before her – that Sean was the image of her.

Lydia had been open and honest with her, but Victoria

had no intention of sharing her own secret with this woman, especially given she lived with someone like James and he was mistreating her. He could get anything out of the woman, for all she knew. No, they would be friends, but there would have to be a limit to their relationship.

By the time they left, Sean and Charles had bonded. Victoria knew that in addition to her lucky escape from James, she and Sean had both found good friends.

Chapter 14

Despite the gas lamps, the dark winter skies cast a gloom over the workroom. Victoria, Milly and Olga had been working late every night for weeks to complete orders for gowns so that their clients could attend the numerous parties and balls being held in the run-up to Christmas. Mrs Hornby-Smythe and her friends had rebooked their appointments, claiming to have cancelled owing to other engagements. Victoria knew she had Lydia to thank for that.

When Mrs Hornby-Smythe had arrived, she'd immediately asked Victoria if there was any prospect of her getting remarried soon. Victoria felt she needed to stop this woman and her jibes, so she'd replied calmly, "No, Ethel, I have no intention of remarrying, ever. *Butt*, I am very happy as I am."

Lydia was right – her face had been a picture – so no need for the pin in the bottom!

She'd heard nothing from James, thankfully. Having changed the time and day she went to the bank, she no longer ran into him. Milly had confided in her that a friend of Anne's had mentioned the rumours during a fitting.

"I put her straight good and proper. I told her you're a respectable widow and that if you ever decided to become involved with another man, you'd have no need to go chasing married men 'cos yer beautiful and kind. Someone as attractive as you – they'd be kicking yer door down. Besides, everyone knows Mr Edward is smitten with you. Why would you need to look anywhere else?"

Victoria squirmed as she thanked Milly for her loyalty. She still felt mortified when she thought about how naïve and stupid she'd been.

She'd deliberately seen less of Edward. Thanks to her father, she'd always had strong reservations about men, and now she had even more reason to be wary of them. The last thing she wanted was for her behaviour to be misinterpreted by Edward, as well.

Victoria was feeling tired and grumpy. Christmas was just a week away and she felt like she could sleep for a week. She didn't even manage a smile for Edward as he unexpectedly walked into the workroom.

Edward took Victoria's elbow.

"Vicky, I need to speak to you, please."

He looked anxious, his breathing rapid. Victoria rose. If there was something wrong, it would be of her own making – of that she was sure. She noticed the girls watching with curiosity. Wishing to escape their stares, she followed him into the parlour.

"I'm busy, Edward. I hope this is important – I've got orders to finish."

"It's important to me, and hopefully to you, as well," he said as he guided her to sit on the sofa.

A feeling of unease bubbled inside her. Edward's hands were trembling as he sat beside her and took her hands in his.

"Vicky, I feel we have become more than friends. You know I am already very fond of Sean. I understand that recently you have been busy and we have seen little of each other. But that has simply increased my feelings towards you."

Victoria's stomach clenched.

"I have missed you, my sweet, sweet Vicky. I want to spend more time with you, not less. Vicky, my darling, you must know by now that I love you dearly. Will you do me the honour of becoming my wife?" he stuttered finally.

Victoria pulled her hands away as though she'd been burned. She stood up and moved away from him.

"Edward, I couldn't possibly get married again. It's out of the question." She hated the sound of her own voice. It was harsh and shrill.

Edward looked hurt, startled. He spoke falteringly.

"I'm sorry. Please forgive me. I do understand. Why would someone like you want to marry me, after all?" He raised his bad hand. "I don't know what came over me. And I've embarrassed you, I can see that. I'm sorry. I'll leave."

After what seemed like an eternity, he picked up his hat and stared at the floor as if unsure of his next move, a brittle silence lingering.

"Edward, I'm sorry, but you must believe me – it has nothing to do with your hand or your leg, or any part of you." She grasped his hand and held onto it, determined to make sure he didn't think this was the reason. "Don't you understand? I can't marry you *or* anyone else. Sean and my business are my life now. But I'm flattered that you asked. Really, I am . . ." She broke off, unsure what more to say, afraid to give him false hope.

"Is it because of James Brakenridge? Anne mentioned

she had heard a rumour during the autumn, but I wanted to believe it was all his fault."

"Edward, I promise you, there is no one else. I simply don't wish to remarry."

"I understand. I only regret that I embarrassed you," he responded quietly.

With that, he left, looking hurt and self-conscious – humiliated.

Victoria was devastated. Edward had become such an important part of her life. She knew that his feelings for her were genuine. He was a good, honest man. But she was confused about her feelings. Now, she'd hurt him. If only she could take the wounded look from his eyes. She cared for him. But marriage – never.

Even if she could set aside her fear of marriage, there was still her other problem. Although in recent years her body occasionally bled, she'd never betray a man by marrying him when she couldn't bear him a child. She was angry with herself, because she'd felt they were getting closer. Rather than just pretending to be too busy to see him, she felt should have made the situation clearer. But she'd enjoyed their closeness. There again, she'd enjoyed James' company, too – and look where that had got her.

There was no denying that a sense of loss gripped her. With Edward in their lives, a potential father for Sean, they could have been a real family. But she had a child and Edward didn't. And he never could have one with her, so there was no point even thinking about it. In the long run, she was being kind. Setting him free. After all, he was still young enough and he'd make a brilliant father.

She went back to the workroom. Struggling to control her voice, she spoke to the girls.

"Tidy up and go home, please."

They looked blank for a moment and then as understanding dawned, they began to cover the half-finished dresses with white cloths and sweep the remnants from the floor, avoiding her stricken gaze.

How much of her refusal had been because of her secret regarding Sean's birth? Was it more about her fear of getting too close to a man? If it came to the crunch, could she ever bear to let her defences down? She'd decided back in Liverpool that men couldn't be trusted and that she'd never marry. Had resigned herself to it, in fact. Yet, she'd made the decision without actually knowing any men. Perhaps she'd been wrong to commit to a life alone.

If only she had a friend in whom she could confide. Perhaps Lydia, she wondered. After all, Lydia had been so open with her. But no, she had to keep her secrets. Her thoughts whirled around in her brain, tormenting her. She was exhausted from overthinking, analysing everything over and over with nothing becoming any clearer.

She tiptoed into Sean's room. He was in a deep sleep and minute beads of perspiration put a sheen on his face. A riot of curly hair framed his face, large brown eyes lying behind those closed lids and long lashes of his. He looked so angelic that she knew she'd make any sacrifice to keep him and their secret safe. He began to stir, so Victoria crept out and went down to the kitchen.

Bridie, who was about to serve a light supper, looked suspiciously at Victoria's anguished face, but for once she refrained from comment. Instead, she chatted about arrangements for Christmas until a loud knocking on the door interrupted them. It was late and the two women paused for a moment before stealing into the shop, where they saw the shadowy outline of a large figure through the blind.

"Who's there? Whaddaya want?" Bridie shouted.

Victoria pulled aside the blind. Patrick, well wrapped against the weather, his arms full of parcels held in place by his chin, grinned back at them.

"Ho-ho-ho! Hello, Vicky," he bellowed. "Merry Christmas. I come bearing gifts. Aren't you going to invite me in? It's cold out here."

"I'm working on it!" Victoria replied, struggling with the lock.

Yanking the door open, she flung her arms around her cousin, almost toppling his parcels.

"Steady, Vicky."

"Patrick. Oh, Patrick. I'm so glad to see you!" she said, taking some of the parcels from him and leading him into the parlour.

"I'll fix a plate of sandwiches and leave you to chat," Bridie said.

Victoria poured them both a sherry as Patrick explained his unannounced visit. Mrs Dawson – or Cybil, as he called her – had wanted to visit her parents in Dorset, so he'd allowed her to take the whole week off.

"Cybil is a fine young woman. Good cook, too. She certainly knows how to look after a man."

Victoria could see she was a good cook, judging by the way his belly now hung over his trousers. She suspected that Mrs Dawson could twist her kindly cousin around her little finger and wondered if it was cause for concern.

They continued to chat into the early hours, Victoria asking about his latest cases, answering questions about the shop and Sean, all the time worrying if he'd be furious with her for hurting his friend.

As the conversation lulled, he finally said, "Now, old girl, tell me what's wrong. I've prattled on, giving you time to speak about it, and you've said nothing. Come on – out with it. Or do I have to drag it out of you?"

"Dear Patrick, you know me so well." Victoria blurted out about Edward's proposal. "Now I've hurt him and I don't know what to do." She watched his face for signs of anger or disappointment.

Patrick said nothing for a few moments, then patting the back of Victoria's hand, he asked kindly, "Do you love him? Would you like to be his wife?"

Victoria's breath hitched as she sighed. "I can't. I won't ever get married. He's so funny and thoughtful, but even if I didn't feel the way I do about men and marriage, it's impossible. I made my choice to live a lie and I have to stand by it."

"That's not what I asked you. Would you like to become Mrs Caldwell? Can you see yourself at his side?"

"Maybe, if I were certain I could trust him not to become like my father. But not if I have to give up Sean or get you into trouble. Besides, I can't give him a child."

"Edward would be understanding about not having children, I'm sure of it. As for trusting him, we can never fully trust anyone. We just have to trust our instincts and follow our hearts. And not all men are the same, you know – just look at me!"

Patrick went on to point out some of the difficulties that might arise if she were to confide in Edward.

"Even forgetting the complications it might cause for us, you must remember that Edward's a solicitor, too, so you'd be putting him in a difficult position, as well," he ended.

She hadn't considered that she'd implicate Edward if she told him about Sean. What the heck was she thinking! All she knew at that moment was that she wanted to apologise to him for her abrupt refusal to his proposal and to ensure that he remained her friend. It was too important to let it slide.

Chapter 15

Victoria tried to concentrate on the orders that had yet to be completed and it was the morning of Christmas Eve before the last gown was dispatched with Bert Gibbs and his cart. Bridie was busy preparing food for the next day and the smell of cinnamon, roasting goose, hams and fresh bread wafted through the house.

"I've neglected you, Patrick, I'm so sorry," Victoria said as Bridie took Sean up to bed.

"Not a bit of it. I've had plenty to keep me occupied, reading and looking around the town. Besides, you've a business to run. Now, why don't I join you at midnight Mass. You don't want to be going on your own and Bridie's told me she's staying here with the little one."

Victoria was grateful for his company as they made their way across town. Several people were lingering outside the church, chatting to friends. She spotted James speaking heatedly with Lydia. As they came close, James stopped talking abruptly and turned to her.

"Vicky, I see you are lighting up my evening with your presence again."

Having not seen him since she'd rushed from the hotel after he'd made advances, Victoria was stunned at how familiar he was behaving. The way he shortened her name, the way he spoke suggested an intimacy that didn't exist between them. Lydia visibly stiffened by his side, but the glance she gave Victoria suggested she understood.

"Patrick Davenport! What are you doing here?" James turned his attention to her cousin.

"James, I'd forgotten you lived around these parts. I see you know my cousin, Vicky."

"Yes, we know each other exceptionally well," he sneered.

His lurid expression made her want the earth to open up and swallow her. Worse was that he knew Patrick! The fact that someone from here was a little closer to her past and her secret – particularly someone as devious as him – made her stomach churn. Victoria was grateful that Bridie was at home with Sean – she didn't want her worrying.

Patrick and James continued chatting for several minutes, James leering in her direction. Victoria noticed for the first time how cold his eyes were. He really is a swine, she thought. And to think she thought he was charming.

Finally, they entered the packed church. As they made their way down the aisle, Patrick gestured to a pew with enough space for them both. She was already feeling unnerved, but as she went to take her seat and she saw Edward, her step faltered. Edward caught her arm to steady her. He smiled and whispered in her ear, his expression closed.

"Can I talk to you later?"

Barely hearing a word of the service, Victoria sent up a silent prayer.

"Dear God, thank you for all the happiness that You have given me in the last year. My friendships, my business and especially Sean, who brings joy into my life every day. Please help me to keep my secret safe. Help me to find the right words to explain to Edward without hurting him why I can't marry him."

At the end of the service, Victoria excused herself and went to light candles for all the special people in her life, making her realise that in the past year, the number of people she wanted God to protect had grown considerably. But with caring came worry, she knew that now.

By the time she'd finished, she could see Patrick and Anne waiting at the entrance. Edward was hovering about halfway down the aisle and as she approached him, he took her arm and guided her into a pew. Taking a seat next to her, he spoke quietly.

"I would like to apologise for my behaviour at our last meeting. I spoke in all sincerity, but it was an impetuous action – I see that now. Not everyone is taken with my obvious charms," he joked, forcing a smile. "Please forgive me. I hope we can remain friends."

"I'd like that a lot. Your friendship means so much to me. I feel I should explain—"

"There is no need, my dear. Please forget it happened."

Relief washed over her. She was about to speak again, when Edward said, "Come along – let's say no more about it. We'll drop you and Patrick home."

She allowed herself to be escorted to the carriage. As the others chatted about the service, Anne cast sly glances at her. They still hadn't made up since their argument and so Victoria smiled at her, in an attempt at making peace and to suggest there were no hard feelings, but Anne turned away without an answering smile. Well, if that was the way Anne wanted things, fine! Victoria decided.

When they arrived back at Centenary Lane, Patrick

invited them in for drinks, but Anne declined before Edward had the chance to respond.

"Oh, Edward, I'm sorry to be a burden, but I have a frightful headache. Would you mind awfully if we went straight home?"

Even though she didn't believe for one moment Anne had a headache, Victoria was relieved they hadn't accepted the invitation. She hoped her relationship with Edward was heading in the right direction, of course she did, but didn't relish the idea of building on those tentative foundations with Anne listening.

That night, she struggled to get to sleep, wrestling with thoughts of Edward and James. After hours of tossing and turning, she came to a conclusion. It was less than a year since she'd moved to Faredene and she'd managed to get herself confused about not just one, but two men. From now on, she'd focus on her business and her son.

As Victoria and Patrick were sitting in the drawing room after their Christmas luncheon, Victoria grinned as she watched him bouncing Sean awkwardly on his knee until Bridie took him for his afternoon nap. He didn't have Edward's natural way with children, but Victoria felt he'd grown to care for him.

"I thought you were mad to take on the child, Vicky, but I think he's a splendid little chap."

"Yes, he is. I can't imagine life without him. I'm so grateful to you for helping me. I love being a mother. I will never be able to thank you enough."

"Think nothing of it, my dear. As I said, I had my doubts. I lost sleep about it in the early days, I don't mind telling you. Even put me off my food."

Victoria stifled a giggle. She couldn't imagine anything putting Patrick off his food, but she knew he was being sincere.

"I'm sorry I caused you worry." She clutched his hand affectionately, suddenly feeling emotional.

"Come on, old girl. Don't take on. I'm trying to tell you I think it was the right decision. You were meant to be a mother."

"Oh, Patrick . . ."

She considered telling him about James' behaviour but was worried Patrick would think she'd behaved badly. Instead, she probed to find out how Patrick knew him.

"I must admit, Patrick, your acquaintance with James Brakenridge concerns me somewhat. How do you know him?"

"I have dealt with some business transactions on his behalf – ones he doesn't want handled locally. He doesn't want local people knowing all of his business. Nothing unusual in that. Although recently he asked me to deal with some unsavoury matters, but I refused point-blank. He took it well enough – no doubt found another solicitor. One who doesn't mind what sort of business he handles.

"There's no reason for him to suspect anything about your past. But if I were you, Vicky, I would steer clear of him. He's not someone you want to be involved with. I don't believe we have anything to be concerned about, but still, it might be worthwhile getting a little insurance against him, if you know what I mean, in the way of information. But you leave that to me, my dear," he ended, tapping the side of his nose with his finger.

Victoria knew Patrick well enough to know he wouldn't divulge anything more about his client, so despite how uneasy she felt, she changed the subject.

"Patrick, did you engineer the meeting with Edward at church?"

"Well, I did happen to call in at his offices. And maybe I mentioned to him that we'd be there. Of course, I had nothing to do with theirs being the only pew with space left – that must have been the work of Him upstairs," he chuckled, pointing upwards.

Smiling, Victoria told him about their conversation.

"Edward's a good man. One of the best," he said.

"Yes, he is. He doesn't appear to have let his disabilities hinder him, either, which is admirable."

"No. And quite right, too. He had a hard time of it at school – mainly down to Brakenridge and his cronies. From what I understand, James gave him the nickname Cripple Caldwell and it stuck. Used to impersonate the way he walked. Always threw the ball in his direction during sports, so he'd miss catching it. That sort of thing.

"But once he got to Oxford, he managed to put it all behind him. Apart from the wobble in his second year. By far the brightest student in our year. He could have gone much further than he has if he'd chosen to move to a city. I tried to get him to come into practice with me in Liverpool, but he was content to stay here."

Victoria wasn't surprised to hear James had behaved badly, but her admiration for Edward had increased.

"Yes, he really is quite special. What was the wobble in his second year?"

"Now, I'm not sure I should be telling you this, Vicky." Patrick remained silent for a moment. "I suppose it won't do any harm. Edward's a fine chap and I think you should know. But you must keep it to yourself."

"You can trust me, Patrick. I'm good at keeping secrets." She laughed softly.

"Well, as I understand it, he had feelings for the young girl from next door – Charlotte, I think her name was. They'd been friends all of their life and became sweethearts. Blonde, petite and effervescent was how he described her. She never made him feel inadequate, or so he said. Always stuck up for him when James and his pals gave him a hard time when they were younger.

"Anyway, at eighteen, Edward asked Charlotte to marry him once he'd finished his studies and she agreed. But when he came home the following summer, she told him she couldn't marry him. Admitted that she was carrying another man's child."

Victoria knew she was staring. Patrick paused and nodded.

"Yes, you've guessed it – James was the father. Edward insisted he still wanted to marry her. Said that he would raise the child as his own. But she refused to saddle him with a child who wasn't his – and especially not one from a man who'd bullied him through his school years.

"Edward was determined not to give up and fully intended to persuade her. But he never got the chance. Charlotte left the family home early the following morning and threw herself under a train. Her family never knew about the pregnancy and everyone assumed she had been suffering from melancholy. Edward had disliked James all of his life, but from that day, his dislike turned to hatred."

Victoria was on the edge of her seat. Poor Edward! Poor Charlotte . . . No wonder Edward had been so upset when she'd spurned him. That was twice he'd been rejected by someone he loved.

Chapter 16

In the three years since Victoria had moved to Faredene, her business had continued to flourish and the purchase of the barber's shop next door when it became vacant had allowed her to expand her little empire. By removing the changing cubicle in the draper's shop, she'd been able to increase the shelving space and could now offer a wider range of fabrics with a new service for making curtains and soft furnishings.

The dressmaking and accessories side of the business was then transferred to the new premises, where quality fittings had been used to create an elegant fitting-room with a waiting area so clients could partake of refreshments. By installing an adjoining door in the back between the two premises, she'd significantly increased the space in both the workroom and the store. Each shop retained a separate entrance and an elegant new sign above the two read "Centenary House".

Victoria was far too busy to be standing in her room reminiscing. She needed to get down to the workroom, so she secured her hair with several pins. Her hair remained as dark brown and glossy as ever, she realised as she appraised her reflection. But she'd lost a little weight and it didn't suit her. Weight fell off her easily, so she was glad Lent was almost over.

She pushed open the door to the workroom and had to strain to hear Grace Brooks above the rhythmic pattering of the new Singer sewing machines. She'd spent a considerable sum purchasing the machines, but they were paying for themselves.

Grace stopped her machine. "I said, would you like me to do the fitting that's booked in for this afternoon? I'm well ahead with me gowns and it'll mean yeh can do some paperwork or cutting."

Victoria accepted gratefully, as Grace was an excellent machinist and seamstress. She'd been eager to employ her when, new to the area, she'd called at the shop looking for work. She had excellent references and quickly became a valuable member of the team.

She was always offering to do extra work and Victoria couldn't understand why Milly didn't appear to have taken to Grace. Victoria suspected it was because Grace had chastised Kitty harshly once, Milly jumping to her defence. Kitty had always been fascinated by the gowns and the sewing machines, calling in several times a week with Teddy in tow – usually when they were hungry or wanted a piece of cake. Bridie was always happy to oblige and Sean adored them both. Teddy and he would play games, while Kitty loved drawing, mainly ladies in posh frocks, as she put it. She'd often tell Sean that one day she'd design posh frocks for ladies just like his mam did. She had a natural artistic talent, but it wasn't something she could do at home, as there was no money spare for paper for her to draw on.

Whenever freed from having to care for Teddy, Kitty would pop into the drapers or the workroom – the couture establishment was strictly off-limits. On this particular day,

Victoria and Milly were passing the workroom on the way to the office, when Kitty, who had been watching Grace sew, had reached out to touch a gown.

"Keep yer filthy hands to yourself, yeh little brat. Get back to that halfwit brother of yours," Grace shrieked.

Kitty responded immediately.

"All right, keep yer hair on. Have yeh swallowed a wasp or summat?"

At which point the other girls had laughed – even Olga, with her limited English – adding fuel to the fire. Grace had lost her head then and walloped Kitty hard across the ear, causing the slight girl to fall backwards. Victoria had been appalled. Grace had been right to stop her, but she was too severe. Under no circumstances would she allow children to be struck in her establishment. Her actions were unforgivable. She marched into the workroom to speak to her.

But Milly got there first and her tone was low, menacing, her accent more pronounced.

"If yeh ever lay yer hands on me sister again or insult me bruvver, I swear to God I'll wring yer bleedin' scrawny neck, you nasty piece of baggage. Got it?" She glared unblinking.

A hush fell over the room until Grace backtracked.

"I-I was only thinking of the gown. Of your profits – not wanting to waste fabric and time doing it over. I acted on instinct. She could have ruined an expensive gown. She shouldn't be in here," she replied nervously, appealing to Victoria.

Victoria instructed everyone to return to their work. The look on Grace's face told her there was no need for her to speak to her – it wouldn't happen again – but she made her feelings clear nonetheless.

"I appreciate your concern for the gown, Grace. But *I*

decide who comes into my shop and workroom. As for striking a child, it must *never* happen again in my premises. Do I make myself clear?"

"Ma'am."

Disgruntled, Grace put her head down to focus on her sewing, but not before catching Kitty sticking the tip of her tongue out at her as she sidled from the room. It didn't go unnoticed by Victoria, who hid a smirk.

Things were never the same between Milly and Grace after that.

Victoria returned her attention to what she was supposed to be doing and spread the green silk on the bench before cutting out the next gown. Normally, there would have been several gowns waiting to be cut. She'd made a big investment buying and refurbishing the premises and although her new venture was profitable, it had greatly depleted her bank balance. Money was tight when she'd first bought the drapers, but now she had several staff in her employ and her monthly outgoings were considerably higher.

It had taken more than a year before she'd felt confident she'd done the right thing by expanding. Of late, however, custom was declining and the takings were dropping. She wasn't sure why and was once again suffering from sleepless nights. Both Edward and Patrick had commented on the change in her demeanour, but neither of them knew about the financial side of her business, which was how she intended to keep it.

Edward continued to visit, but less frequently, his proposal of marriage never mentioned. It had been awkward at first, but gradually, a warm friendship had developed and she now felt completely at ease in his company once again, knowing their relationship would go no further. Anne, however, remained distant and cool with her. When she spoke to Edward about Anne's attitude towards her, he was dismissive as usual.

"Don't let it concern you. Anne has a good, loving heart, but she also has strong opinions on everything, even on things that are none of her business."

It was clear he wasn't going to discuss the matter further.

The little leisure time Victoria had was mainly on a Sunday, which she spent with Sean. He was now a sturdy, mischievous three-year-old, adored by everybody, but sometimes she couldn't help feeling a little jealous of his close bond with Bridie.

At these times she'd remind herself that Bridie had suffered a loss she couldn't even begin to imagine. To lose a child must be like losing a part of oneself, that longing to feel whole again. No parent should ever have to bury their child.

Despite having Agnes to help her, Bridie still insisted on doing most of the baking and jam-making. Victoria could see that caring for an energetic toddler was an exhausting task, but there was something more that she couldn't put her finger on. Bridie appeared to be getting increasingly forgetful and would blame Agnes for things. Agnes always remained quiet and accepted the rebuke, but last week, Victoria had felt the need to intervene when Bridie had snapped at Agnes in front of her. Agnes was sitting at the kitchen table with Sean, finishing her breakfast, when Bridie had marched into the room and crossed over to Agnes, apparently unaware of Victoria's presence.

"Have you moved my knitting again, girl?" Bridie's voice was unusually harsh.

"No, Bridie, I've not seen it. Have you checked in yer room? That's where it were last time." Agnes' voice was unsteady.

"Of course I've checked, yeh cheeky mare. You keep moving it. I know you do. Hiding it so I'll get meself confused."

"No, honest, Bridie, I haven't had it. I promise. I'd never do anything like that to you."

"I know what you're doing. You want me job. I've got yer measure, young lady."

Agnes looked like she'd been slapped.

"Bridie, your knitting is on top of the dresser, where you left it last night. Now, please apologise to Agnes."

Victoria's voice was firm and Bridie turned, a look of shock on her face to see her mistress there.

She mumbled, "Aye, so it is. Sorry, Agnes. P'rhaps I'll show yeh how to make some hot cross buns this afternoon, after we've done a bit of spring cleaning."

Victoria knew Bridie was trying to make amends, but she hoped this didn't signal a deterioration in Bridie's relationship with Agnes. The mood at home was generally so pleasant and she knew what it was like to live in an unhappy house as a child so had no intention of allowing Sean to grow up in an unpleasant atmosphere.

Victoria had invested a lot of time in Milly's training and she now took on responsibility for the running of the drapers. One Saturday evening, Milly was locking the shop door, when Victoria noticed her looking out of the window nervously. Suddenly, she opened the door again and seemed to be beckoning to someone.

"Ma'am, can I introduce me fella? I told you we were walking out and well, he's asked me to marry him."

Dimpling, she stepped aside to let in a sandy-haired, gawky young man with an engaging smile, who Milly introduced as Bob Kellet. "He's just finished his apprenticeship as a clockmaker and watchmaker, so his pay rise means we can afford to get married. Do yeh like me ring? Bought an' paid for, not on the tick," Milly gushed, holding out her hand to display the thin band and tiny red stone.

Victoria hugged Milly tightly and congratulated Bob, who was beaming at Milly.

"I'm gonna start saving for me bottom drawer, and Bob's putting aside for the wedding, some furniture an' a deposit on a place to rent. It's not like me dad'll be able to fork out for anything."

As she showed them out, Victoria decided that her gift to Milly would be a wedding dress. Nothing too elaborate, as Milly was too practical and would think it a waste of money. Knowing her, she'd prefer something resourceful like furniture or soft furnishings, but a wedding dress was a must.

Later that night, Victoria was making a cup of cocoa to take to bed, when she heard a tapping at the side door. It was getting late, so she approached the door with trepidation.

"Who is it?" she asked.

She heard Milly's low voice.

"It's me, ma'am. Can I come in?"

Victoria opened the door, gasping when she saw Milly. Her face was swollen, beads of perspiration mingling with the blood on her face as she spoke.

"Ma'am. I-I need yer help . . . P-please . . ."

"Dear God, Milly, what's happened to you?"

"It's me dad. He went for me 'cos I want to get married."

Victoria herded the girl inside and gradually, between tears and coughing, an account of events unfolded. Wilf, Milly's father, angry at the prospect of losing her contribution to the household coffers, had put up objections to her engagement and ordered Bob out of the house. For once, Milly had stood up to her father and a major row had ensued, after which Wilf had departed for his favourite alehouse.

After closing time, he'd staggered home in a drunken rage and dragged Milly out of the bed she shared with her sisters. He'd hauled her out into the yard, where – despite Edith's screams for him to stop – he'd lashed Milly with his belt, finally kicking her in the stomach before vomiting and passing out. Milly had managed to scramble out of the gate and had made her way to Victoria's.

Victoria helped Milly up the stairs to the spare room.

"You're staying here. Don't worry – I'll take care of everything. Get undressed. I'll be back in a few minutes," she reassured.

She returned with a bowl of warm water, a sponge and a towel. Milly was sitting on the bed, shivering in her undergarments. They were smeared in blood and stuck to her skin. Victoria began to cut them off.

"Don't cut me shift!" Milly said feebly.

"Don't worry about that. The girls can make you a new one."

Tenderly, Victoria sponged off the blood, horrified at the sight of the skin beginning to discolour. As the girl tried to sit up, she winced and held her ribs – Victoria hoped they weren't broken. Once she'd finished, she helped Milly into one of her own nightgowns and tucked her into bed. Speaking quietly, she bent over the girl, caressing her misshapen face.

"I'm going to warm some milk and give you some laudanum to help you sleep."

Popping her head in Sean's room, she was relieved to see he was fast asleep. He rarely woke at night and she had no need to worry about Bridie, as she could sleep through an explosion.

On her return to the bedroom, Victoria found Milly sobbing into the pillow. Victoria gave her the medicine and held the glass of milk to her split lip, insisting that she finish every drop. Her own anger boiled inside her. She had to remind herself that she couldn't allow her own feelings about men and her experiences as a child to come to the surface.

She spoke soothingly. "Everything is going to be all right, Milly. You rest. You're safe, I promise you."

Eventually, Milly's sobs subsided and her lids closed over tired eyes. As Victoria stroked her head, she gave in to sleep.

The following morning, Victoria opened the door to the spare room. The curtains were still drawn, but even in the half-light of the spring sunshine, Milly's face looked misshapen and discoloured. She was twitching and moaning as she slept fitfully.

Victoria closed the door quietly and went downstairs. Agnes had already arrived and was telling Bridie what had happened. Victoria informed them both that Milly was still sleeping and avoided their questions, affirming that it was Milly's business and that it mustn't be discussed with *anyone*. She then told the girls in the shop that Milly was ill and that they'd have to manage without her for a few days. The Gibbs' household was her next stop and she hoped that Wilf had already left for work.

Edith opened the door cautiously, Harry clinging to her ragged skirts. Her face had the same battered appearance as her daughter and she'd lost a clump of hair. Kitty was sitting at the table with Teddy, clutching thin slices of bread and dripping.

"Kitty, take our Harry an' Teddy upstairs and see to 'em, will yeh."

"So I'm not going to school again today, Mam?"

"No, not today."

"Aww, Mam, but I wanna go."

"Kitty, just do as yer told, please, and maybe then you can go in late."

Kitty pulled Teddy from the room, muttering, "Always the bleeding same. I never get to go to school. I'll never get a job as good as Milly and Agnes. I'm just your skivvy."

Clutching his bread, Teddy smiled at Victoria. He was nearly a man now at fourteen and she wondered what would become of him – and of Kitty, who appeared to provide most of his care.

At the sound of a door closing behind them, Edith heaved a sigh and offered Victoria a cup of tea, which she declined. Victoria spoke, choosing her words carefully.

"Edith, I don't think it's safe for Milly to come home."

Edith sat heavily on a battered chair. Her shoulders were slumped and she looked dejected.

"He don't want her to get married. Our Cora's married now and doesn't give anything to our pot. David and Sam are both at the mill full time, but they get paid pittance – it'll be years before they get a man's wage. He thinks we'll never manage without her money. An' he's right. He can't help his temper. He's a good man, really. He don't mean no harm."

Victoria was appalled. She felt angry with Edith for putting up with the situation. For not protecting her children. But then, if her own mother didn't have the strength to escape, how could Edith be expected to do so, with no money and all these children?

"Then perhaps your husband should spend less on drinking." Victoria's tone was steely.

Edith looked taken aback and no doubt nervous of upsetting the woman who employed two of her daughters and herself.

"Aye, ma'am, maybe yer right. But there's not much pleasure in life for a working man. Sixty hours a week he works – I can't begrudge him a pint or two."

Victoria wanted to rail at her. Did she think her children deserved to live like this? But she stopped herself. She knew nothing of what it was like to grow up in poverty. She also felt it was unfair to argue with this already downtrodden woman who relied on Centenary House for part of her family's income. Instead, she came straight to the point of her visit.

"I'd like Milly to stay with me until she gets married."

"Wilf don't like being crossed. He won't stand for it," Edith said, cowering, fear clear in her tone.

"Perhaps not, but please tell him that I won't hesitate to contact the police if he causes any trouble for me."

With that, Victoria returned to the shop, concerned about repercussions for Edith and the others, hoping she hadn't made things worse for them.

As she walked into the kitchen, Bridie spoke quietly.

"I've just checked on Milly. She's tuckered out – still sleeping, the poor lamb. Sure, that bugger wants stringing up for what he's done to that lass."

Agnes turned from the sink, alarm on her generally passive face.

"Don't be looking at me like that, Agnes," Bridie continued. "You know I'm right. He's a swine. Someone wants to sort him out."

Agnes turned back to the sink without retorting.

"Perhaps Agnes can see his good side, too, Bridie." Victoria amazed herself as she spoke, but Bridie was the one who'd told her that her own father had his good side, so she of all people would get that.

Nodding sagely, Bridie said, "Well, p'rhaps you've got a point an' all. But you'd better get through to the shop, lass. They'll need watching without Milly there to keep 'em in line. Agnes and I'll take care of everything here."

Chapter 17

Victoria had a busy morning ahead of her, as one of her best clients, a mother of four daughters, had ordered evening gowns both for herself and her offspring. The cutting out took a couple of hours, after which she gave the girls their instructions. With Olga's help, they drew out the elaborate designs and selected the beading for the bodices.

She turned her attention to the window display next, changing it to include lots of pinks, lilacs and blues. She wanted to encourage her clients to think of putting their umbrellas away and getting out their parasols. That finished, she summoned Olga to her office, knowing what she was about to say would meet with disapproval. She knew that Olga, with her stilted English, struggled to engage some of the more difficult customers, whereas Grace had an excellent manner.

"Olga, I'm going to put Grace in charge of all the fittings over the next few weeks and leave you to manage the workroom. I assume you're happy with that arrangement?"

"As you wish, ma'am."

Olga looked anything but happy.

"I thought you didn't like doing the fittings. Is there something wrong?"

"I feel Grace is bad woman," Olga said in clipped English.

"Why on earth would you say that, Olga? She's here first in the morning, leaves last at night. Or is that the problem? Are you jealous of her progressing?" she asked pointedly.

She didn't have time to deal with squabbles in the workroom or petty jealousies.

"I cannot explain. I mind my own business." Olga folded her arms.

"Right, well, for now she'll be doing the fittings."

The last thing she wanted was for Olga to get upset, but she'd given her the opportunity to air her concerns and she hadn't done so. Thankfully, Grace appeared happy to oblige with the new arrangement – she couldn't have managed two disgruntled employees.

"Just you leave it to me, Mrs Kavanagh. I'll take care of everything. If I need to do extra hours, that won't be a problem," Grace insisted, glancing at Olga.

Victoria couldn't figure out what the heck was wrong with Olga and Milly. She couldn't understand what they had against Grace. She couldn't be more obliging and her work was excellent.

During lunch, Sean asked if he could go through to the shop to see Milly and the girls. Victoria often took him in with her for a few minutes – her son loved the attention and Victoria didn't like to refuse him anything – but this time was different.

"Not today, young man. Sorry, but Mummy's very busy, and Milly's upstairs in bed poorly and has to rest."

"What's wrong with her?" he questioned, inquisitive as ever.

"She has a bad cold. She'll be staying here until she's better, so you can see her soon."

"But why can't I see her now? Want to see her now!" He stamped his foot.

"Because I don't want you to catch it. And that's enough of that attitude, young man."

"Why not? Will I die?" His eyes widened.

"No, of course not. I just don't want you to be poorly, as well."

"Why not?"

"Because I love you and I have enough to do without nursing you," she answered, ruffling his hair.

He was at that age where every conversation involved the word "why", trying anyone's patience, especially now she was even busier with Milly laid up. It was going to be a challenge to keep things from him as he got older but for now, she didn't want him seeing Milly in this state and was sure that Milly wouldn't want him to, either.

Bridie had prepared soup for Milly and as she wanted to check on her, Victoria decided she'd take it up herself. Milly was awake when she entered the room but just stared into the distance, seemingly oblivious to her presence. She even remained still when Victoria drew back the curtains, letting the late spring sunlight flood the room.

Milly squinted, her eyes adjusting to the light, full of pain as she spoke.

"I'm a mess. Me face is swollen an' I can feel a cut above me eye – it'll scar."

"It'll heal. The swelling will go down. You just rest."

"But I can't let my Bob see me like this. He'll want to confront me dad, but Dad'll kill him. Bob's a good man, but he's no fighter."

"I won't let anybody see you until you're back to normal, not even Bob. So don't you be worrying, now."

"But what'll you tell him?"

"Just you leave Bob to me and concentrate on getting better."

"But me mam. Dad's getting worse. He's never gone for me like that before. I don't know what to do for the best. Maybe I'll have to call off the wedding."

"You'll do no such thing."

Victoria wasn't going to let the practical, optimistic Milly she loved and knew so well ruin her chance of happiness for that drunken oaf. Tears trickled over Milly's disfigured face onto the pillow. Her father had, for the time being, broken her spirit, but Victoria was determined that she'd help her to restore it. She coaxed the girl into taking some of the soup then proceeded to bathe her face with salt water, insisting that she rest.

Bob came that evening to see Milly. Victoria could see from his face that her family had already told him what had happened.

"What's he done to her?" he asked, turning his cap in his hands.

"I expect you already know that, Bob. What's important now is what happens next. Under no circumstances must you confront Milly's father. If you do, her family will suffer the consequences and she'll never forgive you."

She didn't feel it would be appropriate to tell him Milly was scared for him. This quiet young man would have his pride.

"But I can't just let him get away with it," Bob retorted, although he looked somewhat relieved.

"He's not getting away with it. Milly will *not* be

returning home. He's already lost her wages and that will hit him harder than you ever could."

"Aye, he takes almost every penny off her. Can I see her, please, ma'am?"

"No, not just yet. She doesn't want to see anyone right now. But I'll tell her you've been round and that you're not going to do anything reckless regarding her father. That will cheer her up."

"All right, but I'll call every night after work to see how she is until she's ready to see me . . . If that's all right with you, of course, ma'am?"

"Certainly, Bob. Now, you get yourself off home and we'll see you tomorrow."

Edward also called in that evening and she told him about Milly's beating.

She was appalled when he said simply, "It's terrible, my dear, but unfortunately, it happens in many homes – and not just those of the poor."

"So, you think that makes it right, do you?" she snapped, her voice rising several octaves.

If he thought it was acceptable for a husband to hit his wife, she was glad she'd never told him about her father's treatment of her mother. Thank God she'd refused his proposal. She was so incensed that she nearly missed his reply.

"No, of course I don't think it's acceptable. How could you even think that of me? I was merely stating a fact." His voice was nearly as angry as her own.

Edward was at a loss as to how he was ever going to get close to her if she thought that about him. He'd always found her such a puzzle – a beautiful, kind puzzle.

His voice softened as he continued, "My dear, I know

you have a big heart and want to help everyone less fortunate than you. But I worry for you, because you can't save everyone."

"I'm sorry, Edward. I should have known you wouldn't approve of his actions. I overreacted. I'm just concerned about Milly, that's all. I haven't had much sleep, but you didn't deserve that. I know I can't save everyone, but Milly isn't just anyone. I care about her. I can't stand by while people I care about get hurt."

She wondered later why she didn't confide in him about her parents. But she couldn't bring herself to tell anyone. It was her private shame, because she wasn't sure which of her parents she was most angry with – her father, the aggressive tyrant, or her mother, the weak victim.

Bob was as good as his word and called at the shop every evening, even bringing Milly a small bunch of flowers on his second visit. Milly had smiled wanly through the bruises at the flowers, but Victoria knew they comforted her.

Victoria didn't know if Milly's girls were just so used to Milly telling them what to do that they'd failed to develop any ability to use their own initiative, or if they were simply taking advantage of her absence. Either way, she found herself constantly chasing between the two shops. Having told Milly that the most she was allowed to do was go to the kitchen or parlour and chat to Agnes and Bridie, she then rushed back to the drapers once again. The two shop girls looked at Victoria as though she were speaking in a foreign language as she tried for the third time to explain the system for reordering supplies, when Grace appeared in the doorway.

"Ma'am, Mrs Parker has been invited to the Continent and needs some evening gowns to take with her. She needs 'em for the fifteenth. I told her I thought we'd struggle to fit it in. Shall I give her your apologies?"

"You're right, Grace. I just don't think we can do it right now."

"Don't worry. I'll explain to her. You're busy with the girls."

Olga and the other girls were hardworking, but most had families to care for. Grace, who was a widow, was able to work late every night, often encouraging Victoria to take a break in the evenings while she carried on working. She'd even lock up before leaving. Victoria was extremely grateful to her, because despite there being more hours of daylight and the gas lamps not needing to be lit so early, there were only so many hours in the day during which they could work effectively.

Victoria knew they could have done with the income the extra work for Mrs Parker would have created, because during the last few months several regular patrons hadn't purchased their usual gowns. But she'd been so tired when she'd replied that she hadn't been thinking straight. Grace assured her the customer had said she was going to Chester anyway and would place an order there. She just hoped Mrs Parker would come back to her afterwards.

It was a few days later that Milly informed her she was coming back to work, but it was still too late to secure Mrs Parker's order.

"It's no good me lying in me pit worrying about you being run ragged, never mind fretting about me mam and the kids. Our Agnes says Dad's behaving, but I need to keep me mind occupied."

After extracting an assurance from Milly that she wouldn't do anything strenuous, Victoria was relieved when Milly returned to work, though the tangible atmosphere in the workroom caused by Victoria's promotion of Grace was still prevalent. It didn't help that she'd decided to leave Grace seeing to all the fittings as the customers liked her, but at least it meant she could spend more time with Sean. No amount of sulking and unhappy faces was going to change her mind – she needed time with her son.

Chapter 18

Victoria had just returned from attempting to corral Sean and Charles as the boys kicked through the fallen leaves. Victoria felt fit to drop – no wonder Bridie got tired chasing after him. After putting Sean down for his afternoon nap, she told Bridie she was going to her office for a few hours. Her brow creased as she pored over the order book. She'd been right and it was as she'd suspected – sales had slumped significantly, from both her couture clients and the sale of fabrics. Yet, they still appeared to be spending nearly as much on fabric and haberdashery, which didn't add up.

In an attempt to make sense of it, Victoria summoned Milly, Olga and Grace to her office and asked if they knew of any reason for the fall in orders.

Milly and Olga exchanged surreptitious glances before Grace answered hurriedly, "No, ma'am. No reason I know of."

Olga and Milly echoed her response, heads bowed, shifting uncomfortably. Then all three, remarkably unforthcoming, left her office.

A while later, Milly slipped back in, closing the door behind her.

"Begging yer permission, ma'am, but I need yer authorisation to conduct a full stock check."

"Why on earth would you want to do that?"

"I'll tell you our suspicions when it's done, 'cos that's all they are at the moment an' it wouldn't be right to say anything unless we're sure."

"Now you're just talking in riddles. I'd rather know right away what you're getting at. Is there anything you need to tell me, Milly? Is something going on I'm not aware of?" She paused a moment. "Milly?"

"Can we leave it at that for now? You trust me, don't you?"

"Of course. There's no question of my not trusting you, Milly. You must know that."

"I'd prefer to get on with it sooner rather than later, if it's all the same with you, ma'am."

"I don't get the urgency, but if you insist, perhaps the four of us could do it together one evening, while the shop is shut. If you're all willing, that is. I like you girls to keep your Sundays to yourselves. I still don't see the problem, though, and why the necessity to get it done so quickly."

"Just the three of us. Not Grace, if yeh don't mind, ma'am. And can we keep it on the quiet, like?"

Victoria couldn't understand Milly's reasons for not including Grace and she didn't like it. She didn't need it and couldn't understand why they couldn't just get along. But she trusted Milly and knew that she was as honest as they came, so she begrudgingly agreed to her request. She'd humour her for now.

The following night, they began unrolling each bolt of fabric.

"Is this really necessary, Milly?" Victoria asked, shoving a bolt of fabric back on the shelf with more force than it needed.

They had a well-established system whereby when a

bolt came in from the supplier, it was marked up to show how many yards it held. Each time a piece was sold or taken to make a gown, the amount was recorded in a book and the ticket attached to the roll was amended accordingly. Any difference should only be from a small amount given to customers as samples.

"Yes, ma'am, I believe it is. Just let's get it finished an' then I can tell you what's on me mind. It might be nowt and I wouldn't want to go causing no trouble or pointing the finger when there's no grounds."

Victoria was exasperated and irritable. She wanted to be with Sean. He loved listening to her reading to him each night. She didn't know how much he understood, but he'd lie transfixed, staring at her until his eyelids could stay open no longer. She didn't like that she'd missed tonight, especially having not seen him all day. Times like these were precious as he wouldn't stay young forever.

As the evening wore on, Milly and Olga exchanged more and more furtive glances until finally, as they finished the last bolt, Milly put down her stock book. There was no mistaking the concern on her face.

"Milly, what is it? Just tell me. You're worrying me. You look distressed. Whatever it is, I'm sure we can sort it out."

"Ma'am, I'm really sorry. Someone's been nicking fabric! Filching it from under our noses."

Olga nodded sadly.

"Stealing fabric? But who would do such a thing? I hope you're not suggesting that Grace has stolen from me. I know neither of you like her."

"That Grace, ma'am. Terrible woman," Olga answered before Milly had the chance.

"Olga, how can you say that? Grace has been marvellous and has helped me a great deal. She's always complimenting your work to me and the way you are with her upsets her. I would have said something sooner, but she asked me not to. And, Milly, I know she should never have hit Kitty, but I believe she was just concerned about the gown. She was wonderful while you were ill and asked after you every day."

Milly tutted and raised her eyes. Victoria ploughed on regardless.

"So, I'm afraid if you believe Grace is responsible, I'll need more than just accusations – I'll need proof. To be honest, I'm disappointed that you're both accusing her behind her back."

"I'd like to think that after all this time, you know us better than that, ma'am." Milly's eyes glistened.

"I'm sorry, Milly. Of course I do. I think the world of you both." She sat down on one of the chairs, suddenly weary.

Milly looked hurt and angry as she spoke again. "That's not all. We believe it's Grace who's doing the stealing, but we think she's pinchin' customers, too. I know you think she's nice but, well, no offence, ma'am, she's pulling the wool over your eyes. We had to wait until we had proof. So, if you'll just hear us out. Even if it means losing me job, I can't turn a blind eye."

Victoria's eyes were wide. Grace had been with her for over two years. Surely they were wrong. There again, this would explain the number of clients who hadn't commissioned new gowns for the summer and winter balls, or the London season.

She'd looked through the books and counted around twenty clients in total. And that was just the mothers –

most of them had daughters, as well. They'd all been thrilled with the last gowns they'd bought from her and she'd been unable to understand why they must have gone elsewhere. Considering they were regulars, it seemed odd that orders had dropped altogether, especially with the Christmas season nearly upon them.

"I am so sorry. What must you think of me . . . Of course I believe you. Let's hear it then, Milly. How did you find out?"

"Well, it was about six weeks after I came back to work after me dad battered me. I noticed the tickets on a couple of the bolts wasn't right. But with me being off, I thought maybe one of the girls had simply made a mistake. If you remember, I said I gave them a right roasting.

"Then just last week, Mrs Tate came in for some lace. You know the one – she has the three girls. Well, she asked me to tell yeh that they were all thrilled with the new gowns. Said that you providing a service where you sent Grace out to do the fittings at home for special customers was inspired."

Victoria balled her fists. How could Grace do this to her?

"But how did Grace manage to get paid for the dresses after she'd made them? Most clients pay on account."

"That's p'rhaps the worst thing. Mrs Tate said that she hoped paying cash in advance was helping you over your little financial difficulties. She thought that the extra she paid for the service was well worth not having to come in."

Victoria put her hand to her chest. She'd been struggling to build her reputation and Grace had undermined it completely.

"Milly, why the devil didn't you tell me straight away?"

Victoria shoved the stock book, sending it bumping to the floor.

Milly jumped back as it almost landed on her foot.

"I'm sorry, girls. I don't mean to take my frustrations out on you."

"I was planning on telling you, really I was, but we know your feelings when it comes to what we think of Grace. We know you think we don't like her an', well, we don't, really. But I always felt there was more to it. I wanted to get to the bottom of it before I approached yeh. I was intending on speaking to you this week, when I'd got some evidence, so you didn't think I was being a cow, ma'am.

"There was no point in telling you without proof, 'cos Grace is devious. She'd have had an excuse ready. And I need me job. If you thought I were causing trouble, you'd have given me me marching orders, and I couldn't risk that."

Victoria felt embarrassed. Milly was right – she had assumed it was simply a case of them not liking Grace.

"I see. And the stock check – that's your evidence. She's been using my fabric to make the gowns," Victoria stated flatly.

She felt hurt and let down. She was also angry with herself that Milly and Olga felt that they couldn't approach her. How could she have got everything so wrong? How could she ever have thought badly of these two?

"I've still not finished telling you everything yet, ma'am."

"Go ahead. I may as well hear the worst of it."

"Well, I got our Cora to ask around, like. You see, Cora's husband works in the bank, so they have a nice little house outside the Rows. Grace lives in the same street. She doesn't know Cora is me sister, 'cos Cora uses her married name, so I asked our Cora to go an' see what she were up to."

"See what she's up to?"

"Yes, ma'am, and what our Cora found out floored me. She has two machinists working in her front room. They're simplifying your designs for women who need to save a few bob, like."

Milly bent down and picked up a brown paper parcel she'd hidden under the counter. After unwrapping it, she brought out a brown two-piece suit. Victoria recognised the fabric immediately.

"I'm not saying Grace is getting all of her fabric from here, but there are big shortages." She gave Victoria the book. "She must have realised we'd twig summat was going on eventually, but my guess is she were planning on leaving before then. In any case, we can't prove it were her. At least not without embarrassing customers, saying they have gowns made out of stolen fabric."

Victoria felt sick. She'd been far too trusting. Milly was right – there was no way she could prove Grace was stealing her fabric without letting customers know what had happened. She couldn't exactly question them. And as for the customers, if she told them Grace had lied and what had actually occurred, she'd embarrass both them and herself. She needed to keep Grace's treachery a secret almost as much as Grace did. To know she'd employed a thief and let a criminal in their homes didn't bear thinking of. There was nothing for it – she had to dismiss Grace immediately and then begin her own at-home fitting service for a select few customers. The stolen fabric and the lost custom amounted to a considerable loss and it couldn't have come at a worse time.

The following morning, Victoria summoned Grace to her office. As soon as she walked in, Victoria noticed the arrogant look on her face. She could barely contain her anger and confronted her immediately, holding up the brown suit in one hand and the stock list in the other as evidence.

"I'm dismissing you immediately, Grace. I've treated you fairly, gave you employment when you were new to the area. I know all about the missing stock, your home visits to my clients and the machinists in your house. How could you be so traitorous?"

Victoria was dumbfounded by her response.

"Don't come the wounded, holier-than-thou nonsense with me. Yeh took me on 'cos I'm a damn good seamstress, an' you know it. Didn't even bother checking me references 'cos you needed me so badly. I'm the best you have here. *I* should have overseen the workroom, not that foreign bitch you've got in there.

"So I were a bit enterprising – so what! I've got me own business set up now and you can't prove I took any stock. As for yer customers, I made their gowns and they was happy with them."

"You made them using my designs, my fabric and my name. Get out of my sight! If I find out you've ever approached any of my customers again, I *will* go to the police, make no mistake. Whether I can prove it or not."

Victoria was seething. She knew the girls in the workroom would be able to hear her, but she didn't care.

When Grace had gone, she put her arms on the desk and lay her head on them. Grace was right – she hadn't checked her references.

Chapter 19

In the seven months since she'd dismissed Grace Brooks, Victoria had worked tirelessly to make up the losses. She'd lost confidence in her ability to choose her employees and was reluctant to replace Grace, meaning she'd been working extra hours, covering her work. She was shattered, spending less and less time with Sean. They say spring is supposed to make your soul sing, but it wasn't happening in her case.

The clients Grace had poached and been providing with her home service had all been visited to ensure they contacted Centenary House direct next time they needed a gown. She could ill afford it, but she'd bought additional fabric and taken out an advertisement in the *Faredene Gazette* with a money-off coupon, in the hope of encouraging some of the less affluent customers back.

According to Milly, Grace was still in business and doing well. As much as it irritated her, Victoria knew there was nothing she could do about it. Grace had used her and she just had to get over it. Only Kitty had come up with a plan for revenge, bringing a moment of laughter into Victoria's troubled world. Grace had been gone a few days, when Kitty had appeared at her office door.

"Come in, Kitty. What is it? I'm busy." She'd instantly

regretted her harsh tone when Kitty stood chewing her lip anxiously. "I'm sorry. Come in, dear. What do you want? Is everything all right?"

Kitty had approached her desk, twirling her long hair between her fingers, her rosebud mouth pursed. She'd surveyed Victoria as though choosing her words carefully for once.

"Well, you know how old Frosty Bloomers has left?"

"Kitty, do you mean Grace? You mustn't call people names – it's not respectful. It's either Mrs Brooks or Grace."

"Right, well, I know *Grace* has left," she grimaced. "An', well, our Milly is keeping her lips tighter than a duck's backside . . ." Kitty paused as if gauging Victoria's mood.

Victoria rolled her eyes at the use of bad language but let Kitty continue. She had work to do and chastising her wouldn't speed things up.

"An' I also know she has upset you in some way. So I wondered if you'd like me to get her back for you, 'cos I thought I could get next door's dog, Shandy, to do a giant plop on her doorstep." She demonstrated the size using her hands. "If he did it right near the door, she might come out and stand in it without noticing, like."

Victoria had had to struggle to keep her face straight. "Kitty, that's kind of you, but it really won't be necessary. Even though Grace might deserve it."

Kitty twirled her hair again, wobbling as she stood balancing with one foot stood on top of the other. "So that's not *really* a no, then?"

"Yes, Kitty, I'm afraid I can't agree to that. But thank you for the offer. Now come here." Taking a coin from the cash box, she placed it in the child's hand. "Go and get yourself, Teddy and Harry some sweets." Instinctively, she pulled her girl into her arms and kissed the top of her head. "Don't let anyone change you, Kitty."

Kitty pulled her head back, her eyes wide. "Really? 'Cos me mam says if I don't change, one day I'll end up in hot water. I told her that doesn't sound so bad, 'cos I love having a hot bath in front of the fire. It's awful when I'm nearly the last in and the water's cold and scummy."

Victoria pulled Kitty close again so the child wouldn't see her smirking. Eventually, she released Kitty from her grasp.

"Run along now – and stay out of trouble."

Kitty disappeared through the door, then she stuck her head back round.

"I'm glad you didn't *really* say no, 'cos I did it early this mornin'. Right in it she went. Nearly slipped on her bony backside. Cursing to high heaven, she was, 'cos it were a real sloppy stinker. I'd made sure of that. I'd given Shandy me cabbage from last night's dinner. Ta-ra, then, and fanks for the money."

With that, she was gone.

Victoria had managed to hold it in for a few moments then, unable to control it any longer, she'd thrown her head back and laughed until tears had rolled down her face. That girl was such a tonic and she prayed life wouldn't change her. She wondered if she should buy Shandy a big juicy bone.

Some customers never returned, but thankfully her coupons had paid off, attracting new business instead. Tiredness was taking its toll and she'd lost weight once again, dark circles almost permanently under her eyes. Both Patrick and Edward had expressed their concern, but she'd refused to slow down. Finally, Edward had lost his temper with her while they were taking tea together.

"Vicky, will you please just *stop*. You will put yourself in an early grave if you carry on. If there is anything wrong, just let me help you for a change. You can't do it all on your own and that fine lad of yours, he needs a mother."

"How dare you! You know Sean is my world. As much as I want to spend time with him, I have to make sure I hold all this together," she retorted, waving her arms to signify the stores, the house, everyone's livelihoods.

"I know. I do understand you're doing this for him, as well. But you've changed. You were really coming out of your shell and now you've closed up again, not letting anyone in. You've barely had time for anything but work. The only time I've seen you smile is when Sean is talking to you."

She knew he was right. It was only on the rare occasion she'd managed to spend time with Sean and he'd put his arms around her neck, kissed her or called her mummy that she'd felt any joy.

"I'm sorry. I know you're just being caring, but everything's fine, Edward, really. Please don't fuss. I can cope." She'd placed her teacup and saucer down on the table with a clunk, causing tea to spill.

"Why won't you let me help you? Bridie told me what Grace did. I can help, if it's money you need."

That was like a red rag to a bull. Since when had Bridie been confiding her business to Edward?

"Well, Bridie had no right to tell you, and I don't need help from you or any man."

"Vicky, why do you always have to be so damned independent? I love you unconditionally, never asking anything of you, getting nothing in return for my devotion.

In fact, you continually push me away. If you don't want my love, my concern, please just tell me and I'll leave you alone."

"Edward, I'm too tired to cope with this right now. I have to deal with my problems myself. I don't want to rely on anyone."

"Not even me?"

"Not even you. I'm sorry, but that's how it is. Why don't you just go home?"

"You know what, I might just do that. At least Anne smiles at me."

That was Sunday.

By the following Friday, Edward still hadn't called round. Victoria regretted her harsh words, but she was determined not to go running to him. But when he came round again – if he did – she'd make more of an effort.

Sean was always taken to the park on a Friday afternoon and Victoria usually took him herself if she could spare an hour, making up the time by sewing when he was in bed, otherwise Bridie would take him. It was a treat he looked forward to, but this week, there was no way she could manage it. She seemed to be failing at everything at the moment. Something would have to give.

"Bridie, I was meaning to take Sean to the park this afternoon. Would you mind taking him instead? I'd hate him to miss out. And if you happen to see Lydia, please tell her I'll try to be there next week. She knows I'm busy at the moment." She rubbed her hands across her face, attempting to wipe away the fatigue.

"Aye, lass, course I will. But you could do with a break. You look all tuckered out. Are you sure you can't go? You'll make yourself ill at this rate."

"Not you as well, Bridie. I simply don't have the time. Why can't everyone just understand what I'm going through and stop . . . stop trying to run my life. And while I'm at it, you had no right discussing my private affairs with Edward."

"I was worried about you. I just wanted to help."

"Well, it didn't. And kindly remember your position in future. Now, please just take Sean to the park and tell Lydia I'm sorry."

Tutting, Bridie wrestled her arms into the unwilling sleeves of her coat. Sean was jumping up and down excitedly, his bear, Tatty, clutched under his arm. Victoria kissed him briskly on the top of his head, guilt already assailing her as she returned to the workroom.

How could she have said that to Bridie? Even though she was still annoyed that she'd discussed what Grace had done with Edward, she knew Bridie was just worried about her – she was family. Still, this was her business, her mess to sort. Thank goodness neither Bridie nor anyone else knew how short of money she was and how the future of the business was hanging in the balance.

Bridie had taken Sean to the park on several occasions. It was some distance from the house with his little legs, but they were always back in time for Bridie to supervise Agnes preparing the evening meal before Agnes went home. However, on this occasion, Agnes was ready to leave and still they hadn't returned, so she went through to the workroom to find Victoria.

Victoria was so absorbed that she didn't look up as Agnes spoke to her.

"What is it, Agnes? I haven't time to stop."

"Ma'am, I don't wish to disturb you, but I've prepared supper for you all."

"I'll have mine after I've put Sean to bed. Has Bridie fed him?"

"Ma'am, that's what I'm trying to tell yeh. Master Sean should have had his by now, but they're still not back from the park. Do yeh want me to go and look for them?"

Victoria's feet froze on the treadle of her sewing machine, her eyes penetrating Agnes. She'd assumed they'd returned hours ago. How could she not have noticed something so important?

"I think perhaps we should both go, if you don't mind coming with me. I know you should have been off home by now. Do you think your mother can spare you a bit longer? Milly will be here if they get back while we're out."

Olga and the other girls offered to help, but Victoria said that for now, just the two of them would go. If she couldn't see them in the park, she'd come back and close the shop, then they could all look. Surely nothing could have happened to them. Unless Sean had had an accident or Bridie had taken ill . . . What if she'd let him wander off?

Her imagination began to spiral. Bridie had been upset when she left and it was Victoria's fault. She'd never before reminded Bridie that she was a servant. Shame coursed through her. She wished Edward were here – he'd know what to do. So much for not needing a man – right now, she wanted Edward by her side helping her. He'd practically begged her to let him help her and she'd spurned him. It seemed she kept messing everything up. He'd probably never come round again after the way she spoke to him.

For over an hour, Victoria and Agnes searched the

almost empty park. Victoria couldn't stem the stream of tears. She'd promised to protect her son – how could she have let him down so badly?

"Vicky. Vicky!" Edward shouted as he rushed across the green towards her, his limp pronounced.

Victoria ran to him. It was like God had answered her prayers once more.

"Oh, Edward, I still can't find them."

"Just calm down a moment, will you. What do you mean? Who are you talking about? And what do you mean, still?"

"Sean and Bridie, of course. What do you think I mean?"

"I have no idea what you're talking about."

"Well, if you didn't know, what on earth are you doing here? I thought when I heard you call that you'd come to help."

Agnes stood by Victoria's side, her head down, eyes averted, biting her nails.

"I often prefer to walk home through the park after a long day sitting in my office. I need to exercise my leg, as you know. But that's not important. Tell me what has happened."

Victoria began to gabble as she tried to explain.

"You should have sent someone to fetch me. If they were still in the park, you would have seen them by now. You head home, I'll grab my carriage and then I'll come to the shop. If they're not already home, it'll be easier to widen the search with the carriage."

"Thank you, Edward. Thank you so much." Salty tears ran onto her lips as she scuttled towards home.

Victoria and Agnes were just entering through the back gate, when Sean came running up.

"Mummy! Mummy! Where have you been?" he cried.

"I've been looking for you, young man." She looked at Agnes. "Thank you, Agnes. You get yourself off. You're late enough already. Edward will be here soon. And, Agnes, thank you."

Bridie was leaning against the gate for support, her jaw working, but she hadn't yet spoken.

"We got lost and I had to find our way home. I'm very clever – I knew the way."

"Don't talk such tripe, yeh cheeky monkey. I've no idea where he got that nonsense from. I wanted a longer walk, that's all, and he got tired. I made it into a game, so he'd walk home without whining." Bridie's voice was harsh and she scowled at Sean, as if daring him to defy her.

Victoria had never heard Bridie scold him in any way. Sean looked crestfallen. Surely Bridie wasn't taking it out on Sean because she'd snapped at her. Well, if she was, it was unacceptable. No, that wasn't it – she could see something else was wrong.

"Come on, let's go in and you can have something to eat, young man. You must be hungry." Victoria led them in.

When Edward arrived, he quickly took in Bridie's anxious face.

"I think we've all had a fright. No real harm done. Come on, Bridie, shall we have a little sherry and a natter?"

With that, he sat patiently chatting to Bridie as if nothing had happened. Victoria could see her visibly relaxing.

After tea, she put Sean to bed, read him a story and assured him he had indeed been a very clever boy. Then she spoke to Bridie, who was adamant that nothing was wrong, that they'd merely gone for a walk to tire Sean out. Victoria could see she wasn't telling the truth. She didn't want to make her feel she wasn't trusted, but she needed to get to the bottom of this – to keep them both safe, if nothing else.

Victoria's exhaustion and fear broke through her reserve later that evening as she cried on Edward's shoulder when she showed him out.

"There, there, my love. He's safe. There's nothing we can't sort together. Please don't shut me out. Why don't you speak to Agnes in the morning and see what she has to say? She spends most time with her, after all."

The following morning, Agnes asked Victoria what reason Bridie had given for being back late. Victoria explained what Bridie and Sean had both told her.

Agnes pulled out a chair for Victoria. "I thought as much. You'd best sit down, ma'am. I don't want to speak out of turn, but I can't say nowt. I think the world o' Bridie, but I think she's losing her faculties, like. The same thing happened to Nan Gibbs before she passed away. But I think she were a lot older than Bridie."

"What do you mean, losing her faculties?"

"Well, forgetting where stuff is. Who people are. She's called me Moira a few times. I don't know who Moira is and when I asked her, she got riled."

Victoria put her hand to her throat.

"You can't do anythin' about it, ma'am. It happens to older folk. You just have to watch her, that's all, 'cos one thing's for sure, she *will* get worse."

Victoria struggled to get to sleep that night. She'd been short with Bridie and just about everyone else. And now Bridie was unwell. Victoria didn't want to be like her father, taking her problems or ill temper out on those around her – she would do better. Be a better person, starting tomorrow. That wouldn't change the situation with Bridie, though.

She hadn't known any older people. She'd never met her grandparents and her own parents never reached their dotage. Did this mean Bridie was going to die, too? She didn't even know how old Bridie was. How much worse would she get? How could she broach the topic with her? She was a proud woman and would be hurt by the suggestion that she was no longer capable. The park was a short, straight walk home if she came out of the right gate. If she used the main gate, she'd have come out on Hampton Heights, which still shouldn't have been a problem. She'd have to ensure that she was always free to take Sean out herself in future.

Chapter 20

Victoria looked with relief at the remaining four gowns hanging in her office, two of which were bridal gowns – all brides appeared to want June weddings. They'd all be collected or delivered within the week, ready for the summer season's round of parties and gatherings. She'd begun encouraging her regular ladies to order their summer gowns as early as possible, claiming that her order book was already overflowing, when in reality she'd merely had one or two orders for the summer collection.

It wasn't that she'd wanted to deceive her customers – she knew they'd order dresses from her at some point – but she wanted to avoid the usual rush, to even out her workload, to avoiding turning away work if she got overwhelmed. More importantly, she needed to bolster her dwindling bank account. To her surprise, this ploy had caused some of her customers to order additional gowns, suspecting that there was to be an event they weren't yet aware of and not wanting to be unprepared.

She yawned, scrunched up her shoulders to relieve the tension and glanced at her watch. It was almost midnight. She'd been working since six. Tomorrow would be another long day. She picked up the box containing the payments she'd received from clients over the last couple of months and carried it with her. She'd deal with it first thing in the morning, starting with paying her local suppliers and taking the remainder to the bank – if there was anything left.

Placing the box on the armchair as she set the pan on the range, she made herself a mug of cocoa to help her sleep. Despite being exhausted, too many worries meant sleep didn't come easily any more. Stifling another yawn, she made her way upstairs.

Victoria turned over in her sleep. A loud clanking and a cry of alarm mingled with her unsettling dreams. Suddenly, she was awake. She sprang out of bed. Her room was the first on the landing and having opened her door, she glanced towards Sean's room at the end of the corridor. The door was closed. Whatever was going on, he was safer there for the moment.

"Milly, quickly!" she called, pushing open the door to the spare room where Milly slept.

Milly was already out of bed, rushing across the room.

"You heard it, too? What if there's someone down there, ma'am?" Milly hissed.

"I think I heard Bridie's voice."

"What's that smell, ma'am?"

Scrambling down the stairs in the dark, Milly stumbled after Victoria, almost falling into her. Spirals of smoke now wafted past them and they could clearly hear Bridie's anguished cries through the crack in the kitchen door, which was ajar.

Victoria burst into the room. Blackened loaf tins lay on the table, flames leaping from them. Bridie was waving a burning pot towel around the room. The next moment she cried out as the flames caught the sleeve of her nightgown. She threw the cloth down on the side, wailing.

Grabbing a mixing bowl from the side, Milly dashed into the scullery, filled it with water and threw it over Bridie's arm, the cloth still smouldering. Victoria pulled Agnes' apron from behind the kitchen door, soaking it thoroughly before wrapping it around Bridie's arms. Victoria could feel Bridie shaking as she began to guide her out of the room into the relative calm of the rest of the house.

"The tins. The cloth. Quickly, Milly!"

Flames from the cloth shot into the air as it reignited.

Milly looked around desperately before running back into the scullery and grabbing a bucket from under the sink. She filled it as best she could from the hand pump and doused the flames. Bridie pulled away from Victoria and started tearing round in circles, muttering, cursing, her hands clasped as she wrung them together, the sodden, blackened apron abandoned.

"It's all right, Bridie. Come now, don't upset yourself. Tell me what happened," Victoria coaxed, attempting to lead her from the room once again.

"I'm no use to you any more. I'll go. I'll go to the workhouse. I'll not risk hurting you or the lad. I could have killed you all. You don't need a useless old biddy like me under your feet."

"Bridie, you'll never go into the workhouse. I promise you. Do you hear me? Your home is here with us."

Bridie was unable to stop her gut-wrenching sobs, just managing to gasp out odd words as she told Victoria how she thought she'd overslept and needed to bake the bread. Then she'd fallen asleep in the armchair and woken when the loaves were ablaze. Now, everything was ruined and it was all her fault.

Victoria decided now was the right moment to ask Bridie about the other instances that had occurred – misplacing things, forgetting the way home . . .

"It's as though sometimes me mind isn't me own any more. Everything is confused, in a fog. I hardly know who I am. Then I'm all right again. It scares me summat rotten, lass, I tell you. I'm not the full shilling no more."

Once again, Victoria assured her that she had nothing to worry about – she'd be taken care of. She was shocked to discover that Bridie was actually seventy-two. Despite the problems with her arthritis, she looked younger and certainly did the work of a younger woman. Or at least she had until Agnes joined them.

Leaving the distraught woman for a moment, she went into the hallway. Milly was already dressed for outdoors.

"Shall I run for Doctor Farrell? It's early, but he'll come. He's not like some of them."

"She's had a narrow escape – we all have. The burns aren't bad, but I think she'll need something to help her sleep."

While Milly was gone, Victoria helped Bridie into a clean nightgown and got her into bed. Returning to the kitchen to make her a cup of sweet tea, she looked at the charred loaf tins and the cloth . . . and the remnants of something else on the side.

Dear God, no!

Removing the blackened cloth, she stared in horror at the flakes of blackened paper representing dozens of payments. She'd left it on the chair when she went to bed.

Bridie must have moved it to sit down and then thrown the burning cloth on top of it.

Victoria's eyes were stinging. No! she wouldn't cry. This was her own stupidity. She should have been banking the money each week. She should have probed more into Bridie's condition and acted sooner.

"They say you learn from your mistakes. Well, you'd better learn from yours, you silly, silly woman, because people are relying on you," she muttered aloud to herself. "What *were* you thinking?"

Doctor Farrell tended Bridie's mild injuries and gave her some laudanum to help her settle. It seemed Agnes' diagnosis that the problem was down to infirmities related to old age was correct and that there was nothing that could be done. Victoria hated to think of Bridie suffering, but the thought that Sean could be injured or killed while in the old woman's care terrified her. If she'd just spent more time with them, instead of making it all about money . . . There was more to caring for people than providing for them, that much was now clear. Money – what did that matter now? It had all gone up in flames, anyway.

Victoria hadn't bothered going back to bed, so when Agnes arrived she was sitting at the table waiting for her. Victoria asked Agnes if she felt ready to take on more responsibility and run their small household as live-in maid-cum-cook. Agnes was thrilled at the opportunity to escape from living at home and accepted immediately.

Ensuring she was up before her a few days later, Victoria took Bridie a cup of tea and sat on the edge of her bed.

"Bridie, you and Sean are my family and from now on, you'll be treated as such. You must never worry about your future. You'll remain with us until the end of your days." She kissed the old woman on the top of her head.

Bridie, her eyes glistening, grasped her hand. "Thank you, lass. You got the best bits of them both, you know. You have your da's spirit and your mam's heart."

A smaller version of the bell used on the front door of the shop was fitted to Bridie's bedroom door, so they would hear if she got up during the night. At first, Bridie had been upset at the idea, but Victoria had insisted it was necessary to ensure there was no repeat of the fire incident. She'd assured her that no one blamed her while tactfully reminding her that the fire could have been worse.

Within a week, despite her trepidation – afraid of making another mistake like Grace Brooks – Victoria had also interviewed several young women for the position of a daily housemaid, with additional responsibility for Sean's care. She'd chosen a well-spoken young Catholic woman who lived alone with her grandparents. Victoria hoped Dora Bates would fit in well with Bridie and Agnes, because something had to change.

Desperately, Victoria had pored frantically over her insurance policy, her heart rate increasing at the realisation she wasn't covered for large sums of money left on the premises overnight. She needed the money – she had suppliers' bills to pay and wages to meet.

In desperation, she'd made a visit to the bank. Mr Heath had looked down his bulbous nose at her but agreed to make her the loan.

"It was foolish of you, Mrs Kavanagh, to keep such a large sum at home. That is what banks are for. Well, it's to be expected, I suppose, when you have women going into business without the guiding hand of a strong man behind them," he'd tutted.

Victoria had had to dig her fingernails into her palms to resist the urge to shove his dip pen up his flaring nostrils. He sounded just like Mrs Hornby-Smythe. "You can't have a single woman in trade." Poppycock! Don't rise to it, she thought. Think calming thoughts. You need this money.

"That said, I find that your business is sound, albeit you appear to have had a downturn in sales and an increase in costs last year. However, you also seem to have turned it back round. Umm, I hope that wasn't just luck . . . Perhaps if you can provide a male guarantor for the loan . . ."

"Absolutely not. Although I could name at least two businessmen who would be happy to vouch for my business, I have no intention of asking them. If you're not prepared to help me when I've been banking with you since I moved to Faredene, I'm sure another bank will be happy to make the loan."

Victoria had jutted out her chin and stared unblinkingly at Mr Heath. She had no desire to tell Edward or Patrick about her situation and definitely wouldn't be asking them to vouch for her. As for another bank, even the thought of going through this process again made her cringe.

"Hmm, very well. We will provide you with a loan on this occasion. However, it must be secured against your premises, Centenary House. But I must caution you. If you default, by missing payments, you could lose both the shop and your home."

"I do understand what default means, Mr Heath, and I will *not* be late with any payments. That I can assure you."

She was extremely irritated by his condescending manner and she felt the interest rate he was charging was higher than it should have been. Granted, she'd made mistakes, but she wondered if he'd have spoken to a male customer in the same tone. However, she wasn't in a position to argue terms with him. Supercilious old boar. She just hoped it wouldn't be the undoing of her business – or affect the jobs she provided.

Victoria resolved never to put herself in this position again. She didn't need anyone's help. She would show him she was perfectly capable of being in business and that she didn't need a man if it was the last thing she did.

She'd just stopped short of telling him to keep his rotten money – that would have been cutting off her nose to spite her face. Although Victoria knew that Patrick or Edward would have loaned her the money if she'd asked, she didn't want them to know how reckless she'd been. She couldn't bear for them to look at her in the same way the bank manager did. So they were given the same story as the staff – that the fire hadn't caused any permanent damage and all was good.

Victoria was determined she would keep her business going and pay the loan off in full at the earliest opportunity, even if it meant going short herself.

Chapter 21

Milly leaned on the counter, wafting herself with the stock book.

"I love summer, but it's too blinking hot. Our David said they're sweating buckets at the mill 'cos there's not enough ventilation."

"I've got Mrs Payne in for a fitting soon. We'd best give her a glass of water. We don't want her passing out in the cubicle. But before she arrives, I wanted to ask you something," Victoria said.

"Yes, ma'am. Blimey! you look worried. Is summat wrong?"

"No. I just wondered if you and Bob had found anywhere to rent yet?"

"No chance. All we can afford is the Rows. I've told my Bob there's no way I'm starting married life there – or anywhere near me dad, for that matter. I want summat better, like our Cora's house, even if we have to wait longer. You're not kicking me outta your spare room, are yeh?"

"Far from it. It's just I think I might have the perfect solution. What about the rooms above Centenary House? They're still sitting empty and they might suit you until children come along."

Milly shrieked with joy and accepted, assuring Victoria that Bob would be delighted, too.

As Milly was under-age, she had to get parental permission to marry. Victoria had asked Edward's advice and he'd suggested that a letter be sent from his office. His view was that a legal-sounding request may be sufficient to persuade Wilf to give his consent. But according to Edith, Wilf hadn't spoken of it to anyone.

"I don't know what to tell yeh, lass. When David read it to him, he never said a word. Just grunted an' put it on the mantelpiece. At least he didn't rip it up."

But it didn't matter what anyone said – Milly believed he'd never sign it.

A few days later, Victoria had just gone through the connecting door into the drapers, when she heard a young voice screeching.

"Milly! Our Milly! Come quick. Come on, I need yeh! Now, not this time next week!"

Thinking Wilf Gibbs had attacked one of his family again, Victoria rushed into the drapers, glad that for the moment there were no customers. Kitty was talking wildly, her face distorted with anguish.

"Aww, Milly, it's them Charnock brothers. The bastards have pissed all over our Teddy!"

Victoria flinched at the use of such a word.

"Teddy! Where is he? Why was he on his own?" Questions tumbled out of Milly.

Kitty took a deep breath. "I were delivering some washing back for Mam an' she said I had to take our Teddy with me. But he walks too slow. So I left him waiting on the corner of Wescott Street while I ran on to Mason Street. Mam'll kill me. I were only gone a few minutes." She pulled at the neck of her faded dress.

"When I got back, he were covered in piss. Stinks like Dad's chamber pot, he does. They told him it were a game. I've left him near yer back gates an' he's skriking. Won't stop," she ended on a sob.

Milly moved towards the door, then she stopped, looking to Victoria for consent.

"Yes, yes, of course, go! And, Milly? Fetch him into the house through the yard. I'll unlock the gates."

Victoria instructed the stunned young shop assistant who'd been listening agog to take over in the shop and not to come through to the back hallway. Grabbing the keys, she closed the door to the shop behind her.

Her heart wrenched at the sight of the poor young lad being led in by his sisters. Tears streamed down his face as his words muffled between sobs.

"We were playin'. Teddy no like that game, Milly. They said Teddy were a cabbage an' they were watering me. Wanted to make me grow."

"I told yeh not to talk to them Charnocks, our Teddy. Why the hell didn't yeh listen to me? Now I'll get me backside kicked," Kitty said, glaring at Teddy.

"But they're me friends, Kitty," Teddy sobbed, wiping his eyes with his filthy sleeve.

"Teddy, love, they're cruel bastards. Kitty's right. You've gotta stay away from them," Milly said.

"Gotta stay away. Teddy stay away," he repeated. "But I ain't got no friends."

Victoria's eyes were stinging. People were so evil at times.

"Yes, you have, Teddy. You have Bridie, Edward, Sean and me."

"Bridie. Old Teddy. Sean."

Milly glanced at Victoria and mouthed, "Thank you, ma'am," before wiping her eyes.

"I'm wet, Milly. An' I stink! Mam'll be mad. But I didn't wet meself. I don't do that no more. Not now I'm all grown up."

"I know you didn't, love. Come on, we'll soon get you cleaned up." Milly gagged.

"Aww, our Milly, what we gonna do?" Kitty paced up and down.

Anger and disgust raged inside Victoria. She pushed open the kitchen door and barked, "Agnes, fetch some clean towels, quickly! Milly, get him stripped off here. I won't let anyone through."

Agnes ran through, touching Teddy's wet shirt and recoiling as Kitty began to retell her story with her usual theatrical flair while together they undid his shirt.

"It's all right, Teddy, we're gonna get you all sorted now. Come on, there's a big lad. Don't cry," Milly soothed as she began to peel off the boy's ragged, sodden trousers that clung to his legs.

"Mustn't cry. Mustn't cry. Won't cry."

Teddy may not be like most young men, but he deserved some privacy. Turning to go into the kitchen and inform Bridie what had happened, Victoria gestured for Kitty to follow.

"Come along, Kitty. Milly and Agnes can manage. Give Teddy some privacy."

Victoria and Bridie shared horrified looks as Kitty, walking into the kitchen, announced, "Oh, it's all right. I've seen Teddy's willy loads of times. I has to help get him ready in a morning."

"Kitty!" Victoria spoke sharply.

"Sorry, ma'am, but I have – an' me dad's, an' me other bruvvers. It's nowt to be ashamed of. They're just like a sausage."

Victoria was speechless. Her smile escaped before she could stop it.

It was Bridie who said, "That may be so, but we'll have none of that talk in this house, young lady."

"All I was sayin' is Teddy's willy isn't summat I haven't seen before."

"Kitty!" Milly shouted from the hallway. "That's enough!"

Kitty threw up her hands, exasperated. Then she tilted her head to the side, suddenly looking at Bridie.

"Bridie, is there any chance of a bit of yer fruit cake while I tell you what's happened, 'cos if I don't get summat in me stomach, I'll starve. I doubt me mam'll give me owt after this an' I'll more than likely get the back of Dad's hand."

"Aye, go on, then, but wash your hands first. I don't know what you've got on them, but you're not sitting at my table like that."

After demolishing several large pieces of cake, Kitty was sent home to tell her mother that Teddy was at the shop and would be home later.

"Rotten little swines! He's harmless. If I could get me hands on them, lass, they'd know about it." Bridie smoothed Teddy's fringe down as she spoke to Victoria.

"I know, it's dreadful. I hope Kitty hasn't got into too much trouble. I know it's hard for your mother, Agnes," Victoria said, turning to the girl, "but Kitty shouldn't have to look after Teddy all the time. She's a bright child – she should be in school. And she certainly shouldn't have knowledge of the male form."

Victoria liked Edith but felt her mothering left a lot to be desired. She knew they were poor, but she wanted to believe that in Edith's shoes, she'd have done what she could to ensure her children had the best possible future no matter what it took, just as she tried to do for Sean. As if on cue, Sean planted a jammy kiss on her cheek. There was nothing she wouldn't do to protect him.

"Begging yer pardon, ma'am, but schooling ain't gonna do much good for Kitty. She'll like as not end up in the mill or skivvying for a living. Many girls her age are already working twelve hours a day for next to nothing. If you ask me, she's been lucky. As for bodies, there ain't no space for privacy in me mam's house. I feel like a princess since I moved in here and got a room of me own."

Victoria felt put in her place. Agnes rarely spoke unless she had something important to say. This was a long speech for her. Her words had hit home. Agnes was right – most of the children in the Rows had little to look forward to in life. Despite being short of cash now she was repaying the loan, she'd still been donating money to the shoe and food fund for the poor that the Women's Guild had now set up. But in her heart she knew that wasn't enough. She'd always meant to get more involved in helping the poor of the area. She should have made more time. She looked at Sean. That may well have been his fate if she hadn't found him. She felt ashamed how easily she became absorbed in her own little world, almost oblivious to the suffering around her unless reminded.

Later that afternoon, Victoria and Agnes took Teddy home, thankful the hot weather had dried his clothes quickly. He'd cried when he'd had to leave, saying he wanted to stay with Milly, which caused Milly to break down.

"I just feel so bad sending him home. I should be taking him back meself, but I don't want to see Dad," she blubbered.

"Give over, Milly. He'll be fine when he gets home. Kitty will be there." Agnes hugged her sister.

People of all ages were sitting on their doorsteps cooling themselves in the evening breeze. Agnes opened the dilapidated front door of her parents' house without knocking. Wilf Gibbs was sitting in the battered armchair, his shirt drenched in sweat and beer stains. Bert was washing himself from a bucket of water and Victoria averted her eyes. Teddy went straight to Kitty, who hugged him and then continued to help her mother, who was preparing a meal of sorts at the table. Kitty was mashing boiled potatoes and Victoria thought her cheek had the trace of a handprint.

Edith was slicing bread. A single plate contained one small chop, two held a thin slice of bacon and the others were empty. A bowl of soggy cabbage was sitting on the table.

"Mrs Kavanagh! Please, come in. Would you like to sit down?" Edith scurried around nervously on seeing Victoria.

"I've got to get back, thank you, Edith. While I'm here, I'd appreciate a private word with your husband, though. But I can see I'm disturbing your meal."

Edith's eyes shot to Wilf, who nodded, so she ushered her family upstairs out of the way. Agnes hesitated by the stairs, unsure what to do, then followed.

"Yer all right. Come in. I've been expecting yeh. Surprised you didn't come sooner, interfering. Edith'll just have to warm it up later," he said.

Wilf, having just come home from work, didn't look how she'd imagined he would. He was sober and didn't look capable of violence. Instead, he looked tired and worn. His large nose, which many of his children had inherited, was bulbous and veined, bumpy from the drink.

"What can I do for yeh, Mrs Kavanagh?" he asked, his eyes wary. "You wouldn't be here unless yeh had summat to say. I know you influenced my Milly to stay with you. It isn't right keeping her from her family."

"Mr Gibbs, I'll get straight to the point. You're fully aware that Milly wishes to be married."

"Aye, so you're here about that, are yeh? I thought it were Teddy you'd have summat to say about."

"No, I'm not here about Teddy. I'd like for you to sign that consent form for me." Her eyes went to the letter on the mantelpiece.

"An' why would I do that?"

"Mr Gibbs, Milly has already left your house. You no longer have her wages. You've already as good as lost her."

"She's me daughter an' I've a right to decide who she marries and when."

"Mr Gibbs, you know as well as I do that Mr Kellet is a good man who loves your daughter. Why would you object?"

"I could make her come back home. She's under-age an' you know it. And there's nowt you could do to stop me."

"Now that's where you're wrong, Mr Gibbs. I'd rather dismiss Milly than allow her to bring her wages back to *this* house. And Edith and Agnes, for that matter."

"Yeh won't do that. Good workers, my kids, the lot of them. Except soft lad. Take after me the rest of them."

Victoria clamped her teeth. Now was not the time to say she hoped to God none of them were like him.

"This town is full of hardworking people, Mr Gibbs, many of whom would be pleased to be in my employ. I am *not* a woman to be tested."

Victoria could see he was struggling to control his temper. She prayed he wouldn't take his wrath out on the womenfolk again, but she had a plan and if it paid off, he'd be placated.

"I've fed and clothed her for years, getting nowt back. Now she's earning a decent whack and she wants to up an' go. Same as Agnes." He thumbed towards the ceiling. "She hardly sends anything home now she's living in. It ain't right. Ain't proper." He shifted irritably in his chair.

Victoria wanted to say that what wasn't right and proper was his drinking away of his family's income and his beating of his wife and children whenever he felt like it. But she knew that would inflame the situation.

Clenching her fists behind her skirts, she continued, "Mr Gibbs, if you sign that form now, on the day of the wedding, following the reception, I'll compensate you."

"Hmm? Is that right. 'Ow much are we talking?"

"One pound." Her stare was steady.

"I dunno. That's nowt, really. Lemme see . . . Now, ten I'd accept." The excitement grew in his eyes.

"Two pounds is my final offer. If we don't agree now, the offer is off the table."

Panic flashed in his greedy eyes. Then slowly, as if considering his options, he said, "Aye, all right, then. That'll do. You drive a hard bargain, missus." He held out a calloused hand embedded with the muck of years of hard work and attempted a toothless smile.

Victoria recoiled at the thought of touching this vile thug but shook his hand anyway, saying, "Our arrangement is to remain just between us. Is that clear?" She didn't want Milly's pride hurt any more than it already had been.

"I won't say owt to no one, yeh can rely on me."

Victoria felt sure he'd keep both the arrangement and the money to himself, no doubt drinking himself into oblivion with it. Removing a dip pen and bottle of ink from her bag, she handed it to Wilf, who penned what would suffice as his name as he marked it with a spidery X.

Back outside, the letter stored safely in her handbag, she and Agnes strode home through the streets. She was thankful for the comfort in which she lived and the safety she provided for her son. She just hoped the money she'd offered him was enough to stop Kitty and Edith from suffering that night.

Milly had been sitting with Bridie and Sean since Dora went home. Victoria assured her that Teddy and Kitty were both fine, omitting to mention the suspicions of a handprint on Kitty's face – Milly didn't need more guilt on her shoulders. She then gave Milly the signed consent for her to marry.

Milly was delighted that her father had authorised the marriage and wanted to know how Victoria had persuaded him. She told her she'd merely reasoned with him and was pleased to see more of the old Milly returning.

The one downside was when Milly said, "Maybe me dad's not so bad, after all."

It rankled Victoria to think he was getting credit for decent behaviour when it was the promise of beer money that had got through to him.

"I've got some other good news, as well. Our David

and Sam popped in while you were out. They've taught the Charnocks a lesson they won't forget in a bloody hurry."

"Tell me they haven't done anything stupid."

"Yeh don't have to worry. Them Charnocks are nowt but big louts. Just as well our David and Sam are strong. P'rhaps getting a clout from me dad so often has toughened 'em up. They've given the Charnocks a good hammering."

"Why didn't your parents speak to their parents?"

"No offence, ma'am, but yeh don't know what it's like in the Rows. You have to stand up for yourself – or have a brother or sister what can do it for yeh. If you let people push you around, life can be hell."

"But your father, he could have gone round, surely."

"That would have done no good. Their dad's built like a brick outhouse. He'd have killed me dad."

Victoria thought that might be a blessing.

Chapter 22

"Now come on, Master Sean. It's too hot to be messing about. If you want to go to the weddin', you have to put on your sailor suit," Dora cajoled.

"Not wearing it!"

"Master Sean, come on now. It's ever so nice."

"Don't want to wear no sailor suit. Want to wear a soldier suit."

"If you don't get dressed, you can't go to the wedding. Then you won't get to see Kitty and Teddy. That's a good boy."

Victoria could hear the relief in Dora's voice as he presumably did what he was told. My son certainly knows his own mind, she thought proudly.

Victoria helped Milly into the ivory lace wedding gown she'd made her as a wedding gift and secured the matching lace veil with a headdress of white roses.

"Will I do, ma'am? I never thought I'd have a wedding dress like this."

"You look beautiful, Milly. Bob's a lucky man. Nervous?" she asked.

"No, ma'am. My Bob's a good man an' I know I'll be happy with him. I'm a little jittery about tonight, though. And a bit excited," she giggled.

"Millicent Gibbs! I'm not sure that's an appropriate topic for your wedding morning." Victoria wagged her finger playfully at Milly before turning away.

"The thing I'm nervous about is letting Dad walk me down the aisle. I've only agreed for Mam's sake. 'Cos if I don't, he'll kick off. I don't want no trouble at me wedding. But after today, he's dead to me. I don't care how much Mam pleads." Milly looked sad but resigned.

Secretly, she envied Milly, who'd also lived with a violent father, yet here she was, happily going into marriage. Even if Victoria didn't have to protect her secret about Sean's birth, she'd still never feel able to trust a man fully – even Edward. She wished she had someone she could talk to about the intimate side of marriage. On occasion, she'd tried to speak to Lydia about it, but Lydia's eyes would darken at the slightest mention of the bedroom and she felt unable to press her. While Victoria felt she was right to have reservations, she also felt a sense of loss of her own chance to be a bride – the opportunity to share a life with someone who'd be there for her no matter what.

That's just nonsense! She didn't need anyone. Just Sean.

The wedding breakfast, a simple affair, was held at a small café close to the church and was restricted to thirty close family and friends. No alcohol was to be served as Milly was worried her father would get oiled. Victoria, Edward, Bridie and Sean were sitting at a table together. It took all three of them to keep Sean entertained and in his seat. A few of the guests looked nervously in their direction, no doubt intimidated by having a solicitor and business owner in their midst. No one came over to talk to them apart from Cora. Victoria was irritated to learn from her that Grace was still doing a roaring trade from her own front room, but at least she was no longer using materials stolen from Centenary House.

As Cora returned to her seat, Wilf sidled over, beads of perspiration running down his ruddy face. Trying not to breathe in the sweaty odour emanating from him, Victoria turned to face him.

"I'm not one for parties, Mrs Kavanagh, but I just wanted to see me girl married. I'm gonna get off home, but I thought I'd pay me respects to you first."

Victoria looked at him with barely concealed contempt. He had no intention of going home. Nor did he want to pay his respects to her. He simply wanted his money and then he'd be straight down the pub. Discreetly removing a small envelope from her purse, Victoria stood and held out her hand containing the envelope.

"Mr Gibbs," she nodded curtly.

Wilf shook her hand, secreting the envelope with the skill of a pickpocket. Then he touched his forelock, making a hasty retreat through the door. Milly frowned slightly as she watched her father speaking to Victoria, her smile not returning until he'd made his departure.

As Victoria took her seat again, Edward raised his eyebrows questioningly. Putting her hand on his, she smiled enigmatically and whispered, "I just made sure Milly had her big day, that's all."

Before he could question her further, Kitty approached their table with Teddy and Harry in tow. Sean immediately jumped down and clung to Kitty.

"Hiya, Tatty Head," Kitty said, rubbing his head affectionately. "I just thought I'd bring Teddy over to say hello, like, and tell yeh me big news." Her proud smile illuminated her face.

"Hello, old Teddy," Teddy grinned as Bridie pulled out a chair and indicated for him to sit beside her.

Harry, who'd always been a surly child, ran off the minute Kitty let go of his hand. Unlike Kitty and Teddy, he hadn't found a place in the hearts of Victoria or Bridie. Even Edward, who had a way with children, struggled to engage the boy. If Kitty brought him with her when she visited, it inevitably ended in tears when he stole Sean's toys or lashed out at him.

"Come on, lass. Out with it. It's too hot to be playin' games," Bridie said. "Tell us yer news."

"Wait for it . . . I'm going into service next week! Scullery maid, in a great big house up the hill. I bet that's shocked yeh." Without pausing, she added, "Faredene Hall, no less. Now what do yeh think about that? Mrs Burns, the cook, well, she were at school with me mam. She put in a good word for me. Me friends are dead jealous, 'cos they're all at the mill."

Victoria's mind was filling with questions as Edward spoke.

"Congratulations, Kitty. I hope you'll be very happy in your new job. Just you be careful, though. Make sure everyone treats you well. If not, you tell me and I'll sort them out for you," he said, smiling and making a fist with his gammy hand, but Victoria sensed the seriousness in his words.

"Ta very much, Mr Caldwell, sir. Mam says I'd better work hard an' keep me trap shut, 'cos if I get the sack, I'll get me backside tanned by me dad. But it won't come to that. I'll work hard, 'cos I'm right excited about working in a posh house."

Victoria was alarmed. Kitty, who wasn't quite eleven, was off to live in a strange house. But not any house. She felt uneasy at what might become of this child in that household. Lydia had spoken of how James took his ease with willing kitchen maids. But what if they weren't willing? Surely Kitty, a child, would be safe . . . She'd ask Lydia to look out for her. Kitty was too attractive for her own good. As for Teddy, without Kitty to care for him, how would he fare?

She was snapped from her thoughts at Kitty's next words.

"Hey, Mr Caldwell, I nearly forgot. Our Teddy's gonna work 'n' all. He'll be with Dad at the brewery – helping with the horses. He's right good with animals, our Teddy – sort of understands them, like."

Victoria couldn't believe Teddy was getting a job. He could barely care for himself.

"That's very good. Are you looking forward to it, young Teddy?" Edward asked.

"Forward to it. Yes. Horses. Teddy like horses. And dogs. I like horses, old Teddy."

"Makes no difference if he is or isn't. Me dad says now our Agnes is holding on to most of her money an' our Milly's giving nowt, me an' Teddy gotta start paying our way – he can't flamin' support us forever," she said matter-of-factly.

Kitty and Teddy took Sean off to play with some of the other children, Sean clinging to Kitty's hand. Over the years, Sean had become attached to this unusual pair. Since his first birthday party, he'd frequently asked when he could see Kitty again. He'd miss them. Victoria, however, wouldn't miss Kitty's influence on his vocabulary. Just the other day, she'd been horrified to hear him ask the startled Dora where his "bloody spinning top" was.

Glancing at Edward, she noticed he looked preoccupied. Was he worrying about Kitty, too? Or perhaps, like her, he was thinking about the opportunity she'd passed up for them to have a life as a family . . .

"You're very good with Teddy, Edward. Very good with children, in fact. Do you regret not having any?" she asked.

"I adore children. I'd be sorry if I never got the chance to have one of my own. But I haven't given up on the idea."

Although his grin was mischievous, it sent Victoria's mind into a flurry. Whether he was harbouring some hope of having a child with her, or thinking that one day he'd marry someone else, she didn't relish the idea of dealing with either scenario.

Once they were alone back at the house, Edward said what was on his mind.

"Victoria, I have something I need to say to you."

He looked so uptight, she thought for a moment he was going to propose again and she'd be faced with refusing him once more – hurting him . . . hurting herself.

"Anne thinks I am wrong to continue my relationship with you. She believes I am wasting my life on a woman who doesn't love me."

"Oh, Edward, but I do . . . Well, at least I really do care for you."

"Yes, I know – I'm just not a man you want to marry."

She was lost for words. What could she say to that? Because he was right.

"It's all right. I understand," he answered for her. "I just want you to know that I still love you. Even if you can't return my feelings, I refuse to give up my friendship with you."

"Edward, I'm so sorry. I don't ever want to come between Anne and you. But you know I will never marry again. I can only ever offer you friendship. And it's not just you – it's any man, if that's any consolation."

"I know. And don't worry about Anne. She's just concerned for me, that is all. She loves me – I suppose someone has to," he grinned. "But it's my life and I will *not* let her or anyone else tell me how to live it." He stood up. "I'll say goodnight."

He looked so dejected, Victoria thought. She got to her feet and held his hands, just stopping herself from burying her head in his shoulder and murmuring, "But I do love you, Edward. More than you'll ever know."

She pulled away as if afraid he could read her mind. To some extent, she understood Anne's feelings. She was being selfish allowing Edward to continue this half relationship with her. Perhaps she should force him to let her go – that would be the kindest thing to do in the end. But no matter how much she reasoned with herself, she knew she wasn't selfless enough to let him go entirely.

Chapter 23

Over the next month, life settled into a comfortable routine. Victoria had been able to make the loan repayments each month and was even saving a little to replenish her bank account. Sean had asked for a pony for his birthday, but thankfully the promise of a kitten had satisfied him. She'd also met Lydia in the park and expressed her concerns about Kitty being in her employ. When Lydia agreed that she was right to have reservations, she felt her stomach lurch.

"James is certainly getting worse. It's as though he has . . . I don't know how to explain it. It's like he has two personalities in one body. One moment he can be a charming gentleman, the next a monster." Lydia clutched her beaded bag, her forehead creasing as she glanced at the boys, presumably checking they weren't within earshot. "James' tastes in the bedroom are increasingly violent and extreme. He'll take advantage of this child if she comes within his notice."

"Will he even see her? I understand she's a scullery maid, so I assume there's no reason for her to leave the servants' quarters. There should be no cause for their paths to cross."

"I haven't met her. I knew the housekeeper had taken

on a new maid, but I prefer not to meet them because I know it won't be long before I hear them groaning behind my husband's bedroom door."

Victoria gave a shaky laugh.

"You think I'm a coward for putting up with it. That's why I've always shied away from more intimate discussions with you. You are such a strong, independent woman. I don't want you to think badly of me."

"No, it's not that at all, I can assure you," she protested feebly.

"Some of the maids enjoy the sense of power they mistakenly believe they have while they're in his favour. As long as they're his favourite, they flaunt their relationship in my face, ignoring my instructions. I've even had to endure him fondling a maid in front of me. I felt no pity for that one when he dismissed her once she fell pregnant. I couldn't bring myself to deny her a reference, though. She'll suffer enough for her mistake, without ending up in the workhouse."

Victoria could contain herself no longer. "So why in the blazes do you stay?"

Lydia placed her hand on Victoria's, her look almost pitying.

"Charles. My son. James would never let me take him. He told me he'd tell the courts I'm an unfit mother. He's even threatened to have me committed. If I were to take him away now, where would I go? I'd need to hide. I've been trained for nothing. Even if there was work I could do, who would employ me with a child? And don't think for one moment he wouldn't be capable of having me committed. He could even claim I'd committed adultery – and I'd have no way of proving it's a lie."

"You could stay with me if I knew he'd never find you. What about your parents? Can't they help you?"

"My parents insisted I marry James in the first place. If I left him, they'd disown me and support his claims on Charles."

"I'm so sorry. If there's anything I can do . . ."

"Charles will be a gentleman whatever happens. He's going to be at boarding school soon. James will have less opportunity to use him against me once he's gone. I must endure my marriage until Charles is old enough for us to leave."

"How does he use Charles against you?" Victoria ground her jaw, unsure if she really wanted to know.

"All kinds of ways. Threatening to hurt him . . . send him away if I step out of line. Perhaps the worst is constantly telling the boy how stupid I am, what a dreadful mother I am." Her lip quivered.

Victoria found it difficult to look her in the eye. It was the first time she'd seen Lydia's resolve breaking.

"I understand. I'm so sorry, Lydia."

"Thank you, but I don't think you can truly understand."

"I understand better than you think. I was very young when she died, but I remember my father mistreating my mother."

"Perhaps you do understand, then."

Lydia assured Victoria she'd make a point of meeting Kitty and would tell the girl she must come to her if she had any concerns. That was the best she could do. If Kitty succumbed to his charms, she would go the way of so many others until he became bored with her or she fell pregnant and was discarded.

Bile rose as Victoria walked home with Sean ambling

happily by her side, leaves crunching beneath their feet. Should she tell Milly about the possible danger Kitty was in? It was doubtful they'd bring Kitty home. Even so, how could she keep quiet about the situation? By the time they arrived home, she'd made her decision.

"Milly, I need you to sit down a moment. You haven't done anything wrong. I just feel I need to tell you something."

"Thank God for that. You had me worried then."

"Actually, it is worrying. It pains me to say that the house where Kitty's working isn't a good place for her to be. I feel she may be taken advantage of, used by men of the house." She couldn't bring herself to tell Milly it was the master of the house she was uneasy about. Taking a moment to let her words sink in, she continued, "Please don't ask questions I can't answer, but I'm troubled. I fear for your sister's safety and I couldn't live with myself if I said nothing.

"I've asked her mistress to look out for her, but please make sure you see Kitty on her days off. If she looks distressed or you see changes in her, we must do something to help her."

To her surprise, Milly answered, "I don't know anything about that house, although I've heard a few rumours. But I've already told me mam that a girl who looks like Kitty isn't safe in service. Even the ugly ones aren't always protected. But yeah, of course I'll keep me eye on her. Thank you, ma'am, I know you just want to help."

Victoria had too many things on her mind. She was glad she'd moved to Faredene. She was happy here. Delighted the Gibbs family had come into her life. But caring for people came at a cost. She couldn't protect them all. And she was confused about Edward. Patrick would visit soon, as it was almost Sean's birthday – she'd talk to him about it then.

Dora and Agnes were well equipped between them to care for Sean's basic needs while she was busy in the stores, but Victoria was glad it was time for his formal education to begin. She disliked snobbery but also admitted to herself that she wanted him to be a gentleman.

Lydia had recommended the local public school called Rockhurst Manor, an exclusive teaching establishment that catered for boys from the age of five to fifteen years. It was where Charles was to attend and they'd be in the same class. Victoria had considered enrolling Sean as a boarder like Charles but couldn't bear the thought of not seeing him every evening, so he was to attend as a day pupil. Was she being possessive? Probably. But she didn't care. He was the only child she'd have and she needed him with her.

Sean loved his tweed uniform and smart cap with its school badge. Taking to school instantly, he'd regaled her with talk of the friends he'd made as she walked him home after his first day.

"We're learning to write our names tomorrow and I already know how to write mine, so I think my teacher will be pleased with me."

Victoria was sorry she'd no longer be able to pop in the back and cuddle him, or simply look at his sweet face whenever the desire took her. But she was happy her son had a strong, independent spirit. He'd babbled happily all the way home, stopping on the doorstep, suddenly serious.

"I'm going to have to call you Mother from now on, Mummy. Mother is what big boys say."

"Oh, I see. All right, darling, that's fine," she answered.

It wasn't really, but he was growing up – she had to accept it. Was she never to be called Mummy again? Unlike most women, she didn't have a string of younger children to turn her attention to.

Patrick didn't visit during the week of Sean's birthday or send a gift. Victoria began to worry and wrote him a letter inviting him to call or requesting that he at least let her know he was fine. When he didn't reply after two weeks, Edward suggested that they take a trip to Liverpool to check on him.

Despite Milly's assurances that everything would run smoothly in her absence, Victoria was concerned. She didn't like the idea of leaving Sean, or the business, especially when she had no idea how long she would be away.

Victoria and Edward took the train on the Saturday morning and arrived in Stanley Square just before noon. The house had an air of neglect, the windows smeared and the brass door fittings tarnished. Edward rang the bell and the door was opened a crack by a woman Victoria assumed to be the housekeeper. All that was visible was part of her face, but it was clear she was young and pretty with a brazen air about her.

"Yes. Can I help yeh?"

"I'm here to see Mr Davenport. Is he home?"

"He's not taking no visitors at the moment. Youse'll have to call another time."

"I'm Mr Davenport's cousin. I've come a long way and I need to see him today."

"As I said, he's not seeing nobody." She made to close the door.

Edward stepped forwards and put his foot in the way.

"I'm Mrs Kavanagh's solicitor and I can assure you, she *is* going to see Mr Davenport today." Edward put his hand to the door and pushed it slightly.

Hitching up her breasts with indignation, the housekeeper stepped aside.

"Well, you'd better come in, then."

Victoria glanced gratefully at Edward and went inside.

"Where is he?"

Without waiting for an answer, Victoria went into the drawing room. The hearth was full of ashes from a fire long since dead and a thick film of dust covered every surface. An almost empty bottle of gin and several glasses were abandoned on the table. Victoria turned on the woman.

"Where's Mr Davenport?"

The woman's arrogant manner faltered.

"He's badly. He's been in bed for two weeks. Wouldn't let me fetch the doctor, so I've been looking after him night an' day. I'm right exhausted. Fetch me, carry me . . . A dog's treated better."

Victoria pushed past her and flew upstairs.

Patrick was lying flat on his back in a dishevelled bed. Victoria instinctively jerked her head back from the smell of the vomit-splattered sheets and blankets. He was sweating profusely. He'd lost weight and a rash was visible above the collar of his dirty nightshirt.

"Patrick. It's me, Vicky," she said softly.

There was no response, so she put her hand to his forehead. He was hot and clammy.

She went onto the landing and shouted hysterically, "Edward! It's Patrick. He's very sick. Fetch a doctor, quickly. And send the housekeeper up to me. I need a word."

By the time the housekeeper arrived, the woman had

tidied her hair and put on a clean apron, but there was no way that she could disguise her dislike of Victoria, or the smell of drink on her breath.

"Bring a bowl of warm water, soap, a cloth and a clean towel. Then fetch a clean nightshirt and fresh linen. And don't dawdle."

Victoria scowled at her. And to think Patrick thought that slovenly piece was a good woman . . . She'd deal with the housekeeper later – for now, her concern was Patrick.

By the time the doctor arrived, Patrick had been washed and was now propped up on clean pillows. As he was being examined, he opened his eyes and when he saw his cousin, his eyes glistened. Victoria took his hand.

"Vicky, you came," he said weakly between great racking coughs, leaving him breathless.

Victoria flinched – had she come too late?

"I'm sorry, Patrick – I didn't know you were ill. I'd have come sooner. Patrick . . ."

But Patrick had lapsed back into unconsciousness, his head lolling to one side.

The doctor beckoned her onto the landing a short while later, his face grave.

"When was he taken ill?"

Victoria repeated what the woman had told her and he snorted.

"She's lying. He would have called me in, without a doubt. He has typhoid. How a man of his standing and wealth has caught it, I don't know. I should have been called much sooner. He should have been in hospital.

"This is neglect, pure and simple. I'm sorry, but I'm afraid it's too late now to move him. All we can do is make him comfortable."

The lump in Victoria's throat threatened to choke her. She stared at the doctor. Words failed her.

"It's all right, my dear, I understand. Would you like me to arrange some nurses? I can have one here in no time."

Victoria nodded her consent before stumbling back into the bedroom to sit at Patrick's bedside.

Chapter 24

The nurse was a formidable-looking woman in her fifties and she had an air of efficiency. Despite the sadness that had enveloped her, Victoria smiled wanly when the nurse informed the housekeeper that the Patrick's bedroom was now her domain and she wasn't to enter the room. Patrick was clearly in the best hands. Edward asked if he could have a few moments alone to say goodbye to his friend. The nurse nodded her approval and stepped outside.

Victoria wandered around the house. Having seen the state of his bedclothes, she wasn't surprised by the rest of the house, with things strewn everywhere. Cobwebs hung precariously in the corners and dead flies littered the grimy surfaces. Finally, she went into the kitchen to tackle the housekeeper.

As she pushed open the door, the putrid stench hit her hard in the face. Heaving, she pulled her handkerchief from her pocket and held it over her mouth. The housekeeper, attempting to tackle the mountain of filthy dishes on the dresser, looked over her shoulder, momentarily embarrassed, before her arrogant demeanour rapidly returned.

"I've not had a minute to do the dishes even this last

couple of days, what with runnin' up and down the stairs to him. I'm a housekeeper, not a nurse."

Victoria's feet stuck to the floor as she marched across the room, looking around her in disgust.

"Couple of days! This place is a disgrace! Some of these pots have been here for weeks. Mould like this doesn't grow in days." She shoved a plate across the table containing the remnants of something that may at some point have been food but was now a congealed, festering mass. "And how may I ask do you intend to wash pots in this sink? Even the flies are fighting for space."

"Yeh can't come in here judging me, it ain't fair. I told yeh, I've been run ragged. Lookin' after him and makin' his meals."

"Making his meals! He's so sick he can't have eaten for days! When was the last time you cleaned this place?"

"I do a bit each day, between the fetch—"

Victoria didn't give her a chance to finish.

"Yes, I know, between the fetching and carrying. Don't make me laugh!" She picked up a plate, dropping it back on the draining board, where it smashed. "Oh, dear God! Vermin droppings! Call yourself a housekeeper . . ." She was tempted to throw her hands up and walk out, but she couldn't do that to Patrick. "You will answer to me from now on. Get this place scrubbed from top to bottom. It's disgusting. This hovel is the last place I want to stay but we have no choice, so I suggest you prepare two beds in the guest bedrooms. And I expect clean linen."

Victoria stared at the woman, daring her to refuse. If there were none clean she'd have to get them washed and out on the line. It was chilly but there was a good breeze to dry them off.

The housekeeper's reply made her blood run cold.

"Aye, I'll do it. But I'll say this an' all. I know yer turning yer nose up at me, but he didn't. No, by God he didn't. Couldn't get enough of me. Never out of me bed. Promised to marry me an' all. Practically begged me to have him," she screeched.

Edward came running through the kitchen door, his foot catching a smear of grease, his arms flailing wildly as he slid into the room.

"What the hell!" He banged into the dirty dresser. "What's all the shouting?" Quickly taking in the mess, he placed his hand on Victoria's arm, guiding her from the room. "Let's go and get dinner somewhere, so we can talk privately. We'll leave the vermin to enjoy Mrs Dawson's cooking."

The corners of Victoria's mouth lifted – she was glad he could always make her smile.

Neither of them relished the idea of staying in the house, but they both wanted to be there for Patrick. Victoria had little appetite but felt she couldn't ask Edward to dine alone when he'd made the journey to Liverpool with her.

They talked while Edward ate and Victoria toyed with her food. How come nothing puts men off their food? she wondered.

Edward explained that while Victoria had been with Patrick, a Mrs Bett Turpin had called at the house wanting to see Victoria.

"The cook from next door, I believe. Inquisitive woman." He smiled weakly. "She said she keeps an eye on things at the house, knowing Patrick's your cousin."

"I'll bet she does. I'll give her a piece of my mind if she comes round again."

"Now, now, Vicky. You've wiped the floor with one woman already today. But what she said was telling. Apparently, about four weeks ago, Mrs Dawson informed her that Patrick was very unwell and that she was fetching the doctor. From what we've learned, she did no such thing."

"I think he must have tried to send for me, as well. You heard him, didn't you? He said, 'Vicky, you came,' as though he'd sent for me. But that woman would never admit it," Victoria sniffed.

"Well, according to Mrs Turpin, in the last two days, three unsavoury types and two blousy women have been in the house – on occasion leaving with bags or sacks. It was then that she suspected something was amiss.

"She'd intended to tell her mistress of her concerns this afternoon but noticed you'd arrived. I don't know if she was actually concerned or just wanted information – she seemed very interested in you. She was even asking if your name was still Kavanagh or had you got married. I got rid of her, but I thought you should know what she said about Patrick."

Victoria paled. Her concerns about what Bett might find out were insignificant compared with Patrick's fate. His housekeeper might not have killed him, but Victoria felt the woman's neglect had contributed to his imminent death. Her sloppy ways may even have caused it. Everyone knew typhoid was spread by poor hygiene and the conditions in Patrick's kitchen were a breeding ground for disease.

"Victoria, are you all right?"

"No. I'm not. Far from it, in fact. You joked about the rats and the dirt, but it's just dawned on me. That's why

Patrick is dying. It's all her damned fault. I'm so incensed with the woman, I could cheerfully throttle her!"

Edward had never seen her so riled.

It was several minutes before she could speak again as her mind catapulted from her own guilt to thoughts of revenge.

Eventually, she said, "What were you saying?"

"I suggest we try to establish what items, if any, are missing before calling the police. As solicitors, it's common practice to advise our clients to list an inventory of valuables for insurance purposes, so I'm sure Patrick will have such a list. Whatever our findings are, this needs to be handled carefully."

"Do you think Patrick was involved with this woman, Edward? Whenever he's visited, he's always spoken highly of her."

"We all have our needs, Vicky, but from what I know of Patrick, I highly doubt it. He never struck me as the type to give in to lustful desires without thought for the consequences. Don't look so shocked. You did ask.

"Besides, I also redrafted his will for him four months ago. I feel sure if he *had* been involved with her, he would have made provision for her," he confided. "But if Patrick *has* recently become involved with this woman, we have to be careful if a scandal is to be avoided. You know Patrick's reputation meant everything to him. Sorry, means everything."

Victoria was inclined to agree with him and wondered jealously if Edward's needs were being met by some other woman, too.

The following day, while Edward was out at Patrick's offices, she kept vigil by his bedside as he deteriorated.

She bitterly regretted her decision to wait until the weekend before visiting him. Despite Edward's reassurances that it wouldn't have made a difference and that Patrick's illness wasn't her fault, the guilt weighed heavily on her. Much of the time he was unconscious, briefly stirring to vomit or cough. At others he was delirious and when he did speak, his words were unintelligible.

Edward returned from Patrick's office that afternoon with a list of Patrick's household goods that had been drawn up for insurance purposes.

"I spoke to his chief clerk. I've met him on several occasions, so he was quite candid with me about the situation. Over a month ago, Patrick sent a note to the office asking him to deal with day-to-day matters and instructing him to refer any new cases to Hawthorn & Bennetts – they're another local firm."

"Was he not concerned about Patrick? Why didn't he come and check on him?"

"Vicky, it's no good trying to look for people to blame. The clerk feels bad enough as it is. But as he explained, he was beginning to get concerned. However, Patrick is a very private man, so he felt it wasn't his place to come round to the house enquiring."

Victoria pursed her lips then sighed loudly. "I suppose you're right. It's just so frustrating."

The housekeeper had been scurrying around all day, putting the house back in some sort of order. Victoria suspected this was how she'd been initially when Patrick first employed her. How could he have misjudged her so badly? He was normally so shrewd. Victoria hated the woman and it was clear the feelings were mutual. Mrs Dawson had the gall to use every opportunity to say the house had only got in a mess while she'd been tending Patrick.

Edward spent the rest of the day meticulously checking the inventory.

"There's no doubt there are pieces missing. Small items, mainly. Easy to move. Silver candlesticks, trinket boxes, his mother's jewellery and Patrick's gold pocket watch."

"That thieving witch. I need to speak to Patrick about bringing the police in, but I'm not sure he'll even understand what I'm saying now."

"The thing is, when I was at Patrick's office, I checked no subsequent will had been made. I realise strictly speaking I shouldn't be telling you this, but you are his main beneficiary. So when he passes . . ." He held up his hand to stop her protest. "He will pass. You have to accept that. But the stolen items will belong to you. So it will be up to you what you do. But please remember, any action will bring publicity. Patrick is respected in the city, as you know."

Later that evening, Patrick passed away in his sleep. Victoria was devastated. He was her only blood relative and she loved him dearly. She felt ashamed that she knew so little of his life. He'd always visited her in Faredene after she'd moved, as she was reluctant to return to Liverpool. Had she been selfish? Probably. They'd chatted for hours whenever they saw each other, but he'd never really opened up about himself. Now, it was too late. She felt like she hadn't known him at all.

Maybe he *had* been involved with his housekeeper. But surely he'd have told her that when she'd been so open with him about her own confusion regarding her feelings for Edward. Then again, perhaps not – after all, she'd never told him about her stupidity regarding James Brakenridge.

Victoria was relieved when Patrick's clerk asked if he could have the honour of assisting with the arrangements for his funeral as his last act of service to him. She wouldn't have had any idea who to contact or where to start. The enormous number of letters of condolence and floral tributes that arrived at the house had astonished Victoria, re-emphasising how little she knew about her cousin's life.

Scores of people came to pay their respects once the coffin was brought home by the undertaker. One of them, Sergeant Gillyburn, a tall, thin man with a drooping moustache, held out his hand.

"My condolences, Mrs Kavanagh. Mr Davenport was a great man. He . . . shall we say he helped me to put away some very nasty people. If there's anything I can ever do to be of service to you, you only have to ask."

Feeling like she'd failed to take enough notice of Patrick's life when he was alive, she determined now that she wouldn't let his reputation be ruined by his dreadful housekeeper. She decided to take the sergeant up on his offer and requested that he make some discreet unofficial enquiries about the missing items.

On the day of the funeral, the housekeeper appeared in the hallway bedecked in widow's weeds with a large feathered hat and veil. Victoria was wary that the woman would say something too intimate, or hint that she'd been in a relationship with Patrick, perhaps even cause a scene. It was with reluctance and undisguised disdain that she allowed her to attend, praying she'd stay quiet.

"I expect you to behave with dignity today. If you do anything to besmirch my cousin's memory, you will be dismissed without a reference. Do I make myself clear?"

"Clear as bloody crystal. Yer not the only one who knows how to behave, yeh know."

Victoria watched the housekeeper swagger out of the front door. Reference! Hell would freeze over before the woman got one of those.

Victoria felt incredibly proud of how well respected her cousin had been. Unlike at her father's funeral, she hadn't felt like screaming at the mourners that they'd been hoodwinked. Back then, she'd wanted to shout that her father hadn't been the *salt of the earth*, or *fair but firm*. She'd wanted to yell that he'd been a lurid, violent tyrant.

Victoria turned from her thoughts to see a tall blond man approaching.

"Vicky! How lovely to see you again. I'm only sorry it has to be under such tragic circumstances. Mind you, any circumstances are more pleasurable if spent with you." He bowed slightly and winked lasciviously.

Victoria was stunned, her heart skipping a beat. She hadn't seen James Brakenridge since midnight Mass some years ago. He was ageing well, but his eyes looked cold and empty. She'd forgotten that he was a client of Patrick's.

"Thank you for coming to pay your respects," she said politely, unable to keep the edge from her voice, hating him for his treatment of Lydia, her concern for Kitty highlighted by his presence. "I trust you're well."

"All the better for seeing you, my dear."

She saw his eyes take in her bosom.

"In your mourning gown, you remind me of our first meeting on the train when you enchanted me. Perhaps I can call on you this evening."

Victoria fumed. Was he insane? How dare he flirt with her! And this Patrick's funeral, of all places.

With as much contempt and dislike as she could portray without drawing attention, she hissed, "Mr Brakenridge, I must assure you that I have *no* interest in enchanting married men or having them call on me, tonight or any other time."

His face darkened. "Don't come the innocent with me, *Mrs* Kavanagh. I've been chatting to Mrs Dawson. Quite the talkative one, is Patrick's housekeeper. Very friendly with the cook from next door. She was surprised to hear of a Mr Kavanagh. I wonder why that is. Mrs Turpin apparently told her you were barely seen outside apart from a daily walk, then not at all for weeks. And the next minute, you were caring for someone else's child. Isn't that odd?"

Victoria gasped. How much did he know?

"Does dear Edward know that you were spreading your legs for someone, maybe even Patrick? That you got yourself landed with a bastard? Who'd have thought – Sean illegitimate. And all this time you were playing the demure widow."

She was shocked and insulted but strangely relieved. He'd got the wrong story entirely. He had no idea that she couldn't have a child – why would he? If it weren't so awful, it would have been laughable – branded as having a child out of wedlock when in reality she was barren. Thank God he thought Sean was hers. Relieved, she held her head high, staring into his stony grey eyes.

"If you'll excuse me, I have guests to look after," she said with dignity, hoping he couldn't see her trembling as she walked away.

She could see Edward glowering at James. She assumed he was still bitter having suffered at the hands of James, and who could blame him.

Chapter 25

Victoria was stunned. Recent profits from her business had improved her financial situation, but she was now an extremely wealthy woman. She was touched that despite Patrick's initial misgivings, her cousin had also thought to provide for Sean's future in his will. He'd even bequeathed him the missing pocket watch.

Although far from Victoria's definition of spotless, the house was now cleaner. Earlier that morning, she'd informed the housekeeper that she'd like to speak to her in the study at eleven o'clock to discuss the contents of Patrick's will.

The woman's eyes had lit up as she'd said, "Aye, well, I'm not surprised he left me summat. I told yeh I weren't just his housekeeper. He'd be rolling in his grave if he could see how you've been with me."

Victoria didn't know if she wanted to laugh or screech at the woman. Clasping her hands together, she'd repeated, "Eleven o'clock," and left the room.

Just before eleven, Victoria sat at Patrick's desk. She braced herself as Mrs Dawson rapped impatiently on the study door.

"Come in."

Victoria fixed her mouth in a firm line. It was bad

enough trying to cope with Patrick's death and missing Sean without all this bother, but she owed it to Patrick's memory.

The door banged back as the brash woman strode into the study. Then her jaw dropped slightly and the swagger went out of her step. Edward was stood to Victoria's left and Sergeant Gillyburn to her right, the sergeant having slipped into the house at ten thirty while Mrs Dawson was still in the kitchen.

"What the hell's going on here?" She puffed out her chest, but there was a tremor in her voice.

Stealing herself for what the woman might say about Patrick, Victoria began.

"Take a seat, Mrs Dawson. I wish there was some way I could make you suffer for your hand in Patrick's death. However, I can't prove it, so I must deal with the other matter."

"You can't prove owt. So, let's hear what he's left me."

Victoria was only too pleased to wipe the self-satisfied smirk off Mrs Dawson's face with what she said next.

"There have been a number of items stolen from this house while my cousin was unwell. I believe you are responsible."

"The bleeding cheek, yeh jumped-up bloody tart, all hoity-toity wi' yer posh airs and graces. Calling me a thief! I already told yeh he were gonna marry me. The stuff were as good as mine anyway."

"Watch your language, woman. Mrs Kavanagh is a lady!" bellowed Sergeant Gillyburn.

"Lady, my backside. Ask her who gave her that bastard child of hers. Everybody round here knows why she did a bunk."

Victoria's chest tightened. Right now, she didn't give a hoot what Cybil Dawson said about her, but she could cheerfully strangle the woman for her part in Patrick's death, never mind trying to taint his reputation.

"One more word like that about Mrs Kavanagh and you'll be sued for slander." Edward glared pointedly.

Mrs Dawson folded her arms across her chest as she huffed.

"You said he'd left me summat in his will."

"Actually, what I said was that I wished to speak to you about the contents of his will. He bequeathed his gold pocket watch to my son. Earlier this morning, Sergeant Gillyburn retrieved it from the pawnbrokers on Cheapside. They advised him it had been pawned by a woman of your description claiming her brother had left it to her in his will."

"You ain't pinning owt on me. He gave it to me before you got here when he knew his time were up."

"Now you've admitted you had the watch, we can get this over quickly. I can see from Patrick's accounts that you're owed a month's wages. The items you've stolen amount to a great deal – several years' worth of salary, in fact." Victoria took a deep breath before continuing. "You will leave this house this morning with nothing but your own personal belongings. The sergeant will check your bag. If you cause problems of any nature or sully my cousin's good name in any way, the sergeant will have you arrested for theft, make no mistake."

"Come on, you." Sergeant Gillyburn took hold of the woman's arm to lead her from the room.

Snatching her arm away, she rounded on Victoria.

"Yeh stuck-up bitch. You turn up here wi' yer fancy clothes an' think you're better than me. Well yeh ain't.

Neither were that fat bastard. The randy bleeder were never outta me bed. Wanted to stick his todger in me every chance he got."

Victoria swallowed, clenching her hands as the sergeant dragged Mrs Dawson from the room, still shouting.

"What about me bleedin' reference, yeh snooty mare?"

After he'd escorted the woman from the premises, the sergeant assured Victoria that he didn't believe a word of what the woman had said and that the whole event would remain between them. Having thanked him gratefully, she slumped back in her chair, relieved she hadn't made the matter public. She was horrified to think it was she who'd suggested Patrick employ a younger housekeeper.

Patrick's business was sold to the firm Hawthorn & Bennetts, who also took on his clerks to cope with the additional workload. Victoria had agreed to parcel up any relevant case files she found in his study and send them to their offices, so she cleared away the final batch that had been stacked on his mahogany desk. Now all she had to do was empty the slim middle drawer of the desk, if she could open it.

She checked the bunch of keys she'd taken from his dresser, but none of them released the lock. Putting her hand under the desk, she felt her way along it, making her way all around the edges until she felt a small key wedged in the rear corner. Not a very original hiding place, Patrick, she thought ruefully.

The only thing in the drawer was a large buff-coloured file. The top sheet was a bill from a detective agency for investigations into the quilt Sean had been wrapped in. Another bill from the same agency suggested that it was in relation to works carried out investigating James Brakenridge.

Was this the information on James that Patrick spoke about obtaining? She rifled through the papers. There were copies of bank statements, share certificates, Land Registry documents. She didn't understand the relevance of any of them.

Then at the bottom of the pile, she came across something far more damning: newspaper clippings about police raids on Liverpool clubs being used as brothels and opium dens. There was also a photograph of Sergeant Gillyburn, constable as he was then, praising the policeman for his part in the arrests. She read through the piece. James Brakenridge had given evidence against the clubs' manager, allegedly completely unaware of how his own establishments were being used.

She continued leafing through the sheets of paper. How the dickens had Patrick managed to get hold of all this? she wondered as she came across invoices signed by James for shipments of tea and coffee. Patrick had scrawled the word "drugs" across one of them.

Finally, there was a report from the detective agency linking Brakenridge to several other establishments where drugs had been found. She wasn't sure how conclusive the evidence was, but clearly Patrick thought it was important enough to lock them away. She threw the invoice relating to the quilt on the fire, placed the remaining papers back in the file, then took the folder upstairs and placed it in the bottom of her trunk.

As Victoria stood in Patrick's hallway surrounded by her luggage and the few items she'd decided to keep, her heart was heavy. Edward would be along soon to collect her. She'd never really know if there was any substance to the woman's claims, but she refused to believe Patrick had been involved intimately with that vile woman. She would remember him as she chose.

She'd been away for five weeks and was desperate to see Sean and Bridie. On the way home, Edward told her he'd called in at Centenary House earlier and they were all looking forward to seeing her.

"Do you think my absence has had a detrimental effect on the business?"

"Vicky, any small loss of revenue will hardly be a disaster considering your new financial position. You are very wealthy. I'm glad you know I've loved you for years, or you might think I'm just after your money."

Edward had travelled to see her several times, staying at a nearby hotel. On occasion he'd seemed preoccupied. She knew he must have wondered if there was any substance to what the housekeeper and Mrs Turpin had said about Sean being the product of a liaison between Patrick and Victoria. Bett had got short shrift from Victoria when she'd called at the house under the pretence of enquiring about Bridie. She didn't care what the woman thought – her connections to Liverpool were coming to an end.

She was jolted from her reverie as they finally pulled up outside Centenary House. Milly appeared with Sean and Victoria held out her arms to him as he ran towards her. She scooped him up and kissed him.

"Mummy . . . Mother, I'm too old to be picked up. Mummy, you're squishing me," he protested as he wriggled.

"I'm so glad to be back. How are you all getting on? No problems, I take it?"

Milly stepped forwards, grinning cheekily. "You always did think you were indispensable. Why don't you at least get in out of the cold. Have something to eat before you start fretting about the business. But I'll tell yeh this much just to settle yer mind. We're gonna be run off our feet next month, 'cos the November order book's full already."

Victoria, who'd lost her appetite and a considerable amount of weight during her stay in Liverpool, felt overwhelmed at the sight of all the food. It looked like they'd been baking for a month. She played with a morsel of pork pie before abandoning it for a slice of cake.

"Come on, eat up. You're as thin as a lat, lass," Bridie said, proffering a plate of sandwiches.

The loneliness she'd felt in Liverpool had lingered on her journey home, even in Edward's company. Looking at these familiar faces, one thing was clear. She may not have any blood relatives left, but she wasn't alone. It was love that connected people, not blood.

Milly massaged her brow later as she updated Victoria about the store. As Victoria had anticipated, Milly had often had to step in to carry out fittings, as several customers had objected to being seen by Olga because of her imperfect English. People were so narrow-minded, she thought.

"Milly, you've got bags under your eyes. I'm so sorry. Has it all been too much for you?"

"Thanks, it's nice to know I'm looking good." Milly forced a smile. "No, ma'am, it's not that." She closed her eyes. "It's just my time of the month an' I thought maybe

I were pregnant. Daft, really. I've not been married long, but I thought I'd get caught straight away, like me mam. Me dad only has to look at her an' she's up the duff." She smiled weakly.

"Oh, Milly, I'm so sorry. But you're young and healthy – there's time."

Even as she said it, she wanted to bite her own tongue for uttering stupid platitudes. She understood the pain of wanting a baby as well as anyone, but she couldn't explain that to Milly.

"I know. I'm just being silly. Maybe it's because I've been fretting about our Kitty."

"Kitty? Why, what's wrong?"

"Oh, ma'am, I don't know what to do. You said to let you know if she were different. And well, she gets one half-day off a month, as you know. But when she came home last, she were really quiet, not chatting about the goings-on up at the Hall. She asked if she could come and see you. She says everything's fine, but I'm not sure she likes it where she is. Maybe she's just tired. Either that, or I'm seeing something that's not there 'cos I'm worn out meself an' it's me monthlies. I've got cramps something rotten. But I feel sure summat's wrong."

Victoria was at a loss as to what to advise. She turned over ideas of how she might contact Lydia. She felt she had more money than she needed and yet all around her people struggled with problems that money alone wouldn't solve. It was apparent she wouldn't have time to mourn for Patrick any longer – people here needed her.

Milly and Agnes expressed concern about Bridie, who had suddenly decided she was going out one day. She'd insisted on going to the grocers around the corner to get sugar and treacle to make a fruit cake for Victoria's homecoming party and had returned with only a quarter of tea. Other than getting a nursemaid or companion for Bridie, Victoria couldn't think what to do. She didn't want her kept prisoner, but she couldn't allow her to go out alone, that much was clear.

"Bridie, I'm going to get someone else in to help with Sean. Take the burden off you."

"He's at school all day. We don't need anyone else. I'm not as daft as you think I am, lass. I know what Milly and Agnes are sayin'. That I can't take care of meself any more. It's one thing that I can no longer pull me weight, but I'm not having you forking out good brass for someone to babysit me, lass. I'd top meself like yer mother did before I'd let that happen."

Victoria was reeling. Bridie hadn't realised what she'd said. Had her mother really been so unhappy that she'd killed herself? Leaving her without a mother . . . How could she do that? Victoria had always assumed she'd fallen down the stairs while running away from her father. Or worse, that he'd pushed her. But it now transpired her mother had *chosen* to leave her.

Victoria's face was ashen. She went to her room, the strain of Patrick's death and now the revelation about her mother overwhelming her. Sitting on the edge of her bed, she felt crushed by the weight of it all. Grabbing her pillow, she pressed it tight against her face, almost stopping her breath as she sobbed unremittingly.

She missed supper later that evening, claiming she had a headache, leaving Bridie and Agnes with the impression she was still grieving for Patrick. In reality, she was now also grieving for a mother who'd abandoned her.

Chapter 26

The following morning, Victoria's head was pounding. It was a few moments before the reality of what she'd learned yesterday hit her. Her mother had killed herself.

She still expected to feel angry with her, but all she felt was overwhelming pity. Her mother had loved her, she knew that. She must have been desperately unhappy, devoid of hope, to take her own life. But to leave her at the hands of her father? She'd have to find a way to forgive her for that, but it would take time.

Refusing breakfast, she took a slice of toast to her office. Trying to take her mind off her worries, she ploughed through the backlog of paperwork on her desk relating to suppliers' bills that had been paid, customers' accounts for finished gowns and a mound of till receipts. As much as she trusted Milly, she still felt the need to check everything had been done correctly.

Mid-afternoon, Milly tapped on the door and opened it a crack before sliding inside and closing it behind her.

"You've done really well, Milly. Business has been good and everything seems to be in order."

That was an understatement. She hadn't found one error.

"That's good." Milly seemed unusually disinterested.

"Ma'am, Mrs Brakenridge is here and she'd like to see you. She's got our Kitty with her."

Her breath tickled Victoria's ear as she whispered the last part.

"Show her in quickly, Milly."

Milly did as she was told then stood by Victoria's side – she clearly intended to be there should her sister be accused of doing something wrong so she could defend her. Kitty squirmed at Lydia's side, balancing on one foot as she generally did when nervous.

"If I may speak to you alone, Victoria. This is a personal matter," Lydia said.

Despite her practised poise, Victoria could see her agitation.

"I'm Kitty's sister. If it concerns her, I should be here." Milly's eyes rested on Lydia, daring her to accuse Kitty of some misdemeanour.

"I understand, dear. But Kitty has done nothing wrong and is quite unharmed. Perhaps you could take her with you for a moment," she suggested softly.

Milly hesitated.

"Please, Milly—" Victoria was unable to finish as Kitty interrupted.

"I ain't done owt, honest, Milly. He tried to grab me, but I scratched his ugly mug for him. Can't keep his hands to himself. But the randy git wasn't getting in me bloomers," Kitty said indignantly.

"Milly, please take Kitty to the kitchen. You can see she is unharmed and I just need a minute with Mrs Brakenridge." Victoria nodded towards the door.

"Fine. If I must. Come on, Kitty. Let's go and get you a drink, love." Milly's face made clear she was going under sufferance.

When they were alone, Lydia took a seat.

"It wasn't actually James who accosted her. It was the second footman. I've dismissed him. James is furious that I've done so without consulting him first. It's not my place, apparently, even if I am supposed to be mistress of the house.

"He made a point of asking the butler to bring Kitty to see him. I saw the look in his eyes. He said he didn't blame the footman, but it was *his* place to service his staff." She gave a sharp intake of breath. "He'll be furious with me when I get back, but I gave you my word I'd look out for her.

"The only way to keep her safe was to bring her here myself and get her out of harm's way. Don't worry, the footman didn't actually touch her as such. She may be small, but she marked his face. She's quite the tigress," she laughed gently.

"What will James do to you?"

"Whatever he intended to do to Kitty – and more, no doubt." Lydia was candid, her jaw tight.

This long-suffering woman before her was stoic if nothing else.

"Lydia, I've inherited some money. I'd be happy to help you get away."

"Thank you, my dear, but the time isn't right. One day I will get away and I'll take my son with me. That will be my revenge."

By the time Lydia had left, Victoria had worked out what to do with Kitty. She could solve two problems in one. She was sure Bridie wouldn't object to a little help from Kitty if it was handled in the right way. She summoned Milly and Kitty to see her.

"Kitty, I believe I've found the very solution for you. If Milly agrees, you may work here and learn to be a machinist, employed part-time as an apprentice seamstress. Olga oversees the workroom and you must do as she says, as you'll be answerable to her. No giving her cheek, or pretending to have an Austrian accent, as you have done in the past." Victoria raised her hand to stop Kitty from interrupting. "I've seen you. No point denying it.

"In addition to your duties in the workroom, I'd like you to be Bridie's companion if she wishes to go out during the day. Or if the weather is bad, you can sit and chat with her in the afternoons."

It was the first time she'd ever seen Kitty speechless, until Milly shoved her shoulder.

"Well, what do you say?"

"Ta very much, Mrs Kavanagh. I'll learn to sew real good. An' I'll take proper care of Bridie, don't you worry. I'm used to looking after our Teddy, an' he forgets stuff all the time an' all. Well, you know what I mean."

Milly shoved her again.

"What? I ain't done owt!"

Victoria stifled a smile. She did have some concern about the girl's tendency to speak before she thought about the language she used, especially as she'd be around Sean. But she was young and Victoria hoped she might have learned to curb her tongue at least a little after her short time at Faredene Hall.

A few weeks later, Victoria once again heard laughter coming from the workroom. No doubt it was Kitty again, settling into her combined role.

"Olga, what *is* going on?"

"Sorry, madam. It Kitty. She make funny joke," Olga replied in her wooden English.

"Kitty, I like to know you're all happy, but we have a lot of orders to get out before Christmas."

"Sorry, ma'am. It's just that I said Mrs 'Ornby-Smythe could never get 'er backside in this without a good pull on her stays."

The other girls snorted, biting their cheeks, turning away, all failing miserably.

"Kitty, I'm disappointed. We definitely never talk about our clients, do you understand? And most certainly not in that manner. I expect better. Have I made myself clear?"

"Yes, ma'am," she spluttered.

Victoria rushed from the workroom before she allowed a huge grin to brighten her face.

She could hear Kitty whisper, "Yeh can put a fancy gown on a pig, but it's still a pig."

More muffled laughter erupted from the others.

Kitty was incorrigible, but Victoria couldn't fault her work or her attitude regarding Bridie. If Bridie thought it strange that Kitty came upstairs every day, she never mentioned it. Sean was delighted to have her around and Victoria found she was no longer jealous of the people with whom she shared Sean's affections. The Gibbs girls were part of her family now.

Edward had been busy in the weeks since her return from Liverpool and hadn't called round as often as she'd expected. She had, however, finally revealed her secret about Sean's birth to him. They'd been friends so long that she felt it would be wrong to keep it from him now she was no longer putting Patrick at risk. Far from being shocked or alarmed, he was full of admiration that she'd given Sean a loving home.

"I know you said you were protecting Patrick and didn't want to implicate me, but do you honestly believe I would have cared? That I would ever have done anything to put you or Patrick in danger? You wouldn't know, but Patrick helped me greatly when I first got to university. I had trouble settling in. Without him, I don't know if I'd have stayed the course. But what bothers me most is that you understand so little about me, about how I feel about you." A muscle worked in his neck.

"Edward, try to understand. I came here with a secret, living a lie. It just never seemed the right time to tell you."

Edward said he understood, but she regretted not telling him before. Life's full of regrets and learnings, she thought sadly, and now she'd hurt him once again. It seemed she was good at that.

Victoria was meant to be catching up on paperwork, but her mind was elsewhere. It was a long time since Edward had asked her to dinner, but tonight he was taking her to dine at a new restaurant. Did he have something special in mind, a question to ask her? If she was truly honest with herself, she couldn't be certain what her answer would be if he proposed, but the thought gave her a shiver of pleasure – she might even say yes this time! Her thoughts were broken when Milly knocked on the door of her office.

"Anne Caldwell has just popped in hoping you're free to do a fitting for her. I've told her Olga or I can do it, but she particularly asked for you."

Victoria considered refusing. Anne had been cold with her for years and hadn't frequented Centenary House for months. But if she was going to be her sister-in-law, she really should make the effort. Thinking of Anne as a potential sister-in-law meant she was seriously considering marriage. Mrs Victoria Caldwell – it certainly had a ring to it. A *ring*!

It was with trepidation that Victoria joined Anne in the fitting room. She was flummoxed as Anne, smiling brightly, greeted her warmly.

"Victoria! It's been so long," she cooed. "Do tell me, how is your dear little boy?"

Victoria told her he was well and enjoying school. Anne appeared genuinely interested. Perhaps she'd realised at last that her friendship with her brother wasn't going to end and had decided to accept it. After taking Anne's measurements, she began to show her some designs.

Anne looked at several, then said, "I adore this one, but is it suitable for Edward's engagement party? What do you think?" she asked pointedly, her eyes piercing, waiting for Victoria's reaction.

"E-Edward's eng-g-gagement . . . ?"

Anne covered her mouth with an air of surprise. "My goodness! Don't tell me I've spoken out of turn? You did know, I take it?" She paused a moment. "You didn't, did you?"

"N-no, I didn't know." Victoria struggled to regain her composure.

Of course Anne had spoken out of turn and well she knew it. To think that at one time she'd actually liked her. She was nothing but a spiteful mare.

"I'm so sorry, really I am. I felt sure you must have known. After all, you and Edward are so close. The lovely Fionn is over from Ireland visiting relatives. They live next door to us and we're almost inseparable. Like sisters.

"They fell in love while you were away in Liverpool. It's so exciting, don't you think? He's already bought the ring. You'll have to see it. There's to be an official engagement party early January and then a spring wedding. Quite the whirlwind romance. She's a year younger than me. Such a catch. Delightful girl. She'll make Edward a *wonderful* wife." Anne paused, titivating her hair in the mirror.

"He's not mentioned it to me yet, but I'm sure he will any day now. In fact, we're due to dine tonight."

She felt sick to her stomach. How could he not have told her? He claimed to love her – they were supposed to be friends. She'd thought he'd wanted more. He must have grown tired of waiting.

"Victoria, you look quite unwell. Shall I send for a glass of water?"

Victoria took Anne's concern for what it really was – fake.

"No, I'm fine, really. It's just such a busy time of year and I get little rest."

Anne stepped back and surveyed her. "I'm afraid I don't believe you, Victoria. I believe you're upset that Edward has moved on with his life. Surely you didn't think he would ask you to marry him again. I know he proposed before – he tells me everything. But I believe you were adamant that you wouldn't marry ever again."

"Yes, that's right – I won't marry again."

"You must understand. Edward desperately wants a son and heir. You've kept him at your side for years, like a puppy waiting to be petted. We both know he wouldn't want to hurt you, so I hope you won't try to spoil this for him. It would be incredibly selfish if you did."

"My relationship with Edward is none of your business and no, I wouldn't dream of standing in his way. As I said, we're just friends, no more."

Her mind was spinning. Anne looked so pleased with herself, Victoria's hand was itching to slap her smug face. It was true they were just friends – she'd never even allowed him to kiss her. But somewhere deep inside she'd hoped maybe one day they could become more than friends. Now that he knew about Sean, that barrier had been removed. If there was a man she could trust, it would have been Edward. But why had he hidden his engagement from her?

The only conclusion she could think of was that Edward was being kind. Not wanting to tell her while she'd been going through a difficult time. He was always so considerate. She'd noticed he was struggling with some internal conflict while she was in Liverpool. She'd been vain enough to think it was his desire for her, when all along it was how to tell her he'd moved on. She wouldn't stand in his way, no matter how much it hurt. He was marrying someone else now – belonged to someone else.

Anne was still talking, her words muffled to Victoria's ears until her voice rose sharply.

"Victoria, I asked you a question."

"Sorry, what?"

"My brother. I'm asking if you'll give me your word that you won't allow your farce of a relationship to stop him from moving on with his life. If you care for him even a little, promise me you will set him free."

Victoria turned away, unable to answer. She knew she'd never deliberately do anything to wound Edward, or deny him a child of his own. But how it hurt! Some of what Anne said was true – she was stopping him. She should have ended their relationship long ago if she wasn't willing to be his wife.

"Yes, Anne, you have my word. Now, have you chosen a design you're happy with?" she asked flatly.

"No. I'm afraid I've quite lost my enthusiasm for a new gown. I'll have to wear something out of my wardrobe."

Victoria wasn't surprised. She knew Anne's visit had nothing to do with acquiring a new gown and everything to do with obtaining her compliance.

"Then if that's all, I must ask you to leave as we are very busy."

Victoria no longer felt like going out to dinner, but she owed it to Edward to be happy for him – he'd done nothing wrong, after all. In fact, in all the years she'd known him, he'd been wonderful. She was such a fool! Clearly, this was his way of telling her he was getting married – a last dinner together. They could remain friends, of course, but going out to dinner, his visits to her home, would be out of the question. She certainly wouldn't be dining with him and the *lovely young Fionn,* no matter how *delightful* she was.

Despite her assurance to Anne, which she fully intended to keep, she wanted to look her best. She needed to feel good, to come out of the evening with her dignity intact.

"Edward, I'm delighted for you. When will the wedding be?" She practised her response in the mirror.

No, that wasn't right. Her face looked taut and her smile forced, lips pinched.

"Edward, I hope you will be very happy."

No, damn it. That wasn't right, either. She'd just have to improvise.

After trawling through her wardrobe, she decided that nothing she had was suitable. Then she remembered the royal blue velvet gown with an elaborately embroidered bodice, which had been made for the new window display. Sod it, as Kitty would say, she was going to wear that. Hopefully, it would give her a much-needed confidence boost.

Having donned the gown, she surveyed herself critically. She swept the hair from her face to secure it with combs, grimacing at the sight of a grey hair among her luxuriant brown curls. Marvellous! Now she was going grey.

Apart from a cursory glance to check if her hair was tidy, she realised she rarely looked in the mirror. She moved closer and scrutinised her face, finding tiny wrinkles around her eyes and faint frown-lines on her forehead. The soft contours of her face had disappeared, leaving her cheekbones sharp, and her chin took on a stubborn look. She suddenly felt old. Old and barren. Of course Edward had fallen in love with someone else.

Victoria took a deep breath before walking into the parlour, where Edward was waiting for her. He looked happy. She had no right to complain, but surely he could have mentioned the young woman who'd stolen his heart before now.

"Vicky, you're enough to give an old man a turn," he said, kissing her hand.

Did he still care for her? He'd been a tremendous friend – he deserved her support. Taking his arm, she smiled encouragingly.

As the waiter showed them to their table, Victoria

couldn't help noticing the smile that lingered around Edward's lips. Clearly, his new fiancée was making him happy. She wanted to be supportive, really she did, but Anne's words were ringing in her ears, blocking out the sound of the quartet playing in the corner.

Her mind was in turmoil as she struggled to focus on the menu. She barely heard a word he was saying until he said, "Vicky, I'm sorry to spring this on you before we have even eaten. But I once asked you to marry me."

Before she could stop herself, the words were out of her mouth.

"Yes, I remember. It almost ruined our friendship. I told you then I would never marry again. Marriage is for those too inadequate to live their lives alone. It isn't an institution I ever intend to enter willingly." Realising she'd upset him, that she'd gone too far, she tried to reassure him. Placing her hand on his, her voice softened. "Edward, I don't think marriage is wrong for everyone. You *should* marry. You'd make some young woman a wonderful husband."

That's better. You're being more supportive to your friend, she consoled herself.

She waited for him to tell her about his forthcoming engagement. She couldn't gauge his expression. Did he think she was being patronising? He appeared to be avoiding eye contact. Then he spoke slowly, deliberately.

"Vicky, you're right. I would . . . I will make someone a good husband. A damned good one. But in order to do that, I must separate myself from you. I need to get you out from under my skin, out of my head. You've been like a drug to me for years and I have to protect myself from you in order to get on with my life. I can't see you again after tonight."

She hadn't expected a sudden end to their friendship, or the flash of anger on his face. She was bereft. That was why he'd brought her here – it was a farewell dinner.

Bracing herself, her voice catching, she said, "I understand. Will you take me home now, please?"

People were glancing in their direction and whispering. Victoria knew she must look dreadful. Putting her hand out to steady herself, she caught the back of a chair filled by a large balding man. His companion's eyes were boring into her. Mrs Hornby-Smythe – of all people, why did she have to be here tonight?

As they reached his carriage, he helped her inside before kissing her hand softly. "My driver will take you home. Goodbye, my dear." He walked purposefully in the direction of his home. He was gone.

Her heart was breaking, the possibility of a life with Edward shattered forever. Letting herself in quietly, she didn't put her head into Sean's room as she generally did. Throwing herself on her bed, she gave way to her misery.

Anne stopped playing her pianoforte and jumped up from her seat.

"Edward! What on earth has happened? You look ghastly."

"I've made a frightful fool of myself again, that's what. I was stupid enough to consider asking Victoria to marry me." Edward threw the ring box on the dresser. Grasping the crystal decanter, he poured himself a large measure.

Anne looked vexed.

"Edward, I'm sorry, truly I am. The last thing I wanted was to see you hurt." She put her arms around her brother. "But you're better than her, you really are."

"You have nothing to be sorry for. And you're just saying that to be kind. Let's face it. You were right about her all along. She's used me. Kept me at her side for whenever she needed help of some kind. She's cruel. She knows how much I love her, despite never getting anything in return.

"I never asked anything of her. Do you know, she recently confided in me. I thought what she told me had been the reason she refused my proposal last time. It gave me hope. I can't understand why she said anything if she still doesn't want to marry me. Women!"

"What did she tell you?" Anne stepped back to survey him.

"Nothing you need to know. Besides, it's not important now. I've told her I can't see her again."

"Good, she doesn't deserve you. Why you would chase after *her* when there are far more suitable ladies, real ladies, who'd jump at the chance to marry you, I'll never know. I've told you already. Fionn who's visiting next door has asked about you several times – she's much more suited to you."

"Maybe it's my leg and hand. Maybe they repulse her."

"Then she's a damned fool. Edward, it pains me to say it, but she doesn't want you. Don't you see? Now you've made the break, you need to move on. I shall invite Fionn to dinner tomorrow night. Please say I can."

"Yes, all right. Whatever you think best. I'm clearly not capable of choosing women for myself," he said flatly before downing his whiskey and sloshing another into his glass.

Part 2

Chapter 27

Faredene, August 1890

Victoria adjusted the angle of her parasol, the glaring sun making it difficult to see what was happening on the scorched pitch. Not that it was bothering Sean, now a gangling teenager, who cheered when his best friend, Charles, hit the cricket ball across the field. It wasn't a game she enjoyed watching, but she never missed the opportunity to support her son, whatever he was doing. He was her life and she was incredibly proud of the young man he'd become. He'd leave home one day, perhaps go to university, marry or even travel, though she hoped it wouldn't be too soon.

Squinting in the sun, she looked around at the other spectators as she sipped her lemonade on the deck of the new Faredene Pavilion. They were without exception the well-heeled and affluent of Faredene. Many looked uncomfortable as their expensive clothes clung to their damp bodies. The pavilion had been bought with money raised by the Women's Guild and over the years, Victoria had become heavily involved in the movement, championing their efforts to provide for the poor. She'd argued that the money spent on the pavilion would be better utilised on the needy, but in the end, Mrs Hornby-Smythe's supporters had won over, claiming that even the poor needed fresh air and exercise.

"How ridiculous! They may need fresh air, but when do they get the time? They certainly get enough exercise working twelve-hour shifts in the mills and mines," Victoria had contended passionately.

Mrs Hornby-Smythe, however, was a manipulative, spiteful woman and many of the ladies were afraid to cross her.

"Ladies, as mothers and wives of the respectable classes, you have to decide where *your* loyalties lie. It's time we did something for our own children and husbands, surely. The pavilion will be for all of Faredene. To not support this project would be a mistake."

Victoria could see from the faces of the ladies present that she'd lost the argument. She resisted giving a parting shot. "*Butt*, Ethel, would your blacksmith father have agreed?"

She hoped maybe the poorer residents of the town would at least get *some* pleasure from the pavilion and that the children would play here. She pondered the idea of a game between the workers and the business owners. Could they ever come together as equals? She doubted either faction would be comfortable mixing with the other.

She, on the other hand, was on the edge of both camps. Neither fish nor fowl, as Bridie would say. She was certainly rich enough now, having invested her inheritance wisely, to be firmly in the higher echelons of Faredene society. However, she still enjoyed the company of her staff more than any of her wealthy neighbours and clientele – except Lydia, that is.

Victoria could see Lydia on the far side of the pitch, sitting stiff-backed next to her husband. No one would guess from the sight of them how wretched Lydia was, or how gambling, drugs and prostitution funded their lifestyle. Not that she blamed her for living off dirty money. Although Lydia hated where the wealth came from, there was nothing she could do to change matters until she was able to make her escape.

Victoria had come to value her friendship, especially as Bridie had withdrawn further into herself. Dear Bridie – the years hadn't been kind to her. A gradual deterioration of her mind had forced Victoria to accept she wouldn't be with them for much longer.

As a cheer went up from the cricket crowd, she was startled from her musings. Her face instantly lit with pleasure as Sean came running over, Charles ambling beside him, shouting, "We won!"

She chatted to the boys for a while and noticed Lydia approaching hastily.

"Charles, come along, darling, we must go," she said, nervously checking over her shoulder. "You know your father doesn't like to be kept waiting."

Both boys screwed up their faces in disappointment. Victoria could see James pacing by the gate.

"I'm sorry, Victoria. I would have loved to have sat with you. But you understand my situation. I'm just so relieved that they won."

Lydia didn't have to explain why. She'd told Victoria how her husband berated Charles if he perceived he'd let him down by not getting top marks or winning at sports. As a result, the boy was developing a nervous stammer.

"May I come and see you tomorrow at Centenary House? I can't be sure what time it'll be," she asked, fussing nervously with the folded parasol.

Victoria detected a note of desperation in her voice and

assured her she could call in at whatever time suited her. She might not have a man in her life, but at least she didn't have to live her life on pins like these two.

The following afternoon, Lydia came to see Victoria.

"Victoria, the time is approaching when I must make my escape. James is beginning to take his frustrations out on Charles. He actually tried to strike him the other day, for sticking up for me. I only just managed to get between them. I truly believe he is insane."

"How can I help? What about those papers I found in Patrick's desk alluding to how James acquires his income? Are you sure you can't use them in some way?"

"No, Victoria, he has too many people in his pocket. If he got off and found out I'd been involved in some way . . . Well, it's just too risky."

"Where will you go?"

"Italy."

"Italy!"

"I have a very dear friend – Madeleine Forbes. Circumstances have kept us apart for fifteen years, since we were both forced to marry. Her husband, who's much older than her, is dying. They live in Dorset but when he passes away, she's moving to Italy. I'll join her there, taking Charles with me. I must go far away, where James can't find us. Charles will have to leave school earlier than planned, but it's the only way we will be safe."

Victoria was trying to take it all in. In all the years they'd known each other, Lydia had never mentioned Madeleine.

"Are you sure? Italy is such a long way. Sean and Charles will miss each other terribly. And you haven't seen your friend for so long. What if you don't get along?"

Lydia giggled softly.

"It's not funny, Lydia. She may have changed."

"Dear Victoria, please don't be cross with me. I fear what I'm about to tell you will change the way you see me . . . But Madeleine won't have changed. She loves me. She's always loved me – and I her."

"Yes, well, I love Milly, but I wouldn't follow her to Italy, especially if I hadn't seen her for . . ."

Lydia's eyes were downcast. Finally, it registered.

"My goodness! I never would have guessed."

"I've shocked you. I can see that. Maybe I should have kept quiet. I couldn't bear for you to disapprove of me."

Once again, she was reminded that you could know someone for years without ever really knowing them. She *was* shocked, there was no denying it. Lydia was staring at her. Pushing her astonishment and discomfort to one side, she placed her hand on top of Lydia's.

"What do you need from me? I'll do anything I can to help you."

"Madeleine and I need to write to each other and the only way that I can see that we can do that is through you. She occasionally writes to me at home, but everything must be written so carefully, in code. The other day, I found James rifling through my desk. I think he suspects I'm less afraid of him now. But he has no idea what might have brought about the change. If he suspected, he would kill me. Charles, too, if he tried to protect me, of that I am certain."

"Kill you?" Victoria repeated sceptically.

She knew he was a nasty piece of work, but murder? Surely Lydia was exaggerating.

"Yes, kill me. He's capable of it. Last time I openly defied him, when I brought Kitty to you, he took his revenge in the bedroom. Then my little dog, Scamper, went missing. She never left the house without me.

"When I was looking for her, he sneered and suggested I look in the woods by the pond. That was exactly where I found her. Her little neck was broken and the birds had eaten her eyes. I am certain he was behind it." Lydia took a handkerchief from her beaded purse, quickly dabbing her eyes.

"Oh, Lydia, I wish you'd told me." She squeezed Lydia's hand.

"What would that have achieved? You would have felt responsible and would have wanted to protect me. Then you'd have felt frustrated that there was nothing you could do. We both know how you always feel guilty about things that aren't your fault. You're forever trying to make life better for everyone. In any case, burdening you wouldn't have brought Scamper back.

"And of course I was never sure how you'd react about Madeleine. You may even have felt I wanted more from *you*." A smile played at the corners of her mouth. "Our friendship was too important. It's you who has got me through it all these years. You and Charles."

Victoria felt so guilty that she hadn't helped her friend that she couldn't speak for a moment.

"See, I knew I was right to keep it from you."

"It's not that. I was just wondering, surely if he's mad enough to kill your dog, you could have him committed."

"Victoria, my dear, I couldn't prove that he was behind what happened to Scamper. As for what he does to me, it is his conjugal right as my husband. He, on the other hand, would find it all too easy to have me certified insane.

"The law is very unfair to women. It is only his belief

that I am completely compliant that stops him. I give him a respectable visage, behind which he can hide his true self and his depraved lifestyle."

"But it's so wrong, so unfair. He's an animal!"

"I don't believe he was born that way. He has scars on his back from where his father used to whip him at the slightest provocation."

"That's no excuse. As adults, we're responsible for our own behaviour."

"You are right, of course. Although perhaps if he had married another woman who shared his appetites, he would have been a different man. We are *all* responsible for the choices we make in life, Victoria. I cannot blame everything on him.

"Although I felt forced to marry him, I accept the choice I made – if you could have called it a choice. But that doesn't mean I'm not going to make other choices now. And besides, I wouldn't have Charles if I'd done something different."

Perhaps her own life would have been different if she hadn't allowed her past to influence her decisions.

"Our friendship has meant a great deal to me also. Tell me what you need. I will do anything to help you get away from him."

"With your permission, Madeleine will address her letters to you and if you could pass them on to me and post my replies, that is all we need for now. She won't leave her husband until he's gone. He's a good man and deserves her loyalty until the end. He knows about me. He understands her. He married her for companionship and they have no children. He bought the Italian estate for us to go to eventually. No one here knows about it. We will still be discreet, but the estate is extremely large. We intend to live a quiet life away from everyone who knows us."

Lydia had been so sure Victoria would cooperate that she already had the first letter written. They weren't leaving yet, but Sean and Victoria were both going to lose a dear friend.

Chapter 28

It seemed as though there would be no end to the rain, sleet and snow that had battered against the workroom windows for weeks. The bleak conditions hadn't lessened the usual rush of pre-Christmas orders, though, so Victoria's day had been a long and arduous one.

"I think we'll finish now, girls. You all wrap up well – it's freezing out there," she said to her staff.

Grateful that the long day was over, they all began reaching for their coats and shawls.

"It's all right for you, Milly, only having to nip next door. I'll have icicles on me nose by the time I get home," Kitty said, pulling on her gloves.

Kitty, now nineteen, was a stunner, with abundant titian hair, a mischievous glint in her eyes and a creamy complexion. Milly often said that Kitty got the entire family's share of good looks and cheek to boot.

Despite her attractiveness and lack of decorum, she was a hardworking girl and was now a full-time machinist, with a great sense of humour. She had no shortage of admirers and appeared to have a different young man wanting to court her each week.

"Well, you know you could stop over, but our Teddy will be here for you in a minute." Milly gestured outside with a quick wave of her hand.

No matter what the weather, after Teddy finished work at the brewery, he'd cut through the park to the other side of town to walk Kitty home. Although she could often be heard telling him off when, as she put it, "he didn't know his behind from his elbow", she was his fiercest advocate and would give her life to protect him.

"Aye, thanks anyway. I'd better get out and start walking to meet him. Ta-ra, all," Kitty shouted as she went out into the cold.

Victoria was thankful that Milly and Bob were still happy living above Centenary House. She'd have been lost without them. Watching them over the years, she'd realised that not all men changed for the worst after they were married. Bob worshipped Milly, but poor Milly had suffered several miscarriages and had never been blessed with the child they both longed for. She'd gladly have seen them move away if they'd been able to have a family, for she knew only too well the ache of an empty womb.

When she got upstairs, Sean was languishing on the sofa.

"Honestly, Mother, I actually think Charles is dreading going home for Christmas. I said to him, what can be so bad about spending your days reading and riding while an army of servants prepare your meals. They don't have to drag the bath up to their bedrooms to bathe, either – they have an *actual* bathroom in their house. It's remarkable! I wanted to get in it right there and then when he showed it to me over the summer while his father was away. But he says he'd give it all up tomorrow to be in a happy home. I think he hates his father."

Victoria understood exactly how Charles felt. She'd

happily have given up the comforts of her own childhood to live with happy parents – even if they weren't hers.

"I expect Charles has his reasons. How is his stammer?"

"If you ask me, it gets worse as the holidays get nearer. I'd have liked him to come here for Christmas, but he says his father would never allow it and I'm not allowed to visit there, either. Charles won't tell me why. His father seems all right to me. He's always really pleasant. I don't think Charles would lie to me, but who knows." Sean sat up quickly, an excited look on his face. "Can *we* have a bathroom installed? Can we?"

She smiled. "I don't see why not. It would certainly be nice to have hot water and a permanent tub. I'll make some—"

Milly and Kitty burst through the door, their faces ashen, the tip of Kitty's nose red from the cold. Sean jumped to his feet and went to Kitty's side. Victoria suspected he was infatuated with Kitty and he'd take any opportunity to engage her in conversation. She wouldn't want to change Kitty, but she wasn't right for her boy. She hated herself for thinking that way, but there was no point pretending she felt differently.

"It's our Teddy! He's been taken away!" Kitty said in a rush, her hands twisting in agitation. "I were on me way home when I bumped into our Harry, who was coming here to fetch me an' our Milly."

"I need to go an' find out what's happened, but I don't want to see me dad. I were wondering if you . . . Well, you know . . ." Milly asked.

Even after all these years, despite lots of urging from her mother, Milly still refused to spend time with her father. It had in some ways divided the family. It was most difficult for Kitty, as she still lived at home. Milly had offered her their spare room, but Kitty wouldn't leave Teddy. He disliked change, it unsettled him, and he was happy living at home, so there seemed no need to change anything, at least for the moment.

"You want me to come with you." Realising what Milly wanted of her, Victoria got up from the armchair.

"Please, ma'am, if you would."

Victoria and Milly pulled on coats and gloves against the fierce cold before all three marched over to the Gibbs' house. Victoria shivered – her toes like ice, her boots were no protection.

Edith was sitting at the kitchen table, her head in her hands, sobbing.

"Mam, where have they taken Teddy? What's going on?" Milly demanded, blowing on her numb fingers to warm them.

"Some money has gone missing from the office at the brewery. They think it were our Teddy. The constable came. They said 'cos he's not right in the head, he won't go to prison. But they've taken him to the asylum. Your dad had to sign the papers." Tears streamed down her lined face.

"He'll never survive in a place like that. He's soft as muck." Kitty grasped the ladder-back kitchen chair for support.

"What's our dad an' Bert said about it? Didn't they tell the gaffer Teddy would never do anything like that?" Milly asked.

At twenty-three, Teddy was gentle and loving, still very much a child in his ways.

"I don't bloody know. Bert and yer dad were arguing.

Going at it 'ammer and tongs. I thought yer dad were gonna kill him. He stormed off to the pub. Then Bert stomped out as well, saying he were gonna see David and Sam. That's when our Agnes sent Harry for you." Edith gave way to weeping and wailing once more.

"Stop bloody bawling, Mam. Summat bloody stinks. There's no way Teddy would ever take owt that didn't belong to him, especially not money. He doesn't have any interest in it." Kitty spat the words at her mother as she dragged the chair back, toppling it, her face furious.

"Watch what you're doing with me furniture. Yer dad'll hit the roof if you ruin what bit we've got."

"I don't give a damn about the stupid chair. Or Dad, for that matter." Kitty kicked the chair leg with her foot.

Milly's restraining hand on Kitty's arm stopped whatever she was about to say.

"I can't get any more out of her," Agnes said, coming out of the parlour. "When I got here earlier, Bert were going crazy at Dad saying he had to put a stop to it. There's definitely more to it. But what can we do?" She lifted her hands in a hopeless gesture.

Milly looked expectantly at Victoria.

Victoria felt like an age had passed before she could collect the jumble of thoughts racing through her mind. Calmly, she said, "It's too late to do anything tonight. But first thing tomorrow morning, I'll go and see Edward and get his help. He'll know what to do."

Since Edward had gone out of her life eight years ago, she'd used another solicitor in town for her legal matters, such as purchasing properties and updating her will. This, however, was too important to think about using anyone else. The only person she trusted to care enough about Teddy's plight was Edward. Although she desperately wanted to see him, she also dreaded it. Seeing him again might rekindle the feelings she'd been trying to quash for years.

That night, she tossed and turned restlessly. What must poor Teddy be going through? He must be scared witless. She could picture his round face, terrified and not understanding what was happening. And how would she feel when she saw Edward? She mustn't do anything to ruin his marriage, that much was sure.

Regardless of how tough it was for her to see Edward, she knew she had to help Teddy and to do that she needed to get some sleep. Shaking her pillow as though that were the problem, she closed her eyes and tried to drift off.

Chapter 29

"Can I go with you, ma'am?" Milly asked as Victoria came into the shop to tell her she was off to see Edward.

"I've already told Kitty and Agnes it's best if I go alone. Please take care of things here. It's where you are needed most. Edward may want to go straight to the brewery and if there are too many of us, it'll be a distraction. I promise that I'll update you as soon as I can." Her tone was firm – the last thing she needed was an audience to her meeting with Edward.

Milly looked over her shoulder to check her assistant was still in the stockroom before speaking.

"All right. I know it will be difficult for you. It's been such a long time since you've seen him."

"I've missed him, Milly. You know that. I can't believe how little I've seen of him around town."

"Aye, the last time were years back at the fayre, wasn't it? When him and that fancy-drawers wife of his were having words."

Milly was right. She and Milly had taken Sean to the fayre. Victoria had been stealing painful glances at Edward, *the lovely Fionn* and their daughter. She felt sure he'd been looking at her, his face pained.

"I still think it's a shame you two never got together. That sister of his has a lot to answer for. I'm glad she took herself off to Hampshire when she got married."

"Perhaps Anne did have a hand in things, but I can't blame her for the choices I made. Well, not entirely."

Victoria forced a nervous smile. Tittle-tattle had soon reached her that Edward's marriage was not a happy one – that Mrs Caldwell missed her home in Ireland, that she didn't like to socialise or wish to be bothered by the affairs of Faredene. Although part of her was hungry for information about Edward, it saddened her to think of him as unhappy.

Victoria's breath misted as she battled to stay upright against the icy winds. She was making her way on foot to the street where Edward's office was situated, needing the walk to steady her nerves. The shops windows were bursting with Christmas treats and decorations. Christmas was the last thing on her mind. Her hands were trembling and felt clammy inside her gloves despite the freezing temperature. She hesitated outside the building.

Right, come on. Sort yourself out, woman. Get inside, she admonished herself.

She turned the handle and pushed the door forcefully before she changed her mind.

An oily-haired, pock-marked young man sitting at a desk looked up, startled, as she as almost fell through the door.

"The wind . . . the door. I mean, the wind blew the door out of my hands."

"Are you all right, madam?"

Victoria pushed her hat back from her eyes so she

could see. "Yes. I'd like to see Mr Caldwell, please." Her voice wavered.

"Do you have an appointment?" he asked, steepling his hands.

"No. My name is Mrs Kavanagh. I'm sure Edward will see me without one."

The clerk stirred in his seat uncomfortably under her gaze. Nodding, he disappeared through a doorway behind him. After a few minutes, Edward appeared.

"Victoria!" he said as he strode across the room, a huge grin splitting his face. "I thought I heard your voice. Come through."

Edward perched on the corner of the desk, so close that they were almost touching. Was that *her* heart pounding? she wondered as the blood rushed to her face.

"What can I do for you?"

"I wouldn't be calling, but I desperately need your help."

"What can I do? Anything, anything at all," he coaxed, extending his hand to encourage her to continue.

She could just take his hand right now and hold it against her face – how she'd missed that smile . . .

He was already on his feet by the time she'd finished explaining.

"I'll send a boy for my carriage. We need to pay a visit to Mr Payne at the brewery at once. That poor boy – it doesn't bear thinking about. There must be some mistake. We'll get it sorted."

"Thank you, Edward. I knew you were the right person to help."

While they waited for the carriage, Edward made notes and asked questions, many of which she couldn't answer. Perhaps she should have brought one of the Gibbs family with her. What she could tell him, though, was that if Teddy took the money, someone must have put him up to it.

When they arrived at the brewery, they made their way through the yard amid glances from curious workers. The smell was pungent and Victoria felt sickly as the combined odour of the dray horses' stables and hops brewing assailed her nostrils. The clerk in the outer office told them Mr Payne would be happy to see them and led them into his dark panelled office with a large window that overlooked the operation.

Mr Payne was a portly man with a ruddy complexion. His manner was affable – like his wife, who Victoria knew from the Women's Guild – as he asked how he could help. When Edward explained they were here in relation to Teddy Gibbs, the man shook his head gravely.

"Bad business, that. I said to the wife I didn't believe that young lad would be capable of pilfering."

"I'm sorry, I don't understand. We were led to believe you accused him." Edward glanced at Victoria, who nodded to confirm that he was correct.

"No. Not exactly. Over the last few weeks, I noticed money going missing whenever the lad had been sweeping the office. Two days ago, a pound disappeared from the security box. The only people who have access to this office are me, Teddy and Smith out there . . ." He pointed through the glass partition at the clerk who'd escorted them in. "Well, I knew it wasn't him. Smith has been with me since he was ten. Good lad. I've sort of taken an interest in him since his mother died. Not the sort to take what's not his – and certainly not from me."

"So why the devil has Teddy been accused, if you don't think he did it, either?" Edward puffed irritably.

"What I mean is, I don't think he'd have done it on his own."

"Perhaps you should explain yourself."

"Wilf Gibbs – I think he told the lad to take the money. Teddy would just do as he was told. No concept of right and wrong as far as I can tell."

Victoria rolled her eyes. "That's exactly what I thought. Well, not that it was his father, but that someone had told him to do it and he didn't understand that it was wrong."

"Did you speak to Mr Gibbs about it?" Edward asked.

"Aye. Got the police in to see him. And he blamed the lad. Bare-faced lie, if you ask me. He said the lad had stolen it to buy sweets."

"Sweets?" Victoria said in disdain. "So you did speak to Teddy?" She doubted that would have helped Teddy, but still . . .

"We did. We had to have his father there – only right with a lad like that. But all Teddy kept saying was, 'I'm a good lad, aren't I, Dad?'"

When Edward asked if they could have a quick word with Wilf, Mr Payne informed them that he hadn't turned up that morning, which had surprised Mr Payne, because although he believed him guilty of theft, he'd never missed a day's work.

Victoria and Edward decided the Gibbs house should be their next port of call.

Edith yawned wearily as she opened the door, her face blotchy from crying. Victoria assumed the tears were for Teddy, until the woman said with a sob, "It's my Wilf. He were proper hurt last night. I can't believe it. His mates fetched him home in a right state. Said they'd found him out cold in the stables. Why did this have to happen to him? I know he's got a temper, but he didn't deserve this."

Victoria tried to control the voice in her head that said he'd got everything he had coming. Especially after he'd let poor Teddy be taken to the asylum. Would this woman *ever* see anything bad in that man? Despite the increased income in Edith's household and having fewer mouths to feed, Victoria knew they still struggled, living hand to mouth each week. Instead of leaving her husband or attempting to curtail his drinking, Edith now joined him several times a week in the pub.

Victoria let her speak. She didn't have much choice if Edith was to be of any help. She was glad Edith seemed oblivious to the fact that she was drumming her fingers against her leg, her frustration mounting.

Edith explained that Wilf's mates said he must have got too close to Samson, one of the huge shire horses, when it kicked him. His workmates had carried him home unconscious and helped to bring a bed from upstairs into the parlour. Wilf hadn't moved a muscle or shown any signs of regaining consciousness in over ten hours.

"But I don't bleedin' believe it were the horse. I think some cruel bugger's done for him. Come and see for yerself the state of him."

Edith led them into the parlour. Even in the dim light, his injuries were highly visible. One side of his face was purpling from the bruising and blood was oozing from a huge gash that had split his nose and cheek. The odour of stale beer filled the room. The woman was useless – she hadn't even sent for the doctor. Victoria asked her why.

"Our David and Sam said not to fetch one. Said that Wilf had probably been up to summat he shouldn't. They said he'd probably be all right, like."

"I really think it would be advisable, Mrs Gibbs. Besides, your husband may have information that could help Teddy. That's why we are here," Edward said.

Edith looked away.

"Don't you think it's gone beyond protecting Wilf now? It's Teddy we need to help. That lad has never so much as harmed a fly." Victoria only just stopped short of saying, unlike the drunken pig in the parlour. "Doctor Farrell *will* be sent for and *I* will be picking up the account," she said firmly as she went out of the front door.

On their return, Victoria summoned the Gibbs girls into the office to update them on what Mr Payne had said.

"Aye, I thought as much," Milly said. "That lad, he hasn't a bad bone in his body. How could Dad do that to him? Honestly, he makes me sick. I'm so ashamed of him."

The girls already knew about their father's accident, as Bert had called in. Victoria noticed none of them had thought to go tearing round there. Agnes stood tight-lipped, looking at her feet. Then Kitty spoke.

"I want Teddy home as much as anyone. I'll break down the door of that bloody place meself if I has to. But we need to go careful, or our David, Sam an' Bert could all end up going along the line for nearly killing Dad. Then it won't just be Teddy who's locked up. Dad got what he bloody deserved. I wish I'd taken the bloody coal shovel to him meself."

"Your brothers did that to Wilf!" Victoria gasped.

"No, but they'll get the blame like as not, 'cos everyone

knew they were gunnin' for him."

"I don't understand."

Kitty explained that Bert had confronted their dad. Wilf had eventually admitted that he'd told Teddy to take the money. Bert was ready to go to the police there and then, but Wilf said if he didn't keep his trap shut, he'd give him a good hiding. Bert was afraid of his dad but wasn't prepared to let Teddy suffer, so he got hold of his brothers and all three of them confronted Wilf in the pub.

"There was a blazing row. The pub was full and loads of the brewery workers were listening," Kitty ended.

"The lads have promised it wasn't them and we believe them," Milly added.

"Dad had already left work, so why would he go back? As for the horse, Dad might be as thick as pig muck, but he knows horses and would never stand where he could get hurt. Besides, Samson's right gentle," Kitty said.

The brothers suspected his workmates had done him over, disgusted at Wilf's treatment of Teddy, whom they all liked.

"If I find out who did it, I'll be happy to stand them a pint. A whole bloody keg if they want. I wish I'd cracked his thick bloody skull with a poker meself." Rage seized her as Kitty clenched her teeth, grabbing an imaginary poker and swinging it wildly, her face contorted.

Edward began writing notes as he explained to the sisters what it all meant.

"Mr Payne is a decent enough man, but he won't want the bad publicity this could bring. If half of his workforce is accused of what could possibly turn out to be murder, while an innocent lad has been locked up, it won't do his business any good. As for the police, it will be far easier for them to prove your brothers are guilty than it would be to accuse men who had no real motive."

None of the girls had any sympathy for their father, so they didn't relish the idea of going back to the house and dealing with their wailing mother. However, Edward explained that he'd asked Doctor Farrell to visit and that it was important they find out the prognosis. If he recovered, Wilf may well be able to clear Teddy's name.

Reluctantly, Agnes and Kitty agreed to go together while Milly, who was pregnant again, tried to get some rest at Victoria's insistence.

"Just get Teddy outta there, please," Kitty begged, grabbing Edward's crooked hand desperately, oblivious to the flash of pain in his eyes. "He's gentle. He won't cope in there."

"I'll get him out, Kitty. Don't you worry."

When they were alone, Victoria turned to Edward.

"Tell me honestly. What are the chances of getting Teddy out?"

"I won't give up until I do, but I'm afraid, even with what we know, it's going to take a while. We must get Mr Payne to drop the charges, or prove Teddy's innocence. That's before we deal with the fact that his father had him committed. That could be difficult to overturn."

He intended to visit Mr Payne at the brewery once more and would call on Victoria the following day once he'd decided on the best plan of action.

It was nearly midnight when Kitty and Agnes returned. Victoria and Milly had waited up together. Bridie rarely noticed anything that was happening around her these days and had gone to bed as usual. Sean was deeply upset about Teddy and had been desperate to help Kitty, but Victoria had insisted he went to bed.

Agnes explained that the doctor had examined Wilf.

"He said he couldn't be sure what had caused the injuries, although it was entirely probable he'd been kicked by either a horse or boots. Whatever the cause, he had a fractured skull and needed extensive care."

"Needed?" Victoria questioned. "Had?"

Wilf had suffered a seizure while the doctor was there and died earlier that evening. Edith was inconsolable and the girls had stayed until she'd finally fallen asleep.

"Good riddance to bad rubbish, I say. Best blinking Christmas present he's ever given us lot. For years he's been beating the sense outta Mam. He nearly killed our Milly just for wanting to get married. Someone should have sorted him out years ago and then Teddy wouldn't be in that place. I nearly gave him a crack with the saucepan after he'd kicked the bucket. Just to make sure he'd gone."

Kitty's face looked anything but lovely as she spoke, twisted with anger. Clearly, she was no longer bothered about staying neutral in family rows, Victoria thought. Everyone had their breaking point.

"Kitty!" Agnes admonished.

"Well, what do yeh expect? Be honest – we're better off without him, aren't we?"

"Kitty's right, our Agnes," Milly said.

Reluctantly, Agnes nodded her agreement.

"Are you all right, Milly, you're very pale?" Victoria asked urgently, pushing a chair towards her.

"Yeah. I'm not bothered about Dad. I'm just worried, because now he's gone, he can't be forced to help clear Teddy."

"Don't worry about that. Edward will sort it. You get to bed. You've got the little one to think about now and stewing on it is no good in your condition."

Not one of the girls would shed a tear for their father. Victoria, for one, couldn't blame them. The man was a swine and she hadn't cried when her own father had passed away.

David, Bert and Sam remained adamant they hadn't touched their father. None of the family wanted to risk the lads getting accused of murder. So left with little option and concurring their father deserved the beating for what he'd done to Teddy, the family had agreed not to involve the police.

"It's like the lads said – it's about time someone put a stop to the rotten old bugger. They deserve a medal," Kitty ended. "We should be shaking their hands. Done us all a right good favour."

Chapter 30

Victoria stood back on the icy pavement and surveyed her handiwork. She'd placed a velvet gown in deep red teamed with coordinating accessories in the centre of the window display. The gloves, shawls and hats would be suitable as Christmas presents for wives and mothers. Normally, the Christmas display was her favourite, but this year she got no joy from it. She couldn't understand why Edith was distraught. She appeared to be so absorbed in the loss of her husband that she'd completely forgotten about Teddy.

The following day, Victoria attended Wilf's funeral out of respect for the rest of the family. It was an uncomfortable affair, and Edith had to beg Kitty and Milly to attend. Disgusted at what their dad had done to Teddy, the older lads hadn't wanted to carry the coffin – only Edith's pleading and sobbing had caused them to relent.

It appeared that the neighbourhood, like the family, were divided over the whole affair, with many who thought Wilf's behaviour despicable. Then there were those who said not too quietly, "What difference does it make? Teddy's as mad as a hatter and is better off locked up."

Victoria had been greatly relieved when she was able to take her leave, hoping it would be a long while before she needed to wear her black gown again. It might not be Christian of her, but she'd hoped Wilf Gibbs was turning in his grave, at least until Teddy was safely home.

Edward confirmed to Mr Payne that Wilf had taken the money, reimbursing the brewery owner for the stolen cash out of his own pocket. Wanting to avoid bad publicity for having an innocent lad locked up, Mr Payne signed a document for the police stating he wasn't pressing charges against Teddy.

The next part was more difficult, getting a reluctant Edith to sign documentation to secure Teddy's release, stating that Wilf had falsely accused their son.

"I don't want to sully his good name," Edith said, turning away from the sheet of paper lying on the table.

"Just sign the blasted thing, Mam, or I swear we'll all be finished with yeh," Kitty warned her mother. "What the hell's the matter with yeh? Teddy's yer son! You should be ashamed."

"I know he's me bleedin' son. I shoved him out, didn't I? I'm grieving. Not that you care. Everything's always about Teddy wi' you."

"Well what do yeh expect, Mam. I've had to look after him all me flipping life!"

Edith scowled at her daughter as she grabbed the document and made her mark.

It took a week following Wilf's funeral for all the paperwork to be reviewed by the asylum authorities and make all the arrangements for Teddy's release.

The night before he was due to be collected, Milly suffered another miscarriage. She came into Victoria as white as a sheet, trembling, still insisting she wanted to go with them.

"You're resting and that's all there is to it," Victoria said.

"I don't think I can stand losing another. I've told Bob he can't touch me again," she sobbed.

Putting her arms around Milly, Victoria stroked her hair.

"I don't know much about it, but I believe there are ways a man and a woman can stop a child from coming. Perhaps you can speak to Doctor Farrell – he's a good man. Just rest for a few days before you make any decisions," Victoria said before she sent her to lie down.

It was agreed that Edward would accompany Victoria and Kitty to collect Teddy, while Milly was to spend the day resting. Christmas rush or not, Milly looked fit to drop. Thankfully, there were just two gowns to be finished and Olga assured Victoria they'd be done on time. Victoria cared little about the gowns or the profit but didn't want to let her customers down.

As the guard had pulled open the heavy iron gates, revealing the immense stone façade of the asylum, Kitty had gasped, her hand going to her mouth.

"Aww, God, it looks like a bloody prison."

Having been permitted access through strong bolted doors, the reek of bleach stung their nostrils. Kitty had gripped Victoria's hand. Muffled shouting and wailing echoed through closed doors as they were escorted to the superintendent's office. It seemed hard to believe there were so many suffering.

Superintendent Wiggins, a thin, gaunt man with cold, dark eyes had entered the room, extending his hand to Edward.

"Mr Caldwell. How nice to see you again. You're here to collect Edward Gibbs, I understand."

"His name's Teddy," Kitty piped up, her mouth set in a stubborn line.

"Yes, Mr Wiggins. I have all the necessary papers here." Edward spoke authoritatively as he handed several sheets of paper to the superintendent.

"I'm sure they're all in order," he said, placing them on his desk without looking at them. Opening the door to his office, he called, "Bring Edward Gibbs through."

As they waited in silence, Victoria could hear clanging and banging. Then Teddy appeared at the door. He was struggling and being held on either side by two burly men. When he saw Superintendent Wiggins standing in the doorway, his struggles became frantic, accompanied by cries of, "Want Kitty. Want Kitty."

Wiggins shifted uncomfortably.

"Teddy!" Kitty screeched, darting from behind the superintendent.

Hearing her voice, Teddy stopped writhing, his eyes wide as he saw Kitty. She flung her arms around his neck.

"Kitty. Kitty. Want to go 'ome. Please, Kitty. Now."

Teddy's face was awash with tears. He put his head on Kitty's shoulder, his body juddering as he sobbed.

Victoria took a handkerchief from her bag, dabbing tears from her eyes. She looked at Edward and saw him swallow as he looked away, seemingly interested in the blank wall.

The two guards let go, revealing red marks and yellow bruising on Teddy's arms. The superintendent waved the men away unceremoniously.

"He was violent and needed restraining," Wiggins said superciliously.

"Teddy's never violent! Yer a lyin' bleeder," Kitty blurted, launching for him.

Edward placed his hand firmly on her shoulder.

"My dear, if he's never been locked up before, how would you know? It can affect *these* cases differently. He's somewhat deranged. In fact, I was unsure about releasing him," Wiggins added threateningly.

"I find it hard to believe Teddy could ever be violent, but we just want to get him home now, if we may," Edward stated. "All the paperwork is in order and there is no reason to detain him any longer than necessary."

"Indeed, we've done our best to care for him. I myself have tried to comfort him. Difficult case, clearly delusional," he said, leading them to the entrance.

"He bloody well ain't!"

Wiggins glared at Kitty.

"These cases can be quite different when they are in a new environment, my dear."

"If yeh call me bruvver a case again, I'll show yeh bloody difficult!" Kitty poked her finger in his chest.

Wiggins took a step back, eyebrows raised, his head jerking round to Edward for support.

"Kitty. Perhaps we should get Teddy home," Edward said, placing his hand on her arm, stilling her.

She nodded, her lips pursed.

Teddy wept all the way back to Centenary Lane, snot seeping into the shoulder of Kitty's coat as she held him close, stroking his hair and whispering endearments between her own choking sobs.

"Take him into Milly's kitchen and stay with him, Kitty, and I'll send Agnes through in a moment," Victoria instructed. Then she turned to Edward. "Edward, did you see the bruises? Do you think they hurt him?"

"I don't know, Vicky. I hope not, but we'll probably never know," he said wretchedly.

"I suppose you're right. It's just the discoloration on his arms . . . Perhaps it is as the superintendent said and he had to be restrained."

"He's home now. That's all we can do. His sisters will take care of him."

"I can't thank you enough for your help. I will of course pay your bill and reimburse any expenses."

"That's not necessary, my dear. I do understand the gratification one can receive from helping others."

Things had been so natural between them while they'd been dealing with the issues surrounding Teddy. Now, Victoria felt they were awkward and uncomfortable. She wanted to invite him in. To ask him to dine with her to repay his kindness. Who was she trying to kid? She wanted to place her hand on his cheek, her lips on his firm cleft chin. To hold him close.

"I'm so grateful, Edward. May I at least take you to lunch as a thank you?" she asked tentatively.

"That's unnecessary, but I am always at your service if you are in need of my help," he said, getting back into his carriage.

"Thank you," she ended lamely, immense loneliness sweeping over her as his carriage pulled away.

Chapter 31

Leaving the occupants of her household to rest following Sunday lunch, Victoria slipped next door to visit Milly. Milly poured her a cup of tea, replacing the woollen tea cosy.

"Doctor Farrell were ever so nice. He told me not many doctors will help people. They think it's a woman's duty to bear children, no matter what it does to their bodies. He's given me a Dutch cap. They've only been out a few years. He said he could have given me some johnnies for Bob, but he said he thinks it's better for women to have control." She made a face. "I were so embarrassed, yeh could have fried an egg on me face."

"I'm glad it's all sorted."

Victoria was keen to change the subject. Despite how close they'd become, she'd never confided in Milly about Sean's birth. So thinking Victoria had been married, Milly had spoken freely to her, expecting her to understand about the intimacy between a man and a woman. She'd wanted to confide in her, but she felt she owed it to Sean to retain his secret.

The kitchen door opened and Kitty's head appeared, her cheeks flushed, flakes of snow melting in her hair.

"Thank God you've got a cuppa ready. My blinkin'

feet are soaked, trudging through the slush. It's cold enough to freeze the snot in yer nose. Sorry, ma'am, but it is."

"That's all right, Kitty, come and get warm," Victoria said, moving to a chair on the other side of the table so Kitty could get closer to the fire. "How's Teddy?"

"He's still jittery and scared of strangers. Teddy's never been like that – he's always been trusting. Too bloody trusting at times. He's back working at the brewery – I hope that'll help. I still can't shake the feeling that they did summat really bad to him in that asylum. He asked me last night if he were going to have a baby."

Kitty had voiced her concerns before. They were all horrified at the thought of what Teddy might have suffered but knew there was nothing they could do.

"Aww, Kitty, don't talk about it. I can't bear thinking about it." Milly pushed a cup of tea in front of her.

Not wanting to continue talking about birth control or what may have happened to Teddy, Victoria tried to change the subject.

"I'm concerned about how quiet the shops have been since Christmas. Our orders for gowns are definitely down."

"I'm not surprised no one is shopping. Bert said they're even scared to take the dray horses out in case they break a leg slipping on the ice. People are daft if they take their carriages out in this. I nearly went flat on me behind twice."

"Get your soaking stockings on my fire guard to dry an' I'll fetch you a pair of mine." Milly held out her hand to take Kitty's wet stockings. "It's not just the cold that's the problem." She wrung them out on the tiled floor. "There's sewing factories sprouting up everywhere. We can't possibly compete with their prices and how quick they can churn stuff out. A lot of it's cheap rubbish, though. Seams all over the place. I don't think half of them know how to sew in a straight line."

"Even so," Victoria said, "it doesn't seem to stop the stores from stocking them. The new department store in town has racks of daywear on display. We'll have to do something if we're to survive."

"But what?" Milly shot Kitty an anxious look.

Victoria understood all of her girls desperately needed the income their jobs provided.

"I've been considering this for some time. We need to get a couple more sewing machines so everyone is using them, including Olga. She won't like it, but she'll simply have to get used to it. That way, we can stock our own larger range of day dresses."

Milly chewed her nails. "That'll help us. But if the mill shuts, there'll be hundreds of men out of work. David says if it happens, him and Sam will take to the road looking for work before they let their families freeze or starve to death. But not everyone is able to do that. Mams can't just leave their kids."

"Are things that bad at the mill?" Victoria asked. She was aware some had already lost their jobs but didn't realise things were so dire.

Milly explained how since Jarvis Erlington had died and his son, Marcus, had been left in charge, the place had gone to ruin.

"Our Sam says Mr Marcus were a decent lad, but he's in a bad way," Kitty added. "Had a fall from his horse and started taking opium for the pain. Now he's addicted. I don't care how sodding decent he were. He's made a right pig's ear of things. Putting jobs at risk. I'd like to give him a kick up the backside – that'd sort him out."

"Kitty, did Sam tell you anything else?"

"Yeah, Marcus is never at the mill these days. Spends all his time in Liverpool drinking, gambling and womanising. An' he's got into debt. Owes thousands to Mr Brakenridge from the Hall. No interest in the business at all. Some flaming folk don't deserve to be rich."

Victoria suspected his opium came from James Brakenridge. That man had a lot to answer for.

During the following weeks while Victoria put her plans for the ready-to-wear range in action, the weather deteriorated further, making matters worse for the poorer people of the town. The day before the monthly meeting of the Women's Guild, she'd asked the girls to tell her more about conditions in the town. If she was to have any chance of getting the ladies to take action, she needed ammunition. Milly had handed Victoria a cup of tea.

"Well, I don't know where to start, really. It's so blinking freezing that everyone needs their fires more than ever, but the price of coal has gone through the roof. Newspaper wrapped round yeh helps a bit, but then most folk can't even afford a paper."

Kitty settled herself in the one of Milly's armchairs. "Yeah, an' most folk use old papers to wipe themselves if they've been in the outhouse. If they're needing them to keep warm, I dread to think what they're using for the other." She held her nose to ensure Victoria got her meaning.

"She wants the facts, not your prattling, Kitty. Anyway, our Harry's got a gang of his cronies working with him. They're doing a four-mile trek with carts just to fetch sticks from the woods. He's selling them to anyone who can afford to buy them. I've warned him to treat people fair, like, 'cos he'd nick the wax outta yer ears, that one."

"Tell her about Hilda Tanner's little 'uns," Kitty put in again.

Milly raised her eyes. "I'm getting to it. The thing is, ma'am, most families have lost someone to the flu. It's mainly the old and babies dying. Hilda's had to bury three nippers in the last month. It breaks me heart to think about a mam burying her babies.

"It's no wonder people are getting ill, because even the ones who are still working can't afford food. They're having to choose between starvin' or freezing."

As Milly took a sip of her tea, Kitty jumped in.

"It makes me so mad, I could spit. I can't believe Smoky Joe has put up the price of his coal, the rotten git. But people won't forget this in a hurry. He's made a mistake if you ask me."

"Well, I for one will be looking for a new coal merchant – that type of behaviour leaves a bad taste in my mouth. Though perhaps the coal mines are charging him more," Victoria said. Everyone seemed to think only of their profit, no matter how it affected others. "What's the situation at the mill now?"

Kitty held up her hand to stop Milly from answering before her.

"First, most of the nippers have lost their jobs. They only earned pennies, but their families relied on it. Now, a lot of the less skilled women have been laid off. Some folks have lost their homes and moved in with relatives or friends. Mam's let out our parlour to a family of six.

We had lodgers before. I thought our house were crowded when we were all living at home, but they're packed in one room like sardines now.

"It stinks like it, too. Yeh get a right whiff every time they open the parlour door. She's not done it for the money, mind. We're all right, like. But she couldn't see them on the street."

"Does she have to charge them at all?"

"Aww, ma'am, yer right lovely an' all that, but yer living in a different world. Folk are poor, but they still need their dignity. The few pennies they're paying is more important to them than it is to Mam. But if our lads lose their jobs, she'll have to get the lodgers to move out, 'cos you can't have one of your own on the street."

Victoria closed her eyes. She was desperately trying not to lose her temper. She felt she was losing the battle, her blood boiling. While many of the ladies from the Women's Guild agreed with her plan, she was sickened by the those who only thought of themselves.

"It's a hard time for everyone and the more you give them, the more they'll drink," one woman said.

Just what the Guild needs, Victoria thought. Another sanctimonious, selfish member. She might be right, but as Edith had once pointed out to her, they had few other pleasures in life. Finally, she snapped.

"Children are dying of starvation while you eat your five-course meals each night and sip your sherry. The biggest challenge you've faced this winter is if it's safe for the horses to pull your carriages. Look at us all with our strong boots and fur stoles.

"At this very moment, some poor mother will be

watching her child die of influenza, knowing there's not a damn thing she can do to save it. If nothing else will get through to you, surely you can imagine how terrible that must feel."

Several of the more unsympathetic women looked ashamed and horrified, and a plan to open a soup kitchen and distribute second-hand clothing was thrashed out. But no matter how many hours Victoria put in working with the Guild, nothing seemed to be enough.

Chapter 32

It was March before the promise of an early spring brought normality to the district and Centenary Lane bustled with activity once more, orders for couture outfits pouring in. Victoria's risky experiment had proved successful. She'd been able to keep on all of her staff and had plenty of high-end ready-to-wear stock to sell as a result.

Kitty and Milly had kept her informed about the situation at the mill until one day, they brought the news that the mill was to be sold at auction. She wanted to make things better for the mill workers, so maybe this was her opportunity – though she was nervous of jumping in too quickly. She'd heard all sorts about mill conditions. Even under old Erlington, Milly had explained that workers were punished for all kinds of misdemeanours.

"You arrive even a few minutes late an' yer wages are docked. Makes no difference if yer wife died that mornin' – yer still expected to turn up on the buzzer."

Mrs Erlington had always had a complete lack of empathy for people, so it was no surprise to Victoria that her husband was the same.

"They look for any reason to dock wages. A bobbin on the floor, making too much waste, a bit of oil spilled. But it's the punishments they dish out to the kids that gets me. The overseers think nowt of using the strap. When our Sam started work there, he were a piecer . . ."

"What's a piecer?"

"They have to take pieces of broken cotton and rub them together until they're joined. I know that don't sound so bad, but their hands get red raw and if they get blood on the cotton, they get the strap. An' they're expected to be grateful they don't get the sack – 'cos if they work too slow or fall asleep 'cos they're knackered, that's what happens."

How does Margaret Erlington sleep at night! Victoria couldn't believe the woman could close her eyes to all this. She must know about it.

"As for accidents, we've heard all sorts over the years. Shuttles flying outta looms, knocking people off their feet. Years back, one of our Cora's mates got scalped there. They've not got all the guards they should have on the machines an' some of the ones they have got are broke. Folk are too scared of losing their jobs to say owt. It's all about how much flippin' profit can be made for the likes of the Erlingtons."

Regardless of the challenges it might bring, Victoria felt compelled to buy the mill.

The following morning, before there was time to let doubts creep in, Victoria called at Edward's office.

"Victoria. Is everything all right?"

"Yes, yes."

"Are Sean and Bridie well?"

She knew she should ask about his wife and daughter, but instead, she blurted, "Quite well, thank you. I'll get straight to the point, if you don't mind. What do you think about me buying Erlington Mill?"

She could see him mulling it over. Would he approve? His approval was important to her. Even if she didn't care to admit it, she was still in love with him.

As Edward read the details she handed over, his face changed, his jaw set, a slight frown lying above his blue eyes.

"I'd heard Erlingtons was for sale. It's always been one of the most profitable in town – Jarvis made sure of that. It would, however, be a difficult undertaking for anyone unless they were extremely experienced in the cotton trade," he added. "Is there any particular reason why you're considering it?"

Victoria thought carefully before replying.

"It would mainly be for Sean. I doubt he'll want to run a dress shop. I'd also like to make sure that the workers get their jobs back, perhaps improve conditions."

Edward got to his feet. "Let me make some enquiries. Find out just how bad the situation is with Marcus and what the mill is expected to fetch. Leave it with me. I'll be in touch soon."

Outside, she stood in front of his offices for a moment. She'd seen him several times now and he'd shown no signs of wanting to renew their friendship. Her feelings were inappropriate – she needed to get a grip of herself.

The following Monday morning, Kitty brought the post through to Victoria's office.

"I was just on me way back from the privy, when I saw the postie."

As Victoria took the letters, she noticed Kitty's eyes were bloodshot and her face puffy.

"Kitty, are you all right?"

"I'm middling, thanks, ma'am." She moved towards the office door.

"Kitty, I can see you've been crying. If you don't feel you can talk to me, why don't you pop and see Milly or Agnes, get yourself a hot drink?"

"Please don't say anything to them, ma'am. I've just been rowing with me mam, that's all. If yeh say anything, they'll interfere, and this is summat I've gotta sort on me own."

"If there's anything I can do, Kitty, please come and see me. Day or night, mind."

Kitty assured her there was nothing she needed and went back to the workroom. Victoria was tempted to push further, but everyone was entitled to their privacy. Hopefully, Milly would whittle it out of her before long.

She turned her attention to the letters. One wasn't intended for Victoria – it was for Lydia from Madeleine Forbes. The last letter Lydia had received had informed her that Madeleine's husband had passed away. Madeleine was now in the process of selling his English estate. Before long, Victoria would lose her friend – to Italy and to Madeleine. Although she'd miss her, she was glad Lydia would be away from that awful man's clutches.

Recently, Harry Gibbs had told Milly that James Brakenridge had said he was a bright lad and would go far as long as he did what he was told without asking too many questions. Milly had expressed her concern that it wouldn't take much to get Harry on the wrong track.

"He could nick the fleas off a dog without it noticing. Lord knows what he'll get up to with encouragement," she said.

Of all the Gibbs children Victoria had employed, only Harry had made her uncomfortable. Weasel-like in both looks and manner, she'd always felt he was watching her, gathering information. Harry wasn't much older than Sean. He'd left school at ten and now worked at Faredene Hall. She didn't like to think of any of Milly's family working for James Brakenridge.

She'd been dismayed to realise she'd been the reason he got the job. After Bert took a full-time job at the brewery, a succession of young lads took his place delivering her gowns. As each one took full-time employment, she'd had to find a replacement. When Milly asked if Harry could have the job, Victoria had been pleased to help the family by giving him the work. That was until he delivered a gown to Lydia.

At the time, James just happened to have an errand he needed running and he sent the boy. Pleased with how promptly he returned with his package, Brakenridge had started using him regularly and eventually offered him a job as a gofer, leaving Victoria to find another delivery boy. Knowing how James made a large portion of his wealth, her real concern was that Harry might get drawn into the same way of life.

Without relaying what she knew, she'd voiced her concerns to Edith about Harry's employer on many an occasion, but her reaction had been to shrug and say, "Work's work. He can't afford to turn his nose up at owt."

At times, she'd despaired at Edith Gibbs.

She returned her attention to the post. The last letter was from Edward's clerk, requesting that she visit his office, so the next day, she found herself sitting in front of him. She felt nervous as she watched him reading papers on his desk and he said nothing for some time.

"I've spoken to the auctioneer about the mill. There's

a lot of interested parties and James Brakenridge is one of them. From what I can gather, he only wants the machinery. He plans to put it in a mill he and a partner are building in Manchester alongside the Bridgewater Canal. I also heard he's been trying to force young Erlington to settle his debts.

"He wanted the machinery in payment, but the young man insists he'll sell up rather than let Brakenridge take everything. There is no love lost between them. Marcus has lost his way, but he's decent underneath it all."

Victoria was horrified. She was more determined than ever to buy it – there was no way she could let that man profit from the mill closure.

"What about the workers? They've got mouths to feed. Does he have no use for the building?"

"No. It would seem he likes to keep most of his business dealings away from the town. I suspect he doesn't like people knowing what he's up to, as it would ruin the genial image he likes to portray around Faredene.

"He'll probably sell the site. I'm sure he couldn't care less about the workers. But then that shouldn't surprise you, surely. The word is that he hopes to equip his new mill on the cheap and eliminate the competition."

"Well then he must be stopped!" Victoria's voice rose. "If I don't buy it, someone else surely will."

Edward shook his head sadly. "He's used his influence with the banks so nobody can get finance. What we *have* got in our favour is that to pay the full value of the mill wouldn't make good business sense for him, if it's just the machinery he's after. He needs to get it as cheaply as possible."

"Do you think I should try to outbid him?"

Edward looked at his watch. "I'll answer that later. A

friend of mine, Matthew Clarkson, will be joining us in a minute. He's been living in New Orleans for years running his own cotton plantation. I'd like you to meet him."

Her head was filling with questions, but she didn't have time to ask, as the clerk showed Matthew in, who bowed slightly. He was lean with strong features, his face tanned, his fair hair long and sun-bleached.

"Right, let me get straight to the point. Victoria, you and Matthew are both interested in buying Erlington Mill."

Victoria was aghast. Surely Edward could have warned her she had competition.

"Matthew would be an ideal business partner for you."

"No offence, Mr Clarkson, but I don't know you at all. How can we possibly work together?"

She knew that she looked cross, but what did Edward expect? She had to be blunt, even if they thought she was rude. He should never have sprung this on her.

"Edward knows both of us and he believes we would work well together," Matthew replied calmly.

"The mill was supposed to be an investment for my son at the same time as helping the workers. You may just be out to make money, for all I know. How do I know you won't just reduce the workforce or cut corners or safety measures to increase profits?"

Edward raised his blue eyes. "If you would just let me explain, Victoria. You're leaping ahead. Before Matthew went to America, he managed some of his uncle's mills for twelve years, but when he objected to workers' pay cuts and bad conditions, his uncle dismissed him. He has some capital, but Brakenridge has made sure that the banks won't lend him anything for this venture."

Edward could see Victoria was beginning to smile.

"Matthew is extremely resourceful. He purchased a run-down plantation in Louisiana. He made a great success of it and has now sold it. His wife's father also owns a plantation as well as a cotton export business in New Orleans, which will allow Matthew to negotiate a good price for raw cotton."

Victoria's mind was churning as she tried to take in all the information. She still had some misgivings about her own ability to run a mill. Her shops had been successful, but this was a much bigger venture. Perhaps this was the solution.

They talked for most of the afternoon, refreshed by frequent cups of tea from Edward's clerk. Matthew produced references from an American bank along with a comprehensive business plan, which included predicted profits, investment costs and an estimated realistic purchase price. He'd certainly done his homework and was clearly serious.

The more she heard, the more she liked Matthew and could see the advantages of a partnership. It would put a stop to Brakenridge's plan. It would also enable her to keep a large part of her capital. Matthew obviously shared her concern for mill workers' pay and conditions, from what Edward said. Then there was his contacts in New Orleans for the supply of raw cotton at a reduced price, potentially boosting the mill profits. As the auction was in two days' time, Victoria suggested they all view the mill the following day before making any final decisions.

When the auctioneer escorted them on a tour of the mill, Victoria was amazed at the size of the place. She soon realised it was hard and physical labour, bending, stooping, stretching, fetching, carrying, scurrying under machines – even worse than she'd imagined. The noise was deafening, and she was overawed by the dust and the stifling heat. The unceasing, unrelenting clash of the machines, hammers knocking shuttles back and forth, huge creaking framework, left her with a headache.

She realised she must have been mad to think that she could have managed it on her own, as it was far more involved than she'd imagined, but then she could see the possibilities for improvement. Noisy and dangerous, conditions would have to be improved. Starting with better wages, reduced hours, education for the children. They could even take apprentices, teach them a trade. This was her chance to help others.

On the day of the auction, Victoria slipped in at the back of the room. The auction began and bidding was brisk at first then tapered off as the price climbed. James Brakenridge was on the front row, looking belligerently at every new bidder. Harry was at his side wearing a cheap but new jacket.

Eventually, there was only Matthew and James still bidding. When Matthew topped his next bid, Brakenridge looked as if he'd combust. The auctioneer looked for a further bid, but Brakenridge shook his head. As he got up, he thrust his catalogue at Harry. Glaring at Matthew, he tripped over his chair as he stalked out.

"Congratulations, Vicky!" Edward said as he embraced her.

She looked around in embarrassment, but people were intent on bidding for the next lot and didn't appear to have noticed. Only Harry, who was following in James Brakenridge's wake, took in the scene.

When they left the auction room, Edward proposed that they dine at Latimers in the evening for a celebratory dinner, suggesting his driver pick her up at seven.

Chapter 33

Victoria was sitting at her dressing table putting the finishing touches to her face and hair. She frowned as she realised Edward might be bringing his wife along to their celebration. But when Sean came into the bedroom to announce Edward's arrival, she felt the tension leaving her shoulders – Sean hadn't said Edward and his wife.

"You look beautiful, Mother. A black satin gown bejewelled with jet-black beads, I believe," he teased.

She stared at him wide-eyed. "Since when did you know the difference between satin and a sack, or jet beads and marbles?"

"The amount of time I've spent in your workroom, I'd have had to be blind *and* deaf not to know. Would you like me to fasten your necklace?"

"Please."

"And these, I believe, madam, are diamonds, which match perfectly with your earrings, completing your ensemble."

"And you, young man, are growing up to be far too handsome and charming and cheeky for your own good."

"I know you're celebrating the purchase of the mill, but is there any particular reason for wearing your finest gown? Could it be that spring is in the air, or is it love?"

She loved his playful moods.

When they entered the parlour, Edward was alone, reading documents. He looked up and smiled, saying briskly, "Perhaps you would cast your eye over the contracts before signing. If we get the formalities out of the way, we can concentrate on our celebration."

He'd not even complimented her on how she looked. So much for all the effort she'd made.

It was after midnight when they bid Matthew goodbye and Edward helped her to his carriage. She'd drank far more than usual and was feeling light-headed and giddy.

"Come on, madam." Edward caught her elbow as she almost tripped. "Let's get you inside before someone sees you tipsy and you cause a scandal."

"You're teasing me! I've missed that."

"Have you? Really?"

"More than you'd know."

Once inside, he closed the carriage door. His face had become serious. Turning to her, he began to speak haltingly.

"Vicky, I've tried to stay away from you. I told myself there was no reason for your feelings about marriage to have changed. But I can't help myself. I've been going crazy. I need you to hear me out.

"I should never have married Fionn. I was in love with you from the first time I saw you. I know you just want friendship, but I need to tell you that my feelings for you have not changed. If anything, they have grown over the years – my marriage was doomed from the beginning. I have to live with that guilt." His voice faltered.

"All we seemed to do was argue. Then Fionn would sulk for days. Nothing I could do would snap her out of it. Then three years ago, she announced she was leaving. She'd already contacted her parents and made all the arrangements. She took Katie with her and hasn't allowed me to see my daughter since." He hung his head.

Had he really just told her he still wanted her? And that his marriage had ended three years ago . . . She hoped the wine hadn't caused her to imagine it all.

She put her head against his and rested it there a moment as he held her hand. Then he twisted towards her and tilted her chin with his hand. His mouth sought hers and he kissed her tentatively at first. She noticed he smelled of cologne and wine, and she giggled then hiccupped. His kiss became more urgent and the carriage came to a halt outside Centenary House far too soon.

"I'm sorry. I shouldn't have done that. Even if you wanted to be with me, it's too late. I can no longer offer you marriage."

Edward helped her down and escorted her to the door.

"Oh, but you should, you sweet man. Don't you get it? I don't care about that, Edward. We've wasted too much time already because of me. I need you to come in a moment, please. There's something I need to tell you. Something I should have told you a long time ago."

She led him into the parlour. Her hands were trembling as she poured them a drink. The room was cold, but it wasn't the temperature that made her shiver – it was the thought of telling Edward the thing she'd never spoken about at length to anyone.

Edward accepted his brandy and stared with shock as she emptied her sherry glass.

"Surely, Vicky, it can't be that bad?"

"It's going to be difficult for me to talk about, but I

hope when I've finished you'll understand why I refused your proposal of marriage, even though I love you deeply."

"But I already know about Sean – and I told you it didn't matter."

"It's not that. You need to let me finish. It's time I told you the truth."

She joined him on the sofa but sat on the edge as though ready to get up again at any minute and flee. Slowly, her voice catching, tears welling, she told him about her mother's life at the hands of her father. Everything spilled out. About the times when she'd seen her mother afraid, the violence. And the countless times when she'd heard her mother cry. She confided in him about her father's drinking, the parties, the women in his room. How he disgusted her. Then finally, she spoke about the night her mother died.

"At the time, I couldn't tell if he'd hit her and she fell, or if she was running away from him. I will never forget her blank, staring eyes.

"Then following Patrick's death, I found out that she'd killed herself. Bridie didn't mean to say anything, but I knew this time that what I was hearing was the truth. It wasn't merely the ramblings of an old woman. Either way, he'd killed her spirit long before that night."

Edward took her hands in his. He looked stunned. But there was also something else.

"Vicky, that's terrible. But you can't think *I* could behave like that. Surely you're not afraid of me."

Victoria pulled her hands out of his grasp, twisting them in her lap, ashamed. She *had* believed that of him. Not just him, but men in general.

"You are a wonderful, kind man, but I must admit that I did worry that you might change if we were married. Bridie told me my father wasn't always violent and that he'd loved my mother."

"I wish you'd told me before – given me a chance to convince you to trust me. We could have been married."

Victoria hung her head now. "Edward, I haven't finished explaining. I need you to hear me out."

He stiffened. "But I can help you to trust me."

"Please, Edward, let me talk. This is difficult enough as it is." She blushed at the thought of the conversation she was about to have.

Edward nodded woodenly and she turned her attention to the day that had set the course of her life.

"When I was younger, Bridie sought the advice of a doctor because my body wasn't functioning regularly as a woman's should." She paused to see if he'd got the gist of where she was heading. "He said I'd probably never be able to have children. So you see, I could never have expected a man to marry me. It pains me to say it, but I'm barren. I could never deprive a good man, you, of the chance to become a father."

"Well, I'm already a father. Not that I've done a good job of it. Fionn has made it very clear she doesn't want me to see Katie. Every time I try, she makes an excuse. If I go to Ireland, I find Fionn and Katie have suddenly gone elsewhere. So, you must believe me when I say I don't care about having more children."

"Oh, Edward. I'm so sorry. That's so unfair to keep you from your child when you've done nothing wrong."

"In *her* eyes, I have. She wants to punish me. She says I've never really loved her and shouldn't have married her. I can't really argue with that, but I feel she's harming Katie, too, by keeping us apart."

"Are you sure you don't feel the need to have another child?"

"Yes. Will you please just stop worrying about your ability to give me a child."

"My . . . my body did eventually begin to function, just not every month – although I can't be certain that it improved my ability to conceive. In any case, I'm thirty-eight now, so it's too late, anyway."

Victoria couldn't believe she'd managed to talk about all the things that had plagued her for years.

"All I want is you, Victoria. I have wasted too many years with the wrong woman. All along, it should have been you."

"I know we won't be able to be married in church, but I want to be your wife. If you'll have me. And if Fionn will release you, of course. You're hardly getting my best years. I am in every sense of the word an old maid – I may disappoint you." She felt her colour rising again.

"Vicky, my love, I promise you, neither of us will come to regret it. I will do everything in my power to make you happy." Edward kissed her gently, as though afraid to scare her off. Then he gently pulled her in towards him. "I've waited this long to get you in my clutches. There is no rush."

Victoria dressed and looked at her reflection in the long mirror, expecting to see a transformation that would match her feelings of having lost a great burden, but no such luck. She just looked tired with dark smudges under her eyes. It might be spring, but she was no spring chicken. Disappointed, she went to her office.

She'd planned to spend the morning cutting out an intricate design for a wedding dress but was unable to concentrate and instead shuffled papers on her desk, counting the minutes until Edward's return. At eleven, Milly popped her head round the office door.

"Mr Caldwell's here to see you, madam. I've shown him into your parlour."

"Please tell him I'll be through shortly." Her voice sounded unusually high.

She checked her hair for the tenth time that morning and looked down at her new day dress in pale lavender linen. It would have to do. She felt jumpy and uneasy, beads of perspiration having gathered on her back. What if he'd changed his mind?

As she joined Edward in the parlour, her nervousness disappeared almost instantly as she saw the look on his face. He was as worried as she was.

"Vicky. Is it true? Are we really going to be together at last?"

"If you still want me."

"Vicky, my darling, maybe this will convince you."

Finally, she knew the excitement of really being kissed, sending a quiver down her spine.

The following day, Victoria and Matthew took a tour of the mill.

"This machine blends what's left of the raw cotton prior to spinning, combining expensive fibres with less costly ones," he explained, wafting tiny fibres released into the air from in front of his face.

Victoria discreetly tried to remove a piece of fluff from her lips. Working here every day, she realised they must swallow mounds of the stuff. It couldn't be good for them.

"So what do you think, Victoria?" He looked at her expectantly.

"To be honest, it's loud, hot and overwhelming." She shrugged – she saw no point in hiding how she felt.

"You really don't have to worry. I'll handle most of the day-to-day running of things. I've written to my father-in-law, Claude Dupont, to make arrangements to replenish our raw cotton from his plantation. I'll get us a good price, I'm certain."

Victoria could only nod, having no idea what a good price was.

By the time the tour was over, her ears were ringing. Even at half capacity, the noise from the spinning and weaving rooms was deafening. She was feeling slightly overwhelmed by it all, deeply grateful she had a knowledgeable business partner. He'd even agreed to change the name of the mill to Centenary Mill.

As they were about to climb in the carriage, she stopped short.

"Matthew, the people waiting at the gate. They must have heard we're here. News travels fast. I'm sure they'll be wanting to know if there will be more jobs again soon. Can you reassure them, please?"

"Leave it with me." Matthew walked up to the gate, speaking to the people closest. "You can get the word out. We'll be getting production up to full capacity within a few months, starting by taking people back on by the end of the month."

As he walked back to the carriage, a murmur spread through the crowd, rapidly gaining pace and getting louder. Victoria could see women crying openly. Even a few of the men appeared to be struggling to contain their emotions. Above the general chatter, she heard one saying, "Thank Christ for that! If we can last until then, we may be able to keep the roof over our heads." The mill might not be somewhere Victoria wanted to be every day, but at least she could at last make a difference to people's lives.

Despite wanting to spend the afternoon with Edward, Victoria felt she had to get home to Bridie. There was a time when Bridie had guarded her place in the house with all the ferocity of a bulldog, but these days she no longer appeared to care. Even Sean, who had the most patience with her, found it difficult to communicate with her at times.

The old woman seemed to have lost touch with reality and had taken to staying in her bedroom for hours on end. When she did leave her room, she often remained in her nightgown, unwashed until coaxed to do so. Despite Agnes making Bridie's favourite dishes, she ate little. She was wasting away and it was as though she'd somehow forgotten how to do basic things. There were moments of clarity, but they were becoming fewer.

Doctor Farrell had said the deterioration in her condition would continue. It broke Victoria's heart to see her fading away. Just last week, Bridie had asked Sean who he was. The boy had thought she was joking at first until he realised his beloved Bridie really didn't know him, at which point he'd rushed from the room on the pretext of having to do homework, but she'd heard him sobbing. She'd wanted to go to him, but he was trying desperately to be regarded as a man in everything he did these days and she felt that to see him crying would embarrass him.

Victoria took a cup of tea in for Bridie. She was sitting

in her easy chair, her gnarled and twisted fingers clasped on her knee, staring unseeing into the distance. She didn't appear to notice her arrival and it was only when the cup was placed in front of her that she looked up.

"Victoria, where have you been?"

"I've been out, Bridie, with Edward."

"Victoria, where have you been?"

Victoria realised Bridie probably wouldn't understand what she wanted to tell her. Days where she was barely aware of her surroundings and unable to hold a conversation were becoming more frequent. But she felt the need to tell her anyway – she was her family.

"I have something to tell you, Bridie. Edward and I are going to be married. Isn't that wonderful news!"

She saw no benefit in mentioning the difficulties of Edward still being married. If Bridie had been herself, of sound mind, she'd have been raging about Catholic marriage being for life and about eternal damnation.

"Are you pleased for me?" Victoria stopped talking, hoping for a reaction.

"Victoria! You're here, lass. Where have you been?" the old woman asked.

Victoria kissed her white hair and left the room, feeling deeply saddened.

When Sean arrived home from school later that day, as always, he went straight to the workroom on some pretext to find Kitty. Victoria was waiting for him.

"Oh, Mother," he said, but he was looking at Kitty, who appeared oblivious as she concentrated on her machine.

When she reached the end of a seam, Kitty looked up. Victoria noticed she'd lost the light usually present in her eyes as she smiled patiently at Sean. It was hard to believe she was only six years older than him. Kitty had always been older than her years, having been expected to care for Teddy since she was five, working at eleven. But even despite the harsh realities of her life, she was like Milly – generally optimistic. Only not today.

"Tatty Head! Have yeh come to give me a hand making this frock? Maybe whisk me an' Olga away to Blackpool on a little jaunt."

"I'll take you to Blackpool or London or even Paris one day, if you want me to, Kitty."

"I could probably come along as yer wife's maid. Hey, that'd be all right. I can just see me, a swanky ladies' maid. I'd have to watch me p's and q's then, though."

"I'll buy you dresses and jewels and *make* you a lady."

My goodness! Victoria thought. He's serious. She was both surprised and slightly alarmed. She knew he held a candle for the girl – she just hadn't realised how much. She'd thought it was just a crush.

"Well, that's right kind, but I think your wife might object."

"No, Kitty, I've told you before, it's *you* I'm going to marry."

Kitty laughed, but there was a sadness Victoria hadn't detected before.

"Gentlemen like you can never really care for a girl like me. When the time comes, you'll find yourself a lovely lady like yer mam." Kitty sounded tired.

"I will *not*! One day you'll stop treating me like a child and take me seriously."

"Sean, will you come with me, please." Victoria led Sean into the parlour.

"Please don't tell me off, Mother. I'm *not* a child. I know how I feel and you won't change my mind."

"Sean, I'm not going to tell you off. I want to talk to you about something. But while we're on the subject, please don't embarrass Kitty like that again. No matter how grown up you feel, you're still a child. More importantly, she's right. You *are* a gentleman. You can't marry someone like Kitty, and she knows it. It wouldn't be right. Besides, she's far too old for you."

"You've always said that Bridie, Milly, Kitty and Agnes are like family." He waved his hand, emphasising each name. "Now they're just staff, are they?" he asked stubbornly.

Victoria ignored his question.

"I wanted to tell you some news, but I didn't want it to be like this," she sighed.

"What is it?" he said petulantly.

"Edward and I are friends again. One day we hope to marry, but I have no idea when that will be, if at all. I hope in time he'll be able to get a divorce. If he can, we will be free to marry. But I could never marry someone you didn't like. You do know that, don't you?"

"I like Edward a great deal – he's really nice. I think he'll make a good husband for you. Just a minute . . . Isn't he nine years older than you? Which completely undermines your argument about Kitty and me. Perhaps we can have a double wedding," he teased.

She couldn't get used to his adolescent mood swings over the past couple of months. Nor could she tell right now if he'd suddenly cheered up because he was genuinely happy for her, or because he really believed she'd lost the argument about Kitty. She considered telling him it was different when the man was older, lots of men married younger women, but decided against ruining their evening. Instead, she reassured herself that Kitty would keep Sean in his place.

Chapter 34

A couple of weeks later, Kitty was sitting between Agnes and Victoria at the kitchen table while Milly paced the floor in front of them. Agnes fiddled with the cold cup of tea in front of her. Kitty was sitting with her head down, tears dropping freely onto the table. Victoria passed Kitty her handkerchief and placed an arm around her shoulder. Milly stopped pacing and gripped the table.

"Kitty, I feel like a right bitch for pecking yer head. But I can't let this go. Summat's troubling you an' I need to find out what it is so I can help. I tried last week but gave up 'cos you were keeping schtum. But I'll not let this drop now – not a second time.

"Mam's been round shouting about you bringing shame on the family. She said you two have had another blazing row. She thinks yer courting on the quiet. She said you've got a posh new frock an' all. Aping yer betters, she calls it. An' one of the neighbours told Mam she saw a gent getting out of a carriage outside our house. Who the bloody hell d'you know with a carriage?"

Kitty just stared at Milly, her eyes filling once more.

"Mam says yer messing about with a married man. Is she right?"

Kitty nodded.

"Aww, love, any man would be attracted to you. Why do you want to be going with a married man? You could get any fella. All the lads are after yeh. I can understand you wanting someone decent – not from the Rows. Mam says Albert Nelson, the new landlord at The Tanner's Arms, is right taken with yeh. And he's a smashing fella. Got money, as well."

Tears rolled down Kitty's face.

"Are yeh in the family way?"

Again, Kitty nodded.

"Dear God, Kitty, what have you done?" Milly faltered, her eyes glued to Kitty.

Victoria gasped.

"Don't start lecturing me, Milly. I've been stupid, I know that." Tears were streaming, her voice defiant. "You can't tell anyone, Milly. Definitely not Mam. If she knows I'm up the spout, everyone will know. I'm not worried about me, but she'll let it slip. An' David and Sam – well, they'll feel like they've got to tackle him."

"Maybe he needs tackling, Kitty. He can't just leave you in a mess," Agnes said as she smoothed Kitty's hair from her face.

"Agnes is right, Kitty," Victoria added.

"You don't understand, none of yeh. I didn't know what he was really like until it were too late. He's a gentleman, but he's no better than the ones he has doing his dirty work for him."

"Who is he?" Milly asked.

"I'm not telling yeh. There's no point. When I told him I were pregnant, he just slapped me and threw some money at me to pay to get rid of it. But I couldn't do it."

"Aww, Kitty, yer gorgeous, but no gent's going to be

interested in the likes of us. They only want one thing. Look, you can trust us. We won't tell a soul. Will we?" Milly said, pacing once more.

Kitty choked back another sob.

"Milly's right, Kitty. We won't say anything to anyone. We just want to help you," Victoria cajoled.

Kitty plucked at her skirt under the table.

"I know if there's anyone I can trust, it's you three and that you'll help me if yeh can, but I still can't tell you who it is. You don't need to know."

"We won't shout. Will we, Milly?" Agnes stared at Milly until she answered, giving her "the look".

"No, I won't shout again, love. So, how far gone are you?"

"It's due November."

"So you're three months gone?" Milly asked.

"Yeah, but I don't want to kill it. I thought about killin' meself, though. Chucking meself in the canal. But I'm too scared and it would kill the baby, too. But I can't keep it, either. I'm not ready to be a mam. Maybe if I can go away I can have it adopted. People who can't have them still want babies, don't they?" Suddenly looking younger than her years, her lip quivered. "I'm frightened."

"No one's going to ask you to kill your baby, Kitty, don't worry about that," Agnes said.

Victoria tried desperately to think of something helpful to say, but nothing came to her. What a mess.

Milly walked to the window. Finally, she turned back to the table.

"Kitty, are you absolutely certain you don't want to keep the baby? Because if you do, I'll help yeh. Me an' Agnes will deal with Mam and whoever else feels they have the right to stick their two penn'orth in yer business."

"I'm sure, Milly. I'm not bothered what people say about me. But I don't want it being called a bastard. Life's hard enough as it is without that stigma, as well."

"Then if yer certain, I'll have it. Bob an' me'll adopt yer baby," Milly said decisively.

Victoria and Agnes gasped.

"Milly, don't be stupid. Have you gone mad? Yeh can't just take her baby. What will Bob say? I hate to break it to you, but he might not want to bring up another man's baby."

"No, Agnes, I've not gone mad. Bob will understand. I know my Bob. If it makes me happy, he'll do it. Besides, he wants a kid nearly as much as I do. He tries to hide it because he doesn't want to hurt me, but I know."

Milly waited. When Kitty didn't respond, she ploughed on.

"Kitty, if you want to keep yer baby, I'll help you in any way I can. You don't have to get rid of it. But if I adopt it, I'll love it like it's me own. Like I love you. Unless you think it will be too difficult for you seeing it all the time – then I'll understand."

"I can't imagine a better mam for it. So yeah, if yer sure that's what you want."

"I do. Definitely. We're so close, it'll feel like mine. And we don't want it going to strangers."

Victoria's mind was whirling. They weren't taking time to think this through – they were jumping in with both feet. But then, isn't that what she did with Sean?

"If yer sure, Milly. At least I'd always know it were loved an' looked after if it were wi' you, 'cos you're not like me. You were made to be a mam."

"There's only one more thing. You *have* to tell me who the father is. I don't want to spend all me life worried about him or her falling in love and marrying their brother or sister one day."

"All right . . . But don't be mad."

Milly and Victoria exchanged glances.

"It's Mr Brakenridge from Faredene Hall, so I guess girl or boy, it's coming from decent stock on at least one side, anyway."

Milly and Agnes were both wide-eyed.

"Oh, dear God." The words were out before Victoria could stop them.

"But, Kitty, he's an old man! What *were* you thinking?" The anger in Milly's voice was clear.

"See, that's why I didn't want to tell youse – I knew you'd shout. It weren't all my fault! But please don't ask me owt else. I know I've been stupid. Let's just leave it at that."

Victoria struggled to hide her shock and dismay. "We're really sorry, Kitty. It's just I-I don't understand. How come you even managed to meet again? You left the Hall! I gave you the job so you could get away from him. How the devil did you get involved with him, Kitty?"

"I didn't want to talk about it, but I can't stand you all lookin' at me like that. So I'll bloody tell you." Kitty pushed her chair back from the table. "I weren't 'involved' with him. Not really.

"He called at Mam's one Saturday night, looking for our Harry. He had an urgent errand for him. But only me an' Teddy were in. He were surprised to see me but remembered me from up at the Hall when I scratched the footman. He were ever so nice to me and right kind to

Teddy. Said I were the prettiest lass in Faredene. Well, all the lads say stuff like that, don't they, but the way he said it were different somehow."

Victoria knew only too well how charming he could be. She'd almost fallen for him herself.

"After that night, he called again a few of times on a Saturday night while Mam an' the lads were at the pub. He came up with all kinds of excuses, like he brought Teddy toffee once. Teddy loved it.

"He said it were a real shame about the way Teddy was and maybe he could help him in some way. At first, he just sat talking to me, like a normal person, not the owner of the Hall. He were really interested in me, honest."

"He was interested all right, just not in what you had to say," Milly interrupted.

"Just shut up and stop interrupting. Yeh wanted to know, so let me finish telling yeh. Anyways, one night he brought me a new dress and told me to put it on. I said no at first, but he were right hurt. And, aww, you should have seen the dress. Honest to God, it would have made a princess green with envy.

"It were like the ones we make here. Not the ready-to-wear – the fancy ones. I thought, this is yer chance, Kitty, girl. Just once in yer life, you can have a posh frock like the ones yeh make for other women. So I said yes and popped upstairs to try it on.

"When I came down, Teddy were gone. Brakenridge had given him money to go and get some sweets."

Victoria was seething. The man was so manipulative!

"Anyway, that was when the dirty old git started sayin' he wanted to stick his gherkin in me. Well, that's not the exact words he used." She laughed nervously.

"I kept saying no. He got angry with me. Said I'd possessed him, driven him mad wi' desire. I told him I ain't possessed no one. But I kept wondering if I'd egged him on, like. I still said no. I weren't having none of it." She stopped talking and scrubbed her wet face with her sleeve.

"Could yeh not just have kicked him out?" Agnes asked.

"Don't talk bloody daft, our Agnes. You've seen the size of her. What chance would she have against a big fella like that?" Milly said scornfully.

More tears spilled over as Kitty said, "The thing is, he were a lot stronger than me. I tried to get away, really I did, but he'd locked the blasted door. He pulled me back by the hair an' shoved me over the table. Pressed me head onto it. And that's when it happened.

"Part of me just wanted it over before Teddy got back. I didn't want him walking in and seeing that randy sod's hairy backside. When he'd finished, he said it were my fault it happened and I shouldn't have led him on."

"Did the neighbours not hear and fetch help?" Victoria asked.

"No. I realised afterwards that he'd once asked me about the neighbours and I told him they all went to the pub with me mam an' the rest every Saturday night."

Victoria kneeled in front of Kitty and pulled the sobbing girl into her arms.

"Now you listen to me. Mr Brakenridge is an evil man. Nothing that happened was your fault. You were raped. You must believe that. That man is a bloody foul swine. Don't let him destroy your life. You must keep away from him in future, do you hear me?"

It was some time before Kitty's sobbing had subsided enough for her to speak again.

"I don't think I've ever heard you swear before. It's really got yer dander up, ain't it?" She gave a weak grin.

"As you say, it's definitely got my dander up."

Victoria kissed Kitty's hair as she had done when she was little. Hatred gripped her. He'd used the same techniques on Kitty as he'd tried on her, flattering her, pretending to be interested in her. The man was a fiend – he'd even feigned interest in Teddy. She thanked God Lydia had a plan to escape from him.

"Have you seen him since you told him you're carrying his child?" Victoria asked, her hand held to her throat.

"He stopped coming round after that. But when I knew I were having a baby, I went to see him. He went mad. Said I had to get rid of it. Said he didn't want any of his bastards roaming around Faredene."

"Oh, Kitty. You're such a brave girl. We'll look after you. You'll be all right, won't she, Milly?" Victoria gestured with her hand for Milly to speak up.

"Yes, Kitty, love. Of course we'll look after you. We need a plan, though, so no one twigs. I want them to think the baby's mine."

The others nodded, waiting to see where Milly's plan was heading.

"I'll need to be getting a bit fatter each month. Kitty, can you make me a kind of pouch to wear under me skirt? One where I can pad it out a bit more each month."

"Bloody hell, Milly, yer getting the best end of this deal, all ways. A baby without having to push it out and now you need to get fat. Hardly seems fair when I need to stay thin with a kid growing in me belly. If I were you, I'd just eat a pile of our Agnes' scones every day."

"Aww, that's the first time you've joked properly in weeks."

"Who's bloody joking!"

"Come on, be serious, now. Bob will be home soon and we still need a plan. We only get one chance at this."

"Sorry. You're right. But I'm serious – I'm really worried about how I'll hide me belly. If I'm the size of a house, people will get wise."

"Simple! You need a corset," Victoria said. "I'm reliably informed by Lydia that it's how ladies hide their pregnancies in similar situations. She's hinted at a few ladies around here who have had to do so."

"Hey, I'll be like Mrs Hornby-Smythe, shrinking as me corsets are pulled in." Kitty mimicked the action by sucking in her cheeks.

"Anyway, if you think about it, you could hardly tell Mam and our Cora were pregnant when they was carrying, so I'm sure we'll get away with it," Milly added, sounding excited but nervous about what they were about to embark on.

Victoria's mind was reeling. James – the father of Kitty's baby! She could feel her face contort as she thought about him. And Milly, finally to be a mother . . . Would this child suffer if it was ever to discover its parentage? Should she be stopping them? Would they have managed to stop her from taking Sean in? Not a chance!

They sat for the next hour ironing out the details. Edith would be told Kitty had indeed been seeing a married man but that it was over and that was why she'd been upset. Apart from Bob, there was no need to tell anyone else anything at this stage. Milly had, however, expressed her concern that they'd involved Victoria in their deception, fearful she'd disapprove of keeping a baby that wasn't hers. It was on the tip of her tongue to tell Milly her own secret. She could so easily have told her right then that she completely understood. But even though she was itching to do so, she stopped herself just in time – she couldn't risk Sean finding out.

Chapter 35

As Victoria finished her slice of toast, Sean picked up his cap ready to leave for school.

"Are you going to the mill today, Mother?"

"Yes, I don't like to leave it all to Matthew. He's there at six and doesn't leave until late."

"He enjoys it. Besides, it's almost summer, so at least he'll see some daylight, even if he leaves late," Sean laughed.

"I just wish I could do more."

"He said you did a great job reorganising the office. He hates all that paperwork."

"That's nice of him, but I also realise that he's the brains behind it. The increase in production and improved morale are down to him."

"I help him as much as I can. You know I go most days after school."

"I'm aware of that and so is Edith, as she's the one who has to get the grease out of all of your clothes."

She was proud of how interested he'd become in the mill since she'd explained that part of the reason for her investment was for his future. Her one concern was that she wanted him to continue his education, while Sean was adamant he wanted to start work as soon as possible.

She hoped his decision wasn't part of his silly obsession with Kitty.

"Ma'am, you need to come now! It's Bridie. She's had a funny turn. Shall I go for Doctor Farrell?" Agnes hesitated in the doorway.

Victoria and Sean tore upstairs to Bridie's room. Bridie's eyes were glazed, her breathing laboured.

"Is she going to be all right, Mother?" he asked.

"I don't know. But I've already explained to you that she will leave us one day before long." She could see how bad Bridie looked and had no intention of giving him false hope.

After Doctor Farrell had examined Bridie, he took Victoria's arm and led her to the far side of the room.

"She's in the final stages of her decline, I'm afraid. There's fluid on her lungs. She may last weeks, but it could be no more than a few days, so you need to prepare yourself. I'm very sorry, Mrs Kavanagh. I know she is far more than a servant to you."

"Is it my fault? Should I have sent for you earlier? Could you have saved her?"

"Mrs Kavanagh, I can assure you. This is none of your doing. I've been visiting Bridie for years and I have nothing but admiration for you and the way you have cared for her. Please don't make this hard for yourself by feeling guilty when there is no reason."

"Thank you, Doctor."

"She'll need constant attendance. Shall I arrange for a couple of nurses?" he asked as he picked up his bag.

"Please, Doctor." Victoria held on to the door as Doctor Farrell went through. "Doctor, are you sure there's nothing we can do? I don't care about the cost."

"Mrs Kavanagh, I'm afraid no amount of money will save Bridie now. You've done all you can for her."

Victoria closed the door and leaned against it. Now, she had to tell Sean . . .

Just three nights later, Victoria was awakened by a knock at her bedroom door. The nurse's face was solemn.

"You'd better come, madam," she urged.

Victoria grabbed her dressing-gown and rushed to Bridie's room. The old lady was delirious, shouting for Moira and Aiden.

Victoria took her hands. "It's me, Bridie," she said, striving to keep her voice calm.

Sean appeared in the doorway. He looked pale and frightened. He'd barely left Bridie's side for days, refusing to go to school. Victoria knew how to pick her battles and hadn't argued with him.

"Bridie . . . Bridie . . . it's me, Sean."

The old woman stared at his face with what looked like recognition in her eyes.

Her voice barely more than a whisper now, she said, "I'm sorry . . . I-I didn't want you . . . May God forgive me . . . I didn't w-want you . . ." Tears rolled down her sunken cheeks.

"Course you wanted me. You've always been here for me." He frowned at his mother, confused.

"I would have sent for the priest to take you away . . . I'm sorry, lad . . . Please forgive me, my beloved child."

Victoria clutched the neck of her nightgown.

Sean glanced at his mother. Then Bridie began to convulse, her face distorted as she began to gasp for air, and then suddenly, she was still. The nurse leaned over, placed two fingers on Bridie's wrist and shook her head.

Sean gathered the old woman in his arms, rocking backwards and forwards. "Aww, Bridie, please don't go. Not yet." His shoulders heaved as if his heart were breaking.

Only when the doctor arrived could he be persuaded to leave. Sean sat at the kitchen table, staring at his mother as though he didn't know her.

As Victoria made his drink, she thought about Bridie, who had been part of her life longer than anyone. Even though in many ways she felt like she'd been losing her gradually over the years as her mind had deteriorated, this final departure was still painful. Although in a strange way, she was glad Bridie had passed away in June, her favourite month. She'd always found the heat of summer unbearable.

"Come on. Drink this. A hot drink will help you sleep," she urged, drawing him to her.

He shrugged her off and twisted from her. His voice was full of anguish when he spoke.

"What did Bridie mean? She said she didn't want me. Why was I going to be given to the priest?"

"She was delirious. She didn't know what she was saying," she lied helplessly.

"Please, Mother. Tell me the truth! I *have* to know. Why wasn't I wanted?"

Victoria felt as if her whole world was about to collapse.

"Was Bridie my mother?" he demanded. "I *need* to know."

"No, Sean. She's not your mother." She clasped her arms around her body. "I mean, wasn't your mother. I don't wish to discuss this now."

"I'm not a bloody child. You can't just refuse to explain things to me." He stormed from the room.

She heard him thumping up the stairs, the house reverberating as he slammed his bedroom door. She needed to let him calm down. Needed Edward's advice. God, what a mess! Bridie, after all the years of keeping our secret, what *have* you done?

When Victoria explained to Edward what Bridie had said, his advice made her blood run cold.

"You must tell him the truth."

"But I don't want him to know. He might not think of me as his mother any more." She shuddered.

"He'll find out one day. If he wants to marry, he will need his birth certificate. I'd have thought you must have realised that. If you lie to him now, he may never forgive you."

She hadn't thought about that. There was no choice – he had to be told the truth.

Edward held her close while she sobbed.

"Would you like me to be there?"

"No. No, thank you. I need to do this alone."

She left Edward waiting in the parlour, her step dragging as she went to Sean's bedroom. He was lying on his bed, his curtains half closed, a shaft of light illuminating his puffy, tear-tracked face.

"Sean, look at me."

"No. I just want to be left alone."

Perhaps it would be easier if he wasn't looking at her. She couldn't bear the thought of dislike, maybe even contempt appearing in his eyes.

Her hands clasped, she explained how she'd found him almost dead in the church, reassuring him that she'd loved him instantly and that she chose to be his mother. She described their departure from Liverpool, the past she'd invented and how she'd pretended to be a widow.

He didn't interrupt at any stage, but his eyes never opened. Tears had rolled down her cheeks and when she'd finished, he sat up and put his arms around her. There was no raging. No tears. His silence terrified her.

Eventually, he muttered, "I'd like to go to sleep now, Mother, if that's all right?"

Squeezing him tightly, she kissed his cheek before leaving his room. She had no words left. The happiness she'd experienced since she found him felt like it had come to an abrupt end.

Chapter 36

Just a month later, Sean stood in front of Victoria's desk, insolence written all over his face. He pushed back his brown waves. No matter what she did, his hair had never laid flat, continually flopping forwards. In the time since Bridie's death, he'd completely refused to talk about his birth. Edward said she needed to give him time – he was coping with the loss of Bridie on top of her revelation.

"If you've called me in here just to lecture me, Mother, don't bother."

"Sean! How dare you! I didn't bring you up to be so rude and arrogant. I called you in here so I could talk to you about this end-of-year report I've received from your headmaster, if you must know."

"What about it?" His mouth was set in a stubborn line, his arms folded.

Victoria sighed. "He says here that your marks have dropped significantly. That you're being rude and difficult. I'm hardly surprised, if you're conducting yourself there as you are right now."

He'd promised her he was fine. That he wouldn't tell anyone about his birth, not even his friend, Charles – or Kitty. But since Bridie's death, she knew he was brooding on the discovery about his birth. She could feel the tension within him and felt like he was permanently on the verge of exploding. She was losing him, she was sure.

"Well, it's not true. He's just picking on me. He's a right miserable old sod."

"Sean, please don't use bad language. And don't treat me like an idiot, either. You liked him a few months ago. I've seen the marks for myself and I believe him when he says you have been impudent, because that's exactly how you're behaving at home. What's come over you?"

"Nothing!"

"Sean!" Victoria rarely raised her voice to him.

Instantly regretting it, she came round the desk, putting her hands on his arms. She tried to embrace him, but he shrugged her off.

"Oh, let me see . . . What could possibly be wrong with me? Could it be that I've found out my entire life has been a lie? In fact, I'm nothing, Mother. I was left like a piece of rubbish."

"Sean, why are you blaming me for that? Blaming me for everything, in fact? *I* didn't leave you in the church. I've shown you nothing but love since that night and your behaviour towards me is incredibly hurtful. It's like you're trying to punish me for finding you and loving you.

"If you think it was easy for me, you're very mistaken, young man! I've had to live a lie, keeping everyone at a distance. At least try to see it from my side. But you know what? I wouldn't change a thing. I wanted to be *your* mother."

"I'm not really your son. I want to be your son."

All of her anger dissolved. "Sean, of course you're my son. I love you more than anything." She pulled him into her arms. "Have you considered that maybe your parents gave you up in the hope you'd have a better life? Maybe they thought it was your only hope of survival."

"Pah!"

"Why are you so sure that's not the case?"

He frowned. "Do you really think that's possible?"

"Yes, I do. In fact, I'm sure of it."

"I keep thinking I'm just another one of your good deeds. You can't save everyone, you know, *Mother*. I'm trying to accept things, really I am, but I need to know who I am. Surely you understand that."

Victoria was hurt. "You *are* my son, Sean. What more can I say?" She clutched his hands. "God gave you to me and there hasn't been a single day when I haven't given thanks to Him for His gift. You were chosen – I chose to keep you – which makes you even more special . . ." Her voice broke.

"So why do I feel as if I have no identity? As if I don't belong anywhere. I don't think I can go on pretending to be something I'm not." He shrugged her off once more.

Victoria struggled to understand his pain, to say something to make him feel better. Did it really matter if he didn't know where he came from? She knew who her parents were – and there were things she'd rather not know.

She was his mother because she chose to be – surely that should be enough. She was too scared to speak for fear of making the situation worse but finally, she looked directly into his face and spoke determinedly.

"Follow me."

Sean made no move to follow her.

"Please."

He did as she asked. Opening the chest in her bedroom, she took out the quilt he'd been wrapped in when she found him.

"Uncle Patrick did everything he could to discover where you came from, but without success."

"What, so he knew, as well? So everyone knew but me!"

"Sean, you know that's not true. It was just me, your uncle Patrick and Bridie. And then later, Edward. And I've explained to you why I felt the need to tell him."

Sean tutted, his arms folded.

"Uncle Patrick had to know. He helped me to move here. Look, it's not much, but it's all I have to give you. You were wrapped in this when I found you. This might be harsh to hear, but if whoever left you there really didn't care, they could simply have dumped you in the River Mersey. It certainly happened to plenty of other unwanted babies.

"At the time I didn't understand *how* they could have left you, either. But since then, as I've understood more about what it is to be a parent, I've come to realise they probably thought giving you up was the best hope for your future. And I think they were right."

He was crying again, but she stopped herself from going to him and hugging him. She needed to get through to him.

"You were a wonderful child and are now a fine young man. I feel so privileged to be a part of your life. You are, and will remain, my son, even if you reject me. Try to forgive your parents and thank God for a happy life. And to forgive me. For with forgiveness will come peace."

"Would you have ever told me if Bridie hadn't blurted it out?"

"The truth is, I don't know. Maybe one day . . . We kept the secret to protect you. To avoid you feeling like you do now."

Sean stared at her for a moment, his face pensive. "But I can't live a lie. I *have* to tell the truth."

"I've loved you since the moment I found you and so did Bridie. That's why she gave you that plaque above your bed. 'May love connect us,' that's what it says. I feel connected to you every bit as much as if I'd given birth to you."

He didn't respond for a few moments.

"I know I'm being a selfish brat. I'm hurting you and I don't know how to stop. This thing, it's eating away at me. I'm so sorry, Mother. I do love you. Please believe me."

"That's all right. I do believe you. I just wish I'd been able to stop you from being hurt. I love you, too – always know that."

She put her arms around him and held him close. This time, he let her. She was desperate to make him understand, but then how can you make someone listen when they don't want to hear it?

There was a light tap on the door. She was about to tell whoever it was to come back later, when Kitty opened the door. As she spoke, Sean pulled himself out of his mother's arms. Standing straighter, he smiled weakly at Kitty.

"Sorry, ma'am, but you're needed in the shop."

"I'll be through in a few minutes, Kitty."

As Kitty closed the door behind her, Sean smiled at his mother.

"I'm all right, really, Mother. I'm just having trouble getting used to it. I guess I'm luckier than Charles. I have you and I know you love me. Charles hates his father. I think he's afraid of him."

Finally, she felt maybe she was getting through to him.

"And there's another good thing – I'm not a gentleman any more. I was the unwanted child of an Irish immigrant, maybe even a bastard, so I'm definitely not too good for Kitty now."

Victoria's heart sank. Given what poor Kitty was coping with, there was no way she could ask her to speak to Sean. She'd just have to pray some other young girl would catch his eye.

Victoria stared at the birdlike woman before her. Milly certainly looked like she had a small bump. And as for Kitty, she was more rounded, even with a corset. Thankfully, no one else appeared to have noticed – or at least they hadn't mentioned it.

"You definitely look like you're carrying, Milly," Victoria said as Milly poured them all a cup of tea.

"It's our Kitty's handiwork. It's genius! Look at this! Undo it for me, Kitty. Everyone's gone home, so we're safe."

Kitty put her hand up the back of Milly's skirt, fiddled around and removed her hand. Milly did a little shimmy and something resembling a round cushion with strings attached landed at her feet.

"I have to hand it to you, Kitty, it's clever," Victoria said, turning the soft pad around in her hands. "The thing I don't understand is why you're not telling people you're pregnant, Milly. Surely you want people to believe you."

"'Cos she's a right stubborn old goat. See, Milly. I told her she should, ma'am, but she won't," Kitty piped up.

"I've already explained this to Kitty, ma'am. I want her to have the chance to change her mind about not keeping it for as long as possible. Then if she does decide she wants to keep it, people will just think I got a bit fatter and slimmed down again."

"But she could never keep it. You do realise that . . . ? Brakenridge would never allow it. She would come to harm. And the baby," Victoria said.

"I've told yeh till I'm sick to death of sayin' it. I won't change me mind." Kitty was exasperated.

Milly was adamant she wasn't telling anyone she was pregnant. She didn't want to attract attention or questions. The other staff tended to refrain from talking about their children when she was around, wanting to avoid the darkness that always descended on her when anyone talked about babies or children.

"The only one who needed to know was Bob and he's right chuffed about it. I've told you before that he wanted a kiddy, but he can't bear to see me go through another loss. He could hardly stand it himself," Milly said, tears balancing on her lashes.

Victoria knew this was true, although she also thought it was likely he'd agree to anything if it made Milly happy. Even though it would have put a stop to his childish infatuation, she was relieved Sean wouldn't learn about Kitty's pregnancy. He didn't need any more shocks right now. He might even think he could gallantly save Kitty by marrying her!

Reluctantly, she'd also agreed to keep it from Edward – the girls had their right to privacy. She wanted to share everything with him but had to accept it wasn't her secret to tell. Sometimes she felt like she'd been keeping secrets her entire life.

Chapter 37

Victoria had been spending one full day and two half days at the mill, trying to ease the burden on Matthew. They were engrossed in discussion as she tried to persuade him to take on a manager and a secretary.

Despite the office door being shut to keep out the familiar unremitting clatter of the machines, they still had to shout to be heard. She wouldn't have been surprised if Matthew went deaf given the amount of time he spent here, there was such a racket. The summer heat outside was making it even more oppressive, but the high humidity was important for keeping the cotton in good condition and preventing the thread from breaking. Her petticoats and bloomers were sticking to her legs. No wonder many of the mill girls refused to wear undergarments.

"Victoria, I appreciate your concern, but I'm not working much longer than anyone else who works here. Most of them are in at six and don't leave until after eight in the evenings. At least the children get to work fewer hours and get afternoons in the school room – that has to be a good thing."

"I know, Matthew. It's not just about you. I don't like them having to work such long hours, either. And you know, if I had my way, we wouldn't employ any children under the age of fifteen. I know they only work in the mornings, but they should still be in school full-time, getting themselves more of an education. It's not just about the three Rs."

Matthew tucked a damp curl behind his ear. "The families don't want it. They want them earning. If we didn't—"

A young man appeared in the doorway. If he *had* knocked, they hadn't heard him. His clothes were dirty and oil-smeared. They waited while he hunched over, desperately trying to gain control of his dry, hacking cough, dust catching in his throat. Gesticulating wildly towards the door with one hand, with the other he pulled a grey rag from his pocket and spat into it, smearing it red. Victoria closed her eyes for a second, once again recognising how naïve she'd been to buy a mill. She'd insisted on the installation of additional ventilation, but for many the damage had already been done.

"Accident! Accident!" he finally wheezed, pointing.

Matthew raced from the office, followed by the young man. Victoria, her heart thumping, lifted her heavy skirts and hurried behind. A crowd had gathered around one of the machines and they broke apart to let Matthew through.

Matthew bound the man's hand tightly in rags, the blood soon soaking through, the man's face ashen.

"Dawkins, fetch the doctor, now. Banes, get this lot cleaned up. The rest of you, out of my way. Back to work!" Matthew shouted above the din.

Victoria was silent, in a state of shock. She followed Matthew as he led the cursing man to his office. It was Sam Gibbs.

"In the cabinet. Third drawer! Quickly, please, Victoria. Pour him a large brandy."

Victoria did as she was bid.

"Me hand! I can't lose me 'and. I've got to be able to work. Me wife's just had another baby. Oh, God, I can't lose me hand," he repeated over and over.

Victoria watched, helpless, as Matthew held a second glass of brandy to Sam's lips. One of the Gibbs family had been maimed in *her* mill! She wanted to run away and never see the blasted place again. Though she disliked brandy, she felt in need of a stiff drink herself.

The doctor arrived and it wasn't Doctor Farrell. Victoria was furious when he said, "You need to leave, madam. This is no place for a lady. I need to get this man sorted."

"I'm part owner of this mill. I'm perfectly capable of dealing with whatever it is you need to do," she said with more certainty than she felt.

"Nevertheless, I will *not* work with a woman standing over me." He looked at Matthew for support.

"Please, Victoria, I will let you know how he is as soon as I can. Get yourself off home. This man needs attention and I don't have time to argue with you right now."

Victoria struggled to control her anger as she rode back to Centenary House, where she had the unenviable task of telling Sam's sisters that he'd been injured, yet was unable to reassure them as to his condition.

"What will happen to him?" Milly asked, frantic.

"His family won't cope without his wages. The baby's only two months old," Agnes added. "But how did it happen?"

"I have no idea. The doctor wouldn't let me stay. Refused to treat Sam unless I left. Ordering me around in my own business! I'm sorry, but I don't have any answers yet."

"Those machines are so bloody slow to stop when

workers get caught up in them. Aww, don't tell me he'll lose his whole arm and he's been flamin' crushed?"

"Kitty! That's not helping! We both know Victoria will do what she can to help, so shut yer gob," Milly said.

"No, I won't shut up! Our Sam ain't like Dad. He doesn't piss his wages up the wall every Friday night. Thelma's just had another baby – that's three they've got now. You know as well as I do that they've already been struggling to make ends meet so she can stay home with the kids. If Sam can't work, it'll kill him . . . just slower than the bloody machine."

"Girls, I promise you all that we'll do what we can for him." She was determined not to let Sam down.

When Victoria joined Matthew in her parlour later that day, he informed her that Sam had lost three fingers on his right hand.

"What will happen to him? How will he manage to work? What job will he do?"

"I don't know what will happen to him. I can see to it that this family have several weeks' wages, to give him a chance to look for other work. That's the best I can do."

"What! We are *not* throwing him out on his ear. Letting his family starve? I'll never agree to that!"

"Victoria, I know this family is important to you, but we can't find jobs for everyone who is no longer able to work. Please be realistic. The machines have guards. You know full well all of our machines comply with the law. He must have taken the guard off or put his arm over it. It's *not* our fault."

"Have you even bothered to find out what happened?"

When Matthew admitted that he hadn't investigated how the accident occurred, she insisted that they get the facts, starting with Sam.

She held a handkerchief to her nose as they made their way to the dingy terraced house on Balfort Row. The height of summer was signalled by the stench of people living in cramped conditions, with open drains and one outhouse shared by a dozen or more families. His wife, Thelma, let them in without greeting them, carrying a baby in her arms. Their two girls were clinging to her skirts. Thelma's eyes were red and puffy as she showed them into the shabbily furnished but clean front room.

Sam's hand was bandaged and he looked pale, deep furrows lining his face. He'd aged overnight.

"You've got to believe me. I-I need me job. But it weren't no accident, guv'nor, ma'am. I'm not stupid. I know the rules. I know how to look after meself and me machine."

He sat on the settle, his wife stood behind him, her hand on his shoulder.

"If you say it wasn't an accident, then what happened?" Matthew asked, his brows knitted.

"Tell him, Sam," Thelma urged. "We've mouths to feed."

"I'd had a row with them Charnocks. It's been brewing for ages. They've been harassing young women. Cornering 'em, like, when they go to the karzy. They kept saying things about our Kitty. And . . ." He hesitated.

"Sam!" Thelma said.

"Well, they've been forcing others to watch their looms while they skive off. But you can't blame people for doing it – for covering for 'em, I mean. Right cruel buggers, they are."

Victoria's face was stony at the mention of the name Charnock. She'd never met these men, but the image of Teddy standing in her hallway covered in urine had never left her.

"I need to work, sir. Anything. I'll do anything. I'll learn to sweep the floors with me other hand if I have to. I know it'll mean less money, but Thelma will just have to work, as well. She'll come back to the mill, if you'll have her. Me mam'll mind the kids."

Victoria found the look of desperation on both faces heart-rending. Despite Matthew's disproving looks, she informed Sam that he wasn't to worry for the moment – his wages would be paid in full at the end of the week and they'd be in touch.

Back at the mill, Victoria told Matthew about the Charnocks and their treatment of Teddy. Then she said firmly, "I want them sacked. They're dreadful men. As for Sam, we can make him an overseer."

"We can't just sack people without reason. You know that's not how we work here. At least let me check out the facts first," Matthew urged.

Despite interviewing several of the workers from the weaving section, unsurprisingly, no one would say anything that would incriminate the Charnock brothers. Everybody said Sam was a good man, hardworking and honest, but without exception, they all said they'd seen nothing. It was clear to both Victoria and Matthew that they were intimidated by the Charnocks.

That evening, Victoria sat brooding, unable to see how she could corroborate Sam's story, until Milly told her a young man from the mill would like to have a word. The lad was no doubt already working a twelve-hour day, yet he looked younger than Sean, she thought as she watched him walk timidly into the parlour, dusty from his day's labours.

"I were wondering if I could talk to you about the accident at mill, like."

"Of course, what is it?"

"I don't like snitching, but it's not right what they've done."

"I appreciate any information you can give me."

From what he said, they hadn't questioned him or any of the children working in the loom room. When she asked his name, he said he preferred not to tell her. He'd looked towards the door as though ready to dart, no doubt regretting that he'd come to see her.

The boy confirmed Sam's story. The lad had been cleaning behind one of the bins, when he saw the Charnocks approach Sam.

"I heard them clear as day sayin' what they'd like to do to Kitty Gibbs. They were saying it were none of Sam's business how they cornered girls in the lav and left their looms, and that Sam should keep his nose out. Only there was a lot of swearing, like." He blushed furiously.

"When he called them lazy so-and-sos and said they didn't frighten him, one o' them Charnocks lifted the guard and t'other shoved his hand in the machinery." He hung his head, looking at his hands.

Victoria fanned herself as she questioned the boy, nerves making him perspire in the cloying heat of early evening. He said he wanted to help Sam because Sam stuck up for people. He'd had enough of how the Charnocks bullied and threatened other workers, especially children or those with no families – anyone who had no one to stick up for them. Victoria thanked the lad for his help, once again assuring him they'd keep him out of it.

She desperately wanted to discuss it with Edward. She felt she'd made a terrible mistake buying into the mill. At least in her shops, she could protect the people who worked for her. She knew all of them well and ensured conditions were safe.

When Edward arrived for supper that evening, he gave her a brief peck on the cheek. Too preoccupied with her own concerns to notice, she told him about Sam's accident. He looked disinterested and she felt a spike of irritation.

"I'm afraid you can't protect the mill workers in the same way you do the shop girls. It simply isn't possible," he said.

"What's wrong with trying to help people?"

"Nothing at all. I love your kind heart, but right now, I think we both need to focus on our own children. Sean's struggling and Katie still wants nothing to do with me. Now, I suggest we have our meal and talk later."

Edward looked drawn. He picked up a spoon and the meal proceeded in a strained silence. What had come over him?

She was still lost in her thoughts when Edward said, "I'm afraid I have to go away to Ireland. Fionn has died. Killed in a riding accident. I need to bring my daughter home."

"Oh, Edward. I'm so sorry. And here I am going on about my worries."

"I know it's not the right time to mention it, but we will be free to marry now. It's what I have longed for, but I didn't want it to be like this. I feel so guilty, as though I have wished her life away."

"Of course you didn't wish for her to die. It's *not* your fault, Edward. You can't *make* things happen to other people. Go and bring Katie home. Then we can be a family."

Looking at him now, she could see the deep furrows

in his forehead, the stiffness around his jaw. She hadn't noticed how tense he was when he arrived and she felt ashamed.

He was to leave the next day, so Victoria determined to use his absence to get her house in order. First, she needed to settle matters at the mill, then she'd focus on Sean.

She met Matthew first thing the following morning.

After listening in silence, Matthew rubbed his chin and said, "Victoria, I can see how much it matters to you. And going into the water closet at the same time as a woman is a sackable offence. We just need to go about it the right way so there are no repercussions. I'll say I saw them myself, so we protect the lad. I presume you're sure as to the accuracy of his account?"

"I'm in no doubt. Those men are animals."

The Charnocks were summoned to the office and informed of their fate. If they'd ranted and raved, it wouldn't have been as menacing as the way they actually behaved. Victoria and Matthew were both seated on one side of the large meeting table, the brothers on the other, their almost identical faces hard, staring. They stank of stale sweat and tobacco, their mousey hair matted. Victoria was sure she saw something moving on one of their heads. They didn't speak until Matthew had made his accusations then told them they were dismissed with immediate effect.

"Aye, we thought as much. We'd heard Gibbs were blaming us for his accident. We know the score – the bloody Gibbs crew are right in the pockets of you bosses. We'll take our wages for last week and get out of yer way," one said.

After a pause, the other brother continued, "Mills can

be dangerous places. Could go up like a pig in a furnace. A lot of people could die. Aye, dangerous places, mills." He gestured to his brother to rise. "You take care of yerself, Mrs Kavanagh. Such a pretty face. And say goodbye to that nice lad of yours for us."

"Are you threatening us?" Matthew had risen from his chair. He was smaller than the brothers by a full head height.

"No, sir. He's just complimenting the pretty lady an' sending our regards to the lad." The first sneered in Victoria's direction.

His words appeared to linger after he'd finished speaking and Matthew escorted them from the building. Victoria was shaken. Surely they wouldn't burn down the mill, attack Sean . . . The truth was that they could be capable of anything. Her heart was in her mouth as she waited for Matthew to return.

Several more things were agreed between Victoria and Matthew that afternoon, including that Sam Gibbs would be given a job as overseer. Matthew conceded he'd been struggling to cope with his workload and Sam's promotion would allow him to delegate more work to his current overseers. Victoria, who had admitted to Matthew she didn't enjoy being at the mill, was also to step back from taking an active role in managing the mill. Instead, they were to employ an undermanager and a secretary to support Matthew. Victoria's new role would be to focus on conditions and safety, working on cost-effective ways to improve working practices for all employees – something that was close to her heart. A couple of watchmen were also to be appointed.

As the weeks went on, they were relieved when no

incidences occurred. The hope was that the Charnocks had merely made idle threats, although when one of their lorries was attacked and a full shipment of fabric stolen, Victoria felt sure the Charnocks were behind it. With no proof, her hands were tied once more. Matthew had gone to the police, but their investigations had come to nothing.

When Milly informed Victoria the Charnocks were boasting they were now working for Mr Brakenridge transporting goods between Manchester and Liverpool, she felt uneasy. The one consolation was that at least the Charnocks were away from both the mill and Sean, who still insisted on spending all of his free time there. He left for school early and had continued going to the mill every day after school. Matthew would drop him off on his way home and Sean invariably went to bed with barely a word.

Chapter 38

Edward pulled Victoria into his arms – the two months since he'd last seen her felt like years. "Please say you will never leave me. I know we can't marry yet – it wouldn't look decent – but I need to know you won't ever leave me." He pulled back so he could see her face.

"Of course I won't. Why? What is it? What's happened? I can see it's more than just missing me that's distressing you."

He buried his head in her hair. She could feel his shoulders juddering as he sobbed. Eventually, he pulled away.

"It's Katie. She refused to come back with me. I thought that with me staying there all this time, she would get to know me and agree to return to England. In the end, I realised it was making no difference. She couldn't have made it any clearer that she wanted to remain with her grandparents. Legally, I could force the issue, of course. But her life is there and she wants nothing to do with me. Have I done the right thing? It doesn't feel like it."

Victoria drew him to the sofa. "Oh, darling, I'm sure you have. She's just lost her mother. It would be wrong to force her away from somewhere she feels safe."

He leaned his head back, staring up at the ceiling. "I've always sent money. But it wasn't enough. I should have insisted on seeing her long before now. Pushed a bit more. I left it too late because Fionn made it so difficult. I knew Fionn didn't want to see me and I didn't want to make her more unhappy by demanding. I felt guilty enough marrying her when I didn't love her. None of that was her fault.

"Who am I trying to fool . . . Regardless of how unpleasant Fionn made it, I should never have given up. But it's immaterial now. I've lost my daughter forever."

"It's not your fault, don't you see?"

"But it is. I made such a mess of my marriage. I've been a terrible father to Katie. I could even go as far as to say I hate Fionn for all the things she's said to our daughter about me. She told Katie I ended our marriage because I didn't love *either* of them. That I never wanted a child. I've told Katie it's not true and that I did want her. That I love her. But she wouldn't listen. Her mother did a good job of poisoning her mind against me. Now, Katie won't even consider coming over for so much as a holiday."

"Don't give up, my darling. She'll come round. One day she'll realise how lucky she is to have you as a father. It's never too late, you know. That's something I've learned of late. Just give her time. We can visit her and rebuild your relationship."

"I hope you're right. But if I have lost her forever, I have no one to blame but myself."

Victoria gathered him in her arms – there was little else she could do.

Victoria was feeling disgruntled as she returned from Mass. Sean had refused to go with her. Unable to face another row and with Edward busy catching up on work after his long absence, she'd gone alone. The service had done nothing to ease her worries about her son or her fiancé.

As she approached the shop, she could see the figure of a young woman, her back against the wall, clutching her stomach. Kitty? She ran towards her, almost tripping on her skirts.

"Arghh! God, help me!" Kitty folded over, her face hidden.

"Kitty, we need to get you inside. What is it? Is it the baby?"

"Quick! Aww, bloody hell, help me in."

Victoria was shaking so much, she struggled to unlock the door. Eventually, she helped her inside, Kitty's arm around her neck, barely able to shuffle.

"Milly! Milly!" Victoria shouted, pushing the connecting door open with her foot.

Milly dropped the cup she was drying and ran to Kitty, her own face suddenly white.

"I need to get this corset off. I-I-I can't . . . b-breathe." Kitty's voice was rasping, beads of perspiration on her brow.

The two of them began unfastening Kitty's clothes.

"You must have it too tight, Kitty, if it's affecting your breathing," Victoria said as she expertly unlaced Kitty.

She was used to ladies fainting having over-tightened their corsets in their determination to ensure their waists were as tiny as possible. But women of Kitty's class rarely wore corsets and she was worried that in an effort to hide her pregnancy, she may now be harming herself or the baby. Eventually, both the dress and the corset fell to the ground and Kitty stood in her slip, her stomach much larger, straining against her undergarments.

"I've had the pains all night. They're getting . . . w-worse. I had to put the flipping corset on this mornin' or me dress wouldn't have fastened and Mam would have known f-for sure. I keep thinking she's twig—Aargh! Christ! I think it's coming now."

"God, Kitty, how the hell have you been hiding that bump? Yer loads bigger than Mam ever was."

"Bloody charming!" was all Kitty could manage as another contraction seized her.

"Kitty. Try to hold on. We need to get you to bed. Milly, let's get her to your spare room."

As Kitty collapsed on the bed, Victoria stuck her head in the kitchen of her own house. Sean was eating a sandwich, his face surly. She didn't have time to deal with him! She beckoned Agnes into the hallway and whispered to her that it seemed the baby was coming. Agnes looked as stunned as Victoria.

"Are you sure it's coming now, Kitty?" Agnes asked as soon as they got in the room.

"How the hell do I know? But . . . B-bloody hell, if it's not, summat's wrong."

"Maybe you got yer dates wrong, Kitty," Milly suggested.

"No, I haven't. It's not due for ages. If I've hurt it with that corset, I'll never forgive meself." Kitty whimpered as another pain wrenched through her.

Milly stepped forwards. "Hold me hand, Kitty."

"Kitty's having a baby!"

The three women stood around the bed turned towards the door. Their faces were horrified. They hadn't heard Sean come in. Victoria rushed towards him.

"Sean, not now. This is no place for a young man. Go back to our house or go and see Bob. Milly, where *is* Bob?"

"He's gone to see his mam and dad. He'll be gone all day."

"How the *hell* is Kitty having a baby?" Sean's face was crimson, his eyes dark.

"Arghh! Lace my corsets!"

Oh, dear God. Not now, Victoria thought. Finding out about Kitty was going to make him even more difficult to live with.

"Sean, I *will* explain to you. But not now. Go to your room and promise me you won't say a word to anyone." She pushed him out of the door.

He looked at her, stony-faced.

"I mean it, Sean. Don't cross me on this."

"Fine. I'll bloody go."

"Maybe we should fetch Doctor Farrell." Milly, on the verge of tears, looked from Victoria to Agnes.

Kitty had barely said a word for the last half an hour. Sweat was pouring from her as pains racked her body.

"Not bloody likely. I've not gone through months of missing out on our Agnes' scones and strapping meself up tighter than a nun's—Arghh! To f-flippin' let the cat out now. Christ that huuurts!" Kitty squeezed Milly's hand tighter, causing Milly to grimace. "I'm all right. It's coming, I can tell. Only, Milly, I think it's a bleeding horse trying to get out, not a baby."

Milly laughed weakly. "Are you certain you don't want to keep it, Kitty?"

For the third time, Victoria refolded the towels that Agnes had brought through, trying desperately not to think of how Sean's mother must have felt when abandoning him all those years back. How was Kitty managing to be so strong? She was basically accepting a life of never being the child's mother, simply watching on.

Would that be harder than just abandoning one – walking away, never to see it again, resigned to a life of wondering?

"I'm sure. I want it to have a proper mam and dad, you and Bob. I want it to be safe, so I . . . Arrgh! Bobbins and pins!

"I-I can't keep it whatever happens. I could brazen it out – I don't care what people say about me – but if him who put the bun in me oven ever found out I went through with having it, he's likely to drown it in his pond. That's what he said he'd d-do! F-for muck's sake!" Kitty tried to breathe through another contraction. "Have yer changed yer mind, Milly?" she gasped finally as the pain subsided.

"No. Course not. Course I want it, Kitty. If yer absolutely sure you don't, that is." Milly's expression was unreadable.

Kitty grasped Milly's hand tighter, pulling her close.

"I'm certain, Milly, honest. You'll be a wonderful mam. Much better than me. It'd be swearing like a navvy before it could walk with me as its mam . . . Arrrgh! For the love of conkers! Just get this friggin' thing outta me!" Kitty said through gritted teeth, pain ripping through her. "Mam never made it look his harrrd!"

Silence descended on the room.

"God, you could cut the tension in here with a knife. Come on, smile! I'm about to be a mam!" Milly said, attempting a smile.

Victoria envied this little woman, who was always so sure of what she wanted. Always certain Bob would stand by her. Then Kitty had them all laughing with what she said next.

"Our Milly, this little sod's fighting to get out. It's gonna give you more trouble than I ever gave Mam," she promised, laughing until another spasm of pain racked through her.

Chapter 39

Kitty looked exhausted as she gripped the sheets, twisting them between her fingers, beads of sweat running down her face.

"Breathe, Kitty!" Milly urged. "You can do this. Not long now. Remember, each pain is one closer to giving me my baby."

"That's very blooming c-comfortin'! It's easy for you to say. I'm the one it's r-r-ripping in half."

"Perhaps we *should* send for the doctor," Victoria suggested.

"No. Not unless she really needs one!" Agnes said, taking charge. "We can't have anyone finding out the truth. Come on, our Milly! We've seen Mam have enough babies and you've had one of yer own," she said to Victoria. "How hard can it be?"

Little did they know, Victoria thought. Little did they know . . .

She felt like an expectant father, pacing between the window and the bed. The baby wasn't due until November, so it was four weeks early. She prayed silently that nothing was wrong and it would survive. She might have been the one who was meant to have had a baby, but she didn't know the first thing about it. To her amazement, unlike herself, the three sisters appeared to be taking it in their stride. Milly was beaming and even Kitty had stopped wailing.

Victoria knew all three of them cared for her, but their bond formed through years of hardship was very apparent now and she couldn't help but feel excluded. She stood staring out of the window into the darkness until Milly turned and spoke.

"Hey, come on, ma'am. I want you part of this. You're family and yer gonna be its godmother. Or at least I hope you are."

"Are you sure we don't need a doctor?" Victoria asked the sisters again.

Kitty looked exhausted.

"There's no need. The baby will be out soon. Its head is crowning," Agnes said knowledgeably.

"If it's all right and healthy, like, yeh can have it, Milly. But if it's like our Teddy, I'll understand if you change yer mind," Kitty gasped between contractions, squeezing Victoria's hand now.

Dear Lord, Victoria felt she would need the doctor herself at this rate. Where did Kitty get her strength? Her hand felt like it was about to snap in two.

Between Kitty's groans and expletives, Milly reassured her that she wouldn't change her mind either way, but Victoria knew Milly must be scared in case there was something wrong with the baby – she knew she would be. Whatever the baby was like, Milly would love it and take care of it, of that Victoria was certain.

"Everything will be fine," Victoria whispered, the fingers of her free hand crossed behind her back.

"Fluffin' Nora!" Kitty screamed as the head was born.

"One more push," Agnes urged.

"I'll give yeh one more push!" Kitty hissed.

And with a small cry, out into the world slid a tiny girl. Perfect and whole.

"You cut the cord, our Milly." Agnes passed her the scissors.

The scissors were shaking in Milly's hand and she could barely see as tears of joy streamed down her face. She cleaned up her daughter with a towel, realising she was as beautiful as the woman who had given her life.

To Victoria, who had never given birth, it was a miraculous moment. She understood how Milly must be feeling, worried in case Kitty changed her mind. In her case, it had been worry that someone would find her out and take the baby away – maybe even lock her up for what she'd done. And worse, Bridie, too.

Milly cradled the baby in her arms. "Just look at her, Victoria. She's a miracle." She turned to Kitty. "Are you sure, our Kitty, 'cos if yer not, say so now. It'll kill me if you change yer mind later."

"I've told you, our Milly. I'm blinkin' sure!"

"I need to know yer certain. Here, hold her and then tell me if you can really give her up." She thrust the baby into Kitty's arms.

Kitty looked down at the baby, who was staring up at her. She gasped, her eyes filled with love.

"Aww, she's perfect." She lifted the tiny bundle to her and kissed her gently on the nose.

Milly stifled a groan, holding her breath.

"I love her so much, even if the little git did just put me through the mangle," Kitty said.

"I understand. Really I do." Milly was nodding, her eyes clouded by tears of sadness.

"I love her nearly as much as I love you, Millicent Gibbs. She's yours and always will be. I will love her as an auntie should." She held the baby out to Milly.

"You really mean it, Kitty? 'Cos it'll have to be done legal – that's only fair to Bob. There will be no going back."

Agnes came in carrying a tray and four cups of tea.

"Right, which one of me sisters has just become a mam?" she asked.

"Milly is," Kitty said, her smile contorting as she grasped the bed covers. "Milly, there's something wrong," she gasped.

Milly looked terrified as Agnes plonked the tray down and darted forwards. Victoria's heart was in her mouth as Agnes pulled back the covers and looked between Kitty's legs.

"Jesus, there's another one!" Agnes cried.

Victoria looked aghast at Milly, whose mouth had dropped open. Milly thrust the baby into her arms, almost falling in her haste to get to the bed.

After a few minutes, with several choice words from Kitty, a second head had appeared, followed by another perfect baby. This time, a boy. Milly cut the last cord while Agnes grabbed a towel. Agnes placed him on it, wrapped it round him and rubbed his back until he gave a cry before handing him to Milly.

The three of them all sat on the bed drinking tea in a stunned silence until Kitty grinned.

"Now, are yer absolutely sure there's no more in there, Agnes, 'cos I think two's enough for our Milly just now. Besides, I'm knackered. If there's any others wanting to come out, they'll have to wait until I've had a kip."

"Crikey! I can't believe it. I've got two children. No wonder you were as big as a circus elephant, Kitty."

"Yeh cheeky cow! I've just given yeh a ready-made family and now yer insulting me."

Victoria wondered if Sean could hear their laughter. Had he *really* gone to his room? She'd have to go through and deal with him soon and she had to admit, she was dreading it.

They agreed that everyone would be told Milly's babies had come early. That she'd kept quiet about her pregnancy because she'd suffered so many miscarriages in the past. No one had guessed Kitty was pregnant. Even if they suspected, they couldn't prove anything. Agnes was going to tell the family Kitty was spending a few days looking after Milly, who was tired after a difficult birth of twins. Bob would register the birth, stating Milly and him as the parents. No one would be any the wiser and the twins would have birth certificates, unlike Sean.

"Now that's all sorted, hand me niece and nephew over, Milly, an' I'll give them a quick feed, 'cos me paps feel like they're gonna burst."

Victoria looked at the sisters. Had they discussed Kitty feeding them? She wondered if they'd both find it difficult. As Milly handed them over, she remembered her own guilt at not getting a wet nurse in for Sean. No matter how difficult it was for them, it was best for the twins.

"What you gonna name them, Milly?" Kitty asked as the babies suckled.

"Master Robert Kellet, after Bob," Milly answered instantly.

They all understood. She'd lost so many babies before they'd had the chance of life, she'd already have thought of names.

"And your daughter?" Victoria asked.

"I've thought of names, but you name her, Kitty."

"Aww, are yeh sure? I might pick summat daft, like Dumpling. Or Shandy after next door's dog – yeh know how much I liked him."

"I'll see what you choose before I say if she can keep it."

"All right, then. But my belly thinks me throat's been cut, so I can only think of food. Can I have summat to eat, Agnes?"

"When you've picked a name and not before."

"Miss Sara Jane Kellet."

"Perfect," Milly said.

As Milly watched her son and daughter being fed by her favourite sister, she couldn't stop smiling. She'd always said she knew she wasn't supposed to have favourites – but she did.

"Just this morning, I was still too afraid to believe it could happen. I were sick of pretending to everyone I were happy when really, more pieces were breaking off me heart. I'll never be able to repay you for this gift, Kitty."

"Aww, yer gonna have me blubbering. I'm glad yer happy, our Milly. You can trust me."

"I know I can, love. Yer the best of us! Always have been."

"I'll never try to be more than their hilarious auntie, teaching them all kinds of mischief." Kitty looked at the twins as she spoke.

"Don't you bloody dare teach my kids to get up to the sort of stuff you did, like pretending you were eating flies when they were raisins – nearly made our Cora puke!"

As Kitty began giving Agnes a list of the mischief she could teach the twins, Milly went over to Victoria and whispered, "I'm made up, honest. I just wish I could feed them." Tears were running down her face. "I'll be back in a minute, Kitty. I'm just nipping to the outhouse," she said, straining to keep her voice upbeat.

Victoria watched Kitty. She understood why Milly had rushed from the room. Giving birth and feeding a child were part of the natural bonding process. She wished she could reassure Milly that all would be fine. That she'd quickly feel like their real mother.

Kitty glanced at Agnes and Victoria nervously and then spoke softly to her babies.

"I really need you to understand that I do love you. More than I'll ever be able to tell you again. It's because I love you that I'm giving you to our Milly, 'cos she'll be the best mam in the world. She'll keep you safe and give you a good home. Bye-bye, me little ones. I love you both. I wish I could keep you. I'll be here as yer auntie Kitty, if you ever need me."

Victoria gulped, almost choking on the lump in her throat as Milly came back in, a broad smile now plastered on her face. How strange it is, she thought, how Milly and I both became mothers to babies that weren't ours. In Milly's case, she got two!

"That poor, brave girl," Edward said when Victoria told him all the details. "I'm ashamed to say that men can be cruel, especially him. But Milly will make a wonderful mother. Then again, so would Kitty if she was given the opportunity. She has a good heart. I think that's why she's the one Teddy always clings to."

"I fear it's not just Teddy who clings to her – Sean is totally enamoured with her. Which is why he's taken this so badly. But you're right – those two are close. Teddy still meets her at the shop and walks her home after he finishes work at the brewery. I don't think it's going to be easy for her watching the babies grow up calling Milly Mother. But she's a strong young woman. I think she'll cope. I hope so, anyway, for all their sakes.

"I'd better go and try to speak to Sean again. You may as well go home – it could be a long night. He's not exactly been easy to talk to recently and this has made him worse."

"Shall I stay? I might be able to help."

"No, I must deal with this myself."

"Why must you? We're to be married. You've got to stop pushing me out."

She knew he was right and after a further discussion, they decided to tackle him together over dinner.

Victoria and Edward were feeling drained after what seemed like an age of trying to get Sean to understand. He stared at her in stubborn silence.

"All right, Sean, so you don't understand and we can't make you. But you still need to promise me you'll say nothing about this to anyone. Everyone is to believe these babies to be Milly's. We must protect Milly, Kitty *and* the babies," Victoria pleaded.

"I'll keep your bloody secret. I'll keep it for Milly's sake. Not Kitty's. She's vile. Filthy. Getting pregnant when she isn't married . . . I hate her."

"Sean!"

"What? It's true. I do."

"Then you should be ashamed of yourself, young man. Kitty has been a good friend to you. She hasn't tried to hurt you. It's not her fault you have feelings for her!" Edward's voice had risen sharply.

Was Sean going to explode at him? Tell him to stop trying to be his father? Even though Sean looked livid, she was glad that for once he stayed silent, his chin resting sulkily in his hand as he leaned on the dining table.

"Hate is a very strong word. This isn't all Kitty's fault," she added.

She didn't elaborate further. She couldn't tell him they were Charles' half-siblings – it wasn't her secret to tell. Nor could she explain how manipulative James Brakenridge could be – he was too young to understand.

"Not her fault. Phfft! Don't make me laugh," he said bitterly.

"Sean, believe me. You don't understand. You will when you're older."

"Then *make* me understand. What is it with you women? Half of you just throw your children away. The rest of you keep children who aren't yours. You're all just bloody liars!" He spat the words.

"Sean. Don't speak to your mother that way! Where would you be if she hadn't kept a child who wasn't hers? She deserves your eternal gratitude, not your scorn," Edward bellowed.

"Thank you, *Mother*!" Sean said as he stormed from the room.

Edward placed his hand on hers. "He's just hurting. Kitty was his first love. He doesn't realise that girls can be used by unscrupulous men. He feels she isn't the person he believed her to be. We have to be patient with him."

"He's had an awful time. Losing Bridie, finding out I'm not his birth mother and now this. His heart's broken. It's so difficult being a mother. You don't realise before you have them how much it kills you to watch them suffer. At least *I* didn't realise. It's worse as they get older – you can't protect them the same. I need to go and check on him." She extracted her hand from Edward's.

Tapping gently on Sean's door, she went inside.

"Sean, do you want to talk?"

He thumped his pillow, burying his face into it. She sat on the bed beside him, longing to take his pain away.

"I know you think I'm stupid 'cos Kitty's older than me, but it's only a few years and I love her, Mother, I really do."

"I know, darling, and you're not stupid. We can't choose who we fall in love with and it can be painful if we fall for the wrong person."

He rubbed his eyes. "I hoped as I got older that she'd stop seeing me as a kid. Now she's had a baby – two babies! *And* given them away. I really can't stand the thought that she's done that. One day, those babies will feel like me. Unwanted. Unloved by their own mother. I hate her for abandoning them. But I don't want to hate her. At least Milly's will know when they were born. I have no idea when I was born," he ended on a sob.

So that was it . . . He was still hurting about his own birth.

She sat with him until he fell asleep. She knew he'd feel self-conscious in the morning, embarrassed that he hadn't handled his feelings as he believed a man should. Yet another problem heaped on his young shoulders.

Victoria walked Edward to the door as he was leaving.

"I hate to leave you alone. I want to hold you, be there for you." He held her hand, reluctant to release it.

"I know, and I need you with me. But tonight isn't the right time with Sean upset. And after all that's happened, I just want to be alone with my thoughts."

She didn't for one moment feel that, but she couldn't give in to temptation. Although it would have been so easy.

"We must marry as soon as we can. I want us to be together. Can we at least discuss it soon?"

Kissing him gently on the cheek, she nodded and closed the door before she gave in to her need for comfort.

She lay in bed, tossing fitfully. Edward had said he understood why she hadn't told him about Kitty's pregnancy, but she was tired of keeping things from him. Ever since she'd moved to Faredene, she'd been keeping secrets. She wanted to share everything with him, be his wife and his partner in everything. Yet, at the moment she was still keeping things from him.

He knew nothing of Lydia's situation, or Lydia's plan to escape – she couldn't break her confidence. She loved him, wanted to make him happy. And she wanted to help him improve his relationship with Katie, but she was at a loss as to what he could do, other than be patient with his daughter. Edward would win her round in the end, she was sure of it. He was so tolerant and caring. She'd been a fool to be afraid of sharing a life with him – so much time squandered.

For the life of her, she couldn't work out how to make Sean feel better about his background, either. Her love for him, the need to protect him, was crushing. She'd do anything for him, yet she felt she was losing him. He'd been stubborn at times, although generally easy, independent, and always kind and thoughtful. Now, he was practically a stranger to her. Perhaps she should have told him when he was younger, controlled how he was told, chosen the right time. Maybe then he'd have accepted it better, if he'd always known the truth, but it was too late now.

And she was worried about Milly, Kitty and the babies, and how it would all work out for them. Would they have problems with the twins one day if they found out who their real mother was? Maybe she *should* tell Milly about Sean, so Milly could learn from her mistake and tell the twins.

Why couldn't life just be simple? she wondered. Suddenly, she pulled herself up as it came to her. She'd had a simple life after her father died. Simple, boring, lonely. Her life might be full of challenges and worries about others, but that was part and parcel of loving people, of having a family. Family!

Chapter 40

The surprise arrival was the cause of much talk in the shop and workroom. Several of the girls commented on how they'd suspected Milly was in the family way but hadn't liked to ask. Others looked suspiciously at the two sisters but said nothing, at least not to their faces.

If Kitty visiting her sister each morning before she began her shift, during her lunch break and again before she went home added fuel to their suspicions, their co-workers kept schtum. Only Edith spoke her mind. She'd walked into Milly's kitchen one lunchtime unannounced while Kitty was expressing milk, so Milly could bottle-feed the twins.

"I thought so. I knew you'd disgrace yerself one day, behaving like a tart, getting yerself up the spout. Why couldn't yeh keep yer hand on your ha'penny until you were wed?"

Kitty looked hurt, but before she could answer, Milly rounded on her mother.

"Kitty never disgraced herself, Mam. Plenty of girls around here are going with their fellas every Saturday night and are crafty enough to use protection. Just because she were naïve and went with a fella once doesn't make her a tart. Besides, it wasn't even her choice! I swear, Mam, if I ever find out you've said a word to anyone, including our Cora, I'll never speak to you again, so help me."

Edith looked stung by her words.

"I might have let youse down in many ways. But I'd never go against youse like that. You should know that, our Milly." She plonked the bootees she'd knitted on the table. "I were gonna make matinee jackets to go with them ready for the winter, if you still want them, that is."

There was an awkward silence until Milly kissed her mam's cheek. "Ta, Mam. Matinee jackets will be perfect."

Even though Victoria had chosen to be a working mother, Milly had surprised her by telling her she didn't want to give up work either, until she explained that she and Bob were determined to give the twins all the things their own parents hadn't been able to afford. While Sara and Robert were still young enough to sleep most of the day, she began training up the shop girls to cover some of her duties. But she had no intention of stopping altogether, even talking about taking on a nursemaid so she could keep working.

The Gibbs family had all been to see the twins. Teddy had sat holding each of the sleeping babies in turn on his knee, closely watched by Milly, who was hovering in case he forgot he was holding them and dropped them. Cora innocently commented on how Sara looked like Kitty as a baby.

Kitty looked nervously at Milly, who hurriedly countered it, saying, "Well, I certainly hope so, 'cos our Kitty got everyone else's share of good looks."

Harry and Bert came round together.

"Aye, they're little smashers all right." Harry had peered into the wooden crib that Bob had lovingly made.

Then he'd pulled Milly out into the hallway that joined the two premises, leaving Bob telling Bert how little sleep he was getting. "Just be careful, our Milly. I know Brakenridge is the real dad. Make sure you keep it secret, 'cos much as I'm grateful to him for setting me up and giving me work, I know what a nasty bugger he can be."

Milly was aghast.

"Shush!" She put her finger to her lips. "How did you find out, Harry?"

"I knew he were after our Kitty. I wanted to stop him, but he's like a madman when he wants summat. He can have his pick of girls in Liverpool or Manchester. I've been there, seen the places he owns. Girls everywhere. Do anything for a few shillings. He's offered them to me an' all, but I don't want to be going wi' no dirty prossie.

"He got it in his head to have Kitty. I dropped a few hints to her when I realised. Told her he was a wrong 'un. But I think it were too late then. I think she were already up the duff."

"Thanks for the warning, love." Milly kissed him on the cheek.

Harry touched his face, seemingly unused to displays of affection from his family.

"I'll get off home then, Milly." He was smiling as he left.

Only Sean didn't want to see the twins. Milly was hurt. She asked Victoria why he hadn't been in and Kitty answered before she'd had the chance to make up an excuse.

"I think I can guess. Is it all right if I go and have a quick word with him, ma'am?"

As desperate as Victoria was for someone to get through to him, she was worried he'd say something to hurt Kitty.

As if reading her mind, Kitty added, "It's all right. I've got skin like old leather. I can take whatever he's got to say."

She found Sean in his room. Knocking on the door, she barged in without waiting for him to tell her to enter.

"Hey, Tatty Head. I didn't wait for you to tell me to come in, in case yeh told me to go away. I just want a quick word."

"What about?" He stood by the window, staring out.

"I'm sorry yer disappointed in me. That I've not lived up to some childish fantasy you have about me."

"I'm not childish!" He spun round.

"Just the fact that yer treating yer mam like you are an' looking at me like you hate me tells it all. When we've been friends for so long – well, it suggests to me yer still a kid. Either that or not very nice. I haven't decided which yet. And I don't want to think about you in that way, 'cos I thought we were mates.

"I'm right sorry if my having the twins has hurt you. But I didn't intend to upset anyone. I can tell you one thing, though. This mess is harder on me than anyone. And for what it's worth, I never willingly let *any* man near me. Do you understand what I'm telling yeh?" she ended, her voice hollow, tears threatening to fall from her long lashes.

She could see Sean was struggling with his thoughts and emotions. Confusion then anger, love, pity fought on his face.

"Who? Who did this to you? I'll kill him!"

"No you won't – and that's why I'm not telling you who it is. Trying to take revenge won't help anyone. While I'm on it, I've got five brothers – and four of them would go for him an' all if they find out. So, you keep what I've told you to yourself. All right?"

"If I must."

"I know you care for me, but yer like a bruvver to me. You can't ever be anything else."

Sean nodded. "I-I'm sorry, Kitty. I'd never want you to be hurt. I wish I could make it better for you. I've been horrible to everyone lately. It's just that so many things have happened and I feel so angry all the time. It's like a storm's going on in my head."

"So I'm yer mate. Come on, Tatty Head, sit down here with me and tell me what's got yer head in a pickle."

They sat on his bed and Kitty listened in silence as Sean told her about his birth, where Victoria had found him and how he'd found out.

When he'd finished, she said, "Aww, yeh don't know how lucky you've been. I used to pray someone would take me away from me dad. I dreamed of living in a clean house with a mam who adored me like yours does you. Of never going hungry, not being clouted around the head for every little thing.

"We can't change who our real mam and dad are, Sean, but I would choose your mam any day of the week. You've got nothing to be ashamed of. I've had to give up me babies because I know they'll be happier with Milly. It's killed something inside me to do it. And I can't even tell anyone how much it's hurtin'. But I'm doing what's best for them and I've just got to take comfort in that."

"Oh, Kitty, I've been feeling so ashamed. It's really helped to tell someone. You're not shocked or horrified, are you?"

"You've got nowt to be ashamed of. And far from it."

"Do you think maybe my mother was raped and that's why she left me?"

"No, I don't. But even if she was, it makes no difference to who you are. If you'd stop being such an idiot and come and see the babies, you'd see they're perfect. Just like you would have been. And with Milly as their mum, they'll grow up smashing, just like you. Although, hopefully, they'll have tidier hair."

Sean gave a small laugh. "I'm so sorry, Kitty. You've been going through such a hard time and I treated you like dirt. I'm a selfish pig. Can you ever forgive me?"

"Blimey, you think highly of yerself! Yer not a pig. Pigs is better lookin' than you are, Tatty Head. You're like that teddy o' yours." She picked up Tatty Teddy off the floor near his bed and rubbed his head with it, ruffling his permanently untidy hair even more.

A small smile appeared on his face.

"Come on, then, let's go and see Milly's babies, Tatty Head. We need to start early, teaching them to be little sods so we can have a good laugh watching her try to cope with them."

"Maybe I should give Tatty to them. I-I only kept it this long because Mother gave it to me."

"Yeah, course that's the only reason he's still near yer bed. Come on, then, you soft sod. Go an' give it to them."

Victoria looked gratefully at Kitty as she led Sean into the room. He looked calmer than he had done in a long time.

As they approached the crib, Kitty plastered a smile on her face.

"I brought them this," Sean said, handing over Tatty Teddy.

"Thanks, love. Do you want to hold one of them?" Milly asked, taking the teddy.

"Erm, all right."

Milly placed Sara in Sean's nervous hands. "Mind you don't drop her."

"Kitty, can I have a word?" Victoria gestured to the edge of the room.

"It's all right. I was nice to him. Well, sort of. I didn't give him a good walloping, if that's what's worrying yeh," Kitty said with a glint in her eye.

"How would you like the opportunity to become involved in the design side of the business? You've been drawing ladies in posh frocks, as you put it, since you were a girl. I think you have a real talent."

"Me? Really?" Her eyes were wide.

"Yes, you. But just on the ready-to-wear collection. Day dresses, suits for the working ladies, initially. You'd need to learn to mind your language before I could let you near any of the couture clients. At the moment, I think you'd cause Mrs Hornby-Smythe to have the vapours if she heard what you come out with."

Kitty grinned. "Cor, that'd be bloody amazing."

"My point entirely," she smiled. "But if it works out, we could move towards you becoming a supervisor. No promises, mind. You're going to have to prove yourself. It'll mean a lot of extra work."

Kitty flung her arms around Victoria and kissed her.

"Thank you. Thank you so much, ma'am. For understanding," she whispered.

Chapter 41

Victoria rubbed her temples. She didn't think she'd ever get used to the noise or the vibrations from the thundering of the great machines. At least it wasn't too hot, but she'd avoid coming to the mill for the next couple of months if she could. Ladies' gowns were hardly suitable for hot weather, never mind when combined with the humidity of the mill.

She closed the accounting ledger – both production and profits were up. She knew that the prosperity of the mill was largely owing to the imported cotton from Matthew's American contact. To think the raw cotton had sailed all the way across the Atlantic . . . Until she'd purchased the mill, she'd never even given it a thought as to where it came from.

The investment in new equipment had enabled them to compete with the cheap imports flooding in from abroad. Their apprentices were no longer orphans who would be bound to the mill for years, for Victoria had insisted that young people were taught a trade and given the opportunity to advance. The increased wages she'd introduced as part of her scheme to improve the welfare of the workers hadn't made a significant dint on profits. Were they grateful for the fans they'd installed? Or would they rather have had even higher wages and inhale the fluff? She couldn't tell.

The one thing she knew the workers and their families all valued was the scheme whereby adult workers could pay a penny a week into a fund for Doctor Farrell to hold two surgeries a week and prescribe cut-price medicines.

Later that same week, Victoria was sitting at her desk in Centenary House finalising the month's accounts for her clients. She wondered what time Sean would be home from the mill this evening. In the year since Bridie had died, his behaviour had improved and although he spent less time with Kitty, their friendship had continued, albeit a little strained. She knew he was still struggling with the revelation surrounding his birth and it pained her that there was nothing she could do to help him. The only person whose company he appeared to enjoy was Claude Dupont, Matthew's brother-in-law.

Claude was twenty-two and the most handsome man she'd ever seen. He was swarthy, with piercing black eyes. He'd arrived in April and spent the last two months visiting other Dupont customers. There was no doubt Sean's friendship with Claude was helping to restore her son's enthusiasm for life, so when Claude had asked if he could take Sean on trips to Chester, Liverpool and Manchester, she'd reluctantly agreed. Each time Sean returned safely, she noticed that she could see a little more of the old Sean – the one she'd thought was gone forever. She dreaded to think what would happen when Claude returned to New Orleans.

Although she was keen for Claude to remain in England, Matthew had his own reasons for wanting Claude to return to America.

"It's my wife, Sophia," he'd confided. "She is reluctant to come and live over here. I fear she will never join me. In fact, she's refused point-blank. I'm guessing she hoped I'd have got bored by now and returned to America. That will never happen," he'd said firmly.

If Matthew left, Victoria knew she could be stuck with the mill to run on her own. Had Sean been older, it might have been different, but right now, she needed Matthew here.

"So, what *are* you going to do?" she'd asked, concerned.

"Claude came over here as he wanted to visit a few of their customers – it's always good to see who you're supplying to. But while he was over here, he and his father thought it might be a good idea if he came and saw our operation. They're both hoping, as am I, that if he can tell Sophia what England's like, she might be prepared to join me. I hope that will be the case, anyway. Our marriage won't survive if she doesn't."

"Well, then we must make sure he feels welcome and takes back good reports to his sister." For all our sakes, she'd thought ruefully.

Sean popped his head around her office door, interrupting her thoughts. He'd just come back from the mill and was looking excited but nervous. The smudge of oil on his face made her smile inwardly.

"Mother, can I talk to you, please?"

"Yes, of course, come in."

He placed a cup of tea on her desk and she stared at it blankly. He'd never done this before. What was up now? she wondered. Something must be coming, she was sure of it.

"What's this in aid of?" she asked as Sean pulled a chair over but changed his mind and plonked himself on her desk right in front of her instead.

"I just want to talk to you."

She resisted the temptation to point out he rarely spoke to her – at least he hadn't until Claude arrived. She smiled cautiously.

"Do you like Claude?" he asked.

"Yes, Sean, I like him very much."

"And you think he's been a good influence on me?"

"Well, yes, you've certainly seemed a lot happier since you've been spending time with him."

Where is this leading? she wondered.

"And you trust him to look after me – when I've been away with him, I mean?"

"Yes. Why? Where does he want to take you now? Not London! I draw the line at you going that far."

Sean fidgeted nervously in his seat. "No, not London . . . Don't be mad. But he's asked me to go to New Orleans with him."

His words came out in a rush and Victoria felt the breath leave her body. She looked at him in horror.

"*What?*"

"He's asked me to go back to America with him in August."

"Well, he had no right doing that without speaking to me first."

"It would be educational, not just fun."

"You can have an education here. I wanted you to stay on at school and go to university."

Sean slid off her desk and shoved his hands in his pockets. "Not that kind of education. This would be things that matter, not just Latin and other stuff I'll never use again."

"Well, if you want to learn about the real world, you can work in the mill. I bought a share of it for you, after all!" she said, her voice shrill.

"But over there, I'd be able to work in the export company and see how cotton is grown. That would help me understand our mill. Matthew knows masses about cotton."

"Well, Matthew can teach you, then. So there's no need for you to go to America, is there?"

"But America is enormous. And I could travel as well, if I get time."

"This is getting us nowhere. Did Claude help you plan your arguments?"

"No. Don't blame him. I want to go."

Victoria strove to keep her voice even. "Well I don't want you to go." But then she lost control. "Claude had no right encouraging you. A gentleman would never do something like that."

"Mother, stop! This is an amazing opportunity. But if you don't want me to go, I won't. I know I gave you a hard time after Bridie's death and I'm sorry for that. But I want to go. I think it'll help me to realise who I am, to enable me to gain an identity of my own. But I love you and will respect your wishes, of course."

The prospect of losing her son even for a short time caused her much anguish.

"I-I need time to think about it," she said quietly.

Sean nodded. "How long do you think you'll need?"

"*I* don't know! You're asking me to consider letting my fourteen-year-old son travel thousands of miles with a man I've only known a couple of months. I need time to think."

"Try to understand," he said gently. "When I'm away from here, I can forget I'm a foundling, just for a short while."

Victoria bristled. "Do you think a trip to America will be long enough for you to come to terms with it?"

"Perhaps not, but I hope so."

"I've said I'll think about it."

Sean kissed her cheek. "Thank you."

When she told Edward about Sean wanting to go on the trip, his response did nothing to make her feel better.

"I can understand your reluctance," he said gently. "But if he thinks that this trip will help him to put the ghosts of his past to rest, you should let him go."

"But he may never come back to me. I could lose him forever." Victoria felt she was being tortured.

"If you don't let him go, you could lose him anyway," he said gravely.

She knew he was right, but the pain at the prospect of separation cut her like a knife. Your children had to be free to live their own lives, she knew that. But she wasn't ready to let him go yet. Would she ever be?

She looked in on Sean a while later, but he was sleeping soundly. He looked so young, with his head resting on his hands, his hair tousled. She felt like waking him so they could talk, but common sense told her that unless she was ready to give him an answer, she should leave him be.

Immediately following breakfast the next day, she'd stormed into the mill office and berated Claude for not speaking to her before making the offer.

"How could you be so stupid, Claude?" Matthew had been equally shocked by the news.

Claude was obviously at a loss to understand their objections and offered to withdraw the invitation.

"Though I have to say, it would be a great opportunity for your son. He'll learn so much, especially about the cotton trade. He'll also make valuable contacts. I will personally guarantee his safety."

Victoria worried she might be letting her love hold her son back.

"How long do you envisage him staying in America?" She steeled herself for the answer.

"It will take at least a year to gain full advantage of the experience, to learn about cotton growing and the export side of things."

Victoria's heart sank. A year!

"It will be advantageous to him in running his mill later, I feel sure of it," Claude continued.

"I'll let you both know when I've made my decision," she said bitterly. It wasn't a choice she wanted to make.

On the way back to the Centenary House, she detoured through the park. She had an envelope for Lydia from Madeleine in her purse. Lydia's husband had become such a tyrant, restricting her movements more and more so that the only way Lydia could be sure to get her letters was to insist that she at least be allowed a short morning walk. Each day, she went briefly to the park at ten in the hope Victoria would be there with some news.

As she approached the lake, Victoria could see Lydia sitting on the bench. Even from a distance, she could see how nervous Lydia was, her hands picking at her skirt. If Lydia didn't get away soon, she felt her poor friend might crack under the strain. Is that what happened to her own mother?

Lydia read the letter hungrily while Victoria sat at her side. She could see emotions playing on her friend's face. Finally, she spoke, her words hurried.

"Saturday. We are to leave Saturday. Do you still have the valises I gave you?"

"Yes, of course. They're stored safely in my attic."

"Thank you. You are such a good friend. Madeleine

has arranged everything. With your permission, Charles and I will come to your home. She's arranged for a carriage to collect us from there at noon. It will take us to London, where she will meet us. From there, we will travel together to Italy via Paris.

"Her home in Genoa is called La Libertà. Very fitting, don't you think – liberty? She named it that because there, she can live her life how she wants."

Victoria had remained quiet throughout. She placed her hand gently on top of Lydia's.

"It's such a long way. I'm frightened for you. For what he might do if he catches up with you."

"It terrifies me to think how furious he'll be. But his temper is getting worse." She pushed up her sleeve to reveal a large purpling bruise. "James thrashed Charles last week – it was the first time that has happened. He hit him hard across the head. It sent him flying across the room, then he kicked him. When I tried to intervene . . ." She tried to gather her composure. "When I tried to intervene, he ripped the new gown you'd made for me. He dragged me to the bedroom, where he tore it off and asserted his manhood. For some reason, that's the way he most likes to show he's in control.

"I *have* to take this chance. Even if I wasn't afraid for myself, I now have to protect Charles, don't you see?"

"You have no need to worry on my part. He will never find out where you have gone from me. I haven't even told Edward. When you've gone, with your permission, I will confide in him, though. Edward has history with James – and not a good one – and I'm tired of keeping things from him."

"Of course you must. You will never know how grateful I am to you."

"You can rest assured I won't tell Sean that I know anything about your leaving."

Another secret I'll have to keep, she thought sadly. Helping others was coming at a cost.

"Thank you, my dear. We will continue to write to you, of course. You can't get rid of me that easily."

Both women had tears in their eyes as they left the park.

Saturday morning, Lydia and Charles arrived as planned. Charles went to Sean's room while Victoria shepherded Lydia into the parlour.

"Does Charles know that you're leaving?"

She poured Lydia a cup of tea. It seemed bizarre to be doing such a normal thing as drinking tea when today was anything but normal.

"No. I told him that he and Sean couldn't go off anywhere. You know how they usually disappear at the first opportunity. Once we're on our way, I'll tell him then. He'll be angry he couldn't say goodbye to Sean, although I feel he'll understand why it has to be this way – or at least he will eventually."

"What will you do if Madeleine isn't there when you get to London?"

Victoria was deeply concerned. If Madeleine let Lydia down, she may have to come back.

"Something grave would have had to happen for her not to meet me. Please don't worry about us. We've loved each other since we were at school. I trust her completely – and Charles will come to love her as I do."

Agnes knocked on the parlour door all too soon to inform them a carriage had arrived for Mrs Brakenridge.

The two women embraced tightly. Lydia wiped her eyes quickly, then she took the two valises and stowed them in the carriage before they called their sons. Both boys had to think this was a normal parting.

Victoria felt terrible as she played her part in front of them – they couldn't know they wouldn't see each other again. Not now. If James questioned Sean, he must honestly be able to say he knew nothing. She hoped this wouldn't cause Sean's anger with her to resurface.

"Charles, I'm afraid I've just received notice that a dear friend of mine is unwell. I must go and see her today, so I'm afraid we have to leave right away."

"B-b-but, Mother, c-c-can't I stay here?" he stammered.

Victoria frowned. Hopefully, the boy's stammer would reduce once he was away from his father.

"No, Charles. I need you with me. Please, you must come now. We must rush. She's very unwell." The fear and urgency in Lydia's voice were real.

"B-b-but Sean ha-has just been tell telling me h-he might be going to A-America. I want to hear m-more about it."

Lydia looked at Victoria. Victoria hadn't mentioned it to her and she looked at Sean crossly.

"As I haven't made up my mind yet, Charles, there will be plenty of opportunity for Sean to tell you about it. *If* I decide he *can* go, that is."

"Charles, we must hurry." Lydia's voice was high.

"A-all right, Mother. B-b-bye, Sean. S-see you s-soon."

Sean sloped off to his room. As Victoria waved them off, she wondered if they'd see them again. She imagined Lydia explaining to Charles about their new life. How would he react to Madeleine's relationship with his mother?

She prayed silently that their journey was a safe one. That they got far enough away before James realised they were gone. As the carriage drove away, she wondered how she'd manage to explain her part in this the next time she went to confession.

Chapter 42

After Charles and Lydia had left, Sean tried to press his mother for her decision on his trip to America. Victoria knew she'd have to give him an answer soon, as Claude was returning to New Orleans in August and it was just two months away.

When Edward arrived in the evening, his face was solemn.

"I have something for you." He joined Victoria on the sofa and handed her an envelope.

She opened it to discover two certificates.

"They're forgeries, of course, but they may help to solve your problem."

She looked at the documents. They appeared to be authentic, declaring that a marriage took place between a Victoria Shaw and a Sean Kavanagh in Liverpool in 1875 and that she gave birth to a son, Sean Christian Kavanagh, in September 1876.

"I thought it would be more realistic if it appeared that you'd named him after his late father," he added.

She was overwhelmed with emotion that Edward was prepared to jeopardise both his career and his freedom by committing a criminal act to help her.

"Do you think they're enough to stop him from wanting to go away?" she asked, looking for reassurance.

"Possibly, but even if you decide he can go to America, from what I understand from Claude, they will need them when they get to Ellis Island in New York. With these papers, he shouldn't have any problems at all, especially as he's travelling with a rich young man of a respectable family. At least he has them and it's better to be safe than sorry."

A loud banging on the door of the shop brought a sudden halt to their conversation. She knew who it would be. She could feel her stomach somersaulting as she rose, her legs shaking. How much more could she take?

"Who the devil is that, banging on the door like that – and at this time of night!" Edward got to his feet.

Victoria followed him through to the shop, taking the door key off the hook as she went.

As soon as Edward had unlocked the door, James Brakenridge barged through, shoving past him.

"Where's my *wife*? I demand to know right now!" He slammed his fist down on the display cabinet. A crack ripped through the glass. "I know you'll have something to do with it, Kavanagh."

"How dare you come in here, shouting at my fiancée."

Edward was a good head height shorter than James and not as broad, but he stood firmly in front of Victoria.

"Mind your own business, Caldwell, you pathetic cripple. My wife has gone. I don't give a damn about her, but she's taken my son."

"That has nothing to do with me, Mr Brakenridge." Victoria clasped Edward's arm.

"They left the house this morning. My butler claims she said they were coming here. She has no right to take my son. Is she here? You've helped her, I know you have. You're just like her."

"Victoria has told you it's nothing to do with her. Maybe your butler misheard." Edward clenched his left fist.

"No, he didn't. He'd lie for her, though. He's a snidey bastard. He knows more than he's saying, I'm sure of it, and he's out on his ear after this."

"They came here in the morning, but Lydia received a note that a friend was sick. A carriage came for them and they left. That's all I know. But if she's left you, I wouldn't blame her. You make my skin crawl, you foul pig."

"You're lying, you frigid bitch! Get that bastard son of yours so I can ask him. Are you hiding them here? If you've nothing to hide, I'll see for myself!" He made to stride through to the back of the shop.

Edward's punch landed firmly on James' chin, sending him backwards into the wall. James staggered, holding his chin. Then he lunged for Edward and lashed out, connecting with his face. Edward rocked backwards, stumbling, his bad leg almost giving way, managing to retain his balance at the last moment. Victoria screamed.

Edward moved towards James as she jumped between the two men. James went to grab the front of her dress to shove her aside, pulling up short as faces appeared in the doorway and Milly shrieked.

"Sean, please tell Mr Brakenridge what happened when Charles was here earlier today," Victoria said.

"What, you mean Charles and his mother leaving to go and see a sick friend?"

"Yes, Sean. Charles and his mother appear to be missing. Do you know where they've gone? Be honest, now."

"Missing? No, I've no idea where they are."

"They're not missing, you stupid boy. They've gone away! And that bitch of a mother of yours has helped my wife to take my son with her."

"Don't you call my mother names! How should I know where they are? They could be anywhere by now. They've been gone hours. Charles would have said something. Why didn't he tell me? We're meant to be best friends!" His eyes blazed.

"Thank you, Sean. I'll speak to you in a moment. Everything is fine. You can all go back inside while we sort this misunderstanding."

"What, and leave him bawling at you? I don't think so, Mother."

"Sean! Milly, please take Sean into the house."

Reluctantly, they backed away. Victoria trusted Milly to ensure Sean didn't stay to listen or interfere.

"Maybe he doesn't know anything about it, but *you* do. When I find her, I'll drag her back and make her pay. And don't think I'll forget your involvement in taking my son away."

This is what madness looks like, Victoria thought, flinching under his furious glare.

"If that's a threat, James, I would be very careful, if I were you." Edward opened the door and stood back to let him out.

James sneered. "Clearly, you're not worried about your reputation any longer, Mrs Kavanagh. Quite happy to have a man in your house at night. If you can call that sorry excuse a man."

Victoria grabbed the sleeve of Edward's jacket, stopping him from lunging at James once more as James marched away, shouting.

"You haven't heard the last from me, either of you."

She locked the door and turned to Edward. Would he be angry with her for getting involved?

"Oh, Edward, let me look at your eye." It was already swelling.

"Victoria, your meddling in people's lives will get us in serious trouble one day. I assume Brakenridge is right and that you do know something. Knowing you, you'll have assisted, as well, you devious, lovable woman, you." He pulled her into his arms and kissed her.

"I'm so sorry, Edward, but she had to get away. They weren't safe with him. I couldn't betray a confidence. And I didn't want to implicate you or Sean. I knew he'd question Sean and believed it would be more plausible if he knew nothing. Please don't be cross with me."

"How could I ever be cross with you, my darling? You can tell me about it later. I know everything you do is done with good intentions – all you ever want is to help people. First, go and see Sean."

He was lying on his bed, staring at the ceiling.

"Has he really gone?" His voice was flat.

"Yes. His mother has left his father. I'm sure he'll write to you when he can. But there's nothing more I can tell you for now. I'm sorry."

"More bloody secrets. Well, then I just want to go to bed, if that's all right." He turned his back on her.

Victoria was at a loss. She felt like she still had a great deal to learn about being a mother.

Edward was sitting at the kitchen table when she went back down, his eye now closing.

"I've got a black eye to add to my collection of disfigurements." He pointed to his face, half smiling.

"Well, I'm sure his will be worse. Where did you learn to punch like that?"

He laughed. "Oxford – boxing club. James and his friends made my school life hell. Cripple Caldwell, he called me. Well, you've seen him. Good-looking, handsome – he was everything I wasn't.

"Except I had brains. But then that doesn't seem much consolation when you want to fit in. Boxing boosted my confidence. That's something Patrick and I had in common – more brains than looks."

"You're very handsome to me."

"I'm pleased to hear it, because you're going to be looking at this face for a long time. Or at least minus the bruise in a week or so. Think you can get used to it?"

"I think I might just be able to."

"I'm glad I punched him. I should have done it years ago when I was at university. You see, there was a girl . . ."

"It's all right. Patrick told me about Charlotte. I hope you don't mind."

"No, I'm glad he told you. Saves me having to relive it now."

"James Brakenridge has ruined so many lives. He's evil."

"He's what he was raised to be. Everyone at school knew his father beat him and his mother. I think we are all a product of our childhood, really."

Victoria felt a trickle of sympathy for James seeping into her. Both Edward and Lydia had made excuses for James, knowing he'd had a difficult childhood. Did that make them better than her – that they were able to justify his behaviour? No, she wouldn't have it. Everyone had a choice.

"That may be so, Edward. But as adults, we get to

choose if we're going to carry on the pattern or make our own choices – new ones."

"You are very wise, Victoria Kavanagh. I knew I was marrying you for something."

"And kind, don't forget kind, because that's why I'm going to bathe your eye."

"My first black eye. Makes me look quite the rogue, don't you think?"

Chapter 43

Victoria felt like she'd taken a step back with Sean. He hadn't even pressed her for a decision on America. In fact, he'd barely spoken at all for days, moping around the house, looking despondent. The following Saturday morning, she was pleased to see he'd already gone out when she got up. She assumed he'd gone to spend time at the mill and hoped the absence of him lolling on the sofa meant things were improving.

When he didn't come home by mid-afternoon, she had an uneasy feeling but told herself he'd be engrossed in fixing a machine with Matthew. Either that, or he'd gone straight to their house to spend time with Claude.

By seven o'clock, she was furious that Sean was deliberately staying out. It wasn't like him. In her head, she'd been rehearsing the dressing-down she was going to give him. If he was staying out to punish her, it proved he was too young to go to America without her. If he wanted to be treated like an adult, he needed to start acting like one.

By seven thirty, the early summer sun had gone down and the sky was darkening when Edward arrived for dinner. Her heart dropped when he told her he'd just left Matthew's house and that there was no sign of Sean.

Matthew had been home from the mill all afternoon playing cards with Claude and he hadn't seen sight nor sound of Sean. All of her anger dropped away.

"Edward, it's all my fault. I should have let him go to America. If anything should happen to him, I will never forgive myself."

"Calm down, Vicky. There could be a logical explanation. We need to make a list of his school-friends. I can call at their homes in the carriage and see if he's there. You stay here in case he comes back."

"He's hardly seen them since Claude arrived. Charles was the one he was closest to."

"I still think I should check, just in case. I'll be discreet, so we don't raise alarm."

"I don't give a damn if we do raise alarm. If he's missing, I want to raise the alarm. If he's just punishing me and it embarrasses him, then it's his own fault." Her voice was shrill, her hands shaking slightly as she wrote down the names and addresses of as many as she could remember.

By half eleven, the men had just returned from scouring the streets. They'd begun the search when Sean's friends confirmed they hadn't seen him all day. Edward sat with his arm around her shoulder.

"Try not to worry, Vicky. I'm convinced he'll turn up, but the next step has to be the police."

Victoria nodded. A fumbling at the back gate had her shooting up from her seat. She flew out of the back door, her heart thumping in her chest.

Thank God! It was him.

Her emotions were in turmoil. She wanted to shout, to scream at him and hold him and kiss him all at the same time. As she got closer, she could smell the alcohol.

"Aww, Mother. I lurrrve you. Have I ever told you that? Not like I lurve Kitty, but I really do lu-u-u-urve you."

"Sean, what *have* you been drinking?"

As he fell through the gate, she put her arm under his, staggering under his weight.

"My real mother didn't want me. Threw me away like rubbish. But *you* – *you* picked me up."

He started roaring as though he'd just told a hilarious joke – one she didn't get, or want people to hear. As they entered the parlour, everyone stared. Not sure if to laugh at Sean's dishevelled state, they stifled their smiles.

"Hello, everyone. Are we having a party?" he asked, gazing around the room once she'd flopped him into a chair.

She began to question him about where he'd been and who had got him in such a state. From what they could make out, James Brakenridge had taken him to Chester Racecourse, where he'd given him money to bet on the horses. Copious amounts of champagne were followed by brandy and a cigar. Her heart sank.

"He wanted to take me out to apologise for getting mad the other day. He's all right, really. He said he'll take me to Liverpool next time and introduce me to girls who are much prettier than Kitty. I don't think that's possible. How's that possible, Mother? Anyway, he said he'll show me other ways to forget about *her*.

"He said to tell you fank you for letting him borrow your son. Hic. Said you understood how difficult it was for him now his own son was gone and that it was sooo nice of you to share yours. He's *such* a nice man. He—hic—was *really* interested in me. Not a bit like Charles said he is."

Victoria couldn't speak. Everyone looked at her. Sean's eyes drooped shut. This was James Brakenridge's revenge. He intended to take her son away, or at least get him into gambling and possibly even drugs. She had no choice – she would *have* to let Sean go to America.

"Someone is going to have a bad head in the morning. I don't think he'll want to drink again for a long time," Claude said, breaking the silence. "We've all done it."

Both Matthew and Edward were furious with James.

"He should have known better than to take a lad out and get him drunk. What the hell is he playing at?" Edward fumed.

But Victoria knew exactly what he was doing.

When Sean woke at noon the next day, she and Edward were waiting for him. He had a sheepish look on his pale face as he joined them in the parlour.

"I feel sick," he said slowly.

"I'm not surprised. What *were* you thinking?" She hoped the way he was feeling might put him off drinking forever.

"Sorry."

"We've all been there," Edward said, smirking.

Victoria shot him an angry look and he continued talking, his face serious.

"Understandably, your mother is upset that you want to go to America. But we've discussed the matter and providing it's for no more than a year, she's willing to let you go.

"Although I'm not sure why after last night's escapade. We were going to tell you last night, but you were in no fit state. If it was left to me, I'd be questioning if you're mature enough."

Sean's face lit up.

"I have one condition. You mustn't see Charles' father again before you go."

"Anything you say, Mother. I thought he was nice. But I have an incredibly bad head. And I hate cigars. My mouth feels like the stair carpet." He stuck his tongue out.

"Very well, you may go to America for a year."

"Thank you, Mother! Sorry about yesterday. Can I go and tell Claude?"

"Yes, but first I want to give you these. Edward has risked a great deal to provide you with these," she said as she handed him the certificates. "They *are* forgeries, but you may need them on your travels and later in life. I'm just sorry they're not real," she said.

"It's all right." Sean stared at the documents for a few moments before shaking Edward's hand awkwardly.

Victoria was resigned – Sean was due to leave before his fifteenth birthday. He was still a child. Fighting to be a man. But she had to let him go, even if it was breaking her heart.

"You're doing the right thing, Vicky, darling," Edward comforted her. "There is no way I can wait a year to get my hands on you, though. And I can't let you go through your wedding day without your son. So, let's get married before he leaves. I know how much it'll mean to you to have him there."

"It's so soon. We'll need a special licence."

"That's right, we will. Do you happen to know a handsome solicitor who can sort that for us?"

"No, but I know a daft one."

"That's amazing."

"What's amazing?"

"That's the second joke you've made in nearly fifteen years."

Suddenly, her laughter stopped. She pulled away from him.

"But, Edward, I've never . . . you know . . . in the bedroom, I mean. Don't you want to make sure things work between us? I don't want you to be unhappy after we're married."

"What *are* you like, my sweet Vicky. You needn't worry about that side of things. I intend to be your husband and love you no matter what. Unless you're bothered about how I'll look without my built-up shoe – now that would be different." Suddenly nervous, his voice faltered.

"No, please don't think that. I don't ever think about it. I never have." She grasped his deformed hand and put it to her face.

"Do you trust me, Vicky?"

"Yes. Yes, Edward. I trust you implicitly."

Sean said he was delighted at the news, pleased that his mother would have Edward when he left. It was a relief that there was something positive to plan rather than his mother becoming more upset by the day as his departure drew closer.

Olga and Kitty had worked feverishly on Victoria's wedding gown, Kitty making the gown, Olga hand-stitching every pearl. Having made clothes for others for so many years, they were adamant she wasn't going to do so much as a stitch on her own wedding gown. Edward had wanted to take her to London to buy one, but she'd refused. This was much more personal. She felt the girls were putting love in each stitch.

With her wedding imminent, Victoria was a jangle of mixed emotions. Excitement at the thought of getting married. Incredible nerves about her wedding night. And overwhelming sadness at Sean's looming departure. At least her concerns about being trapped with a cruel husband seemed foolish now. She was sure of Edward – he was a good man.

Chapter 44

As Victoria stood in the church doorway, she looked at Sean. Their life together had started in a church and soon he'd be leaving. She'd pinned her hair up with the mother-of-pearl hair comb Bridie had bought her all those years ago and could feel her looking down on them.

"Smile, Mother. This is your wedding day, not a funeral." He gave her a lopsided grin as he took her arm to walk her down the aisle.

Edward was waiting at the altar. He'd aged from their first meeting at The Crown Hotel. It seemed so long ago now. Lines had appeared around his eyes and his hair was greying, but to her he looked even more handsome.

As she said I do, she knew for certain she would be happy with him.

Since Lydia had gone away, her only real friends were the Gibbs girls and she hadn't wanted them to feel uncomfortable surrounded by Faredene's finest. With this in mind, Edward had agreed that he'd only invite a few close friends and their wives to the church, followed by a small reception at Latimers.

Victoria picked a canapé off the buffet table. She'd been too nervous to eat breakfast.

"Don't think you can just let yourself go now you're

married, Victoria. My brother doesn't want to be pushing you around in a bath chair because you're too fat to walk."

Victoria's hand halted midway to her mouth. Anne!

"I think I'd have to eat quite a lot before I get fat, Anne." She forced a smile.

"Ha! I was only teasing, sister-in-law. You really must learn to take things a little less seriously."

Victoria pondered before answering. Would Anne go away if she ignored her? Victoria doubted she'd be that lucky. No – she mustn't rise to it.

"How nice for Edward that you could make it," she said instead.

"Wild horses couldn't have kept me away. I can't believe it's taken you two so long to get together. I knew all along you were ideally suited. Fionn was never right for him – I always said so. It'll be so delightful now we're sisters. You'll be able to look forward to lots of visits from me," Anne gushed, air-kissing Victoria.

Visits from Anne – this was a downside to marrying Edward that she hadn't considered. She bit back the retort forming on her lips. Anne was Edward's only close relative – she needed to behave for his sake.

"Thank you, Anne. Yes, I'm sure we'll both enjoy our new relationship." She smiled sweetly.

"Ladies and gentlemen."

Victoria looked astonished as Sean tapped the side of his glass and a hush fell on the room. She hadn't known he intended to make a speech. She moved to her husband's side to listen.

"I would like to say a few words about my mother. As many of you know, I never got to meet my father. But I haven't missed out. My mother has been everything I could ever have asked for in a parent – both a mother and a father.

"From the first moment she held me in her arms, she has loved and cared for me. Protected me. Allowed me to grow and spread my wings. Edward is a very lucky man." He nodded at Edward.

"Hear hear," Edward said.

"Mother, one final thing. I'd like to thank you for teaching me that it doesn't matter to whom we are connected by blood. Our family are all around us in those we choose as our friends, who we *make* our family. I'm about to travel to America. I'm not sure if I've mentioned that to any of you."

Laughter broke out around the room. It was all he'd talked about for weeks.

"Mother, no matter how far apart we are, may our love connect us, always."

Victoria blinked away a tear.

"Ladies and gentlemen, I give you the bride and groom."

Victoria couldn't see her son's smiling face for the tears sitting on her lashes.

"I take it you liked Sean's speech?" Edward draped his arm around her shoulder.

She nodded, unable to find the right words to express how she felt about her son, the boy – no, the young man – who was now chatting to Claude and Matthew. He looked happy. Letting him go to America was the right thing to do. Thankfully, as it was August, the sea would be calmer. Although she wouldn't rest until he'd arrived safely. Not even then – there was no point in pretending . . . she wouldn't rest until he was home again.

"I still can't believe he's going away in a few days. I'm

sorry Katie wouldn't come over for the wedding, darling. But we'll go and see her as soon as Sean has left."

"Let's not worry about her for now. This is our day."

"So, you finally made an honest woman of her, then," Kitty said as she sashayed up to them, balancing a plate on one hand. "Blimey, ma'am, this place is right posh. If yeh hadn't borrowed us lot frocks, they'd never have let us in."

"I can't imagine they could have kept you out, Kitty," Edward said.

"No chance! Not with all this grub on offer. But it took hundreds of these little buggers to fill me up." Kitty held up a canapé for their inspection. "Our Milly said to tell you we need to get off now, as she can't leave Mam with the twins much longer. And we're taking Tatty Head with us."

"Have you taken some cake for Teddy? It's such a shame he wouldn't come," Victoria said.

"Yeah, he still gets scared around strangers, but he'll be happy with the cake. I take it it's all right for me to grab some for me and me mam and . . ." She paused, grinning. "Half our street in case I get hungry on me way home."

When they were alone in their suite, Edward kissed her tenderly and with mischief in his voice, he said, "Well, Mrs Caldwell, it's taken me years to get you to the altar. I hope it's been worth it."

Victoria giggled nervously. "Watch it! You're getting too cheeky by far. You've been spending too much time around Sean. I'll be telling him how you changed the moment you put a ring on my finger." Suddenly, she became serious. "I'm surprised you still wanted to marry me. I nearly backed out when I saw myself in the mirror this morning. I felt far too old to be a virgin bride. Look at me! I'm getting wrinkles and grey hair."

"Are you fishing for compliments?"

"No, Edward. You don't understand – it's different for women. We get old, while men become distinguished."

"Do you never look in the mirror?" Edward shook his head. "You're beautiful. *You* are the only woman I will ever want. I don't ever want to hear you talk like that again."

"Yes, husband."

"Good, because I love your face, your hair . . . And your bosom is magnificent." His lips caressed her neck as he whispered in her ear. "My darling, there is nothing to be afraid of. I will never hurt you," he said, gently brushing a loose strand of hair from her face.

Her feelings fought with each other. She wanted a normal life – the nice thrill Milly had described – really she did. But at the same time, she was concerned that it would be awful and painful, as Lydia had hinted. Or that she'd be overwhelmed by feelings of revulsion that she got when she thought about her father and the women he'd bedded. But she was going to do this even if she was so drunk that she couldn't remember it in the morning.

"Edward, can I have another glass?"

"You can have a whole bottle if you need it." Then he said seriously, "Vicky, darling, if all we do is sleep beside each other, I'll be a happy man tonight and any night we spend together. You do know that, don't you?" he asked, handing her a large glass of Chardonnay.

"I want this. Really want it. Sleeping with you, that is – not the Chardonnay. And no, I don't mean sleeping, either – that would be very boring on our wedding night. I'm just not very romantic, I'm afraid," she said, taking a long gulp.

"On the contrary, it's very romantic that the love of my life needs to be paralytic before she can bear to lay next to me.

"Darling, I hate the scared look in your eyes. In a way, I wish it were over, that we'd already made love and you knew there was nothing to be afraid of. I'm afraid, too, if you must know. Afraid of how you will feel when you realise that without the shoe, I have to stand on the tips of my toes on one foot or be horribly lopsided. I'm so apprehensive about everything, in fact. At this rate, you have nothing to worry about – I won't be able to perform!"

"My darling, neither of us needs to be afraid. We love each other. Perhaps just one more drink each, for nerves."

They both laughed uncertainly.

The following morning, Victoria woke to find her new husband leaning on one elbow, gazing at her face.

"I have a hangover Sean would be proud of," she said, stroking his face.

"That's a great pity. I was rather hoping we could try it again now you are sober, Mrs Caldwell."

For the first time, she felt like a real woman. She might not have carried a child, but she was a mother, and now she knew what real love could be like between a man and a woman. Not scary, after all.

Victoria explained to Edward that she couldn't face seeing them off at the dock and that she wanted to say goodbye to Sean in private, so while Edward went to meet Claude and sort the carriage, she tapped on Sean's door.

"I'm going to say goodbye here. I couldn't bear to watch the ship sail. Edward's in reception with Claude waiting for you. Remember, my darling, that I love you dearly. You will write?"

To her surprise, Sean broke down.

"Mother, I'm going to miss you sooo much. I'm so ashamed of the way I behaved when I found out about my birth. And then there was Kitty – that was unforgivable. Not forgetting me rolling home drunk." He grinned as he wiped his eyes. "I take it I'm forgiven. I love you very much. I couldn't have a better mother. Thank you. I *will* make you proud of me."

"Sean, stop! I'm proud of you already. Finding you saved my sanity, my life. You're a wonderful son. Things have been difficult for you, I understand that."

She held her son close as their tears merged, drinking in the smell of him one last time. She held him away from her. He looked so young and vulnerable. She kissed him swiftly and let him go before she gave in to her need to keep him by her and refused to allow him to leave.

She went back to her room, where she sat on a chair by the window from where she could see the ship that would take her son away. She wondered if she'd ever see him again. She had Edward now, but he'd never be able to take Sean's place in her heart. How would she stand a year without him, maybe longer, without looking at his face, unable to put her arms around him, never certain he was alive and well?

Yesterday, Sean had been in his room finalising his packing when she went to check he had everything. It was just an excuse to look at him again, really. She was desperately trying to memorise his face.

"Can I take this?" he'd asked, lifting the plaque off the wall that Bridie had given him for above his bed on their first night in Faredene.

Victoria had said he could take whatever he wanted,

touched he wanted something with him to remind him of home. He'd also given her back the quilt he'd been wrapped in when she found him. It was all he had to remind him of his origins, but he'd been adamant he wanted no ties to the past.

"The life you gave me and the future are all that matter now," he'd said.

"Victoria, what *are* you doing sitting here while your son sails away?" she said to herself aloud.

Jumping up from her seat, she grabbed the key from the table and her hat from the dresser. Ramming it on her head, she ran from the room and made for the stairs. Her breath was already coming in gasps as she raced through the foyer, bringing startled looks from the manager and other guests.

She could see the entrance to the docks ahead. Her shoes were pinching, totally unsuitable for running. Up ahead, a group of people were alighting from a carriage, the driver lifting down bags.

Please, God, let it be them.

"Sean. Sean!" she yelled. "Sean!"

Suddenly, he was running towards her.

"Mother, what is it? Are you all right?" he asked as he reached her.

"I just wanted to hug you one last time, in case I don't see you again. To wave goodbye to you as you sail and to tell you to have a wonderful time, to enjoy every minute."

Sean, already taller than her, kissed her on the top of her head then lifted her off her feet.

"You are silly, Mother. Of course it won't be the last time you see me. But I will enjoy my trip. Thank you, Mother. I luuurve you."

Victoria smiled. "Reminding your mother of when you got drunk is hardly the way to reassure her that you'll behave sensibly when you're thousands of miles from her watchful eye. Claude's waiting for you, so go on before I send you to your room."

Sean and Claude went onto the promenade deck, from where they could wave goodbye. Sean's grin was wide. Victoria turned to Edward.

"I hope I can trust Claude to look after him."

"You must be finding this hard. I'm incredibly proud of you for letting him go."

"I don't really have much choice. But I'm glad I'm giving him the opportunity to make his own way in life. This way, at least there is a chance he'll come back to me. If I'd forced him to stay, he'd eventually have come to resent me. Perhaps he'd have gone as soon as he was of age and *never* come home. This way, we've parted on good terms and he knows I'm here if he needs me."

Edward put his arm around her as the ship moved out of the docks.

Chapter 45

Victoria thought about Sean several times a day, wondering where he was and what he was doing. The worst part was not knowing if he was safe. At least he'd telegrammed to let her know he'd arrived. His journey had taken four weeks and each day she'd tortured herself with images of his ship wrecked on the rocks, her son lost to her forever. His absence caused a loneliness she hadn't experienced since finding him. She thanked God for Edward and her friends. No, they were more than friends.

Now she was living at Edward's house, she was finding long days at the store more tiring. It was easier when you lived on the premises and could pop in any time to deal with domestic matters. Not that she had much to do in the way of housekeeping, as Edward's butler, Fairfax, ran the house with great efficiency.

When Edward's housekeeper had announced that she'd decided to retire, Victoria suspected it was because the woman didn't relish the idea of answering to a new mistress. This had worked out well, as it meant she'd been able to bring Agnes with her. Agnes had never courted and showed no signs of wanting a husband of her own. Victoria was pleased Agnes had settled into their new home. Even though the house ran with little input from her, Victoria wanted more free time and had been mulling over an idea for days. When she shared it with Edward, he thought it was a wonderful plan and she couldn't wait to put it to Milly.

After work the following evening, she sat on Milly's sofa with Robert on her lap while Milly fed Sara.

"I'll make us a brew as soon as madam has finished eating. They're both teething and right grizzly." Milly looked heavenwards then smiled adoringly at her daughter.

Victoria could still remember nights all those years ago when she'd paced the hotel floor with Sean before succumbing to the lure of undisturbed sleep as he'd suckled whiskey from her finger . . . Was that so bad? She cringed at the thought. That was one piece of advice she was *not* going to pass on.

"I can't believe I've been a mam for a year. Then sometimes I feel like they've been with me forever."

"It goes so quickly, you need to savour every moment. You should give them a birthday tea. I'll never forget Sean's first birthday, when we met Kitty and the others for the first time. I thought you were going to die of embarrassment, the things she came out with."

"She's still the same. I never know what she's going to say next."

"How is she really? I know she seems to be fine about being Auntie Kitty, but I do sometimes wonder if she's just putting on a brave face."

"Aye, I wonder about that 'n' all. But you know Kitty – she can't be serious about anything. The other day the little treasures were both screaming the house down and she turns to me, her face deadpan, an' says, 'You know, Milly, these two are my revenge on you for that time you locked me in the coal hole.'"

Victoria laughed. "You locked her in the coal hole?"

"She deserved it, the little madam. Had told a big fat lad wi' boils all over his face that I liked him. Plagued me for weeks, he did, before I found out what she'd said to him."

"She does like to get revenge. Remember what she did to Grace Brooks?"

"Aye," she laughed. "Right, that's them two fed. They should be quiet for ten minutes." She placed Sara in the crib. "What did you want to see me about?"

"Milly, do you think you could oversee both stores completely, if I worked less hours, maybe even did some travelling?"

"If me mam can manage to do the laundry for half of Faredene while raising nine of us, I'm sure I can cope with two nippers when I've got a nursemaid. Me mam thinks I'm getting too big for me boots."

"How would you like to be a partner in Centenary House?"

Milly almost dropped the teapot she was holding. She laughed nervously.

"I know we're saving up, but I don't have any money to put in a business. Are you thinking of selling some of it off?" She suddenly seemed wary of the changes that might come.

"I don't want you to put in any money and your share of the business would be a small percentage, but it would help you to build your future. Centenary House would no longer be just a job."

"Victoria, I don't know what to say. It would be wonderful! Amazing. But you've given our family so much already."

"And you've given me a family, Milly. From the first day,

you've been loyal to me – much more than an employee."

"Well, you *are* our family. It's not just me who feels like that – Kitty loves you, too. And our Agnes. She might not say much, but she told me God sent an angel to Faredene the day you arrived."

Victoria was deeply touched. She was certain she was doing the right thing. It was unlikely Sean would ever be interested in running the stores, dressmaking or dealing with gossiping ladies.

It was agreed Milly and Bob would move into the living accommodation she'd vacated since her wedding. Milly was delighted. They'd intended to buy a house, but Milly had realised how convenient it was having the twins so close when she was working. She assured Victoria that she'd have no problem with her workload, as she intended to do much of the bookkeeping in the evenings.

Milly's higher salary and small share of the profits meant that even with paying the nursemaid, they could still afford to save. She'd suggested they might send the twins to one of the smaller, less expensive public schools in town. It would mean her current house would be empty, but Victoria would come up with a use for it in good time.

Kitty was every bit as bright as Milly and since the twins were born, she'd changed. She'd always worked hard but now seemed determined to make something of herself. She also worked well with Olga, now running the workroom together. Kitty was still very young, but so was Milly when she was given authority all those years ago. One day, she'd give Kitty a small share, too, if she continued working as hard as she was.

As Edward locked the door to his offices, he noticed a

mist hovering over the gas lamps like a diffused halo. It looked warm and welcoming, but the air was damp and cold. It was the type of weather that made his leg ache and his limp more obvious. He hadn't minded waiting behind to see the new client, but he was annoyed that Mr Styles hadn't bothered to turn up or at least cancel his appointment. Victoria would be waiting and even though he'd sent a note telling her to eat without him, he suspected she'd wait.

He made his way to the park entrance on the high street, nodding to a young couple standing by the gate holding hands and chatting as he rushed past. But for the couple, the park was quiet and eerie.

His stride faltered as he noticed movement in the grey mist ahead. He couldn't make out what it was and strained to see. As the figure came closer, he could just make out the outline of someone short in stature waving.

"Teddy! What *are* you doing in the park at this time of night?"

"Hello, old Teddy. Want to see Samson."

"Teddy, I know you love your horses, but you can see Samson at work tomorrow. He'll be sleeping now. Where's Kitty? I know she doesn't like you to be out at night on your own."

"Kitty with babies. Teddy want see Samson."

"Even so, I don't think you should be out wandering around the park at night." He appraised the lad's thin jacket and trousers. "Teddy, you'll catch your death. I really don't think you should be out. I'm sure Samson will be fine until morning – the park isn't safe. Now, promise me you'll get yourself home quickly."

"Cold. Not safe. Teddy 'ome now," the lad said before

blowing on his fingers.

Edward watched for a moment as Teddy began to walk away before he continued on his own way home.

As he approached the boating lake, visibility diminished rapidly. Noticing the gas lamps were out, he shuffled forwards until his foot connected with the edge of a low iron fence that surrounded the lake. Putting his gloved hand to the curved metal, he realised that if he kept close to the railings, he could use them as a guide through the mist until he reached the other side of the water, where hopefully the lamps would be lit.

A low, strong growl emitted to the side of him and he turned to see the snarling face of a giant of a man. A stench of tobacco emanated from his filthy clothes as he caressed the head of a club hammer.

"What the devil do you want?" Edward demanded just before a second assailant grabbed him from behind and forced a small sack over his head.

Edward struggled to breathe, panic rising in his chest. Despite managing to free his good hand and punch out, he missed making contact.

"Ha! Can't see me, can yeh, you bastard?" sneered the thug, grabbing Edward's arms from behind. "You're done for, Caldwell. Let's have your wallet, for starters."

As Edward's arms were pulled sharply up his back, he felt a large hand being shoved roughly into his pockets. His wallet was tugged out, his watch snapped from its chain.

"Right, let get this over with." The attacker shoved Edward's arms higher, forcing him forwards as he grunted at him.

A searing agony shot through Edward as the hammer

smashed into the knee of his deformed leg. Nausea threatened to overwhelm him as bile rose in his throat and he was allowed to fall to the ground as his leg buckled.

"Gerrup, yeh crippled bastard. It's just a gentle reminder from an old school-friend. Well, perhaps not so gentle. Maybe that bitch of a wife of yours will learn not to interfere in other people's lives when she has to bury you," one of them jeered.

Edward felt a hand clasp his collar and he was lifted off the ground, choking him. Blinded and fighting for breath through the sack, he struggled wildly, his feet sliding on the damp grass as he was dragged around the lake. His body screamed, his mouth so dry he couldn't swallow.

He lurched once more just as the hammer caught him on the side of his head, pulling one of the ruffians off balance. The pair of them began to topple over the low railings. Edward's mugger was pulled back at the last moment, forcing him to let him go or follow Edward into the water.

As Edward's body hit the water, he didn't feel it seeping through his clothing . . .

It was dark when Victoria stepped from the carriage and Fairfax was already opening the front door. She still wasn't used to having a butler, but there was no denying he was efficient and amiable.

"Fairfax, is Mr Caldwell getting ready for dinner?"

"He's not home yet, madam. He sent this note."

He handed her a small, folded piece of paper. No doubt Fairfax could have told her what was in it. Victoria swiftly read the note.

Edward had been asked to meet a new client at seven o'clock and she wasn't to hold back dinner and wait for him. As he didn't know what time he'd be finished, he said he'd walk home through the park.

"Thank you, Fairfax. Has Mrs Gibbs started dinner?"

"You know how efficient she is, madam. I'm sure it's under way."

"Fairfax, if you don't mind, I'd like to wait for Edward before we eat. Would you give my apologies to Agnes – I mean, Mrs Gibbs? I'll get changed and wait for him in the drawing room."

Even if it did befit her new status as housekeeper, she couldn't get used to the idea of calling Agnes Mrs Gibbs.

"Certainly, madam. I've already lit the fire. It's the master's custom to have one every evening from mid-October. I trust that meets with your approval."

Victoria told Fairfax that she was happy for the arrangement to continue and made her way upstairs. She wondered for the thousandth time what Sean was doing. Invariably she imagined the worst. If only she knew he was happy and doing well . . . She shook her head to dislodge the thoughts. As Edward said, she'd drive herself insane before he came home if she didn't stop worrying. Cross with herself, she got changed and went to read a book while she waited for Edward. Everything seemed better when he was around.

At eight thirty, her stomach was rumbling. She wondered if she should have eaten without him, after all.

Fairfax entered the drawing room a short while later.

"Madam, there is a police constable to see you. May I show him in?" he asked, his brow creased.

Victoria felt her stomach lurch – she just knew something

was wrong. The young constable walked into the room holding his helmet, the door left open by Fairfax, no doubt deliberately.

"Mrs Caldwell, I'm afraid I have some bad news," he said, turning his helmet in his hands.

This is his first time, she thought. But first time for what? Is it Sean or Edward? She couldn't bear to lose either of them . . .

"Mr Caldwell was found injured, madam. He was discovered floating in the boating lake by a young courting couple. We think it was a mugging that went wrong."

As he paused for breath, she wanted to scream "Get on with it, man. Tell me if he's dead." But no words came out. It was like she'd lost the power of speech.

For weeks she'd prayed for Sean to make it safely to America. She'd begged God to let him be all right whatever the cost, hadn't she? Was this the price she had to pay for keeping her son safe, widowed after two months?

"Mrs Caldwell, are you all right? Can I get you anything?"

"Sorry, I-I didn't catch that . . ." she stammered finally.

"That's quite all right. It's a lot to take in. Mr Caldwell has been taken to the cottage hospital. The doctors are with him now. It appears he's been injured and robbed. He also suffered a broken leg and a blow to the head."

Edward was still alive? He'd said injured, hadn't he? Not dead. Her blood ran cold.

"Do you have any means by which to get to the hospital, or would you like me to wait for you?"

The constable was looking at her. She needed to respond.

"Thank you, but I'll be fine. We have a carriage."

Was that her hollow voice?

She felt like she wasn't really in the room, instead watching from above. Edward was alive. She needed to get to the hospital. He *must* live. Surely he wouldn't die, not when it had taken them so long to get together. She couldn't lose him now.

Fairfax must have been listening at the door, as he interrupted her thoughts and she realised the policeman had left.

"The footman is getting the carriage ready, madam." His voice was gentle and distant as he guided her out to the waiting carriage.

At the hospital, she was relieved to see Doctor Farrell. He explained that Edward's leg had been very badly damaged and may not heal but that he had set it. The coma was more worrying, though. Whether the blow to the head occurred before or after he went into the water, the doctor couldn't tell. But he'd been very lucky. A young couple had heard the splash and the sound of running feet – what sounded like two pairs. The lad had dived in and pulled Edward from the water. There was no doubt in the doctor's mind that if Edward lived, it was only because of the young man's quick thinking.

Victoria sat by Edward's bedside holding his hand, willing him to come back to her.

"Edward, darling, please wake up. Don't leave me. I can't bear to be without you now," she said over and over.

As the nurses served the other patients their breakfast the next morning, they offered Victoria a cup of tea. Gratefully, she sipped the weak, scalding liquid. She'd kept vigil by his bedside throughout the night, praying for his recovery.

"Mrs Caldwell. If you will excuse us, but we need to

take care of our other patients and prepare them for the doctor's rounds." Matron stood at the bottom of Edward's bed.

"Please let me stay. I need to be with him in case he wakes. I won't be in the way. You won't even know I'm here."

"I understand from Sister you have been here all night. You will be no use to your husband if you make yourself ill. He could be like this for some time and you need to take care of yourself. I'm afraid I must insist you go home for a while and rest." Matron patted Victoria's shoulder firmly.

Reluctantly, Victoria left the hospital. She needed to be with people who cared about Edward – cared about her. She needed someone who would understand how she was feeling. She needed to be with Milly, she realised.

Chapter 46

The girls working in the shop stared as Victoria walked through to the house, saying nothing to them. Her hair was loose, her dress creased. Both Milly and Kitty were in the kitchen trying to calm Teddy, who was refusing to stay seated on the kitchen chair.

"Come on, let's sort yer hair – it's a right mess. Not that you've got much – nine hairs and a nit," Kitty said, flattening it with her hand.

"No. No. Old Teddy."

Kitty looked stunned as Teddy jerked his head away from her.

"Teddy! What's got into yeh?"

"Victoria! What the devil has happened to you? You look dreadful." Milly rushed to her side.

Teddy began waving his arms around, bouncing in his seat as Kitty tried to keep him still.

"Old Teddy's dead," he shouted.

"Aww, flipping heck, Teddy. Will yeh just bloody calm down. Yer not making any sense." Kitty was getting agitated herself.

Teddy never shouts, Victoria thought absent-mindedly as she tried to formulate a response to Milly's question in her mind.

"Ma'am?"

"It's Edward. He's in hospital. Injured. Robbed. Left for dead in the boating lake." Victoria slumped into a chair, tiredness overwhelming her, her legs giving way.

Milly and Kitty gasped.

"Old Teddy dead." Teddy thrashed about.

The three women stared at him.

"Now, Teddy, will yeh just keep yer blooming backside on the seat for a minute and stay quiet while we see what's wrong with Victoria."

Victoria jumped up from the sofa, her tiredness forgotten.

"No, Kitty. Just a minute. Let him speak." She kneeled in front of him, realisation dawning. "Teddy. Did you see something last night? Did you see Edward get hurt?"

Teddy nodded. "Old Teddy dead."

"He's not dead, Teddy, just hurt. Do you know who did it?" Victoria's heart was in her mouth.

"Old Teddy not dead. Teddy glad."

"Who was it, Teddy?"

"Charnocks did it. Teddy saw what they did."

"The Charnocks? They attacked Edward?" Victoria's voice was almost a whisper.

She knew they were evil. She'd seen it in their faces. This was no mugging. The Charnocks were doing James Brakenridge's dirty work. This was all part of his taking revenge.

Edward had heard that James had hired a detective and was still desperately seeking information as to the whereabouts of his wife and son. Just last week, Harry had told Milly that James was demented, lashing out at everyone. According to him, many of the staff from the Hall had resigned, unable to cope with their master's outbursts. She was certain Brakenridge was behind this and she wasn't going to let him get away with it. Not this time. But who would believe Teddy's ramblings? Could he make a credible witness?

Kitty and Milly looked at each other. Then they moved as one, helping Victoria from where she was kneeling in front of Teddy, her arms wrapped tightly around herself.

"Come on, sit here a minute. You look done in. I'll get you a cuppa," Milly said as she gently pushed Victoria onto a chair.

"Aww, good lad, Teddy. Yer a good lad. It's all right now. Come here, Sniff-a-Lot. Let's wipe yer beak," Kitty said, taking a handkerchief from up her sleeve and wiping his runny nose.

"But how *can* Teddy have seen them, Kitty?" Victoria asked, her voice barely audible.

"Last night, I came back here to give Milly a hand with the twins. Teddy came with me, but I sent him home without me when I decided to stay here the night. The little buggers had no intention of settling."

Victoria remembered her own sleepless nights when Sean was teething. She hoped fleetingly that she wasn't putting too much on Milly. Why was she thinking about that now? She needed to focus. She needed a plan.

"Bob's good, but he has to be up early for work of a morning. Well, we all do, but we thought the three of us might manage better between us, taking shifts, like. Teddy must have seen the Charnocks on his way home, because he turned up here just now, all anxious, like." Kitty stroked Teddy's hand.

"Milly, can I go and get something from the crates I left in the attic?" Victoria jumped up.

Milly looked surprised, but Victoria didn't have time to explain. Refusing their help, she rushed upstairs, where she began rummaging through the boxes and crates she hadn't yet collected, throwing stuff around her, stacks of paper scattering across the floor. It must be here somewhere! she thought desperately.

Sean's old clothes spilled everywhere as she opened the last few. She hadn't taken them with her to Edward's house as she doubted they'd even fit him when he returned, he'd been growing so fast – although she hadn't been able to give them away, either. When the last crate was emptied, she found the buff-coloured folder she was looking for among some of her books.

Shouting her goodbyes, she tore out of the door and hurried home, not caring what people who saw her might think of her appearance. She *had* to stop Brakenridge before he killed someone she loved, if he hadn't already.

As Victoria ran through the park, scattering fallen leaves as she went, she averted her eyes from the lake. She couldn't bear to see where Edward had been attacked, knowing it was her actions that had resulted in him being left for dead.

Tearing into the house, she updated Fairfax as to how Edward was and asked for the carriage to be made ready. Upstairs, she quickly washed and changed. If she looked deranged, they were unlikely to take her seriously. Despite her exhaustion, her anger made her resolute. She'd *make* the police see she was right if it was the last thing she did.

It was the first time she'd ever been in a police station. The cramped, green tiled entrance with the small wooden bench against the wall and the high counter with a door to the inner sanctum was daunting. The constable behind the desk eyed her appraisingly.

"Good afternoon, ma'am. Can I help you?"

"Yes, I would like to speak to someone in charge about the attack on my husband, a Mr Caldwell. He was found unconscious last night in the boating lake."

"Yes, I remember. It will be Inspector Gillyburn you need to speak to. If you would like to follow me," he said, sliding the bolts on the other side of the hinged counter and giving her access.

"Inspector Gillyburn?"

"Yes, ma'am."

What was he doing here all the way from Liverpool? she wondered. Surely it couldn't be the same person.

She was shown into a small, dark office, the walls lined with filing cabinets, papers and files stacked everywhere. Behind the desk, the inspector's gaze reflected her own look of recognition.

"Mrs Kavanagh?" he said, tilting his head to one side questioningly, rising from his seat.

"It *is* you! It's Mrs Caldwell now, Inspector. I'm here about my husband. He was attacked last night."

"That was *your* husband? Nasty business. There has been a spate of robberies recently, but we don't get much serious crime around here."

"I'm surprised but pleased to see you here. I hear it's inspector now, not sergeant."

"That's right. Promotion – three years back. Transferred here last year. The wife had a hankering to get the kids out of the city. So, when the chance came up, I grabbed it. Best thing we ever did," he explained, pushing his shoulders back.

Victoria explained her suspicions and how Teddy had witnessed the brutal attack.

"So, you believe the Charnocks and Mr James Brakenridge could be involved in this. It's going to be difficult to prove, as your husband isn't able to give us a description of his attackers. The young couple did say they heard two men running away, but it's not enough."

"Yes. And as I explained, there's Teddy."

"With respect, Mrs Caldwell, but from what you've told me, his evidence won't be much use." He rose from his seat and stared out of the barred window, his back to Victoria.

"Please do what you can. It makes sense – no one else would want to hurt Edward." Victoria rolled her eyes to the ceiling in frustration. "James Brakenridge accused me of helping his wife to leave him. And the Charnocks were sacked from the mill after they injured another worker. Too coincidental, surely. And Teddy *is* a reliable witness, Inspector. Just because he has trouble communicating doesn't mean that he couldn't have seen it. I need you to believe me, Inspector."

It seemed like an age before he replied.

"It was a while ago that you say the Charnocks made veiled threats. And we know they're not the sort to hold their fire. Impulsive type. They might be bad news, but they wouldn't have waited this long to do something. Believe me, I've been wanting to get them on something for a while, but we need to ensure any conviction sticks."

"I believe they have acted before. One of our trucks from Centenary Mill was robbed – that was probably them."

"Aye, you could be right. I had my suspicions the Charnocks had someone protecting them. The thing is, we have no real evidence. And Mr Brakenridge, he's a well-respected businessman." Inspector Gillyburn scratched his long nose.

"Perhaps this will help. I found it among Patrick's things after he died. I don't understand what it all means, but maybe it'll help in some way." She handed him the buff-coloured file.

Inspector Gillyburn opened the folder. The word "drugs" scrawled across the front sheet caught his attention. He rifled through the remaining sheath of papers, linking Brakenridge to one of Liverpool's most notorious criminal gangs. He turned over the last few pieces of paper – documents for shipments of tea to a warehouse owned by Mr Brakenridge. The Liverpool police had been trying for years to find out how the opium was being smuggled in . . . Now this, he couldn't ignore.

"All I can do for the moment is ask you to leave it with me. I *will* get to the bottom of it, that much I can promise you."

Victoria left. She'd done all she could.

Chapter 47

As Matron walked away from Edward's bed, Kitty placed Teddy's cap securely on his head.

"Matron is right, Teddy, it's time we were going. Come on, love. Let's get you home. Mam said she's putting some baked spuds on for us. We can have them with a bit of drippin'. You'll like that, won't yeh?"

"That's me best tea, Kitty. Can old Teddy have some?"

"Course he can. Or at least he can when he wakes up . . . When he's better."

"Teddy got help."

"Yes, love, you did." Kitty raised her eyes apologetically in Victoria's direction. There was no point in trying to explain to Teddy that he got help too late by waiting until the next morning. "Ta-ra, ma'am. Milly will pop in tomorrow to see how he's doing." She nodded towards the bed where Edward was lying. Impulsively, she kissed Victoria's gaunt, pale cheek. "Try not to worry. And get some rest yerself. Mr Edward won't leave you. He'll pull through."

Almost as unresponsive as Edward, Victoria smiled weakly. Then she inclined her head and turned back to her husband once more.

Once they were outside the hospital, Kitty shivered in the damp air.

"Wanna humbug to suck on the way home?"

She held out the small bag to her brother then linking arms, they began the short walk home through the damp streets.

The glow of the street lights was reflected on the wet cobbles, an acrid smell of coal fires filling the air as they approached the Rows. Teddy had been unusually quiet on the walk, so Kitty bent her head to the side and rested it on Teddy's shoulder as they walked.

"You've been a bit of a misery guts these last few days, Teddy. What can I do to cheer yeh up?"

"Can Teddy have a dog? One what sleeps on me bed wi' me."

"Aww, Teddy, love, you know Mam can't stand 'em. She'd never let it sleep in the house, never mind on yer bed."

"Mam can sleep in the yard."

"Teddy, what *are* you like? You're so funny," she laughed as she guided him into the narrow alley leading to the back gate of their mother's house.

"Why is Teddy funny?"

"What you just said, it was funny."

"Teddy not know what he said. Teddy not listening."

Kitty giggled. Teddy looked quizzically at his sister and began to chuckle.

"Yeh daft apeth. Aww, I love yeh, T—"

Kitty's words were cut off abruptly as the gate of a neighbouring house flew open beside them. A blade flashed across Teddy's throat, his warm blood spraying her face red as her screams pierced the air. Grabbing at him, she pulled him into her arms as he fell to the ground gurgling. Kitty stumbled, falling with him as his blood oozed through her coat and blouse. Terror was etched in his eyes, the sound of air escaping.

A large, dirty hand was clasped over Kitty's mouth and nose, muffling her anguished cries as she was dragged away from Teddy and lifted off her feet.

Stale breath warmed her face, clouding in the cold air as her attacker jeered. "You'll be with him soon enough, yeh little whore. You can watch 'im go first."

Flaying and kicking wildly, Kitty fought desperately to get back to Teddy as his blood seeped into the grooves between the cobbles, spreading out down the alley like a spider's web of tiny rivers, his life ebbing away as he bled out. She bit down hard on the nicotine-stained fingers covering her mouth. With a howl, the hand was snatched away. She gasped a lungful of air and screamed until her lungs were on fire.

"Who the bloody hell is out there?" a man's voice called from inside Edith's yard.

A knife swiped at Kitty and she was dropped to the cobbles. Throwing herself forwards, she clutched Teddy's dead body to her as she joined him in oblivion.

Victoria had hardly left Edward's side. He lay unmoving as she talked to him, telling him about all the things they'd do when he recovered, the places they'd visit, how they were going to make up for lost time. After four days, she was beginning to doubt it would ever happen. You could have all the money in the world, but it wouldn't fix this.

She could hear the shouting in the corridor before the doors burst open. Two men carrying a woman laid out on a door barged in. Matted hair was covering her face, her blue coat crimson. Victoria watched, horrified. As they placed the woman on the bed, she realised the men were David and Sam Gibbs.

The woman moaned, her words almost inaudible.

"Teddy," she mumbled.

Victoria recognised the voice instantly and ran to Kitty's side, her eyes riveted to the blood seeping from the gaping wound on her face.

"Dear God, what's happened now?"

"Stand back! Give me room," Doctor Farrell ordered as he ran through the door.

Matron ushered them away from the bed as the doctor bent over Kitty's bloodied face.

Victoria spoke to David, who was pressing his fingers into his temples as though to stop his head from pounding. Sam was bent double, groaning. Victoria watched silently as they grappled with their pain until eventually, David spoke. He held out his hands towards Victoria. Blood was smeared up his arms, the front of his shirt saturated. Surely Kitty couldn't have lost that much blood, she thought, horrified.

"Teddy's dead. Dead! His throat's been cut. They nearly did for Kitty as well. They were jumped in the alley at the back of Mam's house. Me and Sam, we'd just called in to see Mam after work, when we heard Kitty screaming. We ran out. It's them Charnocks.

"We couldn't chase them. Not an' leave Kitty and Teddy in such a state. The blood – it were everywhere. Pumped out of his neck like a bloody standpipe." Angrily, David wiped away the tears as they flowed down his face, merging with the blood from his hands. "Mam's with Teddy. There was no way we could save him. But we had to get Kitty here fast."

Teddy was dead . . .

Victoria moved as if in a trance. After guiding David

and Sam to chairs, she went into the corridor. Finding a nurse, she asked where she could get strong, sweet tea for the Gibbs brothers – she'd heard it was good for shock. It was such a small thing, but there was nothing else she could do. She'd never felt more helpless in her life. There would be no birthday celebration for the twins now . . . Would any of them ever want to celebrate anything ever again?

The three of them were sitting in the ward, Edward still silent, unconscious, Kitty whimpering as Doctor Farrell stitched her face.

David's face was contorted with anger, his features masked by the blood of both his sister and brother. "I'll kill them bastards for this."

Sam sobbed unashamedly, his head in his hands, his elbows on his knees, unable to look at anyone. Eventually, Doctor Farrell moved away from Kitty. Her face bandaged, she was drugged and sleeping.

"She's been very lucky. They slashed her neck, just missing the artery. The blade did most of its damage to her face, if you can call that lucky. But at least she'll live. She'll have one hell of a scar though, I'm afraid. Great shame. She was quite a looker."

It was all her fault, Victoria thought. Everything that had happened was because she'd helped Lydia. Edward said her meddling in other people's lives would cause them serious trouble one day.

Running from the ward, she burst into the visitors' bathroom and sat on the floor, her head over the toilet bowl. Nothing but bile came up. She retched until her throat burned. Her mind was foggy. Surely this nightmare wasn't real. Her body felt so heavy, she knew she couldn't stand. She sat there, gripping her hair. She would just stay here and die.

She heard the bathroom door open but didn't care who it was. She didn't have the strength to move. If it was Matron coming to tell her she was in the way, Matron could go to hell. Hell – that's where she was right now. This guilt, the remorse, the sadness and loss of poor, innocent Teddy . . . It was all too much. Kitty's lovely face ruined. Edward in a death-like sleep. This had to be hell.

Milly put her arms around Victoria's shoulders. She'd left Bob with the twins when Bert brought her the news.

"Victoria, he's waking," Milly said gently, sniffing.

"What?" Victoria replied, her voice hoarse, flat. "Who? Teddy? So it was a nightmare! Nothing more."

"No, my love. It's all real. But Edward – Edward's waking."

It was then that for the first time since it happened, Victoria broke down and sobbed. She'd pleaded with God to let Edward live. Her prayers had been answered – Edward had been saved. But not Teddy.

She hated herself for feeling so pleased that Edward was all right when dear, sweet Teddy was dead. She felt selfish for feeling angry that he could no longer be a witness against the Charnocks. Even though she cursed herself for feeling it, she couldn't help the relief that was flooding her body that Edward wasn't the one who'd died.

Milly supported her as she walked back to the ward.

The following morning, Kitty's siblings gathered around her bed while between sobs, she tried to help them understand how Teddy had been taken from them.

"We'd just reached home when they grabbed us.

Pulled a knife across his throat before I could stop them. He were scared. I could see it in his eyes. He needed me, but I c-couldn't get to him. Oh, dear God! The-the . . ."

They stood silent, helpless, watching as Kitty covered her bandaged face with her hands. Her whole body was shaking as relentless, gut-wrenching sobs tore at her.

"The blood – there were so much of it. I were fighting, screaming that I wanted to get to our Teddy. I didn't care about me. I just wanted to hold him. To stop him from being scared." There were no tears left, her voice hard.

"His blood, it were everywhere. It were pouring out onto the cobbles. I could see from his eyes he were gone. He died quick, but it seemed like a lifetime. Then I must have passed out for a few minutes, 'cos next I remember was youse two carrying me. I can't believe those bastards have killed him."

Only one of Kitty's eyes was visible, the other shielded by the tear-soaked bandage. Milly gathered her close.

Her brothers discussed how they were going to get their revenge on the Charnocks for what they'd done to their siblings.

"We need to be clever about this," Bert said, "or we'll all end up along the line for those bastards. We need to take our time."

"No, we've got to do it now, find them before they get away. They can't have got far, not yet. I did nothing when they did this to me." Sam held up his hand with the missing fingers. "Thelma pleaded with me to let it go. Said she couldn't stand the thought of losing me altogether. In the end, they got the sack and I got a promotion, so there was a good side. But if I'd given them a good kicking then, maybe this wouldn't have happened. And one thing's for sure, there's no bastardin' good side to Teddy's death and what they did to Kitty."

"He's right. So help me God, but I'll gut those bastards if I get hold of them before the peelers!" David paced up and down as he ranted.

"Please give Inspector Gillyburn time. He really is very good. I know him from Liverpool. He *will* get them," Victoria begged, clutching his sleeve.

The Gibbs siblings continued to argue among themselves. Only Harry had nothing to say on the subject, listening quietly, taking it all in as he generally did.

"Promise me you won't do anything for now. All of you, swear to me," Milly said sternly. "This is bad enough without thinking of you lot leaving yer families 'cos yer in clink. I half raised the bloody lot of yeh an' I want you to do as I say."

"Aye, all right, then. We'll give the police a few days. But I don't care what you say – we can't let them get away with this, Milly," David said firmly. "Not this time."

It was two more days before Edward was able to explain fully to Inspector Gillyburn what had happened to him. He'd received a note asking for an appointment at seven o'clock with a Mr Styles, whom he'd never met before. At eight o'clock, when the man still hadn't shown up, Edward had set off across the park as he always did if he was walking home.

He'd stopped to have a quick word with Teddy, who was heading in the opposite direction, before continuing on his way. As he was passing the lake, he'd been confronted by a man carrying a club hammer. They'd forced a sack over his head. When he'd felt the blow to his leg, he'd buckled.

One of them growled something about a reminder

from an old school-friend and my wife learning not to interfere in other people's lives," Edward said, shooting Victoria a look.

She looked stricken when she heard what they said about her interfering, so he squeezed her hand.

The next thing he knew, he'd received a crack on the head. He didn't remember hitting the water.

It was assumed that Teddy had seen the Charnocks going towards Edward and that he'd turned back. But why hadn't Teddy tried to help Edward? Now, no one would ever know.

It was a cold November evening when Inspector Gillyburn called on Victoria and Edward. The ground was covered with frost and breath hung in the air. The Gibbs family were still in deep mourning for Teddy. Kitty was horribly scarred. She no longer laughed, her crooked smile never reaching her eyes. Victoria had to live with her guilt. She'd written to Sean, telling him of Teddy's passing and of what had happened to Kitty and Edward. She didn't even know if the letter would have reached him yet.

The police had caught up with the Charnocks breaking into a warehouse in Liverpool. Eventually, after the police had applied pressure, they'd finally confessed to several crimes, including Teddy's murder and the attempt on Edward's and Kitty's life. Victoria assumed that by pressure, they'd been given some rough treatment in the form of encouragement. They certainly deserved it.

"It was as though they were proud of what they'd done. Reeled it off like a list of accomplishments. But they refused to implicate Brakenridge in any of the criminal activities.

"I still intended to question him based on the

information I'd received from you about his dealings in Liverpool and Manchester, but when we got to Faredene Hall, we discovered he'd been involved in a terrible accident. He was almost dead, his rifle lying beside him. He's in hospital and at this stage, we don't know if he'll survive. Even if he does, with part of his skull blown away, he may never be in any condition to answer our questions."

This was no surprise to Victoria, as she already knew about the fight, though she couldn't admit that. She prayed he didn't make it.

She'd been at Milly's that morning when Harry had tapped on her kitchen window, beckoning her to come into the yard, away from the nursemaid, who was washing the twins. Milly had grabbed Victoria's arm, taking her with her. Harry was breathing heavily as he removed his cap with trembling hands, beads of perspiration glistening on his forehead.

"Harry, what the hell's happened now? Did you find out anything? Has Brakenridge been arrested yet?"

"Just listen to me a minute, will yeh? Give me a chance to speak. I'm scared, our Milly. I had it out with him this morning – Brakenridge. Accused him of being involved. He wouldn't admit he were behind what happened to Teddy and Kitty, but it got real nasty. I think I've done for him."

"Dear God, Harry, what do you mean, 'done for him'?" Milly asked, her face stricken.

"We were in the woods. He's got an old cottage out there where he keeps stuff he needs to hide for a day or two."

"What kind of stuff? What *have* you got yourself involved in, Harry?" she asked angrily.

"That's not important right now," Victoria said, placing her hand on Milly's shoulder.

"No, she's right. It don't bloody matter no more," Harry retorted. "What matters is Brakenridge admitted to telling the Charnocks to get rid of Teddy. Said he were sick of people getting in his way. He kept pointing the rifle at me, saying he had no choice, he had to get rid of me an' all. He weren't making much sense. Kept saying I'd been loyal but that it made no difference in the end, I still had to go."

Milly clutched her throat. "Christ! I could have lost another bruvver."

"He started ranting about how his father did worse to him and it would be a quick death. Said it wouldn't hurt. That were when we heard a noise. It were only a fox or summat, but he turned away. I tried to grab the rifle. We struggled . . . and, well, it went off."

Victoria felt light-headed and surprisingly elated. She had the strangest desire to laugh.

"He went for me. I've left him for dead, our Milly. But I couldn't just stand by and let him get away with everything."

"Bloody hell, Harry. You'll swing for this along with the Charnocks. The police caught up with them two days ago. What *were* you thinking?"

"I made it look like an accident, as though he'd tripped over a rock." Harry's voice was shaky. "He were still breathing. Don't fancy his chances of survival, though.

"I'm not sorry. He deserved it. For what he's done to Teddy an' Kitty, I mean. I might not be close like the rest of you, but I do care about me family."

"Aww, I know you do, Harry."

"I need yer help, Milly. I need to get to Liverpool. Take a ship to America. But I need some money. Can you give me some, Milly? I'll get it back to yeh somehow. Only I need to go today, in case they realise it weren't an accident."

"Of course I'll help yeh, love. It's like you say – you've got no choice, you've got to go now."

Milly ran inside and grabbed the tea caddy off the shelf. Having emptied its contents, she pushed it into Harry's hand.

"I can't take all this. Just enough to get me to Liverpool and tide me over until there's a ship. I'll sign on to work me passage, if I have to. I ain't afraid of hard work, Milly." He pushed most of the money back at her.

"There's no need for you to do that. You'll need money when you get to America, as well. Take it all and just promise me that you'll find a good job. Say that you'll go straight when you get there."

"There's no fear about that, Milly. I've had enough of hanging around wi' bad buggers. They say you can make yer fortune over there. In America."

All through the exchange, Victoria had watched, unable to speak.

Harry had his clothes in a potato sack, so Milly found him a valise Victoria had left behind and packed it, throwing in several items of Sean's old clothes that Victoria handed to her, including a suit. He needed to look like a respectable traveller.

Victoria emptied both the tills and the safe of a few days' takings. Returning to Milly's parlour, where Harry was now waiting, she pressed the money into his hands.

"Aww, there's no need for all that, missus. It's a small fortune. I'm not close to yeh like the girls and I'm not yer bruvver."

"Please take it. That man was evil and now he can't hurt anyone else, thanks to you."

"Aye, he was. Thanks, then. I won't say no, 'cos this'll make it easier," Harry replied, tucking the notes in his pocket.

Just in case anyone did decide to look for him, it was decided he'd take the London train then double back to Liverpool, where he'd change into Sean's suit before purchasing a ticket on the first ship sailing for America.

Milly pushed the twins in their pram as together, she, Victoria and Harry all strolled down the high street towards the train station. Milly managed to chat and smile, despite the realisation that she'd never see Harry again and the worry that he wouldn't be safe until he reached America.

As he boarded the train, Milly waved and shouted with a false cheerfulness.

"Ta-ra. Go make yer fortune in London!"

You never knew who might be listening.

Epilogue

Victoria sat up in bed and placed the letter down by her side. It was a year since Sean went to America. He was due to return home any day now but had written to her weeks before, pleading to be allowed to stay. She'd readily given her consent. He was happy there. He was working in the Dupont family business, and he was living in the Dupont family's plantation house.

The second letter was from Lydia. Despite learning of her husband's ill health, it was clear she felt no obligation to care for him. She'd decided to remain in Italy, where she and Madeleine felt free to be themselves. Lydia had written that Charles was happy and had accepted her relationship with Madeleine, although she'd hinted that he might come back to Faredene one day – after all, James, who was now disabled, was still his father.

Victoria wished that James *had* died. Maybe that was wrong of her, but she couldn't help the way she felt about him. She was just thankful that for now, his condition meant that he was unable to inflict harm on the people she cared about. Lydia had extended an invite for Edward and her to visit them in Italy. Perhaps one day, Victoria thought, but she knew she wouldn't be travelling far for a while.

Edward leaned on his stick as he crossed their bedroom. His left leg had been broken in the attack and would never fully recover. His limp was even more pronounced now, his face one of pain. If the events of last year had taught her anything, it was that she couldn't protect everyone – not even God could do that.

"Victoria, are you sure you're up to going to this wedding?"

"I wouldn't miss Kitty's wedding for the world."

Kitty was marrying Albert Nelson, the landlord of The Tanner's Arms and a widower with two young boys. The Gibbs family were hoping this would be a turning point for them. They'd never recover from the loss of Teddy, though – his passing had left a hole in everyone's hearts. Victoria prayed he was in heaven with Bridie. If anyone deserved to go to heaven, it was Teddy. Harry wouldn't be at the wedding. He'd written to Milly from New York, telling her he was working on the railways and doing well, having been made foreman.

When Kitty had tried on her wedding dress earlier in the week, Victoria had asked her if she was happy.

"As happy as I'm ever likely to be without our Teddy. Nothing seems right. But Albert's a lovely man. I can't believe that he loves me. He's not bothered at all about this . . ." She'd touched the large, ragged scar that ran from the side of her eye all the way to her breast, puckering the skin.

If you looked at her from one side, she was still incredibly beautiful, but when she turned round, it was distressing. Victoria was overwhelmed every time she looked at her.

"My Albert says I'm still the best-looking girl in

Faredene. It's not true, but I like that he says it. I know I've not been courting him long, but he loves me and I love him, and that's what counts. No point in wasting time."

"No, there definitely isn't, Kitty. I've learned that at last."

"Besides, once I'm married, I can eat as much of our Agnes' cake as I like. It won't matter if I get as fat as Mrs Hornby-Smythe, 'cos Albert will be stuck with me."

Kitty was trying to get back to her old self, a joke never far from her lips. Victoria hoped one day the girl's smile wouldn't be one tinged with sadness. Maybe she'd even have more children.

"Victoria." Edward's voice brought her back from her thoughts.

"Yes, dear." She smiled indulgently.

"You've been so tired. I think perhaps you should rest instead. Kitty will understand."

"Edward, I love you so much. I couldn't ask for a better husband. But please don't fuss. I'm not ill. I'm just tired because I've been so busy." She patted the large bump under the covers. "And besides, I'm fine, really. The baby's not due for weeks yet."

THE END

About the Author

Debra Delaney lives with her husband in Shropshire. She took up writing full-time following her retirement and has discovered how easy it is to become obsessed with the lives of her characters. When she's not writing, she's enjoying the surrounding countryside, spending time with her family or indulging in one of her many hobbies.

Now that you're hooked,
why not try

EDGE OF DESPAIR

Part of the Faredene Saga

Here's a sneak preview of
Chapter 1 in the second book
in the saga

NOW AVAILABLE.

Edge of Despair: the second book in the saga

Chapter 1

New York, November 1910

With numb fingers, Sean clutched the icy handrail, mesmerised by the foaming waves and ebony ocean that beckoned him.

"Don't do it, honey. Nothing is as bad as it seems."

As a hand in a silk glove grasped his arm, Sean flinched, jolted from the pit of misery that consumed him.

"Come inside with me. We'll have a drink and talk about it. What do you say?" the woman urged, shouting over the howling wind that whipped across the *Lusitania*'s deck as she eased him backwards.

Sean shivered, suddenly aware of the dark sky and foreboding clouds.

"I-I wouldn't have jumped."

"Well, that *is* a relief. Now, how about that drink before we both freeze to death? Crossing the Atlantic in December is bad enough without spending the voyage on deck." Still holding his arm, the woman edged towards the door.

His steps faltering, Sean allowed her to lead him – someone cared.

As she guided him to a table, long since deserted by diners, she spoke to a stick-thin man hovering nearby.

"Order us two large bourbons, would you, Harry? And leave us alone so we can talk."

Sean sat with his head in his hands. Neither spoke for several minutes.

"Get that down you – it'll warm you," she said as a waiter served their drinks.

Sean's fingers burned, thawing in the warmth of the dining room. He grasped the glass, the amber liquid rippling as his hand trembled.

He remembered the woman from earlier in the day, when he'd gone out on deck to watch as the ship had sailed away. His first-class cabin was conveniently situated on the promenade deck and he'd soon found himself a space among the well-heeled passengers, cocooned in their thick coats and hats against the plummeting temperature.

The Statue of Liberty had become a needle on the shoreline as the ship had picked up speed and Sean had wiped his eyes. It was the wind making them water, he'd decided, too embarrassed to admit even to himself that it wasn't sea salt he'd tasted on his lips. He hated himself for his weakness, ashamed that he was weeping for the future that had been ripped from him.

A loud Texan drawl further down the deck had interrupted his thoughts.

"Gees, Harry, sugar. Even my sable isn't enough to keep me warm up here."

Sean had rolled his eyes before glancing in the direction of the voice. A voluptuous dark-skinned woman wearing a bright orange waggon wheel hat that billowed in the wind had clutched the collar of her fur coat.

"Let's go inside, my sweet. We can order ourselves some champagne. When we get to England, I'll buy you a dozen more furs if you want."

Her beak-nosed escort had placed his arm around her ample waist to usher her inside, away from the elements, and the couple had stared at Sean as they'd passed. He'd made a mental note to avoid the vaguely familiar-looking man and his companion during the voyage back to England, unable to face listening to people bragging about their wealth.

"So, do you want to talk about it?" the woman said now, touching his hand, bringing his attention back to the present.

"I wouldn't know where to start."

"Try telling me your name. Then you can talk about how you got those black eyes and that gash across the bridge of your nose."

"Kavanagh . . . Sean Kavanagh. I-I fought with my friend, Claude," he mumbled.

"Marvellous friend. I hope you gave as good as you got."

He grimaced, unable to put into words his horror about the beating he'd inflicted on the man whom, until a few weeks ago, he'd considered a brother.

"I've made a mess of everything. Lost my money. Even what my mother gave me out of my inheritance. And the woman I love has turned her back on me."

"She's a bloody idiot, then. Without that beard and once the swelling goes down, I bet you're a good-looking fella . . . Don't worry, honey, I'm not making a play for you. I've got my Harry – he's the only man I want."

Sean experienced a stab of envy for this Harry who had someone who loved him.

"No. I didn't assume that – really I didn't."

"I'm just teasing. Have you been out on deck since we left New York?"

Sean nodded. "I needed to think. I had hoped fresh air might help."

"It doesn't seem to have done you much good. I noticed you out of the window while we were eating. I said to my Harry it didn't look as though you'd moved since this afternoon. You've been out there for hours. It's no wonder you're half frozen."

Sean sighed. "I'm so sorry you needed to go out on deck because of me."

"Now don't be worrying about that – I've got plenty of flesh to keep me warm."

"I didn't realise I'd been there so long."

"If you'd stayed out much longer, there would have been no need to jump – the cold would have finished you." She patted his knee.

"Perhaps that would have been for the best."

"At some point, everyone feels like they'll never be happy again. Thankfully, most of us find a way."

"I hope you're right. Because right now, I can't see a clear path through this."

"Trust me – the way doesn't need to be clear. All you have to do is put one foot in front of the other and keep moving. So, why *are* you going to England, anyway?"

"I'm going home to see my mother." He brushed back his wavy dark brown hair with a bruised hand, frowning.

Despite the pain it had caused his mother, she'd still permitted him to go to America for a year. Then, realising how happy he was there, she'd agreed to let him stay indefinitely. She'd been so proud of his achievements. How was he going to explain everything to her and his stepfather, Edward Caldwell? He was dreading it. That he might embarrass them by his failure had caused him to wonder if ending it all was the best solution. Would he have jumped? He'd never know now.

The voice of the woman who had probably saved his life punctured his thoughts again.

"You're doing the best thing. We all need our family when we're in trouble."

She was right. Regardless of how his mother felt about his situation, *he* needed her. Almost as much as when she'd found him all those years ago.

The woman pushed the second glass of bourbon towards him.

"Twice my mother came to visit me in New Orleans with my stepfather and sister, but I've never been back home to see them. She's a wonderful mother and deserves better," Sean said.

"Most mothers do, love. Now, have you eaten since you got on board?"

"I'm not hungry," he lied.

"Your lips are less blue, so let's get you to your cabin and I'll have dinner sent to you. A good meal, a decent night's sleep and things will seem better in the morning."

If only that was all it took, he thought.

Sean allowed the woman to accompany him to his cabin. As she wrote the number of her stateroom, he learned that her name was Jess Gibbs.

"Knock on our door, no matter the hour, if you need to talk," she said.

"I've imposed enough."

"If you don't promise to join us for breakfast, I'll have to spend all night in your cabin watching over you. Now you don't want that, do you, honey?"

Her threat was enough to make him comply.

After closing the door behind her, Sean took the bottle of bourbon from the dresser and poured a measure. Despite his hunger pains, he toyed with his food. Finally, he pushed the plate to one side and drained his glass, then poured another, burning his throat as he gulped it down. He gazed around his plush mahogany-furnished stateroom. Although he was reluctant to give up the finer things in life, perhaps he'd been foolish to spend the last of his money on a first-class passage. No – steerage with a bunk the size of a coffin would have been unbearable.

He tipped the dregs of the bourbon from the bottle into his glass and knocked it back before staggering to the bed and lying on top, fully dressed. He wasn't sure what hurt most – Claude's treachery, losing his fortune or his mistress' rejection. He felt so alone. Maybe not having anyone depending on him, no one loving him, was a blessing. Self-pity wasn't an attractive quality – not one his mother would tolerate. But damn, he was hurting.

The continuous pitching of the ship dragged his thoughts to his growing nausea. After rolling off the bed, he floundered to the water closet, where he retched until he'd brought up most of the liquor. He filled the sink with water and dunked his head before drying his face on the soft white towel. Water dripped from his hair, running down his cheek.

"You need to sort yourself out before you get back to Faredene," he said to his haggard, unrecognisable reflection.

He willed the cabin to stop spinning as he flopped back on his bunk until, eventually, he fell into a fitful sleep.

The following morning, Sean woke with a throbbing head, determined to keep his bourbon intake to a reasonable level during the remainder of the brief journey.

Aboard the *Lusitania*, he'd reach home in far less time than it took him to travel to America, the ship being renowned for the rapid speed with which it could make the crossing.

The liner sped across the ocean, breaking the enormous waves on its bow, making it difficult to keep his balance. As he crossed the dining room, Sean reached out, steadying himself on ornate white pillars. When the ship lurched violently, he staggered towards an empty table. Grasping the starched tablecloth, he pulled it and the gleaming silverware to the floor with a crash. As he stooped to help the waiter pick up the scattered cutlery, Jess waved. Her heavily adorned peacock blue lace and velvet gown, although well cut, was completely out of place at the breakfast table.

Several passengers glanced disapprovingly in her direction as she called, "Sean, over here."

Sean bowed slightly to Jess, then held his hand out to the man who stood to greet him.

"Sir."

"Even with your beard, there's no mistaking you. It's been a long time," the man said, his dark eyes studying Sean's face.

"I'm sorry – have we met?" Sean asked as a memory tickled the back of his mind.

Harold Gibbs laughed quietly, without smiling.

"I told Jess you wouldn't recognise me," he said, straightening his tie ostentatiously. "It's me, Harry Gibbs. Milly and Kitty's brother."

Sean's jaw dropped slightly.

Jess laughed loudly. "Gees, Harry, you've stunned him."

Harry was the youngest of the Gibbs family. He'd been

the least friendly and likable of the nine siblings, many of whom had worked for Sean's mother at some point, either in her shops, home or mill. Shortly after Sean's own departure, Harry had fled England with only the money Milly had taken from her tea caddy and a few days' takings Sean's mother had removed from the till. Yet, if Jess' jewels were any indication, then Harry was now incredibly rich.

Sean's chest tightened. "It's, erm, it's nice to see you. My mother wrote that you'd done well."

"Aye, turns out that bugger James Brakenridge did me a favour when he pointed his rifle at me."

"You were fortunate to get away unharmed."

"He'd have used it on me, no doubt about it. I'd never been so scared in me life. That's why I grabbed for it. Even though he deserved it, I didn't mean for it to go off. I was sure he'd snuff it and I'd swing for it. How he survived, I'll never know. I've been lucky – according to Milly, the spiteful swine claims he can't remember anything about what happened."

"Aren't you worried that one day he might remember about your involvement?"

"No, 'cos I can afford lawyers now and if he tries owt, I'll make sure he pays for what happened to our Teddy and Kitty."

"Are you going home for good?"

Jess answered for her husband.

"We sure are. We're going to set up home there. I've got a hankering for an English mansion. Somewhere real pretty."

During breakfast, Harry told Sean about his time in America, with only occasional interruptions from Jess.

Initially, he'd spent two years working in New York at the docks and running a few bets on the side. Then he and a friend had set out to see more of the country, winding up in Texas, working the drill sites and expanding their gambling ring. When their clients couldn't settle their debts, Harry and his friend often accepted land or stocks and shares as payment.

"We were right there in the thick of it in January 1901, Jefferson County, when the geyser exploded. Reached over 150 feet high, it did. Covered in oil, we were!" Harry said with unusual animation.

As luck would have it, through a gambling debt they'd recently collected, Harry and his friend found themselves in possession of a small part of this largest gusher ever found and were suddenly extraordinarily rich. When his friend had died two years later with no family, he'd left his share in the oilfield to Harry.

As Harry reached the part in his story where he'd gone to a club in which Jess had been working, she took over telling Sean how it was love at first sight for Harry and he'd pursued her.

"It sounds as if you had a wonderful life in Texas. I'm surprised you're leaving."

"It was smashin', but when Jess said she wanted to live in England, I thought why the bloody hell not."

Sean felt another pang of jealousy as Harry glanced lovingly at Jess, who gazed back.

"I'm the luckiest woman alive," she said.

He's got it all, Sean thought. Jess was obviously older than Harry, but she was kind and any dunce could see she adored him.

"What about you, Sean? I expect you did well for

yourself. You moved to America with that toff, didn't you?" Harry asked.

Sean sighed. There was no point in trying to hide the truth – they'd seen the state he was in last night. He hesitated, unsure how to explain.

"Things didn't . . . they didn't go too well after Claude's father died. I . . ."

Jess put her hand on his arm. "I can see it's difficult. You don't have to tell us what happened. Does he, Harry?"

"No, but there's no need to be secretive about it. You've not been in the clink or summat, have you?"

"It's nothing like that. I'm broke, that's all. But it's complicated and I ought to tell my mother first."

"Harry, honey, leave him be. We've all got skeletons in our closets we don't want rattling."

Sean remembered how Harry used to steal his toys and would hit him, calling him a spoilt git. He expected him to appear smug now.

"Well, if the tables have turned, I'm sorry for you. Yer mam has been good to my family. She helped me when I needed to leave Faredene sharpish," Harry said, sounding sincere.

"Thanks, Harry. I'll sort things out."

Somehow, his kindness was a kick in the teeth. Perversely, he wished Harry had gloated. Then he could have hated him instead of feeling humiliated.

In Stepney, London, George Bristow stroked his daughter's blonde hair, kissed her forehead, tucked the covers around her and wandered into the larger room next door. His wife's straw-coloured hair was fanned out across the pillow. He sat on the bed, pulling the covers down to expose her pendulous breasts.

"It took her a while to drop off, but she's asleep," George said.

Pearl touched his face. "She's a good kid, our Daphne. Got your hair and looks more like you every day."

"She's gonna be a stunner."

"Don't go out tonight, George. What's the point of a posh house if you're never home?" she said, her voice wheedling as she played with the hairs on his bare chest.

George tweaked her nipple.

"Most women would be grateful to have a home with running water, three bedrooms and space in the attic for a maid. Or did you prefer living in one bleedin' room with a paper-thin wall between you and the Irish navvies coming an' going at all hours?"

"We ain't got no maid. At least there I had mates. Apart from our Daphne, I don't speak to another soul all day. I get lonely."

"Pearl, there's no point whingeing. I'm doing my best."

George pressed his nails into her nipple.

"Ow! Don't, George, that hurts. It wouldn't be so bad if yeh came home every night."

"If I were working like the rest of the morons who slog their guts out every day for a pittance, there wouldn't be enough money for food, never mind decent frocks and presents."

"I s'pose so, but do yeh have to go out tonight?"

"There's a load of gear that needs shifting."

"It would be all right stashed here for a few days. We've got plenty of room."

"Don't talk daft, woman. The customs officers and police are constantly sniffing around. If I get fingered, I need to make sure this place is clean. Because if they find a load of knocked-off booze and fags, we'll both end up along the line. Then what will happen to Daphne? She'll end up in the workhouse, that's what."

"But I don't even know where you go. What if I need yeh in an emergency?"

"The secrecy is for your own protection. You won't be lonely later. I'll be bringing back a couple of punters. Give Daphne something to make her sleep if she wakes. Make sure you're dressed nice and no talking. They're paying extra to go with a silent lady, not a bit of East End baggage."

"How long have I gotta keep going with all these posh buggers? I want us to be a proper family like yeh promised."

"Don't be so bleedin' ungrateful. It's much 'arder on me than it is you. How do you think I feel letting other men hump me wife? I'm the one making the sacrifices. An' it's all for you two. Look at those Christmas presents I've bought."

"All the presents in the world don't make up for not being with you. And yer not even planning to spend the day here to see us open our presents or to see in the New Year wi' me."

"At least you'll be here with our girl, nice and cosy by the fire, whereas I'll be alone delivering a load of booze to me buyers."

"I don't see why you have to do it Christmas Day. Besides, New Year yer not working – you'll be with that stuck-up piece yer working the scam on."

"That's no bleeding pleasure, either." He pulled away, doing his best to look hurt.

"I'm sorry, Georgie. I don't mean to nag yeh."

"Look, precious, the racket I'm working on might take a year, but if it works out, I'll have enough money to last us the rest of our lives. Then we can be together all the time."

"What if it don't work out?"

"It will. The last one paid off, didn't it?"

"Well, yeah, but before she carked it, you thought the silly cow *owned* this place an' now I have to go with fellas just to pay the rent every week. You're the only man I want in me bed."

George quashed his irritation and stroked her face.

"Don't speak ill of the dead, precious one. It won't be for much longer."

Pearl smiled as she settled herself further into the pillows.

"Tell me again what the plan is."

"Her name's Bella and she's young, wealthy and gullible. The family up north are rolling in it, plus she has a rich auntie in Knightsbridge. If I'm clever, a pile o' money will come our way."

"Do you promise you'll get rid of that Bella girl as well as her family?" She drew her finger across her neck.

"Do you trust me?"

"You know I do, George."

"Good, then shut up an' come here," he said, gently running his fingers up her thigh.

Less than an hour later, as George closed the front door, he shivered as the damp air whipped around his face.

Did the silly bitch think it was easy for him, putting up with her whingeing? Women were never satisfied. He wondered how many times he'd come back here. There was no way Pearl would fit into his plans for Knightsbridge. She'd be surplus to requirements. And the sooner the better – he didn't want to catch a dose from the dirty slut. She was bound to catch something eventually if he kept getting her to go with other men. It would be a shame about Daphne. She was a great kid – and clever like him – but needs must. There was no proof she was his, anyway.

Edge of Despair: the second book in the saga

Now available

EDGE OF DESPAIR

Not everyone makes it back . . .

DEBRA DELANEY

Plans are nothing more than dust in the wind ... and life has a way of dangling happiness in front of you, only to snatch it away.

Victoria Caldwell discovers it's much easier to protect her children when decisions are made for them. Would her son, Sean, really have ended his life? Is her daughter, Bella, old enough to choose the right man? Will her stepdaughter, Kate, allow her insecurities to ruin her life? For Victoria, their pain is her torture.

Sean's life in America was a heady mix of work and pleasure until, faced with betrayal, his world collapses and he heads home, unsure if he can start again. Penniless and facing a lifetime working at the mill, everyone has their breaking point – has he reached his? Confronted with temptation, will he overcome his demons or allow them to consume him?

Bella finds the world exciting, but why do people play games with each other? Surely life would be simpler if everyone was open and honest… When Bella falls in love with a handsome stranger, her happiness is complete. But will her innocence and naïvety be her downfall?

Kate is clever and witty yet filled with vulnerabilities. With her heart broken, can she get off her path to self-destruction? Whatever her reasons for being reckless and selfish while longing for the unobtainable, things have to change. Can she do something worthwhile with her life?

Many reach the edge of despair, but most come back from it. Will these three young people learn that the path ahead doesn't have to be clear – they just need to put one foot in front of the other and keep moving? Or will they give up fighting?

Printed in Dunstable, United Kingdom

80843290R00271